WOMAN IN A MAZE

WOMAN IN A MAZE

Reem Rosheidat

ISBN: 0692855181
ISBN 13: 9780692855188

A Red Sea Place

Have you come to the Red Sea place in your life,
Where in spite of all you can do,
There is no way out, there is no way back,
There is no other way but through?

Annie Johnson Flint

CHAPTER ONE

Scottsdale, Arizona—March 2002

Yasmin drove herself crazy all day thinking about her husband and their last argument. Mahir always stood his ground regardless of his obvious faults and said and did whatever he wanted, and life for him simply went on. But this time Yasmin had a strange feeling that there was more going on than just a bout of bad attitude on his part, especially with him working later than usual. Maybe her feelings were nothing but a result of overanalyzing the situation. Eventually they would go away, and everything would go back to normal.

Once she read about positive thinking and practiced it for a while, but now remembering those days was making her angrier. In her situation it was nothing but trying to fix a reaction rather than a problem. Their relationship as a loving couple had obviously ended a long time ago, but the marriage continued and would probably continue for a long time if not forever. Marriages should be based on two-year contracts and no more, renewable only at the consent of both partners without any consequences whatsoever.

Hopefully no one could hear her thoughts, especially her mother back in Jordan, on the other side of the globe. In a country where living in misery and agony is more favored over the change of marital status.

Yasmin took a deep breath and tried to bring herself back to the present. She looked down at the ingredients she had set on the kitchen island and made sure nothing was missing. Making cookies with her children was the cure for all her heartaches and the best mood lifter. Watching their happy faces while they helped her made her whole life worth living. She glanced at the family room. Sami and Mira sat on the rug facing the big screen and paid her no attention. Nothing in the world distracted them when they watched cartoons. In their stillness, they looked like two live sculptures of small and adorable children. She pulled her long brown curls into a ponytail, opened the red folder that contained her favorite recipes, and flipped through the pages. Some were old, some were new, and some were stained with her greasy fingerprints. When she found her favorite chocolate chip cookie recipe, she ran her index finger down the page and made sure she had not forgotten anything.

"Hey, who wants to help Mama make cookies?" Yasmin called to Sami and Mira.

"Meeeeeeeee," Mira shouted and ran to the kitchen, her dark ringlets bouncing and a smile brightening her face. She climbed up on a chair and sat on her knees. "Fo my burfday," she said and clapped her little hands.

"No, Mira, it's not your birthday. Yasmin overstressed the word *birthday* for her daughter. "Your birthday was in July. Remember?"

Mira nodded and lifted three fingers. "I this many."

Though Yasmin had spoken to her children in Arabic since birth, she wanted to make sure her American-born son and daughter never spoke English with an accent. Kids at school could be mean, plus after the 9/11 attacks she didn't feel comfortable bringing attention to them or to herself given all the stories she had heard about people being mistreated.

Sami hesitated for a few moments before he unglued himself from the screen. He walked slowly to the kitchen, while he glanced back with every other step. He tripped and caught himself.

"Watch where you're going, Sami." Yasmin pushed the long sleeves of her T-shirt up above her elbows and took off her diamond rings and set them on the countertop. One of them was a recent Christmas gift from Mahir. When it came to showing off, he was a master. No one knew he went weeks, even months, without as much as holding her hand. No one even guessed that her marriage was at a place of no passion, boredom setting with every passing moment, leaving deep grooves on her soul.

She then took the butter she had let soften and added it to the mixing bowl. Afterward she handed Mira a measuring cup, held open the bag of white sugar, and let her add a cup.

Sami stood there and watched.

"Don't poke the butter with your finger, Mira." Yasmin shook her head.

Mira giggled, her dark eyes full of mischief. She pressed her fingers into the mixture again and pointed a buttery sugar finger at Sami.

"Don't even think about it, Mira."

Mira lifted five fingers. "Sami is this many."

"One more finger," Yasmin corrected.

Yasmin let each of them add an ingredient until they needed to add the flour. If Mira got hold of it, they would all end up covered in a powdery white dust. After she added it herself and mixed it well, she grabbed cookie sheets from the opposite counter and handed Sami and Mira spoons. This was their favorite part of the whole process.

Big plops of dough covered two sheets in no time.

"Now, into the new oven for fifteen minutes."

Yasmin washed Sami's and Mira's dirty hands and then sent them back to the land of cartoons.

By the time Yasmin cleaned up and mopped the Saltillo floors, the aroma of the melted chocolate and slightly scorched dough saturated the house. She took the cookies out of the oven and set them aside to cool. As she put her rings back on, she wondered when Mahir would replace the old white countertops. She had to admit that, in the past year, he had spent quite a bit on replacing all their appliances, so she needed to wait a little for that. He even promised to buy her a new car, and she looked forward to that although her Ford station wagon was still in good shape.

A quick glance out the window, and the backyard looked as if covered in an orange haze. Two hours just flew by when she spent fun time with her children. She picked up two cookies and two napkins and walked to the family room. It made her smile to see Sami's arm wrapped around Mira. Both of them giggled at something SpongeBob did. They each took a cookie and a napkin.

"You can have another one after dinner. Mama needs to go out to the backyard for a minute. OK?"

With their mouths full, they both nodded.

Before she stepped out, Yasmin took her lighter and a cigarette she kept hidden out of Sami's and Mira's view. Since she arrived in Arizona ten years ago, Yasmin had met more closet smokers than anywhere in the world, and it confused her. She had traveled to a few Middle Eastern and European countries before she moved to America and saw that people smoked everywhere. Smoking was an unhealthy habit that she had to give up, though it comforted her.

Once Yasmin opened the kitchen door and stepped out to the cool evening, she lit her cigarette. Passing by her potted geraniums, she strolled slowly around the pool and stopped where she could see a part of Camelback Mountain. Two turtledoves cuddled close together on top of the yard's slump-block fence to her left, which was mostly draped with the cat's-claw vine. Several pigeons sat on the electric and telephone lines above her and cooed softly or just stared ahead as if hypnotized. Yasmin moved closer to the twin palms and watched the sun slowly descend and cast red and purple stains on the few clouds that hung over Scottsdale. One cloud looked like a titian butterfly that slept on the horizon.

For a few moments, the evening appeared as if sprinkled with gold dust. Though the colors around Yasmin took her breath away, she still believed that nothing was more beautiful than the bright-blue Arizona sky that she loved to paint. Something about it made her feel safe.

When Yasmin finished her cigarette, she went back inside and took a chicken casserole out of the fridge and set it on the counter.

"After dinner we'll go take a bath," she told Sami and Mira.

Mira ran to her room and then came back with a naked doll and sang over and over, "All da fishes are swimmin' in da ocean."

"Stop it," Sami said. "I can't hear."

"I think you watched enough TV for today, Sami. Turn it off."

Sami kept his eyes on the screen.

At the sound of Mahir's car pulling into the driveway, Mira let go of her doll and ran to the family-room window. "It's Baba." She jumped a few times.

Sami went to the window and peeked out.

Yasmin looked at her watch as she sauntered to the front door. Mahir had not come home before eight or nine in a very long time. She opened the door and said hi. The dark circles under his hazel eyes looked darker than ever. But even when tired or overworked, he still had the beautiful and dreamy eyes Sami had inherited.

Both Sami and Mira clung to Mahir's Dockers. "Baba home!" Mira screamed.

Mahir set his briefcase on the floor and kissed Sami and Mira. He took off his blazer and hung it on the coatrack. His elegance was another thing that attracted Yasmin to him in the first place. Though he was not much taller than her and had not worked out in a long time, he still looked fit.

"Dinner will be ready in a few minutes. I made a chicken casserole with garlic and cilantro today. I just have to heat it."

"I'm not going to have dinner." Mahir lifted his briefcase and walked toward the dining table.

"Why not?"

Mahir opened his briefcase and took out some papers. "Remember when we refinanced the house a couple of months back?"

"Uh-huh."

He loosened his tie. "There are some papers that are missing your signature and your initials."

"That's odd. How could that be? Just leave them here for me. I'll check them out later."

Mahir overlapped the papers on the dining table and said, "No, no. I'm going to be very busy at work tomorrow, going in and out of meetings. Actually, this whole week, so we can't take a chance and miss out on the low interest rates. Besides, I promised our mortgage officer that I was going to drop off the papers on my way to the gym." He looked at his watch. "In ten minutes." He held out a pen.

"What gym?" Yasmin widened her eyes. "The last time you worked out was two years ago."

Mira picked up her doll and started to sing again. Sami stared at the screen and then turned up the volume.

"Be quiet, Mira," Yasmin said. "Sami, turn that thing off, will you?"

Mahir looked down at the pen in his hand and smiled.

His smile did not look sincere to Yasmin.

"I know, but...I'm in very bad shape. All these hours I'm putting in at work, all the stress...I need the workout."

Yasmin did not comment.

Mahir smoothed his mustache with his thumb and forefinger a few times and then sighed like he did when he was nervous or in a really bad mood. "Could you sign these real quick? The man is waiting for me."

Still singing, Mira took off her denim overalls.

"Wait, Mira. It's too cold." Yasmin hesitated for a moment and then stepped in Mahir's direction. "Oh, what the heck," she muttered. She took the pen and signed and initialed where it was highlighted with pink.

Mahir gathered the papers and put them back in his briefcase. "I'm going to grab my gym bag," he said, walking toward the hallway.

Yasmin stood still. Something was not right.

When he came back, Yasmin was still in the same place. "What?" She stared at him. "Nothing."

"I'll see you later," he said on his way to the door.

Mira ran after him. "I go with you bye-bye."

Mahir rushed out the door and closed it behind him.

"No, Mira. Baba has to go to work." Yasmin held her hand and walked her to the kitchen.

After dinner and a bath, Yasmin put Sami and Mira in their beds and read them stories until they fell asleep. It was almost nine thirty, and still no sign of Mahir. Later, she took a shower and then picked a few magazines from the family room, sat in bed, and flipped through the pages without actually looking at the contents. She was nervous and had the urge to retrieve a childhood habit of biting her nails. It was not just because Mahir joined the gym at a time when he hardly spent time at home with her or the kids because of work. They lived almost separate lives for years. Something else was going on. Maybe it was her imagination, but he had a look in his eyes that she could not translate, as if all of a sudden his features spoke a new language.

CHAPTER TWO

The moment Yasmin woke up, she realized that Mahir had not slept in their bed. His gym bag lay by the door, and his wallet and keys were not in their usual place on the dresser. There was only some change and folded receipts. The television in the family room was on, and she could hear the faint voice of a news anchor. She thought maybe Mahir was still home, so on her way to the family room she called out for him but got no answer. When Yasmin was about to turn off the television, the news anchor mentioned that seven months had passed since the 9/11 attacks.

It gave her goose bumps to watch the replay of the planes as they pierced the towers and the horrifying collapse afterward. Not just because she believed that the crime was absolutely hideous but also because, worse for Yasmin, followers of her religion had committed it. She had stayed home with Sami and Mira on that day, and it turned out to be a wise decision. Being a Muslim and an Arab, Yasmin was not sure what kind of reactions to expect from teachers, parents, and neighbors. But thankfully, by the next few days, her fears of being judged or held responsible had abated, and no one made her feel like a guilty foreigner. It still bothered her though that ever since the attacks their neighbor Mr. Watts ignored her and no longer crossed the street to talk or to give Sami and Mira lollipops or other treats.

During the commercials, Yasmin turned off the television. For Mahir to come home late after work or after he took a business associate out for dinner was common. But for him to sneak out of the house in the morning was very new, and it got on her nerves. She could not help but think there was more to it than just being busy with his usual deadlines. Yasmin went back to the bedroom and opened the folded receipts. One of them was from Circle K, and the other was a copy of a credit-card transaction from a steak house in Phoenix, dated the night before. Her heart beat fast. Without thinking, she opened his gym bag and brought his neatly folded shorts, T-shirt, and socks to her nose. They all smelled of laundry detergent.

He lied.

Yasmin sat on the side of the bed and pressed her hand to her heart, as if that would slow it down. She had been extremely unhappy with Mahir for a long time and knew one day it was going to end, but not now and not like this. The job she always promised herself to get before her marriage ended was not here yet. Maybe she wanted her marriage to be over so badly that her wish came true. But how come she was so confused and scared now that it might happen? The thought of Mahir being a cheater made her sick. Really? Was that her reward after she put up with his moods and tempers for all these years? Was that what she got after she gave up pursuing a career and dedicated all her time to her children? If Mahir was actually fooling around, she would not only feel betrayed but also have her whole livelihood threatened. What if he refused to help her stand on her feet and forced her to return to Jordan? She could not imagine herself bringing up her children anywhere else in the world. This was where she called home for years, and she loved and embraced every moment of it.

Yasmin felt silly for fighting a little war in her head too soon. There must be an explanation, and Mahir would provide it, although his tactics were no mystery to her. He could argue for hours on end to prove her wrong. Still, Yasmin decided not to go crazy over a receipt. Life would go on, and the change would come later when she was ready. Now it was time to wake up Sami and Mira and get them ready for school. Later she would have the whole thing figured out and resolved.

She walked into Sami's room and tripped on one of his Nintendo games. Lately, Sami's addiction to games and television went a bit too far. The last time Yasmin saw him take his Hot Wheels out of the toy box was months ago. The cars on his curtains and his bed-cover still stood witness to that passion that wavered in favor of tiny cars moving on a Nintendo or Game Boy screen.

"Wake up, *habibi*, my love." She kissed his forehead.

Sami whimpered and rubbed his eyes.

Yasmin caressed his head. "Let's go have breakfast."

"OK." Sami sat up.

Both walked to Mira's room.

Mira was up in bed, her ringlets disheveled. The scribbles of colored chalk on the white dresser assured Yasmin again that buying Mira a chalkboard did not mean cleaning less. For some reason Mira still preferred the dresser as a background for the butterflies she tried to copy from the comforter and the decorations on the wall. Her face still brightened with a smile. Mira slipped out of bed and opened and closed her little palms until Yasmin picked her up.

Once in the kitchen, Yasmin placed bowls of Cheerios in front of them. Not in the mood to wait for the coffeemaker, Yasmin made a cup of Taster's Choice and drank it while Sami and Mira ate their cereal. Although she decided to stop thinking about the receipt and the gym bag, she still did. Her heart beat fast again. She bit off a splinter from her nail and made it bleed. When the phone rang, she flinched and then blinked at the caller ID for a few seconds before she lifted the receiver. It was Mahir.

"Hi. I had to leave early this morning. I didn't want to wake you up," he said, sounding a bit nervous. "What time did you sleep last night?"

"Nine thirty, I think," Yasmin lied. "What time did you finish exercising at the gym?" Yasmin became nauseous and braced herself. She could hear a male voice on the other end, and then it sounded like Mahir covered the phone speaker with his hand.

"A little after that," he said when he came back to their conversation." He lied too but sounded more relaxed. "Listen, I have good news. I'm going to become a partner at the firm."

"That's…good." Yasmin could not think of another reply. Mahir had mentioned that possibility a few weeks ago around the time he had bought new clothes. Yasmin had not taken him seriously back then because it sounded like an excuse for his extravagant purchases.

"But I have to close our joint account, and also some credit cards," he said. "Use only the Visa for now. I'll make a deposit in your account so you can use the debit card from now on. And please, don't spend any money for a while unless it's necessary. I have to go now."

Mahir hung up before Yasmin had a chance to speak.

Their conversation repeated in her head while she dressed Sami and Mira.

Ten minutes before eight, Yasmin handed them their SpongeBob lunch boxes, and they all stepped out the door. Mira tried to run after a bird that flew off a mesquite branch and landed between the saguaro and the other cacti in the graveled area. Yasmin held her hand, and the three of them walked toward her green Ford station wagon. Their neighbor, Lou, was squatting a few feet away from the carport, tending his beautiful flower bed. After Yasmin said good morning and waved, he returned her greeting. His front yard was one of the nicest on their street, and Yasmin loved it. All the neighbors kept immaculate front yards, but no one had as many flowers as Lou. His wife, Beth, once told Yasmin that they had lived all their lives in Arizona and, by now, they were fed up with desert landscaping.

Yasmin drove south on Hayden Road. She paid no attention to the surroundings she passed every day on her way to Sami and Mira's school, like the apartment complex, the strip mall, and the few brick houses that had front yards adorned with queen palms and purple bougainvilleas. Once she reached the gas station, she rolled the window down and turned right on the road that dipped into a golf course and sliced it in half. The air smelled of shaven grass.

"Mama." Sami's voice snapped her out of her thoughts.

She looked in the rearview mirror. "What, habibi?"

"Can you play my *Barney* CD?"

Yasmin was not in the mood for it, but she said sure and pressed the play button. They passed Scottsdale Road and after two more lights turned left and entered the school's driveway. She inched her way behind cars at the drop-off line and tapped the steering wheel with her fingers.

On the way back and before reaching her street, Yasmin turned into a strip mall and parked in front of the Discount Dry Cleaners. Once inside, the lady behind the counter smiled and nodded.

"Good morning." She gathered her hair into a bun and then secured it in place with a pen.

"Good morning." Yasmin handed the woman a yellow slip. The place was warm. It smelled of steamed garments and a chemical solution.

The woman glanced at the slip, turned her back, pressed a button to the side of the mechanized rail, and looked at the plastic-covered garments as they streamed before her. She finally pressed the button again and removed a bunch of wire hangers, holding shirts and pants, all encased in one bag.

"Careful, honey. A bit heavy."

"Thank you." Yasmin took Mahir's dry-cleaning in one hand, supported it with the other, and walked out. While laying the stack on the backseat, her thoughts went back to the time Mahir had bought new clothes and a new aftershave.

She had brought up the subject as a joke back then: "So, what's going on with you?"

Mahir had kept his eyes on the bathroom mirror, while he trimmed his mustache. "Meeting with existing and prospective clients is ninety percent of my job. I have to look my best."

He had never worn pink or yellow shirts before, and no matter how hard Yasmin had tried over the years to make him give up his Paco Rabanne aftershave in favor of one she liked better at a department store, he refused. But since Mahir had always paid attention to his appearance, Yasmin did not think that his last wardrobe update was peculiar at the time.

When Yasmin arrived at the house, she first hung up Mahir's clothes and then looked again at the steak-house receipt and re-checked his gym bag. She needed so badly to talk about it with someone. Her friend Ellen came first to mind, but before Yasmin reached the phone, she changed her mind and turned around. Ellen had her hands full with art shows and three grandchildren. Yasmin did not want to bother Ellen with a doubt at that point. Yasmin learned from living in America that you could not complain all the time. The first couple of times, friends will listen and give advice. Then they will give you a book to read and recommend a few more. If that does not help, then you will have to go seek help from a professional therapist.

As she vacuumed the family-room rug, Yasmin considered calling her Jordanian friend Dina, but Dina was much younger, a newlywed who had no experience. She had lived most of her life in Jordan and spent two years in Arizona socializing only with Arabic women, who sought her fortune-telling talents. Once when Yasmin broke out in hives, Dina insisted that Yasmin was the victim of acts of sorcery, initiated by Mahir's mother. Though Yasmin laughed at Dina's revelation at the time, that conversation pretty much determined the nature of their friendship. Now that Yasmin felt the need to talk to a friend, she really missed having so many around her. Being busy with Sami and Mira all the time did not give her much time to think about how many of her good and close friends had moved out of the state or overseas in the past years. She did not even have the time to contact her best friend, Carole, in Jordan. Now to call her just to bother her with doubts and complain felt very wrong. Carole would worry and feel obliged to call and check on her all the time.

Yasmin put the vacuum away and returned to the family room. She fluffed her embroidered cushions and dusted the television, the shelves of the entertainment center, and some framed photos of Sami and Mira at various ages. After she wiped her wedding picture, she held it and stared at it for a few moments. She and Mahir stood close to each other, holding hands and smiling. She had been twenty-four but had not changed much in the last ten years. Maybe she just lost some of the glow she had in her eyes. Mahir had not changed much either. His hair was now a bit thinner and receded from the sides. Yasmin stared at their joined hands. For a long time, she believed that fate had played a role in their first meeting. Shortly after the wedding, Yasmin not only realized she and Mahir were not the right match but also found out that her mother, aunts, and some of their friends had arranged their so-called chance meeting. So calling her mother back in Jordan or even her sister, Hala, was also out of the question. Hala had been a widow for the past six years and had enough of her own troubles.

Yasmin knew her mother well enough to predict a reaction. What Yasmin really needed now was comfort and words of assurance, but her mother repeated almost the same words every time Yasmin complained: "Don't give me that American-movie attitude and make a big deal every time Mahir is busy working. What do you expect from him? To quit his job and worship your beauty? Always put your children first, and don't be foolish enough to break your home with your own hands."

In the evening, when Mahir came home, Yasmin had just finished bathing Sami and Mira and was about to read them a bedtime story. Mira jumped out of her bed at the sound of Mahir's keys rattling in the door, and Sami ran after her. Yasmin followed them and watched how they both hugged him as if they had not seen him in ages.

Mahir said hi.

"They should go back to bed. It's late."

Mahir held Sami's and Mira's hands and walked to the kitchen. "I want to spend some time with them."

Yasmin could not control the anger that was building inside her all day. She raised her voice. "Then why don't you set your priorities straight and come home early?"

Sami and Mira flinched and then shifted their wide-open and startled eyes between her and Mahir.

"I already told you what's taking place at work," he snapped. "It's not the end of the world if they go to bed an hour late." He opened the pantry and took out a bag of chips, turned, and ushered Sami and Mira to the couch.

Yasmin followed them.

Mahir turned the television on. With his eyes on the screen, he said, "Something else came up at work today. I'm going to volunteer the next few weekends to work on an addition to a mosque in Phoenix."

"What?" Yasmin did not know what to think of that. "Where did this come from? I don't recall you ever having an interest in charity or religion. Mahir, that's unfair to me and to the kids."

Still staring ahead, he said, "I know, but I couldn't refuse the job. It's a favor I'm doing for an old client of the firm, a wealthy Palestinian." He turned the volume up.

"I see." Yasmin left the room.

CHAPTER THREE

The intense smell of oil paint overwhelmed Yasmin when she entered the study. March was almost over, but it was still too cold to leave the window open overnight. She touched the side of her painting to make sure it had dried. Now she had a good idea of where to paint the Arabic verse and where to paint the fish. Enough rocks and bushes were scattered over the terrain, and the horizon was a bright blue. The twin palms, pregnant with the golden dates she had painted last week, needed just a few more touches. When she was about to pick up the canvas and take it with her to Scottsdale Community College, the phone rang. Half an hour before her class, there was no time to chitchat. But suspecting it might be Ellen calling to remind her of the yellow ocher paint she had been out of the night before, Yasmin hurried to the kitchen and lifted the receiver without checking the caller ID. The voice of her mother calling from Jordan came as a pleasant surprise.

"How are you, the children, and Mahir?" Her mother was cheerful.

"We're all fine, Mama. How are you and everybody there?"

"I have some good news. Hala got engaged."

"Oh, wonderful," Yasmin said. The past years had not been easy for her sister, and the whole family. "Let me talk to her."

"She's out now, but I will have her call you later."

"How is she?"

"I've never seen her happier," her mother said. "Unlike all the suitors she rejected in the past, her fiancé, Kamal, is young, educated, and single."

"That's great." Yasmin knew exactly what chance a widow or a divorcée stood in her country. No wonder her mother sounded doubly excited.

"So, you can imagine how some of your jealous relatives started spreading rumors about him. They think he chose a widow over a young virgin because he's after your father's money."

Yasmin laughed to herself. "Of course they do." Though her family had always enjoyed a comfortable life, she never thought her father was wealthy enough to become a target for gold diggers.

"Kamal works for the Holiday Inn," her mother continued. "His father is not rich, but their family is reputable."

"That's good." Yasmin did not know what else to say, but from the way her mother was going on, she figured short comments would suffice.

"His mother is a member of many charitable organizations, and she's also an old client of my new hairstylist's. Isn't that amazing?"

"Yes, it is, Mama. When are they getting married?"

"July sixth."

"Why so soon?"

"I guess Hala and Kamal don't want to wait." She laughed. "Make sure you're all here a few days earlier."

"I don't know if we can come, Mama. I have to talk to Mahir first. He is very busy at work these days."

"Well. See if you and the children can come at least."

Yasmin sighed. "I'll see, Mama. Give me some time to discuss it with Mahir. He's becoming a partner at the firm, and he's been complaining about money a lot lately."

"What's the matter? You don't seem happy for your sister or your husband." The kitchen suddenly dimmed, as if someone had drawn the curtains shut.

Yasmin flinched and turned around. "No, no, Mama. On the contrary, I'm very happy for Hala."

"Anything wrong between you and Mahir?"

"Everything is fine, Mama," she said. "I'm just telling you what's going on. I don't want you to be disappointed if he says I can't travel."

"I see," her mother said. "Well, do your best and let me know soon."

"I will, Mama. Give my love to everyone."

After Yasmin hung up, the kitchen brightened again. A fleeting cloud must have shrouded the sun before it continued on its way. She called Mahir at the office and told him about her mother's phone call.

"I think that's fantastic." Mahir sounded genuinely happy for Hala.

"So, what do you think? Mama wants to know if we can attend Hala's wedding in July."

"I definitely can't with the partnership and all." He was silent for a moment. "But you can take the kids and go. Hala would be very upset if you didn't."

"You're right," she said. "In that case, we'll go for ten days. This way you won't be here without us for too long."

"Don't worry about me. I'm going to be busy, so stay as long as you want."

Under different circumstances, Yasmin would have spent at least a month with her family, since last time she went back home was two years ago. But sensing that he was eager to get rid of her, she insisted. "No, ten days is enough."

"That's fine," he said, defeated. "If that's what you want, I'll call the travel agency right now." For some reason, Mahir did not consider the high price of three tickets for a ten-day trip as an unnecessary expense.

"Great. What time are you coming home tonight?"

"I don't know. I still have a load on my desk. I'll try to come early."

"OK." Yasmin hung up. "No, you won't," she whispered to herself.

It was almost ten forty-five by then, so Yasmin held her canvas and her purse and rushed out the door. She backed from the driveway and headed toward Hayden Street before turning north.

During the class break, Yasmin and Ellen walked to their favorite bench under a paloverde tree and sat down. Dark clouds had smeared most of the sky while they were inside, and the sun made brief appearances. It was cold. Only a few students were out, buying soda from a nearby vending machine. Yasmin reached inside her purse to take out a cigarette and then changed her mind and put it back.

Ellen looked up, rubbed her hands, and blew in them. "Looks like a storm is in the making."

Yasmin grimaced at the sight of the sky.

"Are you all right?" Ellen pushed her silvery strands behind her ears.

Yasmin faked a smile. "Yeah."

"No, you're not." Ellen scooted closer. "What's wrong? Are the kids OK?"

"They're fine." She gazed ahead. "Ellen, I think Mahir is having an affair."

"What? What makes you say that?"

"Just the way he's been acting." Yasmin told Ellen everything. How it all began with them fighting over everything after Mira was born. How Yasmin was overwhelmed with the kids and how Mahir was no help at all and continued to find more excuses to be away.

And how in the past year it had gotten worse with Mahir's late hours at the office, their lack of intimacy, his shopping spree, and his new cologne.

Ellen listened and nodded.

Then Yasmin mentioned his joining the gym, the restaurant receipt, and of course Mahir volunteering his weekends on top of his already full schedule. "One night last week, Sami had a nosebleed, and I tried to call Mahir several times at the office, but he never answered. I even tried his cell and still couldn't get hold of him."

"Did you ask him why he didn't answer or call back?"

"Of course, but he got offended and insisted that he was at the office and said he might have been smoking outside when I called."

Ellen drew a deep breath and stared at Yasmin.

Yasmin knew Ellen understood exactly what was going on, but Ellen was too nice and caring to say it to her face.

"I'm sure you talked about it and tried to make changes that work for both of you."

"Many times, Ellen. He always seemed to have an explanation for everything. He would get edgy and defensive and insist that he was busy at work and stressed because of it. We would have a few peaceful days, and then something would happen and we would argue and go back to the long silence. Now with the partnership and all, it's getting worse, but I don't believe that's the reason for being more absent and nervous around me. If he's so busy, then how come he could make the time for volunteering and going to the gym?"

"Well, I can understand his need for the gym, but I don't know about volunteering."

"It all sounds wrong and doesn't make sense to me. I've noticed in the past two weeks that when he comes home, all he does is play Nintendo games with Sami and Mira. I know he loves to spend time with them, but lately I've been feeling that he's overdoing it just to avoid me." Yasmin sighed. "He says very little when he's home. And he only sleeps in bed on the nights I fall asleep before him. I just feel it's unfair. I know our marriage is not as strong as it was five years ago, but he needs to be honest and do the right thing instead of stringing me along like an idiot."

Ellen had a shocked look on her face. "Yasmin, how come you didn't mention all this before?"

"It took time to build up, so I didn't want to bother you. I always thought it was just a phase, but we never bounced back. And now…"

Ellen held Yasmin's hand. "You don't bother me at all. Look, it's time to head back to class. I'm going to that art-supply store in Phoenix after class. Why don't you come with me, and we'll talk more on the way."

"Sounds good, but I have to be back in Scottsdale around three. I don't want to be late for Sami and Mira."

"You won't. It shouldn't take us more than an hour. Leave your car here, and I'll drive you back."

"That's fine."

At twelve thirty Ellen and Yasmin were on their way. More clouds had gathered in the sky by then, promising plenty of rain.

"Listen, Yasmin. I've been thinking about Mahir during class. I know everything about his behavior might point to something bad or wrong, but I say don't rush to conclusions. I mean, sometimes things just—"

"Ellen." Yasmin turned in her seat. "You don't have to make me feel better. I'm old enough to handle it. I knew for a while something was going on, but I had no proof, and I also chose to let it go. Who am I kidding? Even if I had proof, so what? I can never win with him or with my culture. I'll always be the loser and the one to take the blame."

"That's so wrong. So unfair. I can understand what you're saying." Ellen switched lanes, sped up by the Phoenician resort, and kept her speed until they neared Phoenix. Traffic slowed considerably at that point, and sometimes it felt they were not moving at all. Yasmin looked out the window at traffic, the few pedestrians who were gathered at a bus stop, and the endless line of shops.

Ellen switched lanes again. "We're almost there."

Before they hit Thirty-Second Street, they passed the plaza that had Tomaso's, the Italian restaurant, on its corner. It reminded Yasmin that it had been months since she and Mahir had dinner there, or anywhere for that matter. All of a sudden, she gasped. Mahir was there in the parking lot. He was standing too close to a woman who had blond hair, and all Yasmin could see from that distance was the back of her black dress.

Ellen glanced in that direction and then turned to the road. "What's wrong?" She passed the traffic light.

Yasmin breathed fast. She turned in her seat and looked back but could not see them anymore. "I just saw Mahir with a woman."

"Are you sure? Do you want me to go back?"

"Could you?"

"Sure." Ellen turned the blinker on and tried to take the first lane. By the time she managed that, it became obvious to Yasmin that their attempt to go back and find Mahir still there was hopeless.

"Never mind, Ellen," she said in a shaky voice. "Forget it. He's gone by now. Let's just continue on our way."

"Yasmin, it might be just a coworker."

"Under normal circumstances, yes. But given everything that's been going on, I see this as the answer to it all."

After a few moments, they turned into a shopping strip and parked in front of the art-supply store. "I still say you shouldn't make yourself miserable over it. I mean if they were kissing, then that's another story. Talk to him tonight and give him a chance to explain."

Yasmin shook her head. "I know you're trying to make me feel better, but we both know something is going on."

Ellen took a deep breath. "Yasmin, we don't have to shop for paint now if you don't feel like it. We can always come back."

"No, don't be silly. We're here, so you might as well get what you need. I'll wait here."

Ellen stepped out of the car and entered the store. Yasmin tried to focus and think straight. No point in calling Mahir now. She would deal with him face-to-face.

This had to be the worst day of Yasmin's life. She could not recall ever being so overwhelmed with despair. Not heartbroken! That's for sure, because Mahir had not had her heart in years, so he could not break it. It was the end, and she knew it was coming but tried her best to stall it to avoid confronting her fate, her parents, her society, and most of all her unforgiving culture. She didn't want it to end on a bad note for the sake of the children, but there was nothing she could do now.

It felt like such a big effort on her part to force herself to smile and make the usual conversation when she picked up Sami and Mira from school.

"How was school today, Sami?" she asked and felt guilty for not really wanting to know.

"Fine."

Then her mind went somewhere else. If he had said more, she had no idea. A few moments later, she finally answered, "That's good."

Then she looked at Mira in the rearview mirror. "Did you make a nice drawing today, Mira?"

"Uh-huh, but Gabriella…"

Again, Yasmin's thoughts trailed off. When she could no longer hear Mira's voice, she said, "I see."

Every time she had the urge to call Mahir that afternoon, she restrained herself from doing it. She wanted to look him in eye when she talked to him, wanted to see his face redden, hear him stutter, feel his fear and remorse.

After dinner, Yasmin let Sami and Mira watch television while she stepped outside to have a smoke. It was cold and windy. She lit a cigarette and walked around the pool. She thought about her day and all the weeks, months, and even years that had led to it. The clouds that had appeared in patches during the day had now merged into a gray awning, making the sky seem within reach, about to close in on her. Picturing herself confronting Mahir made her chest tighten. Could Ellen be right? Could that woman be just a client? Yasmin dismissed the thought immediately. She was programed her whole life by her mother, female relatives, and her society to find excuses or look the other way. Living in America for the past ten years and learning about freedoms and rights was more than just a big eye-opener. Whatever consequences might result from talking to Mahir, Yasmin felt more than ready to accept them.

Halfway through her cigarette, a drop of rain landed on her cheek, followed by another on the back of her neck. By the time Yasmin took shelter under the patio roof, the light drizzle that had barely left an impression on the concrete deck turned into fat, rapid drops that created the illusion of a boiling swimming pool. A rising wind spiraled in every direction, forcing the green fans of the twin palms to sway and clash.

Back inside, Yasmin went to close the shutters of the family-room window. The mesquite tree that stood to the side of their brick house was shaking. It scratched parts of the roof with its thorny branches and sprinkled the air with its green confetti. In the graveled part of the front yard, the saguaro and its surrounding colony of smaller cacti maintained their usual stiffness, oblivious to the weather. Sami and Mira continued to watch cartoons, taking no notice of the weather either, so Yasmin took the stack of unopened mail she had left that morning on the dining table with her to the study. She was about to close the blinds when she saw Mahir's Camry pull into the driveway. It was only a little before seven, unusually early for him.

She heard the front door open seconds later, and then Sami and Mira screamed, "Baba!" Sami and Mira were supposed go to bed within ten or fifteen minutes, so Yasmin decided to wait before talking with Mahir.

Yasmin took a deep breath and then shuffled through the stack of mail and opened an envelope. It was a speeding ticket for Mahir, issued in Phoenix, and dated the night Sami had a nosebleed and Yasmin could not get hold of him. She had no doubt about the date. After the bleeding finally stopped, she had written a note on the calendar and a reminder to call his doctor the next day. Mahir had been nowhere near the office that night, and his lie felt like a slap to her face. The ticket shook in her hand while she stared at it with her teeth clenched. Now she could no longer wait. She threw the ticket on her desk and hurried to the family room. Mahir was sprawled on the couch, watching television with Sami and Mira, so Yasmin stepped forward and nudged his shoulder.

"Can you come to the study for a minute? I want to talk to you."

He wrinkled his nose. "Now?"

Sami and Mira kept their eyes on the TV. Cow and Chicken were capturing their complete attention.

"Yes, now." Yasmin walked ahead of Mahir to the study and stood by the computer, facing the door. Mahir entered moments later, looked her in the eye for less than a second, and then turned his face away and stared at the easel in the corner. "What is it now?"

Yasmin pushed her hair back and crossed her arms to hide her trembling. "I know you're having an affair." She made an effort to steady her voice. "You have no right to treat me like this."

Mahir shook his head and traced his mustache. "I'm not having an affair." He released a long exhale. "Anything else?"

Yasmin had never spoken to Mahir like this before, no matter what the subject of their quarrel was. She could tell by his deep frown and the way he stared at her that he was shocked.

"Enough nonsense!" she said, her eyes slightly watering. Mahir had mentioned during their past arguments how the black eyeliner made her eyes fierce and unforgiving, so she tried not to blink. "I saw you today in Phoenix with the blonde." Then she handed him the ticket. "Care to explain this? It's dated the night you didn't answer my calls. The night you lied and said you were at the office."

Mahir's face reddened while he looked down at the ticket.

Yasmin carefully studied his body language: the sweat that started to ooze from his temples, the movement of his chest, his shaky hand. "I saw the restaurant receipt too. Dated the night you were supposedly at the gym!"

He finally lifted his head from the ticket, breathing faster. "If you think divorce is the answer, you'd better keep the children and our families in mind. I don't think it should even be an option."

Yasmin's jaw dropped. She raised her voice. "Is that right? What makes you think you can have your way and get away with it? You don't cheat on me and dictate my options."

Mahir raised his voice too. "I think you're losing your mind and becoming too Americanized. I don't know what you have in mind or why you made up this story. You're crazy."

"Don't call me crazy. I'm not crazy, and you know it." She then recounted to him all his peculiar behavior, starting with his new wardrobe and ending with the ticket. "So, I think you're doing what you're doing because you think you're a man and it's OK for you to have a fling. In the meantime, I'm supposed to either be stupid or just keep my mouth shut. Well, that's not going to happen."

He pointed his index finger at her. "You're just twisting facts," he said and then swallowed.

"Stop denying. I saw you with her today in the parking lot of Tomaso's." She placed her hands on the back of the desk chair between them.

"What? What the hell are you talking about?" He swallowed again as if he were choking on something. "I was there with some clients."

"Clients?" She put her palm up. "OK, you need to stop. I know what I saw and know I didn't imagine it. Don't insult me any further."

Mahir suddenly grabbed her hand and twisted her wrist.

Yasmin let out a cry and snatched back her hand.

Mahir shouted, "Shut up!" and held the desk chair. "You're making this up."

"No, I'm not." Yasmin moved back closer to the window.

He lifted the chair.

Yasmin screamed, crouched, and put both arms over her head. At the sound of breaking, she screamed again. After Mahir muttered something, she heard his footsteps in the hallway and then heard the front door slam. She looked up and saw the broken chair and some pieces of drywall that lay on the floor. Still stunned and scared, she stood up at the same time Sami and Mira entered the study with frightened faces.

"Everything is OK. It was just an accident." Yasmin hugged both of them. Sami did not utter a word. He just held Yasmin tight.

Tears glazed Mira's eyes. "I want Baba! You yelled at him and made him leave," she whined, her lower lip quivering.

Yasmin brushed back Mira's bangs and kissed her. "Don't cry. Baba will be back soon."

She then washed their faces, took them to their rooms, tucked them in, and read each of them a couple of bedtime stories. After they fell asleep, she went back to the study and started cleaning Mahir's mess. The storm had ended by then, but it was too late for the sun to shine.

CHAPTER FOUR

During the first week of April, it seemed like everywhere Yasmin turned she saw signs of spring, of new beginnings, of new life, but she still felt autumnal inside and out. She did not catch a glimpse of Mahir after their argument. Angry and hurt as she was, it suited her just fine not to see him. Actually, the way she felt right now was that she could not care less if she ever saw him again. Her only concern was that his absence was affecting Sami and Mira. Sami's teacher said one morning in the car line that in the past few days he had been very distracted and not as interested in his schoolwork as he used to be. Mira had retrieved a long-forgotten habit of clutching at her tattered blanket and seemed unusually quiet, except when she suddenly cried and asked when Mahir was coming back.

The sound of Mira and Sami screaming snapped Yasmin from her thoughts. She ran to Sami's room, where she found him and Mira both crying. The room looked like a giant had turned it upside down a few times. Not even one toy was inside the toy box. Stuffed animals were everywhere, and the Batman lampshade was on the floor, next to pencils and some crayons.

"What in the world?"

Sami sniffled when he saw her. "She bit me because I didn't let her play with my toy."

Mira covered her face with her hands and continued to sob, and then all of a sudden she lashed out at Sami and tried to snatch a stuffed dinosaur from his hand.

Yasmin picked her up. "OK, stop crying, both of you." She wiped Sami's tears and brushed his hair with her fingers. "Sami, get into bed, now. I'll be back in a minute to tuck you in and clean this mess."

"Mama," Sami said in a quivering voice. "If you don't yell at Baba again, will he come home and play with us more?"

"Habibi, Mama was upset when she yelled, but I promise you there will be no more." She bent down and kissed him, feeling bad, not knowing what to say. "He's very busy at work. He'll come home early sometime soon."

After Sami and Mira fell asleep, Yasmin lay in her bed thinking about them. It pained her deeply to see them suffer because of her and Mahir. All afternoon, Yasmin thought about calling Mahir to discuss Sami's and Mira's behavior but kept deciding against it. That disgusted look he had on his face when he called her crazy, twisted her wrist, broke the chair, and most of all said she was too Americanized never left her mind. Without a doubt, his hurtful words, lame defenses, violence, and accusations were all proofs of how little she or their marriage meant to him, and it saddened her. She had hoped that even though they had drifted apart, there was still some respect left, some compassion. Maybe she was being selfish by not calling Mahir for the sake of her children, and even more so for confronting him in the first place, but there was no way she could have pretended that nothing was wrong.

She slipped out of bed and put on her fleece robe before going out for a smoke. The microwave timer blinked twelve thirty. Yasmin opened the kitchen door and stepped out to the patio and the chilly night. She lit a cigarette and sat down on a patio chair. The moon was a little shy of a full circle, and its reflection on the pool surface looked like a floating disk. Her red geraniums were now in full bloom, fluttering in the breeze and scenting the night. She had been too distracted lately to notice the amount of yellow bells that were scattered all over the cat's claw or the orange blooms on the honeysuckles. Mahir always chose the cat's claw as a background when he took their pictures. Now that she thought about that, she realized how much their lives had gradually changed. How their friends had slowly disappeared and how they no longer went on trips out of town or had pool parties and barbecues. How they ended up now, as if none of their happy memories had ever existed.

Yasmin was lighting her second cigarette when Mahir opened the kitchen door and stepped out to the patio. She flinched. Being so engrossed in her thoughts in the quiet of the night, she did not hear him enter the house.

Mahir pulled a chair, sat across from Yasmin, and lit a cigarette.

Yasmin stared at him with weary eyes.

"I'm very sorry things between us amounted to this." He looked down at the lighter he rubbed between his fingers.

"Are you, Mahir? Then why are you cheating on me as if it's your given right instead of doing the right thing? Since when do you lay a hand on me?"

Mahir banged the patio table with the lighter.

Yasmin flinched again.

"Damn it, Yasmin. I'm not having an affair, and I swear I didn't mean to hurt you. You know I've never done that or will ever. I was just trying to move your hand away from my face."

It had crossed Yasmin's mind several times that Mahir was in some sort of trouble. Something about him working on that mosque addition never felt right. Actually, looking back now, she believed that that was the time when Mahir started changing dramatically, always being in a bad mood, complaining more than ever of too much work and stress.

"Are you in some kind of trouble?"

"No."

"Then what is happening?"

"Please don't do this. I can't talk about it. You won't understand."

"Try me."

Mahir gave her a look. Yasmin could not interpret whether it was anger, sadness, remorse, or a mix of them all.

He traced his mustache with nervous fingers. "You're making this too difficult. I can't continue living like this. I'm going to move out for a while until you calm down. You and the kids stay in the house. I'll take care of everything."

"You selfish bastard. You had it planned from the beginning." Her throat felt like bark when she swallowed. "Did you think for a minute about how this is going to affect Sami and Mira?"

Mahir traced his mustache again. "You know how much I love them." He stood up. "I'll move out as soon as I find a place."

"I don't give a damn what you do anymore. You're never here anyway."

Mahir lingered by the door for a few moments. Yasmin could see from out of the corner of her eye that he stared at her before he opened the door and then disappeared inside the house.

CHAPTER FIVE

Yasmin still remembered Mahir mention moving out at the end of their conversation five days ago, but she did not believe for a moment that he was serious. When she returned from her class on a Tuesday afternoon and found some of the family-room furniture missing, her heart almost stopped. The kitchen cabinets and drawers were open, and just by glancing inside she saw that he had taken some plates, mugs, and silverware. He had left behind a Post-it note on the fridge, scribbled with his new address at the nearby apartment complex.

Yasmin took the note, crumpled it, and tossed it in the trash. Feeling light-headed and out of breath, she picked up the phone and called Mahir.

"Are you out of your mind?" she screamed when he answered.

"Hold on." He did not give Yasmin a chance to say any more, but she could tell that he had his hand on the speaker. Finally, he came back. "You asked me to move, and I moved because you said you didn't give a damn if I moved out or stayed," he said in a low and shaky voice.

Yasmin figured that he had stepped out of the office so no one could hear him. "Liar," she screamed at him again. "That's not what happened. You are twisting my words. "

Yasmin slammed down the receiver. She felt her heart break into a million pieces. Mahir could not wait to leave. How stupid of her to even think that he was going to go out of his way to prove his innocence and stay at least for the children.

When Yasmin calmed down, she picked up the phone, called Ellen, and told her that Mahir had moved out.

"Oh, dear. I'm so sorry. Look, I'm on my way to Sedona, or else I would've stopped by."

"I know, you told me you were leaving right after class. I just didn't know—"

"It's fine. I'm glad you called." She was silent for a moment. "You know, maybe separation is good for both of you right now. I think Mahir needs some time away to reevaluate the whole situation. You also need to clear your mind."

"I never thought that he would do it. At least not this way. The kids—"

"OK, calm down. Let's deal with one thing at a time. For now, you have to be strong for the kids. When I get back, I'll call you, and we'll talk about all the other issues."

After Ellen advised Yasmin on how to break the news to Sami and Mira, they said their good-byes and hung up.

The mess in the family room made the whole house look as if a thief had robbed it in a rush, without any consideration for the feelings of the owners. The love seat was gone, and a side table and a couple of paintings, too. Mahir had taken sheets and towels from the linen closet and emptied most of his closet and drawers. He left behind a shirt that was a gift from Yasmin. The file cabinet in the study had the first drawer opened and half-empty.

Yasmin dreaded the moment of telling Sami and Mira, but there was no use in hiding the truth. They would probably link Mahir's absence to the missing furniture and all the other things.

She ran around the house and cleaned up a little and then tried to rearrange whatever was left of the family-room furniture as if redecorating were her major worry right now. She pushed the coffee table and the couch closer to the television, took the fern from the corner of the room, and put it in the place of the missing side table. A framed photo of Sami and Mira was not in its place on the shelf of the entertainment center, so she repositioned all the other pictures. She made a mental note to hang some of her paintings where there used to be two portraits of Arabic horsemen. Mahir had bought both paintings a long time ago, during his college years on one of his trips to Jordan.

When there was no more that could be done to the room, Yasmin dropped herself on the couch, drained and out of breath. Who was she fooling? Nothing would hide the fact that Mahir was gone. The thought of her living alone with Sami and Mira was confusing and a little frightening. She had depended on her father all her life, and then afterward on Mahir. Now her circumstances had unexpectedly changed, and God knows what Mahir's next move would be.

After Yasmin picked up Sami and Mira from school that afternoon, she pulled into the driveway of her house and then turned in her seat and said, "Mama wants to tell you something. I want you to understand that Mama and Baba love you both very much, but they can't live together anymore."

Sami's eyes filled with tears. He stared down at his clutched hands and then started kicking the back of the passenger seat.

Yasmin reached back and held his chin in her hand. "Habibi, look at me. I know this makes you sad. It makes me sad too. You and Mira will see Baba all the time. I promise you. You will stay at his new place on the weekends."

Sami covered his face with his hands and wept.

At that, Mira pouted her lips and began to cry. Yasmin could not determine whether Mira understood what was going on or if she was just reacting to Sami's sobbing.

Both Sami and Mira refused to eat their lunch, and Yasmin struggled with their edginess throughout the afternoon. Around five o'clock, she drove them to the McDonald's drive-through, bought them Happy Meals, and then took them to Chaparral Park. On the way Yasmin played their favorite *Barney* CD, but that did not change their moods. She tried to attract their attention by pointing at a red Hummer that passed them, and at some ducks that seemed lost on a golf course, but that did not work either. When they got out of the car at the parking lot, Mira held her hand, and Sami held on the hem of her cardigan. They did not run to the playground like they usually did. Normally they would pet every dog that passed them, but they did not even look at the few that went by with their owners.

It would have been a perfect late afternoon at the park if they were not so sad. It smelled of an unusual but beautiful combination of water, grass, pine, and sand. Many children stood near the edge with their parents, throwing bread for the ducks that gathered around. An elderly couple sat nearby holding fishing poles, talking, and laughing. Usually Mira would chase away every bird in sight at the park and make them seek shelter on one of the many mature pine trees around the playground. But she totally ignored the pigeons that pecked at the green grass.

Facing the swings and slides, full of children playing, Yasmin sat between Sami and Mira on a bench and pleaded with them to eat. Mira took a few bites of a chicken nugget, but Sami refused.

"How about you go play then?"

Sami nodded and dragged his legs over the sand toward the slide, his back hunched like that of an old man who was shouldering the burdens of a long and hard life. Yasmin watched as Mira followed Sami and held his hand. They looked at each other and then at the children playing around them, came back, and sat down. Yasmin hugged them tightly, trying hard to hold back her tears.

That night, they all cried themselves to sleep.

The next day Mira woke up cranky. She asked Yasmin for milk but did not drink it. Then she asked for an apple but did not eat it. Sami ate only some his breakfast in silence. On the way to school, Yasmin played their *Barney* CD, but neither one of them sang along or even smiled.

In the afternoon, Mira spent most of her time dismantling one of her dolls, painting her face with markers. Sami watched cartoons hour after hour until Yasmin turned off the television and handed him some colors and a drawing pad. Without protesting, Sami knelt at the coffee table and started squiggling hard on his drawing pad. He slashed through a few pages instead of slowly sketching his favorite portrait of a family with disproportioned arms, standing in the driveway of a house. Yasmin felt her chest tighten. It would have been less painful for her if Sami had taken a pencil and stabbed her with it instead. She turned the television back on. "Never mind, habibi. You can watch TV."

"When is Baba coming back to live with us?" Sami asked.

After standing for a few minutes feeling helpless, Yasmin picked up her cell phone and dialed Mahir. Before he answered, she handed Sami the phone. "Ask him when he's coming back."

Sami put the phone to his ear and waited. Then his face suddenly lit up with a smile. "Baba, when are you coming back?" He was silent for a few moments. His smile became more intense, and then he nodded. "OK." He gave the phone to Mira.

Mira cried when she heard Mahir's voice, and then she nodded and said, "Uh-huh." She listened for a couple of seconds, smiled, and then handed Yasmin the phone. Mahir had already hung up. He did not ask to talk to her. She faked a smile and looked at Sami.

"Baba bought me a Batman sleeping bag, and a Barbie one for Mira." Sami had not looked so happy in days. "He's fixing his apartment now, but he will take us there on Friday." He waited a few seconds before he asked Yasmin, "How many times do we have to sleep and wake up before we go?"

"Only two."

Yasmin was in the kitchen preparing dinner for Sami and Mira when the phone rang. She stepped closer to it and glanced at the caller ID. It was the Mahmouds. A Jordanian couple, Maher and Nuha had long ago moved to California, but Mahir had stayed in touch. Once in a while, he mentioned calling them from his office. When the Mahmouds lived in Phoenix, Yasmin had never really liked Nuha. Though they both came from the same country, they were obviously from different backgrounds. Nuha's conversations had revolved mainly around food, and she constantly sought praise for her complicated recipes, like stuffed lamb intestines.

Yasmin lifted the receiver with reluctance.

"How are you and the children? In good health, inshallah?"

"All fine. Thank you for asking," Yasmin said.

"Listen," Nuha said. "Mahir told us what happened, and I want you to know that we are very upset over this."

Yasmin could not understand why Mahir would call these people and share such private details with them. "Thank you. I appreciate that. Look, I don't mean to be rude, but I left Mira in the bathtub so I could answer the phone. I will call you some other time."

Nuha ignored Yasmin's apology. "Why did you let the problem escalate like that?" she admonished. "You could've handled Mahir in a smart way. You know…you're a woman…you know how it works."

Yasmin squinted. "I'm not sure I'm following."

"Couldn't you stop at Victoria's Secret, the candle store…you know…and work on getting pregnant?"

Yasmin widened her eyes. "And why would I do that?"

"To hold Mahir down and save your marriage, of course. Consider me an older sister, and forgive me for saying this, but a single man with the last name Ahmad, one of the most significant and influential families in Jordan, is not going to have a problem remarrying. But God forbid Mahir divorced you, no one is going to even look at you at the age of thirty-four with two children," she said with conviction.

Yasmin could not believe her ears. Nuha turned out to be more ignorant than she had ever imagined. "You know what? I have to go now." She hung up and stared at the phone in disbelief. It was obvious that Mahir somehow made the Mahmouds believe it was all Yasmin's fault. Just like he claimed that moving out was her idea, which made her wonder whom else he had called so far and what kind of lies he was spreading around. Mahir paid too much attention to what people thought of him or said about him. So that he was twisting facts to protect his image came as no surprise to Yasmin.

Friday afternoon, Sami and Mira prepared for their first weekend with Mahir as if they were leaving on a camping trip. Yasmin helped them pack their backpacks with clothes, pajamas, toothbrushes, and toys and waited for Mahir with them by the family-room window.

"My sleepy bag is pink and has a Barbie on it," Mira told Sami.

"Mine is black and red. Baba bought a new TV for us," Sami said.

When Mahir finally pulled into the driveway, they both ran to the door. Mira held Yasmin's hand and pulled. "Come with us to Baba's new department."

"It's *apartment*, Mira," Yasmin corrected and released her hand. "I can't go with you," she said. "I can't." She opened the door and let them out.

Mahir said hi while he hugged Sami and Mira. He looked at Yasmin as if he were checking her out. "Happy now that you don't see my face anymore?"

Yasmin was enraged at this cheap shot. "Don't you dare turn this on me, Mahir," she said with a shaky voice.

He looked down at Sami and Mira and smiled. Yasmin could tell it was one of his phony smiles.

"Is twisting words and facts your best defense nowadays?"

He gave no answer.

"Nuha called me by the way. Have you told your parents the same lie?"

Mahir's face reddened. "My parents have nothing to do with this. We are old enough to make our own decisions. You are obviously still blinded by your anger, so we'd better wait before we have a serious talk." He then walked Sami and Mira to his car, buckled them into the backseat, and drove away.

Yasmin closed the door. How could the man she had been married to for ten years suddenly become so mean and twice as manipulative in such a short time? At least he let her know that their futures were in their hands and not anyone else's. She wanted nothing more than to raise Sami and Mira in America and make sure they got a good education. Missing them only minutes after they left, Yasmin felt lost. She had never spent an afternoon or an evening without her children, let alone a whole weekend. Though they went to school every day, something about them being with Mahir that night made her feel uneasy.

CHAPTER SIX

On the last Monday of April around noon, Yasmin waited for Ellen to arrive at Starbucks while she sipped her coffee and watched tourists amble by in shorts and tank tops, holding bags from Indian jewelry stores. The smell of food from the restaurants nearby saturated the air. Lately though food had been the last thing on Yasmin's mind. Smoking and drinking coffee seemed to be her only cravings. She hated that.

Her conversations with Ellen over the past weeks were definitely a comfort in many ways but also gave Yasmin a reality check. Mahir said he would take care of everything, but with his vagueness and unpredictability, it was better for Yasmin not to depend on him entirely. Even though Ellen said she believed that Mahir's move was just a temporary situation, she still advised Yasmin to consider finding a job.

"Hello." Ellen's voice came from behind.

Yasmin turned around. "Hi, Ellen." She looked graceful in her blue linen outfit and the serene look she always had on her face. Yasmin liked that.

Ellen placed her cup on the table, pulled a chair, and sat down. "How are you? Anything new since we last talked?"

"Not really. Sami and Mira had another episode of crying and asking when Mahir was coming back. Other than that I've been thinking about our conversation, and I think you're right. Working at Sami and Mira's school, or any school, is my best choice for now. It has to be office work though."

"Good. You see, this way you will have the same hours and same holidays. You won't need babysitters or a daycare." Ellen reached inside her purse and took out some papers. "Here's your résumé and the cover letter. I e-mailed it to you too. Start sending it out now so hopefully you'll hear back from a school before you leave on your trip to Jordan."

"Thanks, Ellen. I always trouble you—"

"Don't say that. Now, speaking of leaving, did you make up your mind? Are you going to inform your parents of Mahir's move?"

Yasmin shook her head. "Not sure yet, Ellen. I'm going to put off calling them for as long as I can. I don't want them worrying while preparing for my sister's wedding."

Ellen pursed her lips and seemed lost in her thoughts. "Will your parents make you stay in Jordan because you are separated?"

"No, not really. I mean...I'm sure they are not going to like the idea of me and the kids living without Mahir, especially my father." Yasmin lit a cigarette. "My parents are very open-minded, Ellen. They still sometimes hold on to a few things of the past, but they're not the type that would force me to do anything."

"What if Mahir wanted you to stay? Did you consider that?"

"I doubt it. I don't think he would like being away from the children. Besides, I know how important Sami's and Mira's education and future are to him. But even if he was considering such a major decision, I'm sure he would've discussed it with me."

Although Ellen nodded while she listened, she had a look of uncertainty in her eyes. It did not surprise Yasmin. Ellen was another American who did not quite understand Yasmin's culture and had her own perceptions, so it was natural for her to fear the worst.

"What's it like for women over there? I mean for a woman in your situation. Would you be able to live on your own and raise your children like single women in America?"

Yasmin took a long drag of her cigarette. "Not really. Usually when married couples separate, the wife returns to her parents' house, and if they were deceased to her brother's house. Though this is the norm, there are, of course, some exceptions. Many divorcées live on their own, working and raising their children. But it's not as easy as it is here. These women are always targets. They are looked down upon, harassed, and criticized like they are some kind of disgrace."

"That's what I thought. So if you and Mahir divorce and you end up going back, you have to live with your parents?" Ellen took a sip of her coffee.

"I'm afraid so. Ellen, the wages over there are ridiculous. Even if my father gave me the choice of living on my own, I don't think I could make it."

Ellen shook her head. "Are you sure that Mahir is not considering the idea of making you move back?"

Yasmin smiled and nodded. Ellen must have heard all kinds of horror stories about parents kidnapping children, but the last thing Yasmin would expect from Mahir was to act in such an uncivilized manner when he really did not need to.

"What is your gut feeling telling you, Yasmin?"

Yasmin did not know what to say. It all happened so fast that she didn't even have the time to clear her head. Instead, she was just going with the flow, trusting that the universe would take care of her.

"Honestly I'm not sure, but I think it's going to be OK."

"Well then, hopefully you'll get a job here and, whatever happens with Mahir, you'll have some sort of financial security."

Yasmin agreed.

⊱⊰

Sami and Mira's last day of school was May 31. When Mahir came to pick them up that Friday, he looked like he was going out on a date, or maybe like he had just came back from one. He wore a pink shirt and navy-blue slacks, his hair and mustache were nicely trimmed, and the smell of his cologne filled the air.

Mahir peeked inside the house first, and then he stepped in and walked toward the kitchen.

"I will bring Sami and Mira close to ten Sunday evening."

"That's too late, don't you think?"

He rolled his eyes. "They don't have school on Monday." He then took a few steps and looked out the french door.

"Yeah, right. That's fine I guess," Yasmin said, though she did not like the idea of Sami and Mira staying up so late. "By the way, I need you to stop by the school on Monday to pay for the first summer session." She smiled at Sami and Mira.

Mahir frowned. "What for? You are traveling."

"That's almost five weeks from today. Besides, they love the summer camp. They swim, go to the park, visit the library, and—"

"Fine." He looked at Sami and Mira and said, "Let's go."

Yasmin locked the door behind them and then walked to the study and checked her e-mail. It had been almost two weeks since she had sent out résumés to several schools, but so far she had heard nothing back. Maybe she should send out a few more résumés. This was not the time to give up or beat herself up for not pursuing a career since the day she landed in this country. She was so angry at herself for waiting so long before realizing how important it was to have some sort of financial security established. What if Mahir had died instead of them having marriage difficulties and left nothing for her and the kids? How come she never even considered that?

She opened an e-mail from her best friend in Jordan, Carole. Yasmin had put off e-mailing or calling her during the past couple of months because Carole was busy with her work at her restaurant, La Bonita, and Yasmin did not have much to share other than her unpleasant circumstances. To explain the situation in just a few lines was not easy, but Yasmin could not hide such news from Carole anymore, especially now that she was going to see her in Jordan soon. After Yasmin wrote a long e-mail to Carole, she signed out and logged off. The time difference between Arizona and Jordan was not right yet to call her parents, so she sat behind her easel and worked on her painting. Close to midnight, she went to the kitchen, took a deep breath, lifted the phone receiver, and called her parents. The phone rang for what seemed like an eternity to Yasmin before her mother finally picked up. After getting done with all the greetings and such, Yasmin confessed to her mother.

"Mama, I'm afraid I have some bad news."

"What?" her mother shouted. "Are the children OK? Is Mahir sick?"

"No, Mama. They're all fine." Yasmin told her mother in detail what had happened between her and Mahir since March.

While she spoke, her mother interrupted her a few times. "That's impossible."

Yasmin kept going on and mentioned the big fight that ended with a broken chair.

Her mother snapped, "I can't believe this is happening!"

When Yasmin finally told her that Mahir had moved out, her mother shouted, "No!"

Yasmin felt anger and despair in her voice.

"How could he do this? How could both of you disrespect us like that and keep us in the dark for so long? How come his parents did not contact us either?"

"I'm sorry, Mama. I just didn't want to upset all of you for Hala's sake. Besides, I'm quite sure this is a temporary situation." Yasmin felt bad for telling such a lie. "So I don't know if Mahir wants his parents to know about this right now."

"When your father comes back from the bank, I will have him call Mahir's father. This is not acceptable. Not acceptable."

"No, Mama, please. I don't think this is a good idea. Mahir doesn't want his parents to know at this point. Let us work on our problems without interference. I promise you we will find a solution and do the right thing."

The next day Yasmin's mother called and began to cry the moment Yasmin answered the phone. Unable to control her sobbing, she handed the phone to Yasmin's sister, Hala.

"I'm so sorry," Hala said. "I can't stop thinking about all of you."

Yasmin pictured Hala's beautiful face, her thick-lashed eyes full of sympathy. "Don't, Hala. I'm perfectly fine, and so are the children."

"Mama sounded like she was announcing someone's death when she told me what happened."

"I'm not surprised. Do me a favor and calm her down."

"I will. Don't worry. Listen, Baba is standing next to me. He wants to talk to you."

"OK."

"How are you managing?" her father asked in his usual composed tone, a tone that always matched his serious features, especially his sharp eyes and his white hair. "I'm very concerned about you and the children. I don't think it's safe for you to live alone like that. I don't know what Mahir was thinking when he made such an arrangement."

"Baba, we are fine. Don't worry about us."

"We can't discuss this problem long-distance. We will talk about it once you get here. For now, I want the two of you to stop this non-sense and deal with your problems in a rational manner that suits our traditions."

As soon as they hung up, Yasmin called her friend Dina to inform her too of her situation.

⊨⊹ ⊹⊨

When Mahir brought Sami and Mira back on Sunday night, Mira clung to Mahir's leg. "Baba stay." She began to cry.

Yasmin gently pulled her hand away from Mahir's leg. "You will go with Baba again next week."

Mira shook her head and continued to cry.

"How about I read you a story before I go?" Mahir asked.

Mira nodded.

Yasmin did not comment. She just moved out of the way and let him in. Mahir stayed in Mira's room until she fell asleep, and then he went to Sami's room and read him a story too. When Sami fell asleep, Mahir came to the family room, where Yasmin was flipping through a magazine.

"The children are hurting." He sounded concerned.

Yasmin heaved a sigh. "What do you plan on doing about it, Mahir?"

"Don't worry. I have it all figured out."

"Really? Care to share your plan with me, or are you still going to keep me in the dark?"

Mahir made a face. He obviously did not like Yasmin's reply. "Why don't we wait until you come back from Jordan? Both of us will be calm enough to sit and talk about everything."

"That's fine."

Mahir opened the front door and stepped out.

47

CHAPTER SEVEN

Just by getting close to the kitchen window, Yasmin could already feel the heat seeping through the panes. Hard to believe it was already July 2, one day before her trip. Too bad she was not staying in Jordan long enough to escape the summer. Jordanian summers were mild and short. The mornings and evening were breezy, and with the exception of a couple of weeks in August, temperatures rarely reached a hundred degrees.

Yasmin had managed to finish most of her packing during the day while Sami and Mira were spending their last day in Scottsdale with Mahir. She also watered her indoor and outdoor plants, took care of the pool, checked her list of reminders, and added a few lines to it.

Dina had promised to stop by around six that evening to say good-bye and take Yasmin's extra key so she could take care of everything while Yasmin was away. Since she still had a little over an hour before Dina came over, Yasmin walked to the study and sat in front of her easel. To the right of the twin palms that had chandeliers of dates hanging from them, she carefully colored a fish floating in the blue sky next to a mushroom. Yasmin smiled as she remembered Ellen's expression when she saw the painting and loved the Arabic calligraphy on the horizon. The abstract letters were a verse from the Koran: "And in heaven is your provision, and that which you are promised." As mentioned in all Arabic dream interpretation books, seeing fish, dates and mushrooms denoted abundance and good fortunes.

When the doorbell rang, Yasmin looked out the window and saw Dina's old Maxima parked in the driveway. By the time she put the paintbrush down, wiped her hands, and reached the front door, the bell had rung over ten times.

"What took you so long?" Dina took off her sunglasses, revealing her heavily lined hazel eyes.

"I was wiping my hands." They hugged and kissed each other on the cheeks. "You're late. It's almost seven."

"Sorry." Dina examined Yasmin from head to toe. "You straightened your hair, and you've been tanning. Lost weight and wearing makeup!" She continued on her way to the kitchen as if reporting a condition.

"Yeah, what's wrong with that? If you don't think I have a right to look good because my husband left me, you can stay over after we have coffee and help me dig my grave," Yasmin joked.

Dina laughed.

"You look different too. Your hair is all one color. I like it better like this. Don't ever spray it with that Sun-In again." Yasmin walked to the cabinet and reached for the turkish coffee canister. "How do you feel like having it today? Just right, or do you want sugar?"

"Yeah, put some in. We have enough bitterness in our lives as it is."

Yasmin smiled. She had known Dina long enough to know that she meant no harm. "Don't act like an old Arabic mother. It's not the end of the world, you know." She filled the special turkish coffeepot with water and placed it on the stove.

Dina fixed her short ponytail. "Don't get mad at me for saying this, but I think you're taking your situation too lightly."

Yasmin frowned. "What am I supposed to do, Dina? Cry day and night? Go beg Mahir to take me back?"

"That's not what I meant. I'm talking about your trip."

"Look, Mahir is negotiating a partnership with the firm right now and has no intention of moving back to Jordan. So no harm is coming from him. My parents know exactly what happened, and I have no worries whatsoever from their side."

"I know, but I'm afraid things will change once you're there. You've been away too long, Yasmin. You forgot how things work over there."

Yasmin did not reply. Dina came from an uneducated family and of course a different background. For her to suspect that Yasmin's parents were showing support only to lure her back came as no surprise to Yasmin. She had heard many stories of unfortunate women in Jordan who suffered because of divorce. Some were even killed by family members in the name of honor as a result. When the water came to a boil, Yasmin added coffee to it and stirred while holding the pot by its long handle over the fire. The smell of coffee filled the air, overpowering Dina's flowery perfume. Yasmin then poured the coffee in small cups she placed over saucers and put them on the island in front of her and Dina. Before she sat down, she opened the window and lit a cigarette. They sipped their coffee in silence for a few moments. Yasmin would have liked more ground cardamom in her coffee, but it still tasted good anyway.

"Dina, are you sure it's no trouble for you to water my plants and pour chlorine in the pool?"

"Very sure."

Yasmin handed her a key.

After Dina put it in her purse, she reached for Yasmin's cup, looked in it, and then placed it back on its saucer. "Hurry up. Finish your coffee."

Yasmin took a drag of her cigarette and then smashed it in the ashtray. "You're not reading my fortune, are you?"

"Yes, I am," Dina said. "I haven't done that in a long time. I want to see what's going on with you." Dina was too impatient to wait for Yasmin's empty cup. She poured whatever coffee was left back into the pot, leaving only a little in the bottom of the cup. She then covered it with its saucer and turned it upside down so the coffee dregs would drain and print images inside the cup.

"You know…something about Mahir simply moving out is very unsettling to me."

Yasmin looked at her watch. It was seven forty-five, and there was still no sign of Mahir and the kids.

Dina picked up Yasmin's cup. "Damn. It doesn't look good. Your cup is too dark."

"What does it mean?" She lit a cigarette.

"I wish you would just sober up and cancel that damn trip. I have a very bad feeling about it. Besides, I dreamed about you and the kids the other day, and I don't like what I saw."

"What was the dream?"

"You were carrying a suitcase, walking with Sami and Mira on a narrow dirt path. To your left there was a desert and to your right green pastures and beautiful houses. Mahir was walking in the distance behind you with a dagger in his hand. Don't go, Yasmin, please. What more of a sign do you need to change your mind?"

Yasmin blew a puff of smoke. Some dreams left her puzzled for days if she could not interpret them. But she also knew that most dreams are only a reflection of fears and overthinking issues and decided that was the case with Dina. She smiled. "Yeah, maybe I should just call my sister and tell her sorry, I can't come to your wedding because Dina saw bad things in my cup and in her dream."

"Hey, you can laugh at me all you want. I know what I'm talking about."

Yasmin stared out the window. The neighbor's black cat was tip-toeing on the fence, and then Yasmin heard the flapping of wings. A lucky bird got away.

"I see you hanging upside down." Dina waved her palm inches from Yasmin's eyes, as if removing a haze. "Do you hear me? Look." She pointed inside the cup.

"Yeah…Yeah, I hear you." Yasmin turned her head. "What does it mean?"

"It means you're going to be in trouble. You'll be in a difficult situation, helpless." She released a nervous sigh. "Give me some white vinegar."

"Please don't tell me this is about your magic theory again, Dina. You remind me of my aunt Nihad and her care packages full of instructions. Burn this, bury that, drink a little, and pour some in his tea! She used to send one every time I made a mistake and told my mother I had a fight with Mahir. "

"I don't understand why you don't believe me. You know very well magic *is* mentioned in the Koran. So don't make fun of me or your aunt Nihad. You do believe in the Koran, right? "

Yasmin nodded. She was not in the mood to discuss religion or what she believed or did not believe in with Dina. "I'm not mak-ing fun. I just don't think it has anything to do with my situation. What's so unusual about having allergies and going through mari-tal problems?"

"Fine. You can believe whatever you want. Just give me the vin-egar, please."

Yasmin stood up, shaking her head. She took out a small bottle from the cabinet and slammed it in front of Dina, who immediately opened it, leaned forward, and started reciting "Surat al-Fatihah," the first chapter of the Koran. "In the Name of Allah, the Merciful, the beneficent," she said aloud and then whispered the rest of the verses into the bottle. She followed with "Surat al-Falaq" and finally "Surat An-nas," two other short chapters of the Koran known to ward off evil. "I'm going to pour a few drops in every corner of the house to cleanse it of negative energies," Dina said when she was done.

"I never heard of this procedure before, but just because it's the Koran, I'm not going to argue with you. Go ahead and do it. If anything, it might cleanse some negative energy."

Dina moved around the house, pouring small amounts into the bottle cap and then onto the floor, first in the kitchen and then the dining area and the family room before she disappeared into the hallway. The smell of vinegar was nauseating. Yasmin looked at her watch again and picked up the phone to call Mahir but decided to wait and put it back.

"What in the world are you painting?" Dina's voice blurted out of the study. When she returned to the kitchen, she said, "You still want me to believe you're not under a spell? Since when do fish fly in the sky?"

"Since I made them."

"You're weird, Yasmin. Forgive me for saying this. I don't know why you waste your time and your money painting unusual things. Sometimes you even talk weird about everything, but I'm not getting into that right now"

"There's more to life than heaven and hell and exchanging recipes and housecleaning tips, Dina," Yasmin said without thinking.

Dina stared at Yasmin, and her eyes said Yasmin was losing her mind.

Car headlights suddenly lit up the family room. Yasmin ran to the window and looked out. "You are not going to believe this. He drove them home with Mira in his lap."

"My God, what is he thinking? He's in Jordan?"

Yasmin opened the door and stepped out while Mahir walked Sami and Mira in her direction. He took his time checking her out. "Whose car is this?" He peeked inside.

"Dina's. Do you want to come in and say hi?"

"No," Mahir snapped. "Thank you for inviting me into my own house anyway." He turned to leave.

"What's wrong?"

Mahir took a deep breath with his back to Yasmin and then turned around smiling. One of his new and fake smiles. "Nothing. Just a little upset about not seeing the children for a while."

Yasmin smiled back and nodded. "What time are you going to be here tomorrow?"

"Don't worry. I'll be here on time." He sat in his car and started backing up.

Yasmin closed the door.

"What was that all about?" Dina looked at Yasmin. "You still want me to think everything is OK? And why is he driving you to the airport?"

"A friend of mine had trouble with the airline counter last year. They demanded written permission from her husband before they let her children on the plane. Safety precautions, I guess, in case the parent is kidnapping the children."

Dina shrugged and then pressed a few kisses on Sami and Mira's faces. Yasmin took them by their hands and walked toward the hallway. "It's too late for a bath now. We'll do it in the morning."

"Baba let us fill the tub and have a bubble bath," Mira said.

Yasmin helped Sami put on his pajamas and tucked him in. She then took Mira to her room and did the same. Before returning to Dina, she stood by the door. "I'll be right back to read you a story, OK, Mira?"

"Mama." Mira sat up. "Are you a *sharmuta*?"

Yasmin was shocked at that. "Where did you learn this word, Mira? Don't ever say it again. It's a bad word."

"Baba said that."

"About whom?"

Mira shrugged.

"Yasmin, I have to go now!" Dina yelled from the kitchen.

"I'm coming." Yasmin walked back to the kitchen. "Did you hear what Mira said? He used the word *whore* in front of the children."

Dina frowned and looked very serious. "Yes, I did. Look, I'm not going to beg you not to go again because I know what your reply is going to be, but please, please, promise me you'll consider everything I said, and try to seek help in Jordan."

"I hate to disappoint you, Dina, but I'm not going to waste my time there looking for fortune-tellers."

"That's not what I want you to do. I want you to find a sheik specializing in exorcism."

Yasmin rolled her eyes. "OK, Dina." She kissed her on both cheeks. "I'll call you as soon as I get back."

CHAPTER EIGHT

The next day a little after four in the morning, Sami woke up crying, frightened by a monster dream. Yasmin sat at his bedside and soothed him back to sleep.

She combed his hair with her fingers. "Monsters only exist in books."

Sami sniffled. Ten minutes later he fell asleep.

Traveling back home was always exciting and a bit stressful, but this time Yasmin felt overwhelmed with anxiety. Ever since Dina left the night before, Yasmin could not stop thinking about their conversation and about Mahir calling her a whore in front of Sami and Mira. Could Mira be mistaken? Mahir might have just uttered the word and Mira misunderstood whom he was addressing. He had certainly snapped at her when she invited him in, but then he immediately apologized, saying he was only upset because the children were going away. Now that that she was only hours away from being with her family, she dreaded how her parents were going to handle the situation.

Canceling the trip crossed her mind many times over the past weeks, but not attending her sister's wedding was unthinkable.

Yasmin still remembered in detail how about six years ago Hala's husband had died in that tragic car accident and how devastated Hala was.

Even with realizing how important it was for her to be with Hala on her wedding day, Yasmin still wished deep inside that she would not go. Instead of counting the minutes to get to Jordan to see her family as she had done in the past, she found herself feeling guilty for counting the minutes to get back even before leaving.

After having a cup of coffee, Yasmin tidied the house, dragged her suitcases to the family room, and then took a shower. Choosing an outfit for traveling to Jordan was pretty much like dressing for the weather; it had to be comfortable and appropriate. Yasmin faced her closet for a few minutes and finally decided on jeans and a black tank top and then tied an oversize denim shirt around her waist to slip on right before landing. Being scrutinized in Jordan by airport officers, security, cabdrivers, or any male could make a woman feel uncomfortable.

It was almost seven thirty by the time Yasmin was ready. She poured another cup of coffee, grabbed a cigarette and her list of reminders, and stepped out to the patio. The moment she sat down on one of the patio chairs, a shimmering hummingbird sped from one plant to another before it flew in the direction of a white half-moon that still hung in the sky to the west. Yasmin took her time smoking and then went over her list and checked the chlorine boxes she had stacked in the shed for Dina. Nothing should go wrong in her absence, and Dina would have no problem keeping the pool blue and a few plants green.

Yasmin was thinking about the strenuous eighteen hours of planes and airports when she heard a gentle knocking. She opened the door and smiled back at Mira, who was standing there barefoot, both arms reaching up. She looked prettier than a perfect doll with her padded cheeks and her soft ringlets. Yasmin lifted her up and kissed her. "Cheerios?"

Mira nodded.

Once they were inside, Mira wiggled in Yasmin's arms and released herself. Sami walked in when Yasmin was pouring the milk over Mira's cereal. "Are you OK?" She leaned over and kissed him.

Sami gave no answer.

Yasmin placed a bowl of cereal in front of him.

He shook his head and pushed the bowl away.

Something was wrong with him, and it had nothing to do with monsters. Yasmin could see it in his sad eyes. "Is there anything you want to tell Mama?"

"Are we going to live in Jordan?"

"No, no, habibi. We're coming back in ten days." She patted his back. "Why do you say this, Sami?" Before he gave her an answer, the doorbell rang.

Mira ran to the family-room window. "It's Baba, it's Baba." She jumped and clapped.

As soon as Yasmin opened the door, Mira ran and clung to Mahir's leg. "Why isn't Mira ready?" He frowned at Yasmin and stepped in. "You have to be at the airport at least three hours before your flight. Didn't you read your itinerary?"

"No, I didn't. Why so early, anyway?"

Mahir walked to Sami and kissed him.

"Security procedures since 9/11." He looked at his watch. "I was planning on being here half an hour ago, but something came up at work." He checked the time again. "We are going to be late. Hurry up. I'll help you dress Sami and Mira so we can still get there on time."

Yasmin cleaned up the kitchen quickly and then took Mira and slipped her into her denim overalls. Then she took a small handbag that she had already packed with a box of wet wipes, snacks, Tylenol, crayons, and coloring books and threw inside it a change of clothes for Mira.

Mahir ran a nervous trace over his mustache. "Are you packing now?"

"Just a change of clothes for Mira."

He waited a few seconds before he asked, "Are you done?"

"I still have to take the trash out and give our neighbor Beth my key. She's taking care of the mail. Can you turn the air off and take care of the suitcases?"

He sighed and walked to the thermostat.

Yasmin rushed out of the kitchen door to the alley. When she came back, Mahir and the children were already waiting in the car. She locked the door and then ran to her neighbor's house.

On the way to the airport, Yasmin kept herself occupied by fumbling with her purse, leafing through the passports and the tickets. Sitting next to Mahir after all they had been through and noticing from the corner of her eye how he glanced at her every now and then felt awkward.

"Are you going to Jordan like this?" he asked.

"I have my shirt." Yasmin pointed to her waist. She had a strong urge to tell him that what she wore was no longer his concern. Saying the word *whore* in front of the children was another thing she wanted to discuss with him, but now was not the right time for it. She would have a serious talk with him once she came back.

After ten minutes of silence, Mahir pointed to the sky. "Look, Sami. Do you see that plane descending?"

Sami did not reply.

At the Sky Harbor parking, Yasmin took care of Sami and Mira, and Mahir handled their luggage. Travelers swarmed around inside the terminal in overwhelming numbers as if the whole town were going on a trip that morning. Some passengers were checking luggage at the sidewalk. They looked angry and frustrated. There was a long line of passengers at the British Airways counter, but after standing there for a few moments, Yasmin noticed that it was moving at a reasonable pace. That was a relief, especially after noticing how some passengers stared at her. Ten months after 9/11, and she still felt uncomfortable when anybody looked at her for whatever reason. Many people not only did not distinguish between Arab and Muslim but also seemed to hold anyone that looked Middle Eastern responsible for the attacks. Eight Americans were killed after 9/11 for that sole reason, one of them a Sikh who owned a convenient store in Mesa, Arizona.

"I'll be back in a minute," Mahir said and walked toward one of the terminal doors before Yasmin had a chance to say anything.

Mira tried to slip away and follow him, and when Yasmin lifted her up, she cried. "I go potty."

"You have to hold it, Mira. I can't leave the line."

Mira continued to whine and squirm in Yasmin's arms.

Yasmin wiped perspiration off her face and kept looking at the glass door for what seemed a lifetime before Mahir finally strolled in. He smelled of cigarette smoke, and Yasmin could not believe that he left her standing there with two children so he could smoke.

"Can you take Mira to the restroom, quickly?" she asked.

"Calm down." He held Mira's hand and hurried in the opposite direction, looking for a restroom sign.

"I want to go with Baba," Sami said in a nagging tone.

"He'll be right back. Don't start, Sami." Yasmin kept her eyes in the direction Mahir took before he disappeared. A few minutes later, she saw him sauntering back, holding Mira's hand. She gestured for him to hurry. There were only a couple of passengers ahead of her by then.

The employee behind the British Airways counter processed their tickets and examined their passports. She then looked at Mahir. "Are you the father?"

"Yes." He handed her his driver's license.

She gave it back on top of the passports, tickets, and boarding passes. "They started boarding ten minutes ago. You'd better hurry up." She smiled.

At the boarding gate, Mahir hugged and kissed Sami and Mira and then took out a stack of folded bills and handed them to

Yasmin. "For you and the kids." He stepped back and waved. "I'll see you soon," he said with a grin.

Yasmin held Mira's hand and let Sami walk ahead of her all the way to their seats. By the time she buckled Sami and Mira, and then herself, the plane started taking off. She looked out the widow and watched as Phoenix got smaller and smaller below them, the wide streets slowly becoming black lines sketched with a crayon and the cars that crowded them turning into mini Matchbox cars. Neighborhoods looked like tiny LEGO houses stacked one after the other, all constructed by the hands of a talented child who was generous enough to give almost every home a bean-shaped pool.

Five hours after takeoff, Yasmin felt like she had been on the plane for an eternity. There were thirteen more hours to endure, and Yasmin's constant checking of the time made the minutes seem much slower in air than they did on land. She closed her eyes and wondered if her wish to unwind would ever manifest. Mira had already dragged her to the toilet too many times, enjoying every moment of walking up and down the aisle while examining the interior of the plane, the passengers, and the flight attendants. She had turned the floor underneath their seats into a landfill of crushed cookies and torn candy wrappers and stood up and jumped down in her seat enough times to force the passengers behind them to complain. Though Sami's Game Boy usually disconnected him from the world, he continued to whine about his ears until Yasmin convinced him that he had swallowed all the gum she had with her.

When the movie *Chicken Run* started and both Sami and Mira gave the screen their complete attention, Yasmin released a long sigh.

CHAPTER NINE

With a hoarse voice, as if just awakened from a long sleep, the pilot announced that they were about to land, adding that it was 4:00 a.m. Jordan time. Yasmin stretched and looked out the window as the plane descended toward the Queen Alia International Airport. Other than the lit tarmac, all she could see was the pitch-black night. In the far distance, some tiny lights flickered like a million candles. Daylight would not have revealed much since the airport was located about twenty miles outside the capital. Landing, as she had in the past, at the old airport in Marka, a suburb of Amman, was a much more interesting experience. Yasmin could still picture flying over the seven hills on which the city had been built, covered in a sea of white limestone houses and buildings, separated by narrow black roads. The nicest part of descending toward the old airport was looking down at the Roman amphitheater and the citadel. Yasmin's first school trip to the theater and the museum had left a powerful impression on her. No wonder she ended up studying archaeology and working for the Department of Culture.

The sound of the overhead compartments opening and closing snapped Yasmin out of her memories. She untied her shirt from her waist and put it on and then helped Sami and Mira into their sweatshirts. Early mornings and nights could get very chilly in Jordan. The passengers were all standing in the aisles by the time she was done, so she stayed in her seat until the last one walked ahead of her.

The airport that had seemed deserted at first glance came to life with the sounds of footsteps shuffling and carry-ons dragging. The smell of sleep and Dettol disinfectant saturated the air. The few people who were coiled on seats or sleeping on benches sat up, stretched, and then walked away. Most were probably workers awakening from a nap since they did not have much to do during the night shift.

Yasmin stopped in the middle of the passport checkpoint and looked around. To her left, some passengers formed a line in front of the "Visa" sign, and to her right, three separate groups gathered in front of the "Jordanians" signs. Trying to determine which of the groups was the smallest so she could tail behind them, she continued to look around.

Facing her sat officers inside glass booths, and behind them stood airport security and men in civilian clothes. When she noticed one in an army suit staring at her, she looked down. After a second she looked back at him and saw that he was still eyeing her. He read from a paper he held in his hand, stepped to the side, and spoke briefly to an officer before pointing his index finger forward. As the officer moved in her direction, her legs felt weak. The first thing that came to her mind was that Mahir had stooped to a level she had always refused to believe possible and used the influence of his family to pull a stunt of some sort. She tightened her grip on Sami and Mira and, without thinking, took a step back. For a few moments, there was nothing in her head except the echo of her heavy breathing and the thuds of combat boots marching toward her.

Once the officer passed her and continued to a disoriented passenger, she flushed, as if everybody around her knew what was going through her mind. After releasing a long sigh, she took out her Jordanian passport that Sami and Mira were added on to and then moved behind a crowd of Jordanians.

⊶ ⊷

"Mrs. Yasmin Nabeel?" the officer asked a moment after she handed him the passport.

"Yes."

With the keyboard in front of him and the screen stationed diagonally on his small counter, he shifted his drowsy eyes between her passport and the green data on his black screen. "Wife of Mahir Ahmad?" His tone carried a hint of admiration.

"Yes."

He smiled and continued at a faster pace. "Do you still reside at the university neighborhood in Amman?"

"Yes."

"Are these your children, Sami and Mira?"

"Yes."

"Welcome to Jordan." He pounded the passport with a cylinder stamp.

Before setting foot on the escalator, Yasmin searched the small crowd on the first floor down below and spotted her mother's short bouffant and then her brother Majid, smoking. They both smiled and waved. Yasmin waved back, descended to the baggage area with Sami and Mira, and disappeared there for fifteen minutes.

Out in the lounge, they all kissed and hugged. Majid said he was going to drive his car from the parking lot to the sidewalk and left. The last time Yasmin saw him, his eyes did not speak of burdens, and not as much of his thick black hair was white. Though it

64

was obvious that he had aged a little, Yasmin liked the changes and thought he still looked handsome.

Yasmin pushed the cart, stacked with her suitcase, and walked next to her mother and the children toward the gate. Though her mother gave all of them a warm welcome, Yasmin noticed a sad look in her eyes. They remained silent for a few moments, but Yasmin knew it was only a matter of time before the look in her mother's eyes translated to words. Her mother had the same sharp and talkative eyes that Yasmin and Mira had inherited.

"I've been worried sick about you and the children. I don't know where this disaster is headed."

"Mama, I'm fine. Trust me. Please stop worrying about me, and while I'm here, just focus on Hala's wedding."

The glass door slid open as they approached it. Once they were outside, it slammed shut with a thud, as if it were announcing that a phase had ended and now Yasmin was standing on the sidewalk of reality. She felt uneasy. The stillness of the dark and nippy night soon ended as the speakers of the airport mosque turned on, sounding of a man clearing his throat for Fajr prayer. "Allahu Akbar" emanated from the mosque and echoed from the ones nearby or in the far distance. For a few moments, all Yasmin could hear were voices praising God, which made every follicle in her body tingle. She had never felt this way before. Maybe it had been a long time since she heard the call of prayer from a real voice, not a recording.

"I hope your misfortune does not affect your sister's happiness," her mother said in a grieving tone that matched her facial expressions.

"Mama, I had no control over any of it, especially the timing."

Majid pulled over and stepped out of his silver Toyota. Yasmin helped him put the suitcases in the trunk while her mother, with the same sad look on her face, helped Sami and Mira get in the car. She then sat in the front seat and rested her jaw over her palm.

A little after they drove off, Majid turned and looked at his mother. He then looked in the rearview mirror and winked at Yasmin.

"Are you doing OK so far?"

Yasmin rolled her eyes and smiled. "Yeah, I'm fine."

The highway to Amman that Yasmin remembered as the never-ending miles of black asphalt slashing through plains was now adorned with red-roofed mansions, elegant farms, private schools, and government departments. Halfway through the drive, Majid rolled his window down and lit a cigarette. As they reached the entrance to the city, an ashy dawn broke over the white limestone houses and buildings. In the east pink and yellow hues streaked the sky. Majid took the main street to their neighborhood, passing a tall Burger King sign as they drove over a ramp and then one for KFC. Office buildings towered over shops on both sides of the street, named after the holy city of Saudi Arabia, al-Mad nah al-Munawwarah.

Yasmin finally broke the silence. "Most of these buildings are new, and even more are under construction. What's going on?"

Majid nodded. "There's a rumor that the United States will invade Iraq. If that happens, then we are expecting many refugees."

Amman, as Yasmin always pictured it, was an elegant city with such open spaces that she could see some of its most significant and large buildings hundreds of miles away. Tall buildings cramped together had never been a feature of the city when Yasmin left Jordan the first time ten years earlier, but she remembered it becoming one right after the Gulf War.

After passing the traffic light by the University of Jordan, Majid turned and entered their neighborhood. In the past, Yasmin had been able to see her parents' two-story house on the top of a hillside. Now an apartment building blocked it from her view. When Majid stopped at the red light, Yasmin looked ahead at the same old crooked juniper and pine trees that lined the left side of the street. Dirt, gravel, and boulders temporarily filled the other side, and from what Yasmin had seen so far, she figured that it was only a matter of time before an investor cramped a few more buildings on it.

The changes dismayed Yasmin. After Desert Storm, many people she had grown up with had left the neighborhood. Some had simply taken advantage of the soaring real-estate prices, sold their homes, and moved. Some had turned their villas into four- or six-story apartment buildings before they sold them and moved as well. Though many new residents rented or bought apartments in the new buildings, Yasmin never had the chance to meet any of them. Her family never got as close to any of the new neighbors as they had with the old ones.

Majid got tired of waiting for the light to turn green, so instead of driving up the hill, he turned right. They passed by the shopping strip at the base of the neighborhood, including the bakery, the Ovens of the University Neighborhood, the Bookstore of Ambition, the Butchery of Honesty, and Frezo, the ice-cream parlor. People were already stepping out of their cars at that early hour, heading to the bakery like sleepwalkers. The smell of fresh bread flooded Yasmin's mouth; she swallowed. Looking around, she could tell that every homeowner or landowner in the neighborhood had jumped at the opportunity of investing in war immigrants and foreign students. Rent signs decorated basements, roofs, and light poles.

When Majid parked his car in front of the house, he centered it between two of the white poplars that interrupted the spread of the sidewalk, making sure all the car doors had the ability to open wide. Jasmines spattered with dew and starry blooms gracefully dangled from the fence. Some of their branches rested on the sidewalk on both sides of the wrought-iron gate. Yasmin took a deep breath, saturated with the smell of the little flowers she had stranded into necklaces as a child. Once they were all out of the car, Majid and Yasmin helped each other with her luggage, and her mother took care of Sami and Mira. They both looked dazed.

Yasmin stepped through the gate and passed the laurel tree and the small sage bush next to it. She made a mental note about drying some bay leaves and sage to take back to Arizona. She looked to her far right at a basin by the fence and was happy to see that her favorite loquat tree was still standing there. From where she stood, she could see the tail of her father's old Volvo. He had let her drive it a few times after she had her license but never after she hit the side of the gate backing up from the carport one time.

"Hey, Majid," Yasmin said while climbing the steps to the balcony. "Remember how Baba used to wait for me here when I missed my curfew?"

Majid laughed. "Baba has changed a lot in the past years. You're going to be surprised."

"So, he doesn't yell and lecture anymore?"

"No more yelling, but maybe some lecturing every now and then."

"That's fine. I'm expecting a lecture anyway."

Yasmin's father had rebuked her in the past when she wore inappropriate outfits or received unsatisfactory grades but only followed with a punishment when she stayed out past seven thirty in the evening.

"Girls go home with the sun," he used to say, wagging his finger.

Yasmin used to walk away, regretting not sneaking in from the kitchen door, the same way she had slipped out.

When they entered the house and stood in the foyer, Yasmin took a deep breath of a smell she could not describe but could only call home.

She looked at her mother. "You can go get some sleep, Mama."

"I can't go back to bed now. I'll go make some coffee and maybe prepare something to eat. Are you hungry?" She turned toward a small hallway that led to the kitchen.

"No, I'm fine. I'll put the kids in bed and have coffee with you." Yasmin passed the family room through a longer hallway and then turned to the guest bedroom that, ten years ago, used to be her own. As a child, she had decorated her room with posters of Mickey Mouse and his friends, and in the far corner next to her bed, she had kept a wooden chest full of miniature tea sets and dolls. Years later as she grew older, she had covered her bedroom walls with posters of famous actors, singers, and fashion models. Her father had called her a silly teenager back then and ordered her to clean up her act and her room. Now a king-size bed took up most of the room, and above it hung a painting of a vase full of flowers.

After Yasmin tucked in Sami and Mira, she opened her purse and took out the bills Mahir had handed her at the airport. She counted $190, shook her head, and threw the money on the dresser. What was he thinking? Thank God she had her credit card with her.

When Yasmin entered the kitchen, Majid and her mother were sitting at the nook. They stopped talking, and both looked at her.

"What's wrong?" Yasmin walked to the coffeemaker, poured a cup, and then sat down.

"I don't think you should remarry." Her mother looked at Majid, seeking his approval.

"I agree with Mama," he said in a kind tone.

Yasmin looked at them in disbelief. "I'm still married."

Her mother stared down at her cup. "Yeah, we know. But just, God forbid, you lose your mind and let that happen—"

"I didn't ask Mahir to cheat on me and move out, and if he decided to divorce me, you know there is nothing I can do about it."

"You *must* prevent that from happening! Divorce is the worst thing that can happen to your children."

Majid cleared his throat. "That's true. Children need both parents around so they can grow up mentally and emotionally healthy." He stood up. "I should go get ready. I'll see you later," he told Yasmin.

"Are you going to the farm?"

"Where else?" With that, he walked out.

"Your father was very saddened by the death of your uncle. He feels lost without him. Since he got sick, Majid had been taking care of everything. I don't know what we would've done without him. He took the responsibility too soon, but that's good for the future of his children too." She suddenly frowned, and her eyes filled with tears. "Why? Why would Mahir do this to his children? No matter how much husbands stray, at the end they return. Maybe you can still—"

"Mama, please don't do this. Mahir is not the first or the last man to leave his wife."

"When I tried to leave your father a long time ago, my mother sent me back in the same cab." Her mother forced out a short laugh.

Yasmin remembered hearing this story from her mother many times before but never thought of it as funny. "Yeah, you told me this story, Mama. Look, you're obviously tired. Why don't you go get some rest? I need to go take a shower."

Her mother nodded. They both stood up and then walked out of the kitchen but in two different directions.

CHAPTER TEN

An hour later Yasmin entered the family room, holding her cigarettes and lighter. She found her mother, dressed in black jogging pants and a white top, watching *The Bold and the Beautiful.*

"We remodeled last summer," her mother said, pointing to the furniture.

"It looks nice." Other than the faint greens and shades of coral, replacing beiges and browns on the couch and seats, the room still had its old and familiar flavor. Family pictures lined the wall-to-wall entertainment center, among them Yasmin's wedding picture. Paintings of ancient Arabic cities, horses, and decorative verses still covered most of the walls. Yasmin noticed a new silver filigree bowl in the center of the coffee table and matching vases and ash-trays on the side tables.

With her eyes fixed on the screen, her mother said, "Do you watch this show in America?"

Yasmin laughed. "No, no, I don't."

"Too bad. You could've told me what's going to happen." She squinted and turned the volume up.

"I'm going to make turkish coffee."

"Wait, I'll ask Suka to make some for all of us. Hala usually wakes up around this time." She remained in her seat and called for the maid. "Go put your cigarettes away, Yasmin. Your father might walk in any minute."

Yasmin walked to the veranda through the family room. It smelled of the cigarette butts that Majid had probably left in the ashtray sometime that morning. She took the seat that allowed her a full view of the family room, lit a cigarette, and waited for her coffee. It had been a long time since somebody had made her coffee. She would not mind having a live-in maid for $200 a month like Suka to take back with her to Scottsdale. That would be nice, but she knew it was impossible in America. A few minutes later, Hala rushed in her direction with both arms reaching forward. Her dark long ponytail rested gracefully on her blue robe. Yasmin loved the changes in her appearance and demeanor. She could sense happiness and optimism in her big dark eyes, and also in the smile that was rooted in her heart. The last time Yasmin saw Hala, she had not only dressed in black but seemed to be draped on every side in the color of mourning.

They hugged, kissed, and sat down. "Yasmin, I know I've asked you this question a thousand times already, but seriously, tell me, are you and the kids OK?"

"Yeah, we're fine."

"If things get complicated and you get divorced, will you still be fine?"

"Yeah, don't worry about us, Hala. Enough of my depressing drama; tell me all about you."

Hala frowned. "Depressing? Did Mama ask you not to discuss your problems with me?" She leaned forward and grabbed Yasmin's hand.

Yasmin laughed. "No, she didn't mention you. I swear."

"Look, I want you to know that, whatever she says, she means well. You know she's a bit forward when expressing her worries, but

I don't blame her anymore. My situation in the past years put her under a lot of stress."

"I know," Yasmin said. "How is Kamal?"

"He's fine. He had a job interview with the Marriott two weeks ago. If he gets the job, we're moving to Cairo."

"That's great. Are you guys ready for the big day?"

Hala nodded with a smile.

"By the way, in America the groom does not take care of all the wedding expenses like here."

Hala widened her eyes. "Really?"

"Yeah, the bride does. Are you happy about moving to Cairo?"

"I can't wait to move away and be on my own again. I miss having privacy. I miss making my own decisions."

"Why? Who tried to run your life for you?" Yasmin reconsidered her question and smiled. "Stupid question, huh? Some things just fade away from your memory if you're not reminded of them every day."

"Everybody I know interfered during the past six years. Whether relatives, coworkers, or friends, they all acted as if they knew better than me and felt insulted when I didn't take their advice."

"You see why I love living in America?" Yasmin sat straight when she saw her mother grabbing the tray from Suka. "Mama is coming. Change the subject. I don't want to hear any lectures about me living there by myself."

Yasmin's mother set their cups on the coffee table in front of them and kept one cup covered with its saucer. "This is for Fatin. She'll be up in a minute to say hello before she goes to work."

"Oh, I didn't know she worked now. Where does she work?"

"At a pharmacy—where else? You still remember she's a pharmacist, right? She started last month." Before her mother returned to the family room, she said, "Hide your cigarettes. Your father is in the shower."

"Where do you usually smoke in this house? In the bathroom?"

Hala laughed. "Yeah, I guess you have to when Baba is around."

Majid's wife, Fatin, came to the veranda followed by her sons Omar and Zaid, two miniature copies of their mother and father dressed in their school uniforms. Even though Fatin was of Arabic descent, she had a petite figure and lightly tanned skin that enhanced her delicate oriental-looking features. After she embraced Yasmin, she sat and reached for her coffee cup, an intense smile adding more slant to her eyes. Yasmin's nephews surrendered to her tight hug and then left to await their school bus on the front balcony. Majid stopped by before leaving for the farm, and soon after, Yasmin's mother joined them.

"Mahir is not a bad person," her mother said as she sat down. "He's a good father and a good provider."

Yasmin became restless in her seat. "I know, Mama. I never said he wasn't."

Majid nodded.

Hala and Fatin looked at Yasmin and smiled.

"I think he has enough good qualities to make up for his negative sides. Nobody is perfect. You just need to be more realistic in your expectations and less judgmental. If you show him you're serious about reconciliation, he will not turn you down."

"I don't know if that will work, Mama." Yasmin took a sip from her cup. "I'm very upset and still feel betrayed by Mahir. I need to see genuine efforts on his side before I consider reconciliation."

Nobody commented.

Yasmin turned to Hala. "Any new family gossip?"

Hala made a funny face. "Cousin Fadi called again to caution me that Kamal might very well be after Baba's money. I guess he and his whole family found it really awkward that a widow like me would marry a young, good-looking, and educated guy like Kamal." Hala's cell phone beeped. She took it out of her robe pocket and read the message. "Hold on," she told Yasmin and started replying. Majid and Fatin excused themselves at that point and said they had to go to work. Yasmin's mother walked them to the front door.

Yasmin was under the impression that her family was still on bad terms with her uncle and his family. So what made her cousin Fadi give himself the permission to interfere in Hala's affairs? Years ago, her uncle and his wife had moved in with Yasmin's maternal grandmother right after her grandfather died, even though her grandmother was still capable of taking care of herself. At the beginning, everybody thought her uncle was carrying on the tradition of taking care of a parent in old age. Only after the death of Yasmin's grandmother did his real intentions materialize. He had pressured his mother into signing over to his name the house and a few acres his father had left behind, leaving nothing to Yasmin's mother and her sister.

In the fifties through the seventies, this was a common practice among men in Jordan. They had always justified their actions as rightful, because they were merely claiming their right by denying the in-laws a share of the family fortune. Yasmin's mother and her sister never sued. Although very upset, they could not bring themselves to shame the family name and scandalize their only brother by taking him to court. The tension between the two families had started long before that, though. While Yasmin's uncle enjoyed living with his mother, his wife made her discomfort very clear from the very first day, especially when Yasmin's mother and her sister visited. She never showed proper hospitality and invented excuses to leave them alone at the house even when Yasmin's grandmother got much older and became bedridden.

Hala put the phone down and turned to Yasmin. "Sorry about that. It was Kamal."

"It's fine. So tell me, why would Cousin Fadi call you with concerns anyway? Did Baba and Mama make up with *Khalo uncle* and his wife? What's going on?"

"Yeah, they actually made up a while back, but their relationship is still somewhat formal. That doesn't apply for cousins Fadi and Lina though," Hala said.

"I can see that. What did you tell him anyway?"

"I just thanked him for his concern and assured him it was unnecessary."

"What? That's it?"

"How else do you deal with such a mentality?"

"My God, Hala. I don't know how you put up with such rubbish. Thank God I'm only here for a few days. I wouldn't be able to listen to such retarded nonsense without losing my temper."

"That's how I reacted when I first came back to live here, but afterward I learned to nod while the words entered one ear and departed from the other."

When Yasmin's father came into the family room holding a book in green leather binding, she stuck her pack of cigarettes behind a cushion and hid the ashtray behind a plant. His ill appearance saddened her. He looked as if he had aged at least ten years since she had last seen him. Diabetes had taken away a lot of his weight, left his skin with deep creases, and made his thick glasses magnify his eyes to an unrealistic size. As he continued toward the veranda, she took note of his thin white hair, slow movement and arched back. When he extended his hand, Yasmin kissed the back of it and placed it on her forehead, carrying on the old tradition of showing gratitude. She then kissed the sagging skin of his face.

"How are you, Baba?"

"*Elhamd-u-lillah* (thank God)." He sat down.

Yasmin smiled at her father as he stared at her for a few moments.

"Have you been working on your problems?" He squinted. "I think you and Mahir should reconcile."

Yasmin gave Hala a quick glance before she answered. "No, we haven't really talked since he moved out."

Yasmin's father fell silent. He stared out at the few thin clouds that striped the section of the sky contained in the wall-to-wall window. In a puzzled tone, he asked, "What was the cause of the misunderstanding?"

"Just what I've told you and Mama." Yasmin looked at Hala again, as if asking for help.

Hala said, "It's not just one thing, Baba. They'd been arguing for months, and then Mahir moved out."

"*Aywa, aywa* (yes, yes)." He nodded. "That's not a big deal. All married couples argue and go through tough times. You should work on your problems and stop this nonsense. You have children. You don't live alone."

Yasmin nodded. "Yes, Baba."

"I don't approve of you and the children living alone. It's not a safe or appropriate living arrangement. Besides, it's against our culture and our traditions."

Yasmin nodded again. "I understand, but you don't have to worry, Baba. This is perfectly normal in America."

"*We* are not *Americans*, Yasmin," he said in a loud and firm tone.

Yasmin flinched. Her heart pounded in her chest. "Mahir decided to move out, Baba. It was his decision."

"I'm going to have a talk with him about this. There has to be another solution. You either make up or move back here—"

"No." Yasmin sat up. "I think we…I mean when I go back, we'll both be calm enough to talk about our problems."

He nodded. "You should."

Yasmin had expected this conversation to take place, but her father's words and his seriousness troubled her. At least he had not insisted on her return as a final resolution. She had a strong urge to end the conversation with him at that, as if afraid he would suddenly change his mind and ask her to move back.

"I have to go check on Sami and Mira." She looked at Hala and gestured with her eyes for her to follow. Her father wiped his glasses, put them on, and opened his book, *The Stories of the Prophets*, volume one. Both she and Hala excused themselves, picked up their coffee cups, and walked to the kitchen.

"Is he really becoming that forgetful?"

Hala stood by the kitchen nook. "Yeah. He writes notes and reminders all the time. You'll see them everywhere around the house."

Yasmin shook her head. "Do you think he was serious about me returning to live here?"

"No, I don't think so. He's probably just trying to convince you to reconcile."

"I hope that's all there is to it." Yasmin put her cup in the sink. "What does Baba do now that he doesn't go to the farm anymore?"

"He spends most of his time reading. He puts the book down for meals and prayers. Sometimes he goes for a short drive in his new car. It's a Volvo too but a newer model. He drives his old car to his doctors' appointments in the morning and once a month to the bank to cash his retirement check. At night, he watches the news on almost every channel."

"Interesting. What about Mama? Is she always glued to the TV like that?"

Hala laughed. "No, she records the soap opera every day and watches it in the morning, and after lunch she watches *Oprah*. Usually she goes out in the morning and sometimes in the afternoon."

"Every day? Where does she go?"

"Hair salon, alterations, and shoe repair. And like Baba, in between all her activities, she makes time for meals and prayers."

"Are you serious?"

"Yeah, basically that's it. Sometimes she goes out with Auntie Samira and their cousin Nihad. Sometimes they come over and smoke hookahs."

"Mama smokes hookah? Since when?"

Hala laughed again. "Since the Gulf War. It became a fad in the country, and Mama became hooked."

"Too many things have changed since I last visited. Unfortunately, not the things I care about."

Yasmin's mother entered the kitchen with the phone in her hand. "It's your aunts, Samira and Nihad. They want to say hi." She handed it to Yasmin and walked out.

CHAPTER ELEVEN

Two days after arrival, Yasmin adjusted her sleep and no longer awoke at two after midnight or spent the whole day dazed and yawning. Her father did not discuss her situation anymore, so her concerns somewhat abated. Other than her mother's endless advice on how to win back Mahir, the only thing that accounted for her uneasiness was that eerie feeling that came over her. She felt that all she wanted to do was to cower in a corner until she boarded the plane back to Scottsdale. Subtracting the two days that she would spend on her trip back, Yasmin calculated with relief that she had four more days left of her very short vacation.

With the exception of Carole, Yasmin did not intend to see any of her old friends. She did not feel it was the right time in her life to do any catching up and was not in the mood for hearing more advice than she had already heard. So with everyone out of the house that late afternoon and not expected to be back before seven or eight, Yasmin invited Carole over. Yasmin's mother had left earlier with her aunts to get their dresses from the tailor. Hala and Kamal were taking care of last-minute wedding preparations.

Sami and Mira went out with Fatin and their cousins for ice cream and a long drive. The circumstances seemed perfect to Yasmin. She would have enough time to talk without interruptions before Carole went back to work at her restaurant, La Bonita.

The early evening brought a pleasant breeze to the front balcony along with the faint sound of music and of children playing somewhere nearby. Yasmin set her cigarettes and lighter on the patio table and then paced back and forth, as she waited for Carole. She could hear the laughter and the chatting of the neighbors across the street and assumed they were sitting under the grapevines, behind the limestone fence. At the sound of bells jingling, mixed with ba'as and mehs, Yasmin stepped closer to the edge of the balcony and watched as a herd of sheep and some black goats hurried up the hill. Their shepherd rode a donkey, clucked his tongue, and directed the herd with a stick. Some goats stood on their hind feet by the gate and nibbled on the jasmine before they continued on their way, leaving behind their smelly excrement.

When Yasmin saw Carole's car approaching, she stepped down and stood by the gate. She had not seen her in years and immediately noticed how much she had changed. She had frosted her hair and cut it short. They embraced on the sidewalk and then climbed the steps side by side to the balcony.

Carole took her blazer off before she sat facing Yasmin. "I have to look serious and dress conservatively now that I work with a male staff."

Before Yasmin had the chance to comment, she turned to the sound of a car pulling over. Her mother stepped out of a cab, holding a big bag in her hand. She climbed the stairs and stopped to say hello to Carole.

Carole stood up and kissed her on the cheeks. "Hi, Auntie," she said. "How are you?"

Yasmin's mother sighed. "I'm fine." She turned to Yasmin. "Did you offer Carole something to drink?"

"Not yet. She just arrived."

Yasmin's mother stepped closer to Carole. "Talk some sense into your friend." She pointed to Yasmin. "I wish you could get through to her because we gave up. Tell her that if she doesn't wake up and do something about her marriage, her life will crumble over her head."

Carole smiled and nodded.

Yasmin lit a cigarette, took a drag, and then released it as a tornado toward the sky.

"Look at her. All she's been doing since she arrived is drinking coffee, smoking, and staring. She refuses to go out of the house."

"Mama, you make it sound like I've been here for weeks or months. Besides, I'm here for Hala's wedding, not to rediscover the country."

Yasmin's mother was about to start a new sentence when a bang startled Yasmin. "What was that?" She looked around.

"Calm down; it's just fireworks. It must be an early wedding."

"A wedding? Are you serious? Since when are fireworks allowed at weddings? Last time I saw fireworks in Jordan was on Independence Day." She considered her comment and then said, "Don't you think it's ironic that people celebrate independence and marriage the same way?"

Carole laughed.

"I hope Hala didn't plan anything like that for her wedding."

Yasmin's mother squinted. "No, she didn't." Before going inside she said, "I'll go tell Suka to make coffee." She closed the door behind her.

"What's going on?"

"She's in denial, I guess. She doesn't want to understand what's happening between me and Mahir. She wants everything back the way it was overnight. She says it's all in my hands."

"Well, that's expected."

"I don't care what's expected. These are my circumstances right now. She might as well accept them."

"You talk as if you were born in America. By no means will your mother accept divorce as a way of life. Never." Carole gave Yasmin a look they both understood as well as they understood their culture. They had talked many times in the past about the things they never liked about their parents and their society, but talking about it when it had not affected either of them was different.

"I know what you're thinking, Carole. I'm not going to live in misery, knowing Mahir is cheating on me, because my mother on the other side of the globe thinks of divorce as a disaster."

"So you're going to start a revolution and change an ancient perception overnight? Who's happy anyway? Look, there is no such thing as a perfect life. You just have to be smart enough to know how to live yours without headaches."

"So that's my problem. I'm not smart enough to know how to play the game? What was I supposed to do? Pretend I didn't notice he was cheating? Pull him back when he moved out?"

"No." Carole thought for a moment. "Don't make a big deal out of it. We all went through similar situations at different points in our lives. Having children is a big challenge."

Yasmin held her head. "You too, Carole?"

"Yasmin, let's be realistic. We were not raised to be independent. You know if it wasn't for our parents we could have never lived on the poor salaries of the Department of Culture."

"I know. Finding a job when I go back is actually one of my biggest concerns. Things are going to be very difficult without Mahir's full financial support, but I'll make it."

"If you can't calm down, take something that will make you."

"I'm not going to get medicated so he can have his way. Damn him."

"Look, there's nothing wrong with that. Almost every woman I know here either took, or is taking, some kind of antidepressants."

Yasmin's mother came out with a tray, set it on the table, and started serving. After she handed Carole her wedding invitation, she placed an extra cup in front of a vacant chair and sat down.

Carole picked up her cup. "Any plans for tomorrow?"

"Not really. I don't feel like doing anything."

"What is wrong with you? You don't go out, and you make me apologize when somebody calls and wants to come over," her mother snapped.

"Nothing is wrong. I'm really not in the mood for our nosy relatives who are looking forward to interrogating me."

"Your relatives are going to be offended if we keep turning them away, especially your aunts."

"I already talked to my aunts. They understand my situation. Besides, if I don't see them now, I'll see them at the wedding, or sometime after."

Yasmin gave up on her mother leaving her alone with Carole. She turned to Carole and asked her about her sons, her restaurant, and some of their old friends, whom Yasmin had no intention of calling or seeing during her stay.

CHAPTER TWELVE

S ami stood like a stunned scarecrow inside his little black suit. "My toes hurt. Can I wear my flip-flops?"

"To the wedding? No, you can't. Why don't you go down to Khalo Majid's house and watch TV with Omar and Zaid."

"OK." Sami turned and walked out of the room in penguin steps.

Mira came in, holding the hem of her ruffled white dress. She twirled once and then stared at Yasmin through the mirror. She had been wandering around for the past half an hour, seeking an audience to admire her dress. When Yasmin reached for the lipstick, Mira moved closer. "Me too," she said.

Yasmin dabbed some color on her pouted lips. "Happy now?"

Mira nodded with her mouth open as if afraid her lips would fall off if she uttered a sound. When the doorbell rang, she ran out and, a minute later, returned with Yasmin's mother.

"Are you ready?" The hair spray that stiffened her mother's bouffant glistened under the light.

Yasmin took the last roller out of her hair. "Almost."

"You should've been with your sister at the hair salon."

"Mama, please. We already discussed this. Hala understands my situation. She didn't think leaving the children with Suka half a day was a good idea either."

Her mother shook her head. "I'm going to get dressed," she said, leaving the room.

Yasmin slipped on a long black dress that hung on her shoulders by thin straps. It had a slit on the left side that revealed her knee. Her mother reentered, holding a pearl necklace. She took one look at Yasmin and choked on her breath.

Yasmin lifted her palms as if surrendering. "I have nothing else to wear. You know how much I hate dresses, Mama, so don't make a scene. You're the one that insisted I should wear a dress."

"Do you want to give your father a heart attack? Couldn't you buy a more decent dress?"

"They don't make formal dresses with sleeves. Besides, everybody dresses like this nowadays."

"I don't care about everybody. You are not leaving the house like this. You look like a bar singer, Yasmin."

Her mother left the room and returned shortly after with a big black shawl that she threw over Yasmin's shoulders. She then turned around and asked Yasmin to help her fasten the pearl necklace.

Trilling cries of joy announced the groom's arrival in the evening. Hala looked like a mermaid in her white sequined dress, and the joy that sparkled in her beautiful eyes reminded Yasmin of her wedding night. It seemed so far away now, and after what she and Mahir had been through, Yasmin could not relive that incredible feeling of pure happiness. It saddened her a lot, but she immediately snapped herself out of that thought. Tonight was Hala's special night. She looked at her, smiling, knowing that her heart was pounding with love and anticipation. Hala smiled back, her eyes shining with a tear.

"Don't even think about it," Yasmin said. "Let's go." She held the tail of Hala's long veil and walked behind her to the living room where relatives and close friends gathered to watch the first part of the wedding celebration, the *zaffeh*. Along with Kamal, his family, and friends, a wedding troupe arrived at the house to perform wedding songs and dances before Kamal and Hala led a convoy of honking cars to the reception party. When Yasmin and Hala faced the crowd, more trills erupted from almost every mouth. Yasmin's mother, and her aunts Samira and Nihad, in their short bouffant and their almost identical dresses, patted the corners of their eyes with tissues. The room smelled of the many flower bouquets that filled it and the entrance, and the burning of incense. Hala led the way to the front balcony, and everybody followed.

Kamal kissed Hala on her cheeks and then stood beside her. He was a few inches taller and looked charming in his black tuxedo. His slicked-back hair shone like Chinese ink under the sun. They held hands and smiled as they watched their zaffeh begin with the sound of Irish pipes. Six members of the wedding troupe clutched at each other's shoulders and blocked the street while they performed a dance. They all wore red and white kaffiyehs on their heads and the same caftans of black and gray stripes that parted below their cloth belts, revealing their black genie pants. As they moved in a circle and beat the asphalt in a rhythmic motion with their black boots, two others stood clapping and singing by the piper.

The singers started with a song that glorified King Abdullah, the Hashemites, and the country and then sang for the bride, the groom, and their parents before doing some folk wedding songs. Neighbors watched from balconies or peered from windows, and the drivers who preferred not to split the crowd pulled over and stepped out of their cars. The loud music made everybody's efforts at chatting useless, but that did not stop some of Yasmin's relatives from expressing their feelings about Yasmin's situation. A distant cousin of her mother's gave her a few disapproving headshakes, and another older woman faced her with a challenging glare and wrinkled her hooked nose as if bothered by a bad smell. Yasmin assumed that both women had heard something about her separation from Mahir and about living alone in America.

As soon as the troupe finished their routine, Kamal and Hala climbed into a Silver Mercedes-Benz decorated with ribbons and white roses and led the honking convoy of relatives and friends to the reception party at the hotel.

At the InterContinental hotel, Hala and Kamal proceeded to the elevator, followed by a photographer and his assistant. Fatin and Majid took their places next to Yasmin's parents and Kamal's and greeted the arriving guests. Kamal's mother looked like royalty in her turquoise dress and her chignon. Yasmin could tell that she was once a stunning beauty. Kamal's father was a couple of inches shorter than his mother. He had thick white hair and bushy eyebrows. He gave Yasmin a gentle handshake and a warm smile.

The hall smelled of incense, most likely sandalwood or whatever was potent enough to word off the evil eye. Yasmin eyed the entire place before she walked with her children and Carole to the far corner. Since flowers sprouted from vases placed in the center of every table, when Yasmin sat down, she stationed herself at an angle where she could hide from her nosy relatives but still have a view of the hall.

Carole set her purse on the table. "Aren't you going to take off your shawl?"

"No, my mother made a scene at the house."

"What for? Look around you. Half the guests are in spaghetti straps."

"My mother sees the other half. I don't want to upset her now for Hala's sake." Yasmin gazed at the entrance. "Oh, great. My cousin Fadi just arrived. I hope he doesn't see me. I'm not in the mood for his attitude."

"Fadi? Since when has anyone from your uncle's family attended your occasions?"

"My mother made up with my uncle when he moved his family from Irbid to Amman a while back. She decided to bury the past since he's her only brother."

"Interesting."

"More interesting is the way Fadi had been acting ever since. When Hala got engaged, he acted like he was her guardian or something. He even wanted to be one of the witnesses when Hala and Kamal had the official wedding procedure at my parents' house."

"What? Your cousin is so full of himself."

"Hala told me that even the marriage official seemed annoyed at Fadi's sudden appearance when they were signing the marriage certificate. Though he is well aware of how private and formal the procedure is, he had come to the house that day and barged into the living room without being invited. My father and Kamal's father were there of course, and Majid and a cousin of Kamal served as witnesses, so he was very out of place."

Carole made a face and shook her head.

Fadi was thin enough to look sick, and although not very tall, his body hunched. The whites of his eyes were yellowish, which always reminded Yasmin of a cunning animal. The thing about him that bothered her the most was his constant interference in the private issues of relatives and friends. He also liked to appear like someone who had a lot of status, so at all times he wore three-piece suits that his tailor copied from famous designers, carried an empty Samsonite briefcase, smoked cigars, and held agate prayer beads.

Yasmin had heard a few years back that Fadi had settled for a degree in sociology after he had given up on law school. Shortly after his graduation and with the help of an old acquaintance of his father's, he found a job with an insurance company that paid a mediocre salary. In order for him to maintain the living standards he had always set for himself, he got himself into the business of recruiting clients for some of his friends, who were lawyers, realtors, or merchants, in exchange for small percentages.

The sound of the pipe got louder as Hala and Kamal approached the hall, and by the time they entered, the tunes completely silenced the guests. Trills erupted from many tables, and before each one completely died, a hand cupped a mouth and released another one. The troupe repeated the same routine on the sidewalk as they led the bride and the groom to their table.

As soon as the DJ played the first song, Hala and Kamal took to the dance floor, then their friends and some relatives followed, besieged them in a circle, and danced along. Nihad and Samira performed a traditional troupe dance in honor of Hala and Kamal and then left the dance floor that remained swarming with twisting and turning bodies. Yasmin carefully planned her route between tables when she chased after Mira who insisted on going to the restroom, ran around with Omar and Zaid, or hid under tables. Yasmin smiled, nodded, and occasionally stopped to shake hands with guests before chasing after Mira again.

During dinner, Carole volunteered to take Sami and Mira to the buffet so Yasmin could take a break and go smoke. When Yasmin stood up and turned in the direction of the restrooms, she was startled by the way her cousin Fadi stood behind her and glared. He held a cigar in one hand, and with his other hand, he thumbed his agate beads. They exchanged a handshake and a couple of cold kisses and stepped away from each other.

"Mother is sitting there with my sister, Lina, and my aunts." He pointed his cigar in their direction. "Come and say hi."

"Oh, really? I'll stop by later.

Still looking ahead, he said, "By the way, we need to discuss your situation."

"Need? I don't discuss my private issues with anybody, Fadi." She left him baffled by her answer and walked away.

When Yasmin returned, her mother was standing by the table Fadi had pointed out earlier. From that distance, she could see Fadi and his mother talking and her mother nodding with different unpleasant expressions alternating on her face. Yasmin knew that her situation with Mahir was the subject of discussion, so when her mother looked around the hall as if seeking a savior, she waved at her. Fadi and his sister, Lina, looked like they had started an argument as soon as Yasmin's mother left their side. Yasmin walked in her mother's direction and met her halfway. "What's going on, Mama?"

"What do you think?" she snapped. "What else would anybody be talking about?"

From the corners of her eyes, Yasmin could see the focused faces around them. Without uttering a word, she walked away from her mother.

The hall was almost empty after dinner. Hala and Kamal moved between tables and shook hands with the remaining guests. Then-unmarried young girls stood in a half circle behind Hala and reached out for her flying flowers. The girl that caught the bouquet left the wedding clutching at the satisfying prediction of her future, followed by her very relieved parents. Shortly after, Hala and Kamal left the hall, and the few remaining family members followed suit and walked out in the direction of the parking lot.

"I don't know what Fadi told my mother, but I don't like the way she talked to me after dinner," Yasmin told Carole as they stood by her car.

"I noticed. You'll soon find out." Carole made a face and smiled. "We'll talk about it later. Majid and Fatin are waiting for you. You'd better go."

Yasmin hugged and kissed Carole. "If I don't see you before I leave, I'll call you when I get there."

CHAPTER FOURTEEN

Seven hours before her midnight flight, Yasmin began packing her suitcases with great relief and some apprehension. Though she was curious to know what exactly Fadi had told her mother at the wedding, she did not attempt to find out. She feared that an argument with her mother over the subject might get out of hand and jeopardize her return to Arizona. So during her last two days in Jordan, she had avoided discussing the subject with her mother and spent most of her time with Fatin and the children.

She was packing her second suitcase when her mother pushed the door and entered the room. "How long do you plan to go on with this attitude?" she snapped.

"What attitude, Mama?" Yasmin folded a blouse.

"Ignoring everybody around you as if they didn't exist. Couldn't you at least acknowledge the presence of your relatives at the wedding? It's not enough that I turned them away three times when they wanted to come and welcome you back?"

"Didn't you all see me running after the children like a shepherdess?" Yasmin grabbed her bag of toiletries from the dresser.

"If they're so genuine about their feelings and really miss me, why didn't any of them bother to come forward and talk to me?"

"Don't give me excuses. You're younger than all of them and know what appropriate manners are."

Yasmin started piling up clothes in the suitcase. "You know as well as I that most of them have big mouths and are only interested in gossip."

"Whatever their motive is, I think you still should treat your relatives and your family with respect."

"I didn't mean to disrespect anyone. I just didn't find it necessary to please some people who think I should go out of my way to attend to them. I honestly don't understand why you give so much consideration to what they think."

Yasmin's mother hit the dresser with her palm. "Enough nonsense. You are in no position to pass judgments. They all know what you did to Mahir back in Arizona. Did you think he would never tell his parents? Honestly, Yasmin, I don't know why you never think ahead and account for things."

"What are you talking about? And why are yelling at me like this?"

"Your cousin Fadi told me everything about that court order you signed to prevent Mahir from coming near you—"

"What?" Yasmin shouted. "There's no such thing. Since when do you take what Fadi says at face value? Is this why you snapped at me in front of everyone at the wedding?"

Her mother wagged her finger. "He said you have a boyfriend back in Arizona. Do you want me to go on?"

"OK, that's enough, Mama. I'm not going to stand here and listen to these outrageous lies. I know Mahir would never make up such stories, either, at least for the kids' sake. Obviously Fadi is playing one of his dirty games, and for some reason you chose to believe him."

Yasmin left the room. She banged the bathroom door behind her and refused to come out despite her mother's knocking and begging. She remained in there smoking until her mother summoned Fatin to help get her out. Yasmin finally opened the door.

"Take her out with the children for dinner and a long drive," her mother said in a low and sad voice. "I made her angry."

"Sure, when Majid comes back." Fatin looked at her watch. "He just left, but he should be here in an hour or so."

"I don't want to go out. I have to finish packing."

Yasmin's mother walked away, patting her eyes.

Fatin followed Yasmin to her room. "Your Mother is upset because you've been avoiding her since the wedding."

"Honestly, Fatin, I don't feel like talking to her. I don't appreciate the way she lashed out at me, believing all these stupid accusations." She zipped her suitcases shut. Fatin helped her drag them to the front door, and then both of them went downstairs to Fatin and Majid's house to have coffee.

As Fatin boiled the coffee, Yasmin stood by the kitchen door and watched Sami, Omar, and Zaid play soccer on a tiled area between the lawn and the closed gate, while Mira harassed them on a scooter. After Fatin poured the coffee in cups, they walked into the yard and sat under a canopy of entangled grapevines, surrounded by potted geraniums. Pale orange and hints of yellow colored the afternoon and camouflaged it with a soothing serenity.

"I don't think your mother believes Fadi, but his mother has been calling her since the wedding with a new issue every day, and I guess your mother just finally exploded and took it out on you."

"Where did all that rubbish come from anyway? Who gave Fadi and his mother all this information?" Yasmin snapped a cigarette from her pack.

"Abu Mahir."

"What? Mahir's father?" Yasmin sat forward. "How come you didn't tell me before?"

"I didn't know. Your mother told me only half an hour ago. It seems that Abu Mahir has been visiting with your uncle and Fadi since you and the children arrived. They say he's really angry."

"This doesn't add up, Fatin. Mahir's parents did not bother to contact me, whether to hear my side of the story or to see the children. So why would Mahir's father be angry? Besides, I'm sure he's constantly in touch with Mahir and knows the truth." Yasmin took an intense drag from her cigarette.

Fatin had a look of extreme uncertainty in her eyes. "Are you sure Mahir is not behind all this?"

"You know Mahir, Fatin. Do you think he'd ever do something like this?"

"I don't know. Men can flip a hundred and eighty degrees when they get mad because things are not going their way."

Yasmin considered Fatin's reply. "Yeah, I guess you're right. I can't believe he let us travel overseas with less than two hundred dollars. I'm sure he counted on my credit card, but still, he would've never done something like that if we were still on good terms," she said. "What else are Fadi and his mother are saying?"

"They really made your mother angry when they told her that your father's leniency with you caused things to get out of hand between you and Mahir."

"Why would Mahir's father discuss the issue with my uncle instead of Baba?" Yasmin rubbed her temples and then squinted.

"I guess your uncle volunteered to listen."

The boys were still running after the bouncing ball and Mira was still getting in their way when Yasmin and Fatin entered the house with their empty cups.

"I'll wash the cups; you make more coffee. I have to stay up all night," Yasmin said.

"OK." Fatin set the pot on the stove.

A minute later, the sound of the gate shaking startled both of them. "Did you hear that?" Yasmin tried to lean over and peek out of the kitchen window.

"It sounds like one of the children hit the gate or tried to open it. I'll go check." Fatin walked out.

"Baba, Baba," Mira shouted outside.

"What's going on?" Yasmin washed the soap off her hands.

Fatin stood pale by the kitchen door. "It's Mahir." She swallowed.

"No way. This is a joke, right?"

Fatin shook her head. "No. I swear he's outside."

Yasmin wiped her hands on her jeans and ran out. Standing behind the gate with one of his cousins, Mahir was reaching out for Mira's hand. Yasmin had a very formal relationship with that cousin and had not seen him in years, but he still wore his pants so high above his waist and buttoned his shirt to his throat. Both he and Mahir did not acknowledge her presence, even when she stood next to Mira. Mahir looked extremely tired, as if he had not slept in days, which made Yasmin assume that he had arrived in the country that same morning. Yasmin had never felt so frightened in her life, and whatever she felt in her stomach was not the gentle brushing of butterfly wings; it was more like the tearing of wild claws. As if she were a body of liquid and somebody threw a bolder in her center, in a matter of seconds, hot and cold flashes passed through her body in rings.

"Open the gate," Mahir said, tightening his grip on Mira's hand. His arm was the only part of him on the inside, the only part the iron rods allowed.

Yasmin sensed a fabricated toughness in his voice and decided to seize the moment. She swallowed the bitterness of every curse she considered but held back.

"Hi, what's going on?"

"Open the gate," Mahir snapped.

Without thinking, Yasmin reached for the lock and opened it. "Let go of her hand. Let me slide the gate."

Mira jumped and hugged Mahir's leg as soon as the gate slid opened. Mahir lifted her up, secured her between his chest and his arm, and then grabbed Sami by his hand, stepped out, and walked away in a confusion of unbalanced steps. Mira did not realize what was happening, but Sami kept his head turned, looking with fearful and confused eyes at Yasmin. Mahir's cousin placed both hands on his waist and faced Yasmin, as if declaring that he was ready to become a human shield if the situation demanded.

At that point Mahir took faster steps toward his father's blue Mercedes, parked a few houses down. Sami had a hard time keeping up with Mahir. He tripped and fell down, but Mahir yanked him off the asphalt and continued to flee.

"Why are you doing this? Stop and talk to me," Yasmin shouted and rushed after them. Mahir's cousin ran after her, held her wrist, and stopped her. He asked her to keep her voice down. Yasmin snatched her hand back, and with both hands, she banged his chest. "How dare you?" she screamed and walked down the hill.

Mahir did not bother to look back. Yasmin watched him get in the car with Sami and Mira, who stood up and turned around in the backseat as the car drove away. Mira smiled and waved goodbye to Yasmin like she did when Mahir picked them up on the weekends they spent with him. Yasmin's eyes followed the car until it entered a web of narrow streets lined with tall buildings. She screamed out Mahir's name and began to run but did not get far and fell on her knees and hands. While she cried and picked herself up, Mahir's cousin passed her and continued in the direction Mahir drove.

The far hills had swallowed most of the sun by then and splashed the sky with bloody streaks. Yasmin tried to take a deep breath, but her lungs failed her. She tried very hard to concentrate, to comprehend what had just happened, to predict the consequences, but her attempts were futile. Her heart pounded, tightened, became as hard as a rock in her chest.

After a few seconds of panting and staring ahead, Yasmin turned around and walked toward the house. Majid was pulling over at that same moment. Omar and Zaid looked frightened; they held Fatin's hands and shifted their eyes between her and Yasmin. When Majid stepped out of the car, Fatin told him what happened.

He frowned. "Are you OK, Yasmin?"

Yasmin could tell how angry he was from the tone of his voice. She shook her head and wiped her tears and then entered the kitchen and went through the other door and upstairs to her room. Majid and Fatin followed her. She heard Majid call for her father. A few moments later, she heard her mother yell something and then call for her. "Yasmin."

When Yasmin entered the family room, the whole family was discussing Mahir. Her father stopped talking and said, "Calm down, Yasmin. Let's not jump to conclusions." He squinted at his watch. "It will take them about an hour to get to Irbid. I will call Mahir's father tonight or tomorrow."

Yasmin nodded.

"Why would he come and take the children unannounced like that?" her mother asked in a shaky voice. "Are you sure you told us everything, Yasmin?"

As Yasmin related to her parents, Majid, and Fatin in detail what had taken place between her and Mahir since March, her mother kept interrupting her with the same question: "Are you sure?"

"I wouldn't lie to you," Yasmin would say and continue while they all listened and nodded, exchanged worried and angry looks, and shook their heads. When Yasmin explained how Mahir ended up moving out, her mother asked again, "Are you sure this was his decision?"

Yasmin said, "Yes. Yes it was."

CHAPTER FIFTEEN

During the few hours of sleep Yasmin had, she dreamed of herself floating in the sky with her hands tied behind her back. Against her will, she was lowered from the sky into a battlefield full of horsemen, charging after women and children. Under different circumstances, it would have been just a dream. Dina would have said it meant this and that, but Yasmin knew better.

Her dream did not need any interpretation. Just thinking about it and about Mahir taking Sami and Mira, Yasmin felt her heartbeats become frantic, as if one beat were tripping over the other. She closed her eyes and tried to force herself back to sleep, but her horror did not allow it. Then all of a sudden she leaped out of bed and stood there for a few seconds. She was disturbed and confused, like she were standing in a room that remained intact after a massive earthquake, unable to assess the overall damage. Trying to take it all in made her skin tighten, and all she could think of at that moment was tearing her skin off. She held her head in her hands and cursed herself for being so trusting of Mahir, so stupid.

When she entered the kitchen, her mother was on the phone, annoyed by whatever was being said to her. Yasmin poured a cup of coffee and stepped out of the kitchen door. She took her time smoking a cigarette, drinking coffee, and thinking and then returned to find her mother still on the phone.

"That still doesn't make it right," her mother said to whoever was on the other end. "I have to go now." She slammed the phone down and turned to Yasmin. "Fadi and his mother haven't stopped calling all morning."

"If you keep listening to them, it's going to be a long and miserable day."

"They insist that you forced Mahir out of the house."

"That's not true, but I'm not surprised they think they know better." As she had done the night before, Yasmin retold the events that led to her dispute with Mahir to her mother, insisting that Mahir had moved out on his own. There was nothing she could have done about it because it was obvious that his mind was already set.

Yasmin thought about Mahir's actions and speculated on his next step all morning. She called his parents' house a few times but got no answer. When Fatin came into Yasmin's bedroom and asked her to join the family for lunch, Yasmin was standing by the window, smoking.

"You go ahead. I'm not hungry." She put her cigarette out and pushed the ashtray to the side. "If Mahir had done this in America, Sami and Mira would've been back in an hour."

"The police?"

Yasmin nodded.

"This is Jordan, Yasmin. The police are not going to knock on someone's door, let alone an Ahmad's, and take away their own flesh and blood. It just doesn't work that way; you know that."

"It should."

"They didn't commit a crime. Besides, your father would not allow it, or even Majid. People will butcher them with their tongues."

Talking to Carole did not calm Yasmin's restlessness either. Carole basically repeated what Fatin said but in different words.

Yasmin stayed in her room all afternoon, replaying in her head the moments of Mahir's sudden appearance by the gate, and with every playback, the horrifying feelings would come back, as if it were happening all over again.

That evening, Yasmin's mother came to her room with the phone receiver in her hand and said that Fadi wanted to talk to her. At first, Yasmin told her mother to tell him she was not available, but then she changed her mind. She could not stand the sound of Fadi's voice, but she decided to stop his interference. From the way he had commented on Hala's engagement, and the way he had approached her at the wedding and afterward kept tormenting her mother with his calls, Yasmin figured that he had more ego than he could actually handle. As unfriendly as she could be, she lifted the phone to her ear and skipped hello. "Fadi, why are you interfering?"

"I'm just trying to help."

"Thank you, but that's not necessary."

"I need to come over and have a talk with you."

"No."

"I need to know your plans," he said.

"I have none," Yasmin shouted. "I have to go now."

"Wait, are you going to file for divorce?"

Yasmin pressed her teeth. "That's none of your business." She hung up.

Half an hour later, Fadi called again and told Yasmin's mother that Mahir and his father were going to pay Yasmin's parents a visit tomorrow. Since Fadi did not give an exact time for the visit, Yasmin's mother asked Majid and Fatin to stay home, and they both agreed.

⊷ ⊶

The next day when the doorbell finally rang around three thirty, Yasmin was in her room staring at her suitcases. She heard some voices and figured Suka had greeted the guests and let them in. Yasmin's father was reading on the veranda at that time, and her mother was watching *Oprah* in the family room. There was no sound of Sami and Mira, and Yasmin dreaded what that meant.

Yasmin's mother called Suka from the hallway and asked her to go downstairs and call Majid before making coffee. Yasmin stayed in her room as her mother had instructed that morning. Her temper might worsen the situation and ruin everything, so it was better if she waited until the situation demanded her presence. Yasmin could hear voices coming from the family room, but from that distance, it was impossible to grasp a complete sentence. When she heard Majid's voice in the family room, she moved to the hallway where she could hear clearly.

"I have no doubt the problem is going to be handled the right way, the way all men handle such situations," said Abu Mahir. "We don't want to start a family feud like the al-Basus War. I think you agree with me on that."

Yasmin thought the statement was typical of Abu Mahir, a man living under the shade of his big family name, savoring the delusion of greatness. But that did not surprise her a bit. Abu Mahir grew up in the forties, a time when, unfortunately, Jordan lacked a significant urban center of its own, such that the social organization of the country was basically tribal, based on trade and the exchange of protection between the seminomadic tribes and the villagers. Though Yasmin was used to Abu Mahir referring to incidents from history that were tribal related, this time she found his example irrelevant. She could not see the resemblance between her problems with Mahir and that ancient Al-Basus War that was named after an old woman. It had started over the neighbor's camel crossing to her garden and her brother killing it. Later he was killed by the owner of the camel who belonged to a different tribe, which ignited a war between the two tribes that lasted over forty years.

When Yasmin's mother questioned the accusations Fadi and his mother had annoyed her with over the past days, Mahir's voice got loud. He defended himself and denied making up these rumors. He explained that Yasmin never issued a court order to keep him away from her, but he said that she could have if she wanted. He also spoke of the law in Arizona and explained how Yasmin could have taken advantage of it if he had not moved out of the house by choice.

Yasmin's mother raised her voice too when she demanded an explanation about the boyfriend rumor that increased gossip in the family.

Abu Mahir interfered at that point. "This is my opinion and not a rumor," he said. "Because Yasmin had no sufficient evidence to prove Mahir was cheating, which I don't think is a reason for breaking up a family anyway, I suspect that she started the whole charade as an excuse to get her freedom and be with someone else."

There was a loud commotion after that. Yasmin had a hard time matching words to voices.

Suka stood by the family-room door with a tray full of turkish-coffee cups. Yasmin's mother took it from her and went back to the room.

Minutes after, Yasmin's mother came out and approached Yasmin. "They put me through hell for nothing. Come and sit with them and make sure you tell his father the truth."

Yasmin entered the room behind her mother. Without greeting Mahir or his father, she took the seat by the door.

Mahir's father had reached the age of sixty-three, living up to a reputation of having a sharp temper and a ruthless mouth. Most of his hair and his thick mustache were gray, and his hooked nose and the deep creases that mutilated his face made him look like a villain from an ancient Arabian fairy tale. He smoked triple the amount of cigarettes Mahir smoked a day, so it was almost impossible to sight him without a cloud of smoke lingering around him. One time in the past, he had been involved in a fight at a gas station for refusing to put out his cigarette. He had slapped the Egyptian worker in the face, and some of the bystanders had to separate them after they both wrestled over dirt, oil, and gas.

Knowing Abu Mahir, Yasmin had no doubt that some type of tranquilizer, and not inner peace, had caused his warped smile. She had seen him boil with rage in the past for reasons much less important than the crumbling marriage of his son.

"Tell him how it all started," her mother said.

Yasmin spoke with an upset tone. "He has barely came home in the last few months and was always inventing excuses to stay away and then shortly after that started sleeping on the couch—"

"That's ludicrous," Abu Mahir shouted and hit the coffee table with his lighter.

Yasmin attempted to speak again, but Abu Mahir cut her off. "She was never a good wife or even a good mother, but my son kept her because he loved her and respected her family. She never even cooked him a decent meal."

Mahir looked down, avoiding Yasmin's eyes. This was the second time she had seen him in Jordan, again with a wrinkled shirt, no trace of cologne, and dark circles around his eyes.

Yasmin squinted. "Really? What did we eat all these years?"

"From what I hear, mostly canned foods."

Mahir traced his mustache with his fingers, still looking down.

"You're a liar," Yasmin shouted in Mahir's direction.

"Shut up," Abu Mahir said. "You don't raise your voice at my son in my presence." He wagged his index finger and continued, "Or behind my back."

Majid pressed his teeth and stared at Mahir and his father.

"Take it easy," Yasmin's father said, addressing all of them in a calm pitch. "We need to understand the problem in order to solve it."

Mahir gave him a side-look and smiled. "She's always out with her friends. That's the problem."

"That's not true. Stop lying."

Mahir lifted the ashtray as if he were going to slam it, but when Majid stood up and Yasmin's mother sat forward, he put the ashtray back on the side table.

"What are you doing? No wonder things got so bad between you two," Yasmin's mother said.

Mahir crossed his legs. "Yeah? Why don't you set your daughter straight, then?"

"Don't you dare be rude to me, young man. There is nothing wrong with my daughter's manners." She sat back.

"That's not the attitude of someone who wants to solve a problem," Yasmin's father said. "Let's deal with the situation in a respectable manner for the sake of the children."

"Yeah? Why don't you tell your daughter not to raise her children on welfare then?"

"What welfare?" Yasmin could not believe her ears.

Majid rubbed his temples. He heaved a long sigh.

Mahir looked in Yasmin's direction without making eye contact. "I don't care what you do in order to make money; you'll never make enough to take care of yourself and two children. I'm not going to let you raise my children on welfare."

"Stop lying, for God's sake. You're only making things worse."

"Unless you've been stealing from my son, I don't know how you're going to manage," Abu Mahir said.

"OK, that's enough. I will not allow you to cross the line with my daughter, not in my presence. You both know that's not true," Yasmin's father said, his face reddening.

"Oh yeah? What do you know?" Mahir's question overflowed with sarcasm. "Why don't you resume your silence? I don't think you even know where God placed you in the middle of all this."

Majid finally jumped off his seat, held Mahir by his wrist, and started twisting his arm. "I'm going to bash your brain and cut off your tongue for insulting my father."

Yasmin screamed, and so did her mother. What Mahir had stated was very insulting. Mahir had used that phrase in the past to describe disoriented or senile people as unaware of their surroundings or their position with respect to the four cardinal directions.

Mahir tried to release his hand, but Majid tightened his grip. "I kept my mouth shut for the past half hour out of respect for our fathers and for the sake of my sister, but you obviously took it the wrong way."

"Leave him, Majid; he is not worth it," Yasmin's mother said.

Abu Mahir laughed. "Calm down, all of you. Mahir, apologize," he said but obviously did not mean it.

Majid released Mahir's wrist and pushed him back in his seat.

Mahir smiled, "Sorry."

"You both had better leave now," Yasmin's mother said. "There's no use in going on like this. It doesn't take a genius to figure out your intentions."

"Our intentions are to keep the family intact," Abu Mahir said. "You," he pointed at Yasmin's parents, "should have more control over your daughter, and since none of you are getting through to her, maybe it's our duty to teach her a lesson."

"A lesson in what? In letting your son have his way without paying the price?" Yasmin's mother shouted.

"He is a man after all. If she were raised properly, she would've known better than to scandalize him and humiliate him for no reason. We are Ahmads, and nobody steps on our turf."

"I think it's best if you both leave now."

Yasmin could tell that her mother could no longer tolerate their arrogance. She had never asked anyone to leave in her life.

When Mahir and his father stood up, Yasmin left the room. She stood by the end of the hallway as they both walked toward the front door angry, muttering insulting and threatening words.

Abu Mahir looked at Yasmin's father. "I am being insulted and kicked out of your house, Abu Majid. I expected more respect from you."

Yasmin's father nodded. "I feel the same way, Abu Mahir."

"I'll show you," Mahir shouted to Yasmin's back before she disappeared from the hallway.

When Yasmin's mother slammed the door behind them, Yasmin came back to the family room and sat silent and appalled. There was no room for speculations in her head anymore. Mahir, coached by his father, had tricked her, and now that she was in the country of her birth, unprotected by American law, she was as vulnerable as any Arabic man would want his wife to be. Now that Mahir was showing his real colors, the ones he had never dared to expose in a country that granted rights to women, Yasmin decided that the end of her story would only be written with her own hands.

"I'm going back with my children at any cost," she told her parents. "If Abu Mahir wants to deal with the situation as a tribal issue, then I'm going to fight his stupid war to the end."

CHAPTER SIXTEEN

When Fadi's sister Lina called and asked to speak with Yasmin the next morning, Yasmin was surprised. "What does she want?" she whispered.

Her mother shrugged, put the phone on her nightstand, and left the room.

Yasmin stood there for a moment staring at the phone receiver. Fadi was the one more likely to call for one stupid reason or another. Though Yasmin had only seen Lina on a few rare occasions during the past years, they had both maintained a semiformal, but friendly, relationship with one another. Lina was very picky when it came to people and was not much of a sociable person. She either loved someone to death or hated someone for no reason. The ones she loved were fewer than the fingers of one of her hands, and it was not necessarily permanent. Her feelings could change all of a sudden for reasons unknown to her or to anyone.

Yasmin finally picked up the phone and talked to Lina. It turned out that she had called to tell her about the other meeting Mahir and his father held at their house.

Lina told Yasmin that, in addition to her parents, her brother Fadi, Mahir, and his parents, a mix of people affiliated with both families by close and distant kinships and friendships had gathered at their house. She added that, minutes after they arrived, Abu Mahir telephoned one of his relatives, who was their family lawyer and also an international referee, and invited him over. She complained about how all the guests had crowded the house, choked it with their smoke, and cluttered it with too many tea and coffee cups. She then told Yasmin that everybody acted like an expert on marital affairs, psychology, law, and many other related subjects. Some participants had nothing to say other than some unsubstantial comments every now and then. Women spoke mainly about Yasmin's ill manners, and all agreed on how unfair to Mahir she was.

"They said it wasn't like Mahir had ever come home drunk, beaten you up, or brought a woman into your bed," Lina said.

"Oh really? All other mistreatments are OK?"

Lina laughed. "Mahir told everybody what went on at your house. Is it true Majid wanted to hit him?"

"I wish he did. Mahir was very rude to Baba."

"Abu Mahir said you're the one that needs a beating. He also swore you'll never set a foot in Arizona again as long as he lived."

"Mahir must have explained the divorce laws and told them how much I got in the settlement. But Abu Mahir has no tribal influence in Arizona, so he can take his threat and…never mind."

"Yeah, everybody was shocked. No wonder he followed you here."

Yasmin contemplated the thought of how, by law, divorced women in Jordan got only their postponed dowry, a certain amount of money that is usually specified in their marriage certificates like a prenuptial agreement. And of course, they got it upon divorce if the man was generous enough not to make his divorcée sign away that right in return for a fast divorce, free of hassles. Yasmin had heard that in the past some men had punished their ex-wives by giving them their dowries in small payments stretched over years.

"Lina, did anybody mention how the children were doing?"

"No, they didn't. Abu Mahir threatened to never let you see them, though."

"Well, maybe somebody can point out to Abu Mahir that women have the right to custody in this country."

"He said he will never let Mahir divorce you. He would do whatever it took to keep you hanging. Neither married nor divorced."

"I don't have to be divorced to get custody, Lina. That's not his concern anyway. He's only worried about me getting the house or money from Mahir. Trust me. By the way, what did Mahir's mother say about all this?"

"Nothing. She didn't look upset though."

"That's typical. What else do I need to know?"

"They all agreed with Fadi when he said that you had adopted too many American values and almost forgotten where you came from."

"Really? Tell Fadi I know exactly where I came from. I think where I came from should update those ridiculous manuals they still use, especially the section that deals with women."

"He said even if you had American citizenship, that doesn't mean you can act like an American woman."

"That frightens him? I think it frightens all of them." Yasmin recalled Mahir once telling her about some of his Arabic friends in college and how they drooled over American women and fantasized about courting them. But they never considered a long-term relationship, and they all ended up marrying women from their countries. Now Yasmin could understand why the idea of marrying an independent woman that was protected by the law did not appeal to them.

"I think Fadi is upset because you didn't let him help," said Lina, interrupting Yasmin's thoughts.

"It doesn't take a genius to know that Fadi didn't want to help me. I think he is fond of the way things work here, which shouldn't surprise me; he's a male after all."

"I don't know what else to tell you, Yasmin. Until the meeting was over, everybody talked about you like you were an infidel that challenged their religion."

"That just shows you how much they understand their religion. If Abu Mahir knew his religion, he would know his plan to leave me hanging, neither married nor divorced, defies a specific divine order. It's not religion they are so concerned about. It's these social rules that a bunch of illiterate and egocentric men invented while reclining in their tents hundreds of years ago."

"I know, but I still feel bad, Yasmin. I don't know what to say or how to help. What are you going to do?"

"I don't know. I guess I have no choice but to wait for now."

Before they hung up, Lina promised to call whenever another gathering took place.

Yasmin wiped perspiration off her warm face. Though she was furious with the nonsense she had heard, she still made sure not to question Lina about Abu Mahir's previous visits with her father in fear of offending her. She did not want to risk losing her as her sole informant since she had remained as neutral as a camcorder throughout the meeting, listening and memorizing scenes in her head.

Yasmin's mother was enraged when she found out about that meeting. "Why would they all squeeze their noses into our affairs?"

"It's genetic, Mama. Some people thrive on grief and drama. If fate didn't grant it, they would go out of their way to borrow it," Yasmin said. "You see why I refused to see any of them?"

Yasmin tried to call Mahir at his parents' house that day, but no one answered. She missed Sami and Mira and worried about their mental and emotional states. She feared that if they missed her and asked to be with her, Mahir's father would take out his anger on them. They had left without their clothes and their toys, and she could not stop wondering if they were eating what they liked and if they cried for her at bedtime. She could only console herself by thinking how much Sami and Mira loved Mahir and how much Mahir loved them.

⊨⊣ ⊢⊨

Three days later on Mira's birthday, the morning of July 16, Yasmin let her nephew Omar call Mahir's house and ask to speak with Sami and Mira. She thought maybe this way she would stand a chance of talking to them and wishing Mira a happy birthday. But Mahir's mother told Omar that Sami and Mira were still asleep and hung up. When Yasmin tried again after her nephews returned from school, Mahir's mother told Omar that Sami and Mira were out. Yasmin remained restless and heartbroken all day, wondering what Mira's day was like. If she had a good time, if she thought about her, missed her, and cried for her. That night Yasmin tried to call again but still could not get hold of anyone.

The next day she tried again, calling Mahir's house during the day, but no one picked up. Even though Yasmin did not doubt that everyone in her family sympathized with her, she felt very lonely. No one mentioned the kids, asked her about her plans, or discussed solutions. Her father moved his bookmark to the middle of his book. Her mother carried on with her daily routine and went out with her sister, Samira, and her cousin, Nihad. Majid and Fatin went to work in the morning and became soccer parents in the afternoon. They either received their friends at home in the evenings or went out with them. Yasmin wished her father or Majid would at least threaten Mahir, tell him to bring back the children or else. Then she would have felt that she was not alone, and Mahir would probably reconsider and account for his next step.

At one after midnight, Yasmin took the phone receiver to her room so she could call her friend Ellen in Arizona. The phone rang several times before she heard Ellen's voice.

"Ellen, it's me, Yasmin."

"Oh, hi, Yasmin. I'm sorry my hello didn't sound very welcoming. I was staring at the long and foreign number wondering who it might be at this early time."

"I'm sorry. Did I wake you up?"

"No, no, don't worry about it. Tell me what's going on with you. How come you're not back yet? I called your house twice this week."

"Oh, Ellen…" Yasmin's words melted down her throat.

"Gosh, Yasmin. Your parents didn't let you come back?"

"No…it's Mahir."

"Please don't tell me he did something stupid."

Yasmin sniffled. "I'm afraid he did, Ellen. He took Sami and Mira, and there's nothing I can do about it."

"Why? Can't you just go to the police?"

"No, Ellen, I can't. It doesn't work that way here. What am I going to tell them? My husband came four days ago and took our children to his parents' house. They're going to say, 'So what?' My parents won't let me do something like that anyway. It's almost unheard of here."

"Gosh, Yasmin. Can you call a lawyer?"

"I can, but that would only be for filing a lawsuit, either for divorce or custody. But since Mahir is not telling me exactly what he's planning, I don't want to do something that might worsen the situation. Besides, I have to get my father's consent before taking any serious steps."

"I thought they were on your side."

"They are, but…I don't know how to explain this. Going to court is not a common option here. Solving the problem among families is more the custom."

"What? That must be killing you. What are you expected to do then?"

"Sit back and wait for Mahir to act before I react in a proper way. This is his winning territory. I have to calculate every move, or I'll lose."

"Gosh. Is that ridiculous or what?"

"*Ridiculous* is not the word, Ellen. If it were up to me, I would've denied him touching the children in the first place. This is not America. What he did is very acceptable here, and that is smashing me to fragments right now. I want to beat myself up for even thinking about bringing the children here under such circumstances."

"Yasmin, please calm down. You need to be strong now. Stronger than I've ever known you. Listen, did you call the embassy?"

"No. I didn't."

"Why not? I'm sure they can help."

"I don't think so. I heard once that they don't get involved in personal matters, especially if the person asking for help was born here. The Jordanian laws apply."

"Well, that is the stupidest thing I've ever heard."

"My God, Ellen. I'm so angry and confused."

"Oh, dear…listen, I want you to call the embassy anyway. They might at least recommend a lawyer or something. You have to do something, anything."

"I will." Yasmin took a deep breath. "Listen, Ellen, I need to ask you a favor. Could you call my friend Dina and tell her that I don't know when I'm returning? She's taking care of the pool and my plants, and she's probably called the house a million times by now."

"Sure. Give me her phone number."

Yasmin dictated Dina's phone number to Ellen.

"I will call her now. Don't worry. Promise me you will do something, Yasmin. Don't let the current push you. And keep in touch. Let me know what's going on every day if you can."

"I promise you I will, Ellen."

For Sami and Mira's sake, Yasmin thought she would swim against the current of a mud river. In the morning she would talk to her father about hiring a lawyer.

CHAPTER SEVENTEEN

Yasmin and her parents took their after-lunch coffee in the family room since, by mid-July, the afternoon sun almost turned the veranda into a sauna. Yasmin's father opened his book, and although the television was off, her mother still stared at the black screen while she sipped from her coffee cup.

"I wish Mahir would call you," she said, breaking the silence. "He must communicate with you and explain his plans."

"That's typical of him," Yasmin said. "When he doesn't want to confront a situation, he just shuts me out."

"The children are paying the price." Yasmin's father took off his glasses and put his book down. "I have to call Abu Mahir."

"No, Baba. I don't think that's a good idea. They're both rude and disrespectful."

Yasmin's father squinted. "Maybe I should go talk to Fadi and your uncle. They seem to know more than we do."

Yasmin's parents looked at each other, and Yasmin understood the meaning of that look.

This was not the first time Yasmin's mother had felt betrayed by her only brother. She shook her head with sadness. "He didn't have the decency or the courage to call me from the beginning when he found out about all this from Abu Mahir. I don't see why we should even consider talking to him. That dirty streak of meanness in him does not know limits, even when it concerns my children who had nothing to do with my old dispute with him."

"I agree with Mama. I don't think that's a good idea either, Baba. They're both on Mahir's side." Yasmin adjusted in her seat. She was about to discuss the court option with her father when the doorbell rang. They all looked at each other.

"Who could it be at this time?" Yasmin's mother looked at her watch. A few seconds later, Suka entered the room. "Man outside for you, madam," she told Yasmin.

Yasmin hurried to the door, her parents right behind her.

A man was standing on the balcony with a motorcycle helmet under his arm and a green dossier in his hand. He wiped his forehead with his sleeve before he stepped forward closer to the door to talk to Yasmin.

"Are you Mrs. Yasmin Nabeel, wife of Mahir Ahmad?" He read from a paper he took out of the dossier.

"Yes. How can I help you?"

"I'm here to serve you. Your husband filed a lawsuit against you."

"Divorce?"

"No. Visitations with the children, Sami, six, and Mira, three," he read from the same paper.

Yasmin trembled, and so did her voice. "The children are with him."

The server took a step back. "I'm sorry, but I have nothing to do with this. Usually men file this lawsuit to prevent the children from leaving the country."

Yasmin could feel the sympathy in his voice. "Sorry, I didn't mean to be rude. What am I supposed to do now?"

"You need to appear in person on the date specified in your papers. You can have a lawyer represent you on the second hearing, though."

The court server let Yasmin use his helmet as a clipboard when she signed two copies of the court order. He then placed one in the dossier and handed it to her. When he left, Yasmin noticed that she did not see or hear a motorcycle. She stepped forward to the edge of the balcony and watched him walk down a couple of houses and turn left. When the sounds of a car engine disturbed the quiet afternoon and then slowly faded away, Yasmin figured that the server must have parked his motorcycle somewhere far away and had someone drive him to her house.

"I bet you anything in the world that Fadi drove the server back and forth," she told her parents as they followed her to the family room.

The green dossier shook in her hands while she stared at Mahir's signature on the first page. She put it down on the coffee table, unclipped the little stack of papers inside it, and read the first one. The subpoena had a brief explanation of the lawsuite Mahir filed aginst her. It listed her name, Mahir's name, and both children. At the bottom of the page, there were a few mail stamps, a signature, and the court stamp.

A typed document from Mahir's lawyer had a handwritten draft stapled to it, and Yasmin had no doubt it had been written by Fadi. He had very distinctive handwriting that resembled her father's, and everybody in the family knew that. Fadi not only drove the server to her house as she suspected but did Mahir the honor of arranging the lawsuit on his behalf.

Yasmin's mother called Fadi and asked his sister Lina to wake him up from his afternoon nap. "Have you no shame? She's your cousin for God's sake. What did she ever do to you or to your family to deserve this? You're an animal, and you're going to pay for this," she screamed into the phone handle before she slammed it.

Fadi called right after and spoke to Yasmin.

"What do you want now? The lawsuit is not enough?"

"I tried to help, but you refused to talk to me."

"Why would I? It didn't take a genius to figure out from the beginning which side you were on."

"I'm as neutral in the middle of all this as I was from the beginning."

"What are you getting out of all this, you mean little backstabber? Or should I say how much?"

"I told you I'm not taking sides. As the old saying goes, all of you are nothing more to me than figures of pottery that can go ahead and smash one another."

Yasmin hung up. "*Hmar* (donkey)," she muttered.

After Yasmin's father looked through the file, he lifted his head and looked at her. "I think you're going to need a lawyer." He seemed as confused as he was angry. "I don't know of a lawyer that processes marital cases, but I will ask around and see if any of my friends can make a recommendation." He wrote something on a small piece of paper and stuck it in his pocket.

Still trembling, Yasmin nodded.

A couple of hours later, Lina telephoned and told Yasmin that a meeting to discuss the court issue had been held at her house. Mahir's father had proudly informed all the people who gathered that the lawsuit was the first punishment Yasmin would receive for messing with his son. Lina said that some relatives and a few friends resented that action on behalf of Mahir and found it unethical. It was one thing to gather and gossip, but when things took a serious turn, they decided to withdraw and pledge their support to Yasmin.

"They can go to hell," Yasmin's mother said when told about the meeting. "It's too late for them to feel sorry now. We don't need the support of a bunch of worthless mercenaries anyway."

Yasmin's aunts, Samira and Nihad, came over that evening to console her. When they walked in, they first stood next to her mother and with saddened faces looked down at her, sitting on the couch, her eyes full of sadness and despair. They looked like an athletic trio in their jogging pants, colorful shirts, walking shoes, and their hair that was puffed up like helmets. Though Yasmin was in no shape to make such observations, she still wondered at their appearance, keeping in mind that she knew for a fact that none of them had ever gotten close to being athletic in any way, not even by watching a game on television. They hugged her and kissed her. When Yasmin's mother said that their hookahs were ready in the backyard, Yasmin excused herself and said she would join them in a few minutes and went to her room to get her cigarettes. By the time she was in her room, she could hear them in the backyard mention her name and then whisper a few sentences. Right after that she smelled the incense and knew what her aunts were up to. She remembered how over the years every time she complained to her mother about Mahir and his temper, Auntie Nihad's "care packages" arrived in the mail soon after.

The contents always came in tin containers of Mackintosh's Quality Street Toffees and Chocolates or Royal Dansk Danish and Butter Cookies. Sealed with a few rounds of tape, the tin containers had a small plastic bag full of incense, the kind Yasmin has never seen in Scottsdale or Phoenix, not even at the Middle Eastern stores. They also had some tiny rocklike objects Auntie Nihad called the incense of the good-spirited people, along with sage, wheat, barley, salt, and round red seeds with a black dot on each of them that she called the eye of the jinni. If those jumped out when they burned, then may God have mercy on Yasmin's poor soul. That was an indication that the evil work of Satan was in full effect. A paper folded into a triangle needed to stay folded, or else the spell would reverse. Yasmin had to soak it in a glass of water for fifteen minutes or until the ink seeped out. And there was no need for Yasmin to be alarmed since the holy verses were written with a mix of saffron and rosewater. She just had to drink half of the water and pour the other half in Mahir's Arizona Iced Tea because he was not a water drinker.

Auntie Nihad always included a list of instructions, mostly to explain how to burn the incense, inhale it, set the burner on the floor, and cross over it. And of course instructions on how to dispose of the ashes afterward. Yasmin had to dump them in the middle of a four-way crossing out of her normal route. The first time Yasmin received the package, as a desperate young newlywed, she followed the instructions to a T, but as she expected, there was no change. When she protested her aunt's rituals to her mother and called them nonsense, her mother warned her against blasphemy and said that Nihad assured her that she consulted the best spiritual healer and gifted psychic in the country, and she was not cheap!

"When Allah loves one of his human creations (meaning Yasmin), he lets her suffer longer so he can hear her beautiful voice over and over again begging for his mercy," her mother quoted Nihad. So Yasmin had to be patient. Nothing changes overnight.

"Yasmin, where are you?" Her mother's voice brought her back from her memories.

"Coming," Yasmin left her room and went to the backyard.

After many tall buildings had blocked the view, the cool breeze, and most of the sky from the backyard, Yasmin's parents had heightened the fence and installed a canopy of blue canvas above it. It protected them from the afternoon sun and the ever-prying eyes of nosy neighbors. At the base of the eastern and northern walls, Majid had built brick planters and filled them with geraniums and sage bushes.

As soon as Yasmin sat down, Nihad turned to her. "That Mahir was spoiled to a stink. His mother raised him to feel superior because he was an only child. You're better off without him," she said, trying to lift Yasmin's spirit. "Don't let grief eat you up. You're still young and beautiful, and any man would wish to marry you."

Yasmin's mother widened her eyes. "What do you mean she's still young? She's thirty-four. No one is going to marry her with two children."

"Thank you for pointing that out, Mama." Yasmin shook her head.

"I'm just being realistic, Yasmin. I've been trying to make you understand this from the first time you complained about Mahir years ago. I knew the children would be the ones to pay the price."

Before Yasmin had a chance to reply, a distant bang startled her. Though the explosions of fireworks turned out to be the routine of almost every evening, the sounds still made her edgy.

Her aunt Samira patted her back. "It's true that absence makes a heart grow fonder. The more Mahir keeps your children away from you, the more they'll love you."

As they fixed the coals on their hookahs, Yasmin's mother and her aunts talked about the worsening economy. Nihad blamed it on President Bush and his speeches that implied a war against Iraq. Yasmin's mother and her aunt Samira agreed with her and said that life was becoming unaffordable and that people were struggling for necessities. Though Nihad was only a couple of years older than Yasmin's mother and her aunt, Yasmin noticed how she seemed more informed than both of them on many subjects. They listened to her attentively and perceived her statements as facts.

Suka set the table with baskets full of fruits and a few small tubs of mixed nuts. On her last trip out of the kitchen, she brought out a teakettle on a tray, surrounded by small glasses, each with a few fresh mint leaves placed in the bottom. Hookahs gurgled, releasing different aromas from the flavored molasses, making the air smell of sweet apples, mint, and licorice. In a small brazier to the side, the flaming charcoals crackled as they burned and became small and red like little dusty scoops of watermelon.

Yasmin took advantage of a moment of silence and moved closer to Nihad. "Do you know anything about courts, *Khalto* (Auntie) Nihad?"

"I've never been to one, but I hear all kinds of things about them, not all too encouraging." She took a long drag from the hookah and released it. "They say many judges judge by appearance first and then by the last name."

Yasmin understood exactly what Nihad was saying. The last name indicated not only tribal significance or wealth but also whether one's origins were Jordanian or Palestinian.

"That's unfair. That means justice is only for the privileged."

"Isn't it always? But things can work out better for you if you know the judge or someone that knows him."

Yasmin frowned. "What about lawyers?"

"I heard many stories in the past about lawyers who took money from clients but never appeared at court hearings. They never reimbursed the poor people who lost their cases as a result, either."

"Oh, how encouraging." Yasmin did not like what she was hearing but still did not take Nihad's comments as entirely true. She had lived in her country long enough to know that gossip was the fuel of people and how a simple rumor could ignite it, sometimes turning a small lie into a dangerous reality.

"I know you must be shocked from all this, but as sad as it sounds, it's true," Nihad said. "By the way, lawyers are usually allowed to become judges after studying for only two years at the judicial institution. Did you know that?"

"No. Actually I don't know anything related to the subject." Yasmin pulled her chair closer to Nihad.

"Many of these young judges they assign at courts are recent graduates of the institution. Believe me, some of them have no clue about processing a case." Nihad adjusted the coals on her hookah, drew a deep breath, and released the smoke away from Yasmin's face.

"How am I going to find a decent lawyer then?"

"Word of mouth," she said. "That's the only way to get around in this country. You know someone, you are someone."

Yasmin slipped away from her mother and her aunts, grabbed the phone receiver from the kitchen, and took it to her room. She took a picture of Sami and Mira from her wallet, stared at it for a long time, and kissed it. She called Carole and told her how her discussion with Nihad frightened her. Carole said she had heard all kinds of things too but told Yasmin that she should get some facts from a trusted lawyer.

"My father said he would find one, but it's taking him forever," Yasmin said.

"I have the number of a lawyer a friend of mine used years ago. She said he was good and very knowledgeable and won the case for her." Carole dictated the number to Yasmin. "Go for a consultation. He's been divorcing people for over forty years, so I'm sure he has an answer for every question. If you like him, you can ask him to represent you at the second hearing."

"I don't know about hiring him, but like you said, I should at least get a consultation. All I've been hearing so far is 'I heard' or 'They said.' I'll call him first thing in the morning." Yasmin took a deep breath. "Carole, do you think if I called the American embassy as an American citizen they would help or tell me what to do?"

"I don't think they would, but let me make a few phone calls and see what I can come up with. My sister's friend used to work there. She quit a few months back when she started chemo."

"I see. I wonder if the embassy would at least have a list of trusted lawyers that they recommend to the American community here."

"Never heard of such a thing either. It's better to find out about it from an insider. I'll call my sister and ask."

"OK, I'll wait then," Yasmin said, but she did not truly want to. Every passing moment she spent separated from her children was filling her with panic, despair, and frightening thoughts of how far she was willing to go in order to get them back.

CHAPTER EIGHTEEN

Half an hour before her appointment with the lawyer, Mahmoud Saleem, Yasmin strolled down the hill, dressed in her jeans and her oversize denim shirt. A couple of houses down, a Sri Lankan maid stood on the windowsill of a second floor and wiped the panes. The roar of a vacuum cleaner came from another house, muffling the voice of the late Farid al-Atrash singing about spring. Yasmin walked for less than five minutes before she stopped a yellow cab. Sweat was already trickling down her forehead and her back by then.

She opened the back door and asked the driver, "Wast-el-balad, downtown?"

The cabdriver, an older man in a stained caftan, first made a face and then nodded and turned the meter on. Yasmin knew how much drivers detested downtown on any day, but more so on a chaotic Thursday, a day before the official holiday, Friday. The driver drove by the shopping strip in the neighborhood, passed the green light, and then turned into University Street. There were no seat belts in the backseat, and even though the front seats had them, the cabdriver chose not to buckle up for some reason. Both his and Yasmin's unbuckled bodies shook in every direction as he zigzagged his way between cars and buses. His unnecessary racing talents passed the stare of a police officer and skipped two stop signs that did not have enough commands to even slow him down. They passed tall buildings on each side of the street, towering over shops, restaurants, and sidewalks full of pedestrians walking or going in and out of stores.

A woman wearing a long dress and a white scarf suddenly crossed in front of the cab with her four children, the youngest running ahead of her.

"Watch it," Yasmin screamed.

The driver screeched the asphalt before he stopped. Angry drivers behind him honked.

"Don't worry. It's normal," he told Yasmin. He held a miniature Koran and a few rosaries that hung from the rearview mirror to stop them from swinging. He looked at Yasmin. "You must be a summer visitor."

Yasmin did not answer. She only nodded, staring at a postcard glued to the dashboard. It had a blurry face of an oriental woman that kept winking. When other jaywalkers surprised the cabbie, Yasmin tightened her grip on the back of the front seat and closed her eyes.

Cars quadrupled in the downtown area, and the air became thicker, almost suffocating. Yasmin rolled down the window and moved her head closer to it. Cars crawled for a long time before they stopped, and the honking never stopped. Hawkers held out socks, men's blazers, shoe polish, cigarettes, and SB gum and screamed out their merchandise to the passersby. Deliverymen in white aprons held aluminum trays full of tea glasses and coffee cups and rushed in and out of stores.

A man who pushed a steaming cart of boiling corn stopped every few seconds and yelled, *"Durayeh! Durayeh!"* When no one approached him, he continued to push, yelling the name of his yellow vegetable. Just a few feet away, another man stood behind a big wooden tray balanced on a stool, stacked with baked *ka'ek* that looked like big sesame bagels. To the side of the tray, he placed a few boxes of cheese triangles and a pile of ground thyme.

Once they passed the gold market, Yasmin asked the driver to stop. When she had asked the lawyer's secretary for his address, the woman gave Yasmin the name of the main street and half a page of directions. It included a major mosque and a fabric store close to the gold market. She handed the driver a dinar, almost $1.30, and then stepped out. When she saw the Big Husseini Mosque ahead of her, she turned left and started looking for the lawyer's office. She passed shops that used parts of the sidewalk to display endless piles of underwear, towels, sheets, kitchenware, home decorations, and Taiwanese electronics.

The old and darkened buildings across the street had signs hanging under every window. On the fourth floor of one of them, Yasmin spotted the rusted sign that had the lawyer's faded first and last name. A young boy holding a box of black socks with Chinese or Taiwanese tags on them followed her as she crossed to the other side. When he lifted the box to her face, Yasmin waved her hand. "No, thank you." The air smelled of meat and burning fat. She felt her stomach turn.

"Please, madam, *mishan Allah* (for God's sake)," he begged. "I'm hungry. Please buy some for your husband so I can buy lunch." He pointed behind her.

Yasmin turned and saw a few men standing in line behind a man in a dirty white apron, holding a knife as long as a sword, facing a shawarma stand. The big stack of sliced lamb, interwoven with chunks of fat, revolved on a skewer that had some sort of a grill attached to it. To the side there was a glass case, where rows of chicken were roasting.

Yasmin handed the boy a dinar. "Keep the socks," she said and entered the building.

When she reached the lawyer's office, breathless, she walked through the abandoned reception and stood facing the lawyer. He was sitting behind a desk, working his way through the greasy bones of a whole chicken that he had placed over a newspaper section. Stacks of green and beige files covered most of his office walls and left little room for his desk.

When the lawyer noticed her, she took a step back. "I'm sorry if I came early."

Still chewing, he dismissed the need for apology by waving his hands. He then pointed to a seat.

"I'm Yasmin Nabeel." She sat down.

"Mahmoud Saleem. Nice to meet you." He asked her for a case briefing and started cleaning up. During the removal of oily deposits from his padded fingers and full lips, his fast nods accompanied Yasmin's short, but apparently common, story. Every time he burped, he rubbed his rounded stomach and apologized.

"What is your husband's name, Madam Nabeel?" he asked when Yasmin finished her briefing.

"Mahir Ahmad."

"Ah…I see. I'm going to be honest and straightforward with you." He smiled the way people do when they feel sorry for someone. "From the many domestic cases that I have processed in the past, I must confess the small chance you stand as a woman, especially when you don't have a powerful last name, money, or the right connections."

Yasmin sat forward in her seat.

"I'm saying this because I'm sure you are fully aware of the influence of your husband's family."

Even though Yasmin and Mahir had the same Jordanian descent, he had always bragged about belonging to one of the seven most influential tribes of the North. The way that had such significance to him had never bothered her before, but now it was crushing her.

Mahmoud Saleem explained Mahir's lawsuit for visitations, the one Yasmin already knew he filed just to prevent Sami and Mira from leaving the country. "If the judge rules in favor of your husband, which I suspect he will, the names of your children will be added to a computer list on all ports." He joined his hands over his desk. "Someone in the army with a high rank, however, could easily erase their names, as I have observed in the past. Fifty dinars, which amounts to seventy dollars, would have the same effect too." He opened his eyes as wide as he could.

Yasmin was appalled at how easy it was to break the law, but at the same time, and with a bit of a guilty feeling, she was relieved that such options were available.

"A bribe?" Yasmin folded her arms and smiled at him.

Mahmoud Saleem nodded, stuck his pinkie nail between his teeth, and started digging out a stuck piece of chicken. "If divorce is what you have in mind, I advise a case like yours to file for a *khuloe* divorce. You would be divorced within six months, but you would have to give up all your rights. Since your advanced dowry, as you explained earlier, is one dinar and the postponed is only five thousand, I say it's not worth filing for."

Yasmin nodded. Not knowing much about divorce laws in her country somewhat bothered her. She remembered studying some of it years ago in school, but that was the end of it. No one in her family or among her friends was ever divorced.

Mahmoud Saleem looked for a more effective tool on his desk to relieve his teeth. He smoothed out a paper clip and put it in his mouth.

"Correct me if I'm wrong, but I know I have the right to custody, proper housing, child support, and my dowry," Yasmin said.

After he succeeded in picking at his teeth, he threw the paper clip in an ashtray, chewed a little, and swallowed. "You are right, but let me remind you that such lawsuits could drag on for years, and there is always the possibility of husbands hindering the procedure by trying to prove the wife unfit. Some even accuse their wives' honor. Men have done that in the past with the help of witnesses. With a small amount of money, you'll be amazed how many men and women are willing to sell their conscience."

This was the second time Mahmoud Saleem had mentioned money in his consultation, but this time it was not to Yasmin's advantage. Actually, the idea of losing her children along with her reputation because someone was willing to lie in exchange for a few dinars mortified her. "Some women are killed in this country in the name of honor, and their killers walk away free."

He nodded.

"But according to the Koran, it takes the sworn testimony of the four witnesses who catch a woman and a man physically joined in the middle of an act of sin to prove them guilty."

"That's true, but when the accuser is the husband, his solitary testimony is enough. But the good thing is that his accusation cannot stick if the wife swears that he was lying."

Yasmin sighed and shifted in her seat. "I have a hard time imagining it's as simple as you put it. Don't they investigate matters before making decisions in courts?"

"Unfortunately, they don't."

"So what you're saying is women in this country have rights, but men have the power to deny them."

"One more thing to keep in mind, Madam Nabeel. There is a big chance that your looks might work to your disadvantage."

"What do you mean?"

He smiled and nodded a few times. "Most judges have a formula in their heads for respecting a woman, and that is the hijab, the scarf, and the long robe. Now we all know that not all women respect and honor that outfit, but judges deal with what's in front of them. They don't speculate on what goes on outside the court walls." Mahmoud Saleem gave Yasmin a "do you understand what I mean" look and leaned back in his revolving desk chair.

Yasmin understood exactly what he was saying. It was so typical of Jordanians and Arabs in general to judge by appearance. Showing off was and would always be a big part of the culture. No wonder people went out of their way to borrow, steal, and even sell their testimonies for a few dinars.

"Why do they bother with having laws, then?"

"Look, Madam Nabeel. I'm not trying to scare you or discourage you in any way. I'm trying to show you every scenario that you might come across. You need to know it all."

"I understand," Yasmin said. "What I don't understand is why we are even discussing these possibilities. I know divorce is among the many cases processed in this country according to the Islamic law, sharia, but that's not how divorce laws are stated in the Koran."

Mahmoud Saleem laughed. He picked up the phone and looked at Yasmin. "Coffee, Madam Nabeel?"

"No, thanks."

"Get me coffee, extra sugar," he asked of the person on the other end and then looked back at Yasmin. "Unfortunately, only certain laws follow sharia, the Islamic laws stated in the Koran, contrary to your and other people's expectations. When it comes to divorce, even though all cases are processed under the same law, there is no such thing as one solution for all."

Yasmin shook her head.

Mahmoud Saleem leaned forward. "Also, keep in mind that, in many cases, not all court orders are implemented, for one reason or another."

"In other words, even if I win the case, that doesn't mean I get my rights?"

"Madam Nabeel, even if you win the case, your husband can pay your dowry in little amounts stretched over years. Knowing how to hide his income, the twenty-five dinars per child you'd get as child support that is commonly granted by the court would not be enough to feed one of your children for a week. In my opinion, filing for spousal maintenance and housing would cost in lawyer's fees more than you can ever gain."

Yasmin remembered Nihad's words. "It sounds to me like justice is either a privilege or matter of luck."

A young lady wearing a scarf on her head walked in with a cup of coffee. She greeted Yasmin with a smile and then set the cup in front of Mahmoud Saleem. He immediately picked it up, brought it to his lips, and sipped, making a whistling sound.

"I need to ask you one more thing. I think I know the answer to it, but I just want to make sure."

"Go ahead, please."

"Does the fact that I have American citizenship and my children were born in America help me in any way?"

Mahmoud Saleem pressed his lips and shook his head. "No such thing. In Jordan, everyone is subject to the Jordanian laws. Besides, the American embassy does not interfere in personal disputes." He took another sip of his coffee. "Look, Madam Nabeel, there are always other ways for dealing with a situation like yours," he said. "I would like to bring to your attention the famous Magboola family case. The man killed his wife, and the children were deported from Jordan with the help of high official powers and placed in the custody of their only aunt, who happened to be a bartender in Turkey."

Yasmin took the hint and nodded.

Mahmoud Saleem then stood up, announcing the end of the consultation. "Before you make a decision, I have to remind you that this is a strange country and knowing the right people can sometimes even help you make your own laws, as I have observed in the past."

Yasmin paid him a consultation fee of ten dinars, about thirteen dollars, and left his office. She put on her sunglasses, and as if the chaos around her were just an illusion, twenty minutes passed before she realized how far she had walked. When she stopped to wave down a cab, a young boy pulled at her sleeve and begged her to buy safety pins. She reached in her purse, scooped out some change, and placed it over his pins.

On the way home, she felt small and stripped of dignity. She had a strong urge to kick and scream inside the cab, but she did not. She felt as if somebody had wrapped her whole body in a tangle of heavy chains and the big lock that held the chains together pierced her lips. She took out the photo of Sami and Mira from her purse and stared at it all the way, tracing their little smiles with her finger. She thought about what Mahmoud Saleem had said about the embassy. Though he appeared to be very informed, she still found what he had said hard to believe. There had to be something the embassy could do for her.

When she arrived at the house, she entered the study, sat behind her father's desk, took out her phone book, and looked for the number of the American embassy. The big window behind her lit the room of dark wood shelves that covered every inch of wall from floor to ceiling. It took her a few moments to adjust to the light and a few more to slow her breath, but she failed to regulate the pace of her pulse. She did not know what to expect from calling the embassy but hoped it would be her way out of the country with her children. She had promised Carole to wait and see what her sister's friend had to say, but after listening to Mahmoud Saleem crush her hopes she did not have the patience to wait anymore. She finally lifted the receiver and dialed.

"American embassy," a man's voice said.

"Good afternoon. I'm an American citizen, and I need to speak with someone who can help me with a problem."

"What kind of a problem?"

Yasmin gave the man a brief explanation.

"Stay on the line."

She sighed with relief. "Thank God," she whispered to herself. This was the call she had to make from day one.

Seconds later, the same voice came back on the phone. "Here are the numbers of the two American centers," he said. "One of them will help you."

As soon as she hung up, she dialed one of the numbers.

A woman with a young voice answered. "American center, can I help you?"

Though the secretary spoke in English, Yasmin knew right away from her accent that she was Arabic. It did not matter though; it was common for embassies and foreign organizations to hire locals. To eliminate any chances of a misunderstanding on the secretary's behalf, Yasmin explained her situation with every bit of boring detail.

"I can give you the name and number of the lawyer we deal with," the secretary said.

That was not what Yasmin had expected to hear. She expected an appointment with somebody at the center if not at the embassy but figured maybe that was how things worked in such situations.

"Go ahead. Give me the number. I'm ready," she said.

Yasmin immediately called the lawyer and set an appointment for Saturday morning since the next day was Friday, the country's official holiday. She then walked to the veranda, where her father was sitting, his glasses on and his book in his hand. On the day Yasmin had arrived and her father failed to remember the details of her fight with Mahir, she had not imagined that his forgetfulness was that serious. But a few days later, she began to notice how he documented events and placed little notes and reminders everywhere in the house.

"Baba, can I talk to you?"

He put the book down and sat straight. "Sure."

"Did you find a lawyer?"

"Not yet." He looked embarrassed and began to search his pockets. "I should go call my friend and ask him, now."

"That's OK, Baba." Yasmin knew he was looking for that reminder he wrote, but he obviously could not find it. "Don't we have a phone book? Yellow pages or anything like that."

"We do, but it's no good finding a lawyer that way. How are we going to tell if he's a good lawyer if he wasn't recommended by someone?"

"I see," Yasmin said. "Well, I hope you don't mind, but I called the embassy and they recommended a lawyer for me. I set an appointment just for a consultation."

"That's fine."

Yasmin smiled. "OK, then." She was overwhelmed with hope; her feet barely touched the floor as she walked away. That night when she stared at the photo of Sami and Mira, a smile came to her face.

"Soon," she whispered before she put it away. She opened one of her suitcases and took out Mira's tattered blanket and Sami's bear from it. She brought them close to her nose and breathed into them for a long time. When she went to bed that night, she held them close to her heart and then closed her eyes.

CHAPTER NINETEEN

Saturday morning Yasmin's father insisted on driving her to her appointment in his old Volvo. After they buckled their seat belts, he turned to her and said, "The new car has air-conditioning, but it's automatic. It has too many confusing switches, and I didn't get a chance to figure them all out yet."

Yasmin dreaded the long and sweaty trip. "It doesn't make a difference to me, Baba. I feel bad for troubling you like this. I could've taken a taxi."

"Take a taxi and go by yourself?" Yasmin's father put his glasses on, held the steering wheel with both hands, and eased down the hill.

Yasmin laughed. "What's wrong with me going by myself?"

"We don't know the lawyer. What if he's not decent? Besides, the city has changed quite a bit since your last visit. I don't think you can find your way around."

Yasmin nodded. "I see."

At the red light, a man in rags holding a big bag full of tissue boxes moved from car to car repeating, "Four for a dinar." When he approached Yasmin, her father waved him away.

"I'm going to take al-Madeenah Street to Jabal Amman (Amman's mountain)," her father said.

"Whatever is easy for you, Baba."

Even though the capital was initially built on seven hills, people referred to them as *jabals* (mountains). A long road known as Zahran Street sprung from the bottom of Amman's mountain, and miles of it streamed through eight areas. Each one was named after one of the roundabouts that interrupted its flow. Some of the roundabouts had fountains, statues, or small gardens in their center. Later on as new areas developed, the city progressed in age and size, and its inhabitants multiplied, traffic lights replaced most of the roundabouts. But people still referred to them when giving directions.

While Yasmin's father continued to stare at the red light, two young girls engrossed in a conversation crossed in front of them. One had her hair covered with a scarf, and the other wore a tank top and tight jeans. Two young men walked right behind them, carrying backpacks. Yasmin assumed they were all college students since they all proceeded to the university entrance. She remembered how, after Desert Storm, wearing head scarves became very popular among young women in Jordan. This came across to Yasmin as more of a fashion statement than a religious duty. The scarves came in all colors and styles to complement makeup and the fashionable and modern clothing. She wondered how the two girls that had just passed them perceived each other. Did the one in a scarf look down on the one in a tank top, and what did the latter think of her friend? She also wondered what the guys who walked behind them thought, too.

When the light turned green, Yasmin's father drove out of the neighborhood into mild traffic. "From the sixth roundabout, I'll go down to the lawyer's office between the first and the second roundabout. It's not as busy as the other streets."

"That's fine, Baba." She looked at her watch.

"It will take us probably the same time going any other way if you think of all the traffic lights and traffic jams."

They passed by banks with foreign names, American fast-food restaurants, and many tall buildings, plastered with hundreds of signs that made their fronts and sides look like newspaper ad sections. A few miles down the road, watermelon stands appeared in vacant lots on the right side. The front of every canvas tent there was a high stack of the big green fruit. Some of the merchants displayed more of it on the sidewalk in the shape of pyramids, the top watermelon cut in half, red side facing the street. Yasmin's father got stuck behind a car that suddenly stopped in the first lane. The driver stepped out of the car, ignoring the honking of Yasmin's father and all the cars behind him. While the man continued to bargain with the watermelon vendors, Yasmin's father struggled to change lanes. As he stared in the side mirror awaiting an opportunity to switch lanes, Yasmin wiped her sweaty face and looked at her watch.

From the sixth roundabout area, they drove south, passing the fifth- and the fourth-roundabout areas that housed old neighborhoods of palaces, embassies, and five-star hotels. Mature eucalypti and weeping willows guarded a few extravagant villas on both sides of the road. Traffic slowed a little as they approached the third roundabout, where pedestrians ran or just walked between cars. Yasmin checked the time again.

"We still have time," her father said.

"Yeah, I know, Baba."

Since the moment Yasmin called and set the appointment with the lawyer Thursday evening, she had not stopped producing scenarios of how he would handle her case. She pictured herself in his presence and gave him features and a character. By the end of every little sketch she wove in her imagination, she saw herself on the plane with Sami and Mira, heading back to Scottsdale.

Once they arrived at the old building described by the lawyer's secretary, Yasmin's father could not find a parking space. He drove past that building and then, half a mile away, pulled over and parked between two cars. Yasmin took a tissue out of her purse and wiped more sweat from her face and neck. When she stepped out of the car, she peeled her shirt off her back and let some air pass through. Her father walked ahead of her along the narrow sidewalk that led to the entrance of the building. They climbed the stairs side by side to the second floor and entered a waiting room that smelled of cigarettes and fresh paint. A small vacant desk sat in the corner.

As soon as they entered, the lawyer came out of his office and introduced himself. "Faris Bader." He extended his hand to Yasmin's father. "You must be Mr. Nabeel."

Yasmin's father nodded and shook his hand.

"Mr. Nabeel, you are called Abu…?" Faris allowed himself to get formalities out of the way and address Yasmin's father in a more casual manner, as if he were a family member or friend.

Yasmin's father did not mind. "Abu Majid," he said.

"And you must be Sister Yasmin." He shook her hand and then stepped aside and made room for them to walk into his office. Yasmin thought that his brilliant green eyes looked out of place on his dark Middle Eastern face. She could tell he was very aware of that asset by the way he dressed. He wore an olive-colored three-piece suit, a starched mint-green shirt, and a green-striped tie.

The bare office walls were white and shiny. Breathing in the fresh paint somehow left a taste in Yasmin's mouth. Faris stood behind a large lacquered desk that had brass corners. A picture of a woman wearing a scarf and full makeup hugging a girl and two boys between the ages of three and seven showed through the big sheet of glass that laminated the desk. Beside it lay a picture of an infant that Yasmin assumed was the last addition.

Next to the undressed window behind the desk, an old oak case shelved big volumes in leather bindings, stamped with golden scales. Faris Bader pointed to the two seats in front of his desk before he sat down and asked Yasmin for a briefing.

Yasmin told her story as briefly as possible, starting back in Scottsdale and ending with the lawsuit filed against her by Mahir. When she finished, she looked at Faris with eyes full of hope, but he stared back at her as if waiting for her to continue.

Faris rested his elbows on his desk and asked, "You want to file for divorce?"

"No." Yasmin's father sat forward.

"I actually came for advice since both my husband and I are American citizens, and I was told by the lady at the American center that you were recommended by them and by the embassy."

Yasmin noticed concern building up in his eyes.

"There must be some kind of misunderstanding here. I'm not a divorce lawyer," he said and combed his fingers through his hair. "I wish I had the privilege of representing the embassy, but as far as I know, the embassy does not get involved in personal disputes." Faris puckered his lips and sat back. He confessed his limited knowledge of the English language as if it were a major vitamin deficiency. "I very much regret not paying attention during English classes. Sister Yasmin, that doesn't mean I can't recommend someone who can help in a case that involves an English-speaking continent." He smiled and gave her an assuring nod.

Yasmin could not think of anything to say. She just stared at Faris, devastated that she was not going to see her children as soon as she had imagined.

"What kind of cases do you process?" Yasmin's father crossed his legs. "Yasmin is going to need a lawyer for the second hearing."

"Since I moved into this office, I've only been accepting business cases, Abu Majid, but my old partners still take domestic cases, disputes, divorces, and custody. Sister Yasmin mentioned earlier that she is married to Mahir *Ahmad*. Don't get me wrong for saying this, but she needs aggressive lawyers to represent her. I'll be more than happy to give my old partners a call on her behalf."

He explained his old partners' education, experience, and fees to both Yasmin and her father.

"OK." Yasmin's father seemed satisfied with their credentials. He uncrossed his legs. "Go ahead and give them a call. I will stop by their office first thing in the morning."

"Now as you know, Sister Yasmin, your husband will have a lawyer representing him, but you are going to appear in person before the judge on the first hearing."

Yasmin already knew that. She just nodded.

Faris took out a cigarette from his pocket and lit it. "I want you to know that you have the right to ask for a case postponement until you hire a lawyer. It's a routine procedure hardly ever rejected."

Yasmin sighed with relief for not having to appear at court more than once.

"This way you'll give a chance to my old partners to deal with the court hassles on your behalf. And remember, when you stand before the judge, don't speak unless he asks you. Don't forget to address him as Your Honor."

"Don't worry; I won't."

"Just in case Sister Yasmin loses the case, she can always file for custody. It's a simple procedure. Policemen will bring the children to her on the same day."

"No, no, no." Yasmin's father waved his hand in the air. "We are not discussing that option at this time."

Yasmin did not comment. She looked at Faris, who was about to say something but looked at Yasmin's father and stopped. He thought for a moment and then said, "I'm going to explain Sister Yasmin's situation to a friend of mine who owns a translation company and has good connections at the American embassy just to get his opinion on the situation." He smiled at Yasmin. "Language barriers must not delay the actions necessary for solving the problem."

Yasmin smiled back. "Perfect."

Her father agreed by nodding.

The word *embassy* had a promising tone in Yasmin's ears. She immediately sent her thoughts on another journey concerning her great return.

Faris walked Yasmin and her father to the door, shook their hands, and asked Yasmin to keep him informed of her court appearance. He refused to charge them a consultation fee, and when Yasmin's father insisted, he said, "Please, Abu Majid, we are like family; there is still goodness in this world. It gives me great honor to be of help."

CHAPTER TWENTY

Tiny streams ran down the moistened glass like sweat, and the potted geraniums outside sparkled with dew. Yasmin drew the curtains further to the sides and closed the window partway, leaving only a one-inch passage for the chilly and damp morning air. The sounds of early masons hammering their chisels into white stones in a nearby vacant lot quieted down, but the sounds of children playing while awaiting summer-school buses still crept in. Yasmin ached for Sami and Mira. She had not seen them or heard from them in ten days. She pictured them walking behind her to the car in the morning, clutching at their lunch boxes. She longed to hold their faces for a kiss and a hug.

While rubbing her arms, Yasmin moved away from the window and stood facing her opened closet. She carefully studied her clothes and tried to mix and match enough decency into an outfit she could wear to court. Besides the dress she wore for Hala's wedding, she had only packed enough jeans and casual tops for the few days she had planned to spend with her family and maybe an informal outing with Carole. Her long-sleeved tops revealed too much chest. The ones with more decent necklines had no sleeves, and the few that concealed the most stretched with her curves. Giving up, she turned to Hala's closet in the next room and looked through her leftovers.

"Mama." She stuck her head out of the room. "Can you come to Hala's room for a second?"

Her mother tied her robe belt as she entered the room. "You're not dressed yet?"

"I don't know what to wear."

"Wear dress pants or a long skirt. Anything casual but conservative."

"I don't have anything like that."

"Don't be foolish. Let me go look in your closet."

Yasmin heard her mother mutter something in her room before she came back. "What is wrong with you? Ten black tops and four pairs of jeans. Is that what you call clothes?"

Yasmin kept her eyes on Hala's closet.

"Let me go ask your father and see what he says."

Yasmin could not make out a word her parents said in the hallway before they entered Hala's room.

"Your father said you can't wear jeans. It's inappropriate."

Yasmin reached with reluctance for a flowered summer dress. "This is good."

"Spaghetti strap?"

"Calm down, Mama." She found a white knitted cardigan, folded on the shelf. "Here, I'll wear this over it. You think Hala would mind if I borrowed these?"

"No, go ahead. She wanted me to give away everything she left behind."

"I've never been to a court before, but I think you should cover your hair," her father said.

"What?" Yasmin looked at her mother for help.

"No, no, she doesn't have to cover. Let's not get too carried away here."

"OK, then. Get dressed fast. We have to be there at eight," he said.

Yasmin slipped into the dress, buttoned the sweater to her throat, pushed up the sleeves, and walked out of the room, pulling her hair back into a ponytail. Her father was already by the door, holding his keys and the green dossier that the server gave Yasmin. "You didn't wear heavy makeup, right?" He handed the dossier to Yasmin.

"I'm not wearing any."

"I'll pray for you, Yasmin," her mother said. "Be careful driving."

When Yasmin's father drove down the hill at seven thirty in the morning, the sun was a splash of faint yellow behind an overlay of haze, and the neighborhood had not fully awakened yet. Garbage collectors in orange overalls pushed their wheelbarrows from house to house, picking up garbage bags to unload at the Dumpsters nearby. All the stores in the small strip had their fronts concealed behind corrugated-iron doors, except for the bakery that already had a line of cars parked in front of it.

Yasmin's father leaned forward in his seat and gripped at the steering wheel with both hands. "Remember what the lawyer said. Ask the judge to delay the verdict until you hire a lawyer."

"I remember, Baba."

"When you talk to the judge, you address him as Your Honor."

"I know, Baba."

"It's good that we left early enough to beat morning traffic." He stopped and carefully inspected the intersection before proceeding to the main road. Only a few cars honked at her father on the way and tried to race him, and very few pedestrians startled him by jumping in his way while crossing to the other side. Yasmin rolled down the window as they neared the roundabout named after the Department of Interior Affairs.

"They built bridges and dug a tunnel, and nothing changed. The roundabout still gets jammed any time of the day," her father said.

Yasmin looked ahead. It was overcrowded with people and cars, as if all had expelled from the earth at that very moment. Her father inched his way toward a brand-new Mercedes-Benz and a green truck that had collided, causing a commotion and traffic delay. The driver of the truck was arguing with the driver of the Mercedes, a woman, who did not seem to give him any attention. Holding a cell phone to her ear, she pointed her finger to her car, as if explaining what had happened to the person on the other end. Men surrounded her; some stood too close, touched her car, gazed inside it, and leaned on it. Clutching tightly to her purse, the woman looked around in despair for whomever she had called to get her out of this mess and deal with the man who was yelling at her, as well as the women and children who had stepped out of the back of the truck and were cursing her.

The jam began to loosen when two police motorcycles finally arrived on the scene.

Yasmin's father drove out of the roundabout and turned right as soon as the cars ahead of him decided they had seen enough and started moving.

"We're almost there," he said after a few minutes. "Some people are so irresponsible. They think they own the streets. I bet you that woman was talking on the phone when she hit the truck."

"God knows what happened, Baba. It might not be her fault." Yasmin held her stomach and took a deep breath.

"Are you OK?"

"I'm frightened."

"Calm down. It's just a routine procedure. No verdict today."

"I know," she said, but her fears did not lessen.

Yasmin's father drove a few more minutes. "I think I'll park here." He looked out from her side.

"I don't see the court."

He pulled over and parked in front of a building.

The night before, Yasmin had envisioned the courthouse as a huge building with massive columns in the front. The type of structure that implied by its haughtiness that justice could never bend. Upon arrival, however, she did not have a glimpse of that design and did not sense the metaphor, either. On the sidewalk of the commercial building, a few men sat behind small folding tables that had black umbrellas stabbed into their corners. Each man had stacks of forms, sheets of stamps, and a small metal safe placed in front of him. Yasmin figured they were most likely notary publics.

Yasmin and her father climbed the stairs to the second floor and entered the court. A long hall had three rooms on either side and two at the opposite end. To the right, a small counter served as the court's canteen, and behind it, an aged Xerox leaned against the wall. After making some copies and handing them to a young man, the man behind the counter moved to the coffee and tea station, poured some in cups and glasses, and rushed with his tray to deliver. His rolled-up pants revealed long black fluffy hair, and his plastic slippers made a loud noise that turned every head he passed.

The office rooms Yasmin and her father passed had judges and crowds of people, a few sitting down and many standing up. Most judges dressed in Muslim habits and topped their heads with fezzes wrapped with white cloth, and a couple wore suits. In a small foggy waiting room, men of various ages smoked and drank coffee. A picture of the king hung high on a wall and was secured in place next to a flag of Jordan by many pieces of Scotch tape. Women remained out in the hall, pacing back and forth, their eyes looking tired and full of worry and despair.

Waiting for the announcement of her case number, Yasmin and her father stood in a corner where they underwent curious inspection by people standing around or passing by. A crying young girl held a newborn in her arms. She looked about eighteen and was dressed in sequined jeans, a pink top, and high-heeled sandals showing the chipped nail polish on her toes. A middle-aged woman in a stained scarf and a long embroidered dress approached the girl and smiled.

"Divorce?"

The girl turned her wet eyes away.

The woman looked at Yasmin. "Divorce?"

"No, no. I'm waiting for someone," Yasmin lied.

"Oh!" She stepped away, leaving behind an aroma of sweat, fried onions, and cheap perfume. Then she started a conversation with another woman.

"What are you here for?" she asked her.

"Custody. What are you here for?"

"I'm suing my husband for child support. He never paid."

"Oh? I didn't know you could do that. Would that make him pay?"

"No, not really. They'll just send him to jail for a couple of months. That should teach him a lesson, at least."

A man approached the sobbing girl, holding a paper in his hand. "He insists," he said.

"Why should I sign away my rights?" the girl snapped. "He's the one who dragged me here to divorce me." She wiped her smudged cheeks and looked away.

"He says if you don't sign, he will sue for custody and never let you see your son again."

The girl started wailing.

The man put the paper in her hand before he turned and walked away.

After waiting on their feet for more than an hour, Yasmin feared that she might have gotten the time and date of her court appearance wrong. She checked her court order. It said eight o'clock. She looked at her father. "Don't you think we should go talk to someone about this? We've been standing here for an hour."

Her father laughed. "You think you're in America? They assign all cases here to the same hour. That way if a case is canceled, the next is waiting."

Two and a half hours later, a man called the number of Yasmin's case. Yasmin and her father followed him into a room full of men. Yasmin knew none of them and didn't understand why they were in the room. She had heard once that anyone from the public, including law students and trainees, were allowed to sit in courtrooms. She felt so uncomfortable and exposed. The judge that sat behind a big desk, dressed in a three-piece suit under an opened black robe, already looked bored and tired.

Yasmin stepped in. "Good morning."

The judge did not reply, as if Yasmin's voice had gotten lost on the way between her insignificance and his sacred importance. He motioned for her to sit on one of the two benches facing his desk. Her father remained standing by the door since none of the men who immediately started inspecting Yasmin offered him a seat. After she sat down, she kept her eyes forward on a picture of the king that hung behind the judge next to a framed script of Allah, stitched in gold over black velvet.

Mahir's lawyer entered the room soon after and sat on the other bench. She wore tight blue jeans and a not very buttoned up shirt and threw a long black robe over her shoulders. Yasmin felt betrayed by her appearance since she felt like a curtain in Hala's old dress and her small cardigan. There was no dress code for the court after all.

The judge briefed Yasmin on the lawsuit filed against her by Mahir and looked at her for response.

"Your Honor, the children are with my husband," she said, hoping the judge would consider that fact and cancel the case.

The judge did not comment.

She expected him to at least question Mahir's lawyer, who seemed too busy removing a splinter from her nail, but he did not do that either. When Yasmin looked back at him and saw him flipping through the papers on his desk, she realized that the routine according to which all cases were processed was going to prevail, regardless of the facts and the lies.

Her voice shook, and her hands grasped at the dossier as she addressed the judge. "Your Honor, I wish to postpone the case until I hire a lawyer to represent me."

The judge made a displeased face. "Case postponed until the court is notified by the assigned lawyer," he said and then signaled a man by the door to call the next case.

Mahir's lawyer leaned to the side and picked up her briefcase as Yasmin was getting up. "The children are with your client. If he said otherwise, then he lied to you, Miss," Yasmin said.

Mahir's lawyer looked up with a face of no expression. "I was hired to represent him, not to find out the truth." She then walked away.

Still standing by the door, Yasmin's father shook his head, appalled by the whole procedure.

Once outside the building, he said, "They call this justice? Their procedures are not even fit for a post office. Make sure you call Faris Bader when we get home to let him know how the judge handled the case so he can have his partners prepared."

CHAPTER TWENTY-ONE

On the afternoon of Yasmin's second hearing and while waiting for Faris Bader to call, she paced back and forth under the canopy in the backyard with the phone receiver in her hand. Faris had promised to call the moment her lawyers left the court. From what she had seen at the court and what the old lawyer Mahmoud Saleem and her aunts had told her, she knew her chances of defeating Mahir were close to nothing. But listening to Faris Bader speak of his talented and successful previous partners had revived her hopes and left her with the conviction that winning the case was possible.

When the phone finally rang around two o'clock and Faris told her that she had lost the case, she couldn't utter a word.

"Sister Yasmin, are you still there?" Faris asked in a compassionate tone.

"Two lawyers were not enough to convince the judge that my husband is a liar?"

"Sister Yasmin, I assure you they did everything in their power." He was silent for a moment. "Forgive me for saying this. I don't think your husband needs lawyers to deal with him but rather a villain to slit his throat from ear to ear. We know he only filed for visitations so he can prevent the children from leaving the country, but that could be worked around."

"How? The court order would still be effective even if I win a custody case."

"That's not important if you have the right connections when departing the country. Why don't we discuss this further at my friend's office? The one who has connections at the embassy."

"What time? What's the address?"

"Is three o'clock good for you?" Faris dictated the address to Yasmin. "It's on the fourth floor, the door facing the elevator."

"I'll be there."

Yasmin tried to pull herself together before entering the house. She sat under the canopy, held her head in her hands, closed her eyes, and took deep breaths. Sami and Mira had never spent time away from her, save for a few weekends with Mahir. She had not seen them in almost ten days and not only missed them but dreaded the thought of them suffering and crying themselves to sleep every night the way they had done when Mahir moved out. She checked the time. Her heart beat fast at the thought of meeting with Faris and his friend in forty-five minutes. The idea of them helping her get back her children, break the law, and escape reminded her of Sally Field in *Not without My Daughter*. Her heart beat even faster. The movie was a heart-wrenching story of a mother's struggle to escape Iran during the Iran-Iraq War and return with her daughter to America.

Yasmin thought back to the day when Mahir and his father left her parents' house after they had that dreadful meeting. She had vowed back then that she would go back with her children to their home at any cost. Now that the opportunity had arisen, she wanted to make sure nothing was going to jeopardize her return. If her father and Majid knew she was planning to flee the country, they would object and say that such plans were unethical and dangerous. It would also put them in a bad position once Mahir and his father found out. Yasmin did not look forward to disgracing her father and her brother in any way, but by putting their reputation first, they left her no choice. Telling her mother was also out of the question. Aside from her negative reaction, there was always the risk of her sharing the news with Nihad and Samira. One of them might unintentionally slip a word in front of a family member, who would not only run to Mahir with the news but would have the whole country talking about it in no time.

After coming up with a plan, Yasmin called Carole. She told her about losing the case and about her alternative solution.

"For the next few afternoons, I'm going to lie and say I'm with you. I don't think my mother will call you unless there's an emergency, but just in case, be careful."

"Don't worry," Carole said. With a tone full of doubt, she asked, "Are you sure Jalal and Faris are related to the embassy?"

"Honestly? I don't care if they're related to the devil. I want to get out of here with my children."

When Yasmin entered the house again through the kitchen, her father was in his usual place at the head of the table, placing a napkin on his lap. Her mother was standing next to him pouring water in his glass from a carafe.

"Majid and Fatin will be up in a minute with the children," her mother said. "Sit down; lunch is ready." She pointed to a stuffed chicken and a dish of rice covered with ground lamb and pine nuts.

"Faris Bader called. I lost the case."

Her parents both gasped and then stared at her.

"Did he say why?" Her mother put the carafe down.

Yasmin shook her head.

Her father turned and looked at the clock up on the wall behind him. "I will call the lawyers after lunch."

Yasmin nodded, doubtful that he would remember to do so unless she or her mother reminded him.

"Sit down," he said. "We'll discuss it later. I promised you I would find a solution."

"I'm not hungry. I have to go see Carole at the restaurant in fifteen minutes. If I get hungry, I'll eat there," she said and walked out of the kitchen.

At two thirty, half an hour before her appointment, Yasmin strolled down the hill, wearing a buttoned-up shirt over her T-shirt. The sun quickly warmed her face and her body, and she felt drops of sweat roll down her neck and her back. A few houses down, one of the neighbors parked under an olive tree, stepped out of the car, and opened the trunk. A young boy came up to him and helped him unload grocery bags. Something about his posture reminded Yasmin of Sami. She felt a pinch in her chest. She was dying to see Sami and Mira.

When she reached the intersection, she waved down a cab. The cabdriver put down his cell phone the moment she approached the passenger-side window and asked him if he would drive her to Jabal al-Hussein (Hussein's mountain). He nodded and turned the meter on. Once inside the car, she gave him further directions. The car smelled of his lunch, something fried and cold. It made her stomach turn, so she rolled down the window. The driver took a shortcut and drove inside the neighborhood all the way to the roundabout named after the Department of Interior. Yasmin's trip to the downtown lawyer had only cost three dinars for both ways, about four dollars, and now she estimated much less than that for her destination, maybe one dinar. Though cabs were cheap in Jordan, whatever she had left from the money Mahir had given her was not going to last long.

Traffic was light that time of the day. People were either having lunch or taking their afternoon naps. Tourists usually doubled the cars in the capital during the summer, but Yasmin noticed too many black-and-white Iraqi cabs, and also private cars with Iraqi license plates, roaming the streets. There had been no official announcements yet by President Bush regarding a war, but the rumors had given people enough reason to believe a war was inevitable.

"I should've taken a shortcut. These summer tourists get on one's nerves," the driver said, interrupting her thoughts. He lit a cigarette and looked in the rearview mirror, anticipating her reply.

Because the office was less than ten minutes away, Yasmin assumed that that would not leave much room for a conversation or a display of driving talents, but the short distance did not make a difference. Staring at the dashboard, covered with shimmering stickers of verses, Yasmin said, "They give a boost to the economy, at least."

"Tourists? They use us as a station and go spend their money in Europe. I drive around all day, Miss. These people bargain with the meter."

"Yeah, that's too bad."

"Making money is getting harder every day. Prices keep going up, and incomes stay the same."

Yasmin wanted to roll her eyes. His phone was the latest version of a Motorola, which probably cost him over three hundred dinars, yet he still complained of lack. She did not comment. The moment they approached the area Faris Bader had indicated, Yasmin kept her eyes glued to the window. On both sides of the street, tall rectangles of limestone with Arabic signage under every widow in thick three-dimensional metal lettering made all the buildings look the same to Yasmin. After paying the driver, she stood on the sidewalk scanning the front of the office tower and looked for the translation office's sign but found no trace of it. She took the elevator to the fourth floor and walked straight toward the opened door facing it, as Faris had instructed. There were no signs by the door either.

Faris was waiting behind the secretary's desk, dressed in different hues of green. After shaking her hand, he let her walk ahead of him through a sliding door into a spacious room. Yasmin assumed it was the office of the director. Though all the oak furniture looked well-placed, it still reflected its old age. The desk, the side tables, and the bookcases could use a coat of stain. One of the large bookcases was missing a section, and Yasmin remembered seeing that part at Faris's new office.

Faris stood in the middle of the room and pointed both hands at the two seats facing the desk. Yasmin sat on the one closest to the window.

"Jalal will be here any minute." He pushed up his sleeve and looked at his watch. "Official hours of business here are eight to one thirty."

"That's fine, Mr. Bader."

"Please call me Faris. We are like brother and sister. No need for formalities."

"OK." Yasmin smiled. "What type of services does this company normally provide?"

"Ah…they translate official documents to English, but mostly they fill out applications for American universities, immigration… that type of thing." Faris rubbed his hands and grinned. "And they help with other things of course."

"I see." Yasmin folded her arms and stared ahead at a poster of the Statue of Liberty.

"Sister Yasmin, whatever goes on in here must remain between us. Helping you and your children flee the country can have very serious consequences for all of us."

"I understand." She wiped sweat from her forehead. As she waved away a fly that hovered by her ear, she turned around and saw that the big window was open. The office tower next to the building left no room for the air to move freely, which made the room hotter than it should have been.

A man with red hair, styled in a comb-over, entered the office at that moment and walked straight to Yasmin. He shook her hand. "Hello. I'm Jalal."

"*Ahlan*," she greeted him back in Arabic.

Jalal took his suit jacket off, sat behind his desk, and lit a cigarette. This was definitely not the right time for Yasmin to make certain observations, but she could not help it. Jalal struck her as being one of those men who cheated their shirts out of a few sizes, which stretched the fabric between the buttons and exposed flesh. The skin on his chest and further down looked as if it had been pinched with chopped and rusted steel wool, and the roundness of his stomach made Yasmin very aware of his breathing.

"I already explained to Sister Yasmin how secrecy was important for the success of the plans," Faris said.

She nodded.

"Yeah, yeah, this reminds me to call the American consul right now." Jalal picked up the phone and dialed a number.

Yasmin sighed with content.

Jalal waited a few minutes and then hung up. "I can try later. I need to brief him on the situation before we start the real action." He smiled at Faris and then turned to Yasmin and asked her to bring a copy of the following: her passport, Sami's and Mira's passports, her marriage certificate, and the court order. He also asked for photos of Sami, Mira, and Mahir. Yasmin took out her little phone book and took notes.

"We are going to run a check on your husband in the United States," Jalal said. "I know he's an Ahmad, but from what I've heard so far, he's acting a bit strange. Just to be on the safe side, I'm going to need his Social Security number."

Yasmin lifted her head. "I don't know it, but I'll try to get it."

"Very well then," he said. "It looks like there isn't much we can do today. Why don't you stop by tomorrow around the same time with all the documents I requested and we'll go from there."

"That's fine." Yasmin stood up, shook hands with Jalal and Faris, and walked out. She was down in the lobby when she realized that neither Jalal nor Faris had mentioned fees for their services but thought it definitely depended on what the American consul had to say. She hoped that the amount they were going to charged her would be reasonable so she could borrow it from Carole.

Though the meeting was short, and no mention of the actual traveling plan took place, Yasmin found herself overcome with joy, as if she were already on the plane with Sami and Mira. Or even in their driveway in Scottsdale, unloading their luggage. Yasmin tried to stop a cab outside the building, but none that passed her were vacant. As she walked up the sidewalk, she kept turning and looking for one. When Yasmin was ten or eleven, every Thursday her father used to take all of them on a late-afternoon drive in the suburbs of Amman. At the end of the drive, he used to bring them to Jabal al-Hussein for an ice-cream treat or a falafel sandwich. She smiled at the memory of looking forward to Thursdays and wondered if eating at McDonald's every Friday after school meant the same to Sami and Mira. Oh, how she ached for them!

No sign of a vacant cab yet. She stopped for a few moments, looking down the street, and then turned around and continued on her way. A man walking on the sidewalk in her direction took faster steps when he noticed her. Yasmin tried to get out of his way, but he still bumped into her.

"Nice breasts," he whispered.

"Animal," she muttered, feeling her face reddening. She looked down at her chest and fastened one more button. A few seconds later, she finally stopped a cab. The driver was a bearded older man and had the radio turned to some news station. He remained silent all the way, and Yasmin was grateful for that. She was still shaky from that sidewalk idiot and was not in the mood for cab talk. When she arrived at the house, her father was reading in the family room. He lifted his head and greeted her back. He told her that her mother was in the backyard with Nihad and Samira and that Majid and Fatin were out with their children. Yasmin nodded and went to the study. She closed the door behind her, called Carole, and talked about her afternoon with a voice full of optimism.

Carole still kept her reluctance. "I hope you get what you want from these meetings, but I doubt these guys are related to the embassy."

"Why do you say that? Did you get a chance to talk to your sister's friend?"

"No. My sister said her friend is in very bad shape right now, but I'll keep trying."

"Oh, I see." Yasmin was relieved that Carole's suspicions were no more than a hunch. "Look, Carole, the embassy's operator gave me the number of the center. The secretary of the center gave me the number of the lawyer who introduced me to the owner of the translation company. So what do you think?"

"Something doesn't feel right to me. How much are they charging you for their services?"

"I don't know yet. Look, of course it doesn't sound or feel right. You don't expect the embassy to deal with such cases in the open."

"I don't know what to say, Yasmin. I just don't want anyone to take advantage of you. It will devastate you. Call me tomorrow, and let me know how it goes."

"I will." Yasmin hung up. She would not waste a second thinking about it. She had to stay focused on getting her children back and returning with them to their home.

CHAPTER TWENTY-TWO

The next day, Yasmin's father did not mention the lawyers, and though it pained Yasmin that he could forget something of such importance, she still did not remind him. She knew nothing would come out of it and looked forward to seeing Faris and Jalal that afternoon. While she got all the documents and photos ready for Jalal, she imagined one scenario after the other involving her departure with her children. They all had a smooth and successful ending even though she was anticipating much anxiety and stress at the beginning. But that was expected. It wasn't like she was going on a vacation under normal circumstances. Yasmin added a copy of her passport, and Sami and Mira's too, to the other documents, put them in a small manila envelope, and hid it in her closet for now.

⊷⊹ ⊹⊶

Yasmin opened the door for her mother when she returned from the hair salon around one thirty that afternoon.

Her mother said a quick hi and walked through the hallway.

Yasmin followed her to her room and stood by the door.

"I'm not having lunch today, either. I'm going downtown with Carole. She wants to buy some damask for the tables, and I promised to help her pick a color."

Her mother took off her shoes.

At that, Yasmin went to her room, put the manila in her purse, and left the house.

Minutes after Yasmin arrived at her meeting, Jalal called the American consul again. The phone rang for a long time before he hung up. He then looked through the envelope Yasmin handed him.

"Be prepared any day now to drive with us to Mahir's hometown, Irbid. We cannot get the children without you. Otherwise, it will be considered kidnapping." He wagged his finger. "No suitcases. Pack a small handbag, and make sure you keep the passports in it. And money of course."

"How much money?"

"Enough to buy tickets from a neighboring country if we end up taking a ground route."

"I'll call the airlines tomorrow and see if I can cash out our unused return tickets."

"I don't think that's possible. It won't be enough anyway. Keep in mind that it's more expensive when you buy tickets the same day," he said. "Don't worry about that now. We will let you know ahead of time."

Yasmin nodded.

"Hours after I get ahold of the consul, you and the children will be in a jeep, heading to the border." Jalal looked at Faris and continued, "Either plan A, the Syrian border, or plan B, the Israeli border." He then winked at Yasmin. "You might get lucky and leave from here on a special flight." He waved his hand in the air, pretending it was a plane.

"It's up to the consul, though," Faris said.

"How are you going to contact me when you know the exact plan?"

"I will call you, Sister Yasmin," Faris said. "Your father already knows who I am. I can always say it's related to the case."

"That's fine."

Yasmin sensed some stage effects in the way they spoke this time. They sounded like they were performing rather than having a normal discussion, and that reminded her of Carole's suspicions. Yasmin did not want to even contemplate the thought of Carole being right. She leaned forward and looked at Jalal.

"You never mentioned your fees so far. I was hoping you would give me an estimate so I could decide if I can go through with this or not."

Faris looked alarmed. He stood up and left the room.

"It's too soon to determine that now. As Faris said earlier, it all depends on my conversation with the consul. I will try him again tomorrow morning. He is a very busy man, as you know."

Jalal lowered his voice. "Look, you don't have to worry about my share in the fees right now. In the future, when you settle down and would like to show appreciation, you could send me a small gift." He smiled. "But I think you should keep *him* in mind." He pointed to the opened door. "As you have noticed, he is devoting most of his time to your case and is very eager to help. He has a big family to take care of, and...you know."

"I understand. How much money should I set aside for him?"

"Eight hundred dinars," he said looking out the window.

The amount shocked Yasmin, but she did not comment. It was about $1,100.

When the meeting was over, Yasmin walked out of the office with many doubts and a confirmed appointment for the next day. By the time she stepped out of the building, it was early evening, that part of town was swarming with pedestrians, and the air smelled of frying oil. Just about every store on the street played some Arabic music. All of it playing at once sounded like a frantic medley of voices and tunes. The chaos of the sidewalks was overwhelming. People of all ages and genders, dressed in all sorts of modern and Muslim clothing, walked back and forth, talking, laughing, or eating watermelon seeds. Seed shells were all over the sidewalk in addition to candy wrappers, napkins, cigarette butts, and plastic bags.

Long lines formed by ice-cream parlors, and even longer ones at the fronts of falafel shops. Workers in grungy white coats stood behind large fryers, using a flattened spoon and a copper gadget to mold the falafel mix into cylinders before throwing it in the boiling oil. Yasmin paced amid that chaos, pretending not to notice how some men stared at her and made her feel like a cut of meat. She finally stopped a cab.

When she arrived at the house, she went straight to the family room. Her mother was on the phone with Hala. When she finished talking to her, she handed the receiver to Yasmin.

"They're back from the honeymoon. They're coming tomorrow to have lunch. Kamal's parents too."

Yasmin said hi to Hala.

"I can't believe Mahir did this to you," Hala said and began to cry.

Yasmin knew from conversing further with Hala that her mother had informed her of Yasmin's news with every bit of depressing detail her memory could recollect.

"Calm down, Hala. You are overreacting. It's not as bad as Mama made it sound."

"Really?"

"I wouldn't lie to you. So, how was the honeymoon?"

Hala told Yasmin that she and Kamal had a great time and that they were staying with her in-laws for a couple of days. They were packing and shipping more of their things to Cairo, where Kamal was starting his new job. Yasmin and Hala ended their chat by agreeing on having a more detailed talk the next day.

As soon as Yasmin hung up, her mother turned to her and asked, "How is Carole? Is she done redecorating?"

"Decorating?"

"Haven't you been helping her pick tablecloths?"

"Ah, that. She decided to do it tomorrow," Yasmin stammered. "I helped her add up some receipts today. She has an accounting problem of some sort."

"I see," she said and then turned on the television.

"Mama, have you heard anything about Mahir and the children from Nihad or anyone in the family?"

"Nothing. Your father is looking for someone to mediate. Let's see what happens."

"Did he call the lawyers?"

Her mother gasped and placed her palm on her mouth. "It's my fault. He asked me to remind him. Forgive me, Yasmin. I will remind him tomorrow, first thing in the morning."

"It's OK, Mama. I was just wondering."

When Yasmin called Carole that evening, she spoke with a different tone. She was less optimistic. Carole urged her again to be careful and let her know what happens at the next meeting.

"I will call you tomorrow," Yasmin said. "I know nothing is for sure so far, but at least it's something."

Though Yasmin was glad to see Hala, she had a hard time socializing with her in-laws. Forcing herself to smile, she felt it a difficult task to show interest in their conversations. She did not want Hala to notice how restless she was. Yasmin would have loved nothing more than to have Hala by her side at such a difficult time, but that would be unfair. Hala had enough on her plate, and bothering her now just did not seem right. For a while, Yasmin managed to act as if she had no worry in the world in front of Hala and the guests. Then when she started thinking about her next meeting with Jalal and Faris and began to daydream, she excused herself and went to the kitchen.

Hala followed. "I still can't believe Mahir is capable of such cruelty," she said, her eyes casting sadness all over Yasmin.

Yasmin added some lemon juice and a drizzle of olive oil to the salad and mixed it. "Look, you've been through enough in the past years. I don't want my problems to affect your new life in any way. Smile, go back to the living room, and sit with Kamal and your in-laws."

"I can't stop thinking of you and the children."

Yasmin moved away from Hala. She took out some pickled cucumbers out of a jar and placed them on a plate. "Getting angry is not going to change a thing."

"I wish I could stay for another week, but Kamal—"

"Don't be silly. I'm fine. The children are fine too. I'm going to see them soon."

"Really? Is Mahir going to let you? Mama said—"

"Of course he will," Yasmin lied. She turned her back to Hala and leaned over the opened oven. "Never mind what Mama says." She poked the leg of lamb in a few places. When she looked up again, she noticed that her lies did not seem to erase the worry from Hala's eyes.

Yasmin smiled. "Come help me set the table."

As soon as Hala and the guests left, Yasmin ran to her room and started getting ready for her meeting. Saying good-bye to Hala had not been easy. They both became emotional when they hugged and kissed each other. Yasmin knew that Hala did not believe a word she said and did not buy the fake smile she put on her face, but she thought she did the right thing by not giving Hala the chance to get involved. Yasmin washed her face and fixed her hair and then put on a loose white shirt that she found among other tops in Hala's closet.

Before leaving the house, Yasmin told her mother again that she was going to see Carole.

When Yasmin arrived at her meeting, she found Faris waiting in the lobby.

"What a coincidence, Sister Yasmin. I just walked in." He pulled up the sleeve of his forest-green suit and looked at his watch. "Jalal spoke to the consul after you left yesterday. He briefed him on the situation, and the consul said he would get back to him." He stepped aside and let her enter the elevator.

"Really? That's great. I hope he contacts Jalal soon."

Jalal was already behind his desk when Yasmin and Faris walked into his office.

"Look, Mrs. Yasmin." He sounded nervous. "I know you can't get us your husband's Social Security number, but I was hoping you might fill us in on his financial situation. It's very important to study a case from all sides."

Yasmin did not like Jalal's tone and did not see how Mahir's finances related to her escape. She waved away a fly as if slapping someone.

"There isn't much to say, really. All I can tell you is that he is an engineer." She did not admit that she and Mahir had a mortgage and were going to own a house in twenty-two years, and she did not think it was necessary to discuss Mahir's partnership or the company shares he owned.

Faris tried to end the awkwardness of the several silent moments that followed. He took out his pack of cigarettes and extended it opened to Yasmin.

"Sister Yasmin." He expressed his invitation in English. "Take your rest," he said, pronouncing the last word as *wrist*.

Yasmin knew he meant to say *feel comfortable*. He must have realized that she was a smoker when he stood close to her inside the undersized elevator.

"No, thank you," she said and took out her own cigarettes before settling her purse on the side table next to her seat.

After offering her a light, Faris looked closely at her purse. He seemed impressed with the brand name carved on it because, right after that, he turned to Jalal, smiled, and nodded.

"Sister Yasmin, now when you go back, inshallah, you might need our help over here in some judicial matters. I suggest that before you leave, you give me full power of attorney so I can process things without any delays."

Yasmin squinted. "Process what?"

"Sister Yasmin, in case you decide to divorce your husband after you arrive in Arizona, I could take care of it here in no time."

"I see. Let me think about that and get back to you."

Jalal looked at his watch, and then he stood up. "I just remembered a very important appointment." He gave Faris a look.

"Yeah, yeah, we should get going."

Yasmin immediately excused herself and walked to the door.

"Sorry about this, Sister Yasmin," Faris said. "Tomorrow, inshallah, at the same time, we should discuss going to Irbid to get the children, and also your departure plan."

The following morning Yasmin's father called one of her lawyers and spoke to him for over twenty minutes, but when Yasmin asked him for details, he did not have much to say.

"They insisted that the children were with Mahir, but the judge ignored their remark. He proceeded with the case as if he were certain that Mahir's sole reason for filing the lawsuit was to prevent the children from leaving the country. Apparently it's a case that gets processed repeatedly by the court, so they go about it in a routine manner without paying any attention to the details." He shook his head. "Leave Mahir to me, Yasmin. As I promised you before, I will make sure your problem is resolved outside the court."

"As you wish, Baba," Yasmin said.

During lunch, her father mentioned his phone conversation again and repeated what he had told her earlier to Majid, Fatin, and her mother. Little comments went around the table, but as Yasmin had noticed since the beginning of her ordeal, nothing she heard from her family involved a real solution or even gave her any kind of assurance or comfort.

After lunch, Yasmin repeated the rituals of the past few days, got dressed, lied to her mother, and left the house. She thought about how excited she was on her way to see Faris and Jalal the first time and how distraught she felt after returning the day before. She knew deep down inside that getting her life back with the help of Faris and Jalal, if ever, was not going to happen anytime soon. Whenever it did, it was going to have a very high price tag. One she probably could not afford. The meetings gave her hope, although false. Hanging on to a straw while drowning in the middle of an ocean felt much better than not hanging on to anything at all.

When Yasmin entered the office, Faris was sitting behind the secretary's desk, smoking, and drinking from a can of Pepsi.

"Jalal is on the phone, Sister Yasmin." He stood up and motioned to her to take the seat near the desk. He then pointed to the Pepsi can. "Can I get you a cold Bibsi?"

"No, thanks." She sat down. "Jalal is on the phone with the American consul, I hope."

Faris adjusted in his seat and cleared his throat. He took a long drag of his cigarette and released the smoke toward the whiny ceiling fan. "You know, Sister Yasmin, I once represented a nice lady like you in another case. I have to say I still admire her courage and her generosity. She actually helped a friend of mine get his green card through legal matrimony."

Yasmin nodded. She was sure her face expressed enough disinterest to make Faris end his story at that, but he carried on.

"They never lived as husband and wife, of course," he said. "You know, Sister Yasmin, I've always dreamed about waking one day in Amreekia."

Yasmin had that much figured out by then. She frowned and bit her lip. Sometimes at the beginning of the meetings, she felt as if she were acting a part in a movie. And she did not mind that as long as she, the heroine, was going to end up triumphant. But now, she decided that the movie was very badly directed, the actors not at all talented, and the ending just another devastating disappointment.

"You know what?" She stood up. "I'm leaving."

Faris jumped off his seat. "Sister Yasmin, we are doing our best to hasten the procedures."

She saw a desperate look in his eyes. "I'm sure you are. Why don't you call me after Jalal really gets hold of the consul and we'll go from there?"

CHAPTER TWENTY-THREE

While resting her elbows on the windowsill, Yasmin stared at the drab and depressing sky through the spirals of the black wrought iron. People in Jordan were fools to have thought of the sky as blue all these years. Maybe they had never lived under a different sky. She wiped a tear from her face with the back of her hand.

The smell of food saturated the afternoon air, and the sound of pots clanking came from a kitchen somewhere nearby. In the distance, she could hear the faint voice of a news anchor and the crying of a baby. She lit a cigarette. Ever since Mahir had driven away that evening with Sami and Mira, life had become like a massive ball made out of newspaper pages. Trouble never ceased to unfold as Yasmin peeled the pages off that ball, yearning for the prize in the center: her children.

The past two weeks seemed unreal. There was no justification in the world for what she was going through. Even if she had done something wrong in the first place, this kind of punishment would still count as inhumane. Mahir had never been perfect; he had always had a temper, but he had never been so cruel. She had seen him change a little when they had visited Jordan in the past, especially around his father and his old friends. He would talk to her in a formal tone and criticize her in front of their families. He would not spend much time with her and would stay with the men, as if spending time with her would make him less of a man. But what he was doing now was something beyond her comprehension. And the way everyone around her was gliding through the events as if it were the norm was slowly wiping off whatever she had left of her sanity.

Yasmin detested the thought of Mahir having so much control. It was no secret how much he loved the fact that he had a powerful last name, but now he was getting more than that. He was living the role, reaping the rewards. She had seen how the airport officer, old lawyer Mahmoud Saleem, Jalal, and Faris Bader all reacted to Mahir's last name. It saddened her to be in her own country, among her family and her friends, yet feeling lonelier and more estranged and worthless with every passing day.

Yasmin squashed her cigarette and moved the ashtray to the closed side of the window. She felt exhausted, as if she had been swimming against a current upstream or walking for centuries down the wrong maze. None of this would have happened if she had stayed in Scottsdale, but the moment she had set foot on the plane, she had handed Mahir her neck. Dina was right: Yasmin had been away from her country too long. She forgot what it was like to be a Jordanian woman, supported by her parents or otherwise. Now more than ever, she felt the privileges of being born or even just living in a free country. Yasmin held her head and closed her eyes.

"Yasmin."

Fatin's voice startled her. She turned around.

"Please come and have lunch."

"I'm not hungry." She sat on the side of the bed. Sami's bear lay on her pillow next to Mira's folded blanket.

"You hardly ate anything in the past few days. I know how you feel—"

"No, you don't, Fatin. And I hope you never will."

"Your mother said your father hasn't been sleeping because he's worried about you. Can't you at least pretend you're eating in front of him? He's very concerned."

Yasmin did not comment. All the arguments she had heard since her arrival were about how her problem was affecting everyone else.

"You know we all want to help—"

"How, Fatin? Can any of you give me back my life? Can you send me with my children back to our house?"

Fatin looked down. "You can always file for custody."

"I know I can, Fatin, but that's not going to be easy. I haven't worked in years, and I know what the wages are here. Whatever I do, I'll never make enough to eat. Even if I did, do you think Baba will let me live outside this house with the children? Do you think Abu Mahir will allow it or let Mahir support me?"

Fatin put her arm around her. "Everything will be all right."

Yasmin shook her head.

"You'll see. He can't go on like this forever. He knows the children belong with their mother. He is just being mean because he can. He'll come around and realize what he did was wrong."

Yasmin lifted her head to the sound of footsteps approaching. Her mother stopped by the door and looked at her with sorrowful eyes, her arms dangling on her sides. "We're all going crazy over this too, but what can we do?"

Yasmin gave no reply.

Her mother looked at Fatin. "We have to send somebody to talk to Mahir."

Again, the lame solution to Yasmin's problem was to find someone to settle the matter, and she was getting nauseous from hearing it over and over.

"Please come and have a bite for your father's sake, Yasmin. He has enough of his own things to worry about; he's too old and too sick to bear this," her mother said.

Yasmin nodded and walked to the kitchen, followed by her mother and Fatin. Her mother sat across from her, and Fatin sat next to Majid and their sons, Omar and Zaid. Yasmin's father looked up, and when their eyes met, he smiled. He cleared his throat. "Would you grant your old and sick father a wish?"

She looked at him, trying hard not to let her tears find their way out, and nodded.

"Promise me you will sit with us for every meal."

"I will, Baba." She looked down.

"I'm sorry if I seem to stand helpless in the middle of all this. I think about you and the children day and night. We've never had a situation like this before in the family. Never."

Yasmin sensed the genuine sadness in his voice. She knew her father was not helpless by any means, but he was right about never encountering a situation like hers before in the family. Hala had told Yasmin how their parents reacted to the fact of Hala becoming a widow with confusion, bafflement, and the same inability to make a decision. Yasmin was beginning to believe that her parents probably awoke every morning of the past two weeks hoping for a miracle that would turn everything around.

"Let's eat now. We'll talk about it later," her father said.

She placed some stuffed grape leaves on her plate and picked up her fork.

Her mother slapped herself on the cheek. "Only three?"

"I'm not hungry," Yasmin whispered.

Her mother and her father exchanged worried looks. As soon as they finished eating, they walked out of the kitchen. Majid, Omar, and Zaid followed right after. When Yasmin finished the last small bite of her grape leaves, she stood up.

Fatin moved to the stove and started making coffee. "Will you have coffee with us?"

Yasmin nodded and left the kitchen. When she passed the family room on her way to the bathroom, she overheard her parents talking and caught only two words: *depression* and *doctor*. When she returned to have her coffee on the veranda, her mother was in the family room watching *Oprah*. Fatin and Majid stopped talking to her father the moment she entered. Yasmin took her cup from the tray and sat down.

Yasmin's father took his glasses off before he spoke. "I wish your uncle, God rest his soul, were still alive. I miss having him stand by me. I miss his advice and his support."

After two weeks of lawyers, a court hearing, and meetings with Faris and Jalal, Yasmin could no longer listen to more comments, wishes, and pieces of wisdom that did not and would not change a thing. Never before in her life had she felt so let down. Her father continued to sip his coffee and stare out the window. After several moments of silence passed, she stood up.

"Smoke it here," her father said. "I don't like the idea of you smoking, but if that's the only way to snatch you out of your solitude, then I have to live with it."

Yasmin felt her face redden and didn't know what to say. Her mother always said that if her father evr found out about her smoking he would get a heart attak.

Yasmin sat down. "I wasn't going to smoke." She looked down for a few moments and then back at her father. "Baba, why can't I sue Mahir and get back Sami and Mira?"

He took a deep breath. "I want nothing more than to see you reunited with the children, but I would rather have the situation resolved within both families." His eyes shone with tears that made them look glazed. His voice weakened, and the words came out with effort. "Mahir is angry, and all his actions are reflecting that. If we go to court, that will only make him angrier. It will cause more grudges between you two, and between the two families. Give me some time to think it over, and I promise you I will find a way to deal with the situation in a more peaceful manner."

Yasmin nodded though not a bit satisfied. She knew her father meant every word he said, but with his increasing forgetfulness, she doubted he would keep his promise. That saddened her and made her feel even more helpless.

A few hours later, as Yasmin curled on her bed, staring at the closet door, Majid came to her room. He took out some folded bills from his pocket and placed them on the dresser. Yasmin knew he was doing it out of duty, as he did with Hala when she returned to live with them as a widow. That was probably what he was discussing with her father when she entered the veranda that afternoon. Yasmin appreciated that Majid was not the kind of brother that ever abused that duty by making it seem like charity or expecting some kind of obedience in return.

She lifted her head.

Before she spoke, Majid smiled, "Don't say a word."

"Thank you, Majid."

"I'm taking Omar and Zaid to soccer practice. Can I get you anything on the way back?"

"No, thanks."

"Cigarettes?"

"I still have some."

Majid nodded and left the room.

A few minutes later, Yasmin heard the doorbell ring three times, followed by a commotion of voices in the house. She knew her aunts Nihad and Samira had come for a visit. "The team has arrived," she muttered and closed her eyes. She was not in the mood for more meaningless statements and useless opinions.

Her mother called from the hallway. "Yasmin, come to the family room. Fatin and your aunts are here."

"In a second, Mama."

As she expected, when she entered the room, they were talking about her. She said hello and sat next to Fatin.

Nihad looked at Yasmin with eyes full of sympathy.

Yasmin had already gathered enough sympathy to last her a lifetime. What she really needed seemed beyond anyone.

"There must be someone you know in their family who can talk some sense into him," Nihad told her mother.

Yasmin closed her eyes. Not that lame solution again. She wanted to scream.

Nihad then turned to Yasmin. "Why don't you sue for custody?"

Yasmin's mother nudged Nihad with her elbow. "We don't want to escalate matters any further. We are going to try to solve it peacefully with Mahir first. If we just go straight to court, people will butcher us with their tongues."

"Who cares about what stupid people think? Am I ever going to come first to you, Mama? I want my children back," Yasmin snapped.

"Well, I tried my best not to make you lose them in the first place, but you never listened. Despite my college degree in English and home economics, you still think of me as an old-fashioned retard," her mother said.

"My God, Mama. I can't believe we're having this conversation again. You know what? I don't care what anybody thinks: I'm suing for custody."

Samira tsked her tongue a few times. "Calm down. What good does it do now bringing all this up?"

Yasmin felt her chest about to tear open. She gritted her teeth and stared down at the floor.

"Give her a break, for God's sake. That's not fair." Nihad slapped her own thigh. "She will get a heart attack or lose her mind if she goes on like this."

Yasmin's mother frowned.

"She is turning yellow; her hands are shaking. Give her something to calm her down," Samira said.

"We called the family doctor today. He suggested Valium." Yasmin's mother did not sound too thrilled with the idea.

"So what are you waiting for?" Nihad extended her hands.

Yasmin's mother left the room. When she came back, she gave Yasmin a small pill. Yasmin flipped the ten-milligram pill between her fingers before she swallowed it.

As if that pill were the solution to Yasmin's problem, a few minutes later she felt completely ignored by her mother and her aunts. They talked about fashion, recipes, the economy, and the war. They even discussed the last episode of *The Bold and the Beautiful*, as if they had no other worry in the world. In the meantime, Yasmin sat silent, savoring the delusional serenity that the little pill provided.

When the voices in the family room faded into the back of Yasmin's head, she slipped out and went to the study, locked the door behind her, and called Carole.

"How are the meetings going?"

"They're not. You were right about them," Yasmin said.

"What are you going to do now?"

"I decided to sue for custody."

"I think you should. It's about time you did something. Your parents agreed?"

"My father said to give him some time, but at least he did not reject the idea completely."

"Good," Carole said.

"It would've been great if the stupid meetings led to something. I was hoping to be back in Scottsdale with Sami and Mira by now. By the way, did you hear anything from your sister's friend who worked at the embassy?"

"My sister's friend passed away."

"I'm sorry," Yasmin said and meant it.

CHAPTER TWENTY-FOUR

The muggy morning of August did not seem to agitate Yasmin as this kind of weather usually did, even though she woke up drenched in a sticky kind of sweat. She had slept with the window open all night, hoping the early-morning breeze would seep through, but by now she was accustomed to having her hopes crush concerning everything. The weather was her last worry this morning. She had prayed most of the night that this new hope of suing for custody was not going to vanish during the day for one stupid reason or another. If she won a custody case, she would never have to wake up to the horror of what Mahir had done. Today, hot or otherwise, she was not going to let anything get to her and spoil her mood.

She lay on her back and closed her eyes. In her mind's eye, she began to picture the moment she would see Sami and Mira again and imagined herself holding them in her arms, kissing them, running her fingers through their hair. Telling them it was all over and that no one would ever take them away from her. She saw the three of them on the plane and then in their house in Scottsdale, going about their lives as if nothing had ever happened.

Yasmin opened her eyes and smiled at the ceiling. She was wondering how Mahir and his father were going to react to her lawsuit right when her mother entered her room panting. She held the phone in one hand, choked the speaker with the other, and whispered, "It's Mahir." The look on her face was of someone who had just encountered a miracle or had a sighting of a saint or even a prophet.

Yasmin sat up in her bed and grabbed the phone from her mother. "Hello."

"I need to talk to you about the children," Mahir said. "Can we meet somewhere?"

"How are they? Let me talk to them."

"They're out with my mother. Maybe next time."

"We can meet at La Bonita, Carole's restaurant, if you like."

"That's fine. I'll be there at five."

Yasmin's mother lifted her head to the ceiling with her palms facing up. "*Al-Hamdu-Lillah* (thank God)," she said and walked out of the room.

Yasmin telephoned Carole immediately, told her about Mahir's call, and asked her if she could meet her at the restaurant ten minutes before five.

"Don't worry. I'll be there," Carole said. "I'm going to call the restaurant now and arrange with the manager."

Carole called ten minutes later and told Yasmin that she had instructed the manager to reserve a table for Yasmin and assign two waiters to attend her. One in charge of taking orders and the other just to stand nearby and be alert at all times.

Half an hour before leaving to meet with Mahir, Yasmin's aunts held an emergency gathering and promised to be there when she returned. Nihad insisted that Yasmin should wear some makeup and borrow from Fatin a top that had a cheerful color.

"She looks as if she's in mourning in her black top and with her clean face. Don't you think I'm right?" She looked around the room, seeking approval.

"He's not going to look at her clothes. She should do something about her face, though. Maybe put a smile on it instead of having a cigarette sticking out of her mouth all the time," Yasmin's mother said. "Be nice to him. Try to reconcile."

"Really, Mama?" Yasmin laughed. "I'd do it in heartbeat for the children's sake if it were that simple."

Her aunts continued with their suggestions.

"She should let her hair down."

"I think she can use some makeup."

"She's fine. She just needs a different outfit."

Yasmin's face shifted between her mother and her aunts, as if following a tennis ball. She could still hear them discussing their last-minute makeover plan as she and Fatin walked out the door.

Twenty minutes before five, when the whole city seemed to come to life, Yasmin sat in Fatin's red Renault, rolled the window down, and lit a cigarette. The faint sound of a melody repeating in the distance was becoming louder by the second. A young boy stood behind a gate a few houses down, and when an older model of a white Toyota truck with a big speaker mounted on its roof became visible, the boy stepped out and waved to the driver. Fatin eased down the hill, passing by the truck that inched its way up, stacked with propane tanks.

At the red light, hawkers carrying Styrofoam boxes full of figs ran to the car. "Figs. Two dinars," a teen shouted in Yasmin's face, holding up the box.

Fatin leaned out from Yasmin's side. "Too much."

Yasmin took the money out of her purse and swapped it for a box.

"You could've bargained."

"I know, but the price is good. Do you know how much these cost in Arizona?"

"How much?"

"I don't remember." Yasmin laughed. "But I know it's much more than what I paid." She set the box on the backseat. "He's a kid, for God's sake. Who cares how much?"

"What do you think Mahir is up to?" Fatin honked at the car in front of her and shouted, "Move."

"Who knows what the donkey is up to now?"

Fatin tapped at the steering wheel, laughing.

Yasmin looked out, amazed at Fatin's ability to maneuver through University Street in her little car. She zigzagged her way between cars, yellow cabs, and buses without making sudden stops, even when jaywalkers jumped in her way. From the roundabout named after the Department of Interior Affairs, Fatin took a right, passed through a tunnel, drove a little farther, turned at the third roundabout, took the second right, and parked. When they entered the restaurant, Fatin went inside to look for Carole, and Yasmin stayed on the terrace.

A waiter dressed in a black suit, black tie, and white shirt came rushing out of the bar.

"Good afternoon, madam," he greeted and then ushered her to a table that had a full view of the entrance.

"Good afternoon." Yasmin sat down.

The waiter waited for a moment and asked, "What can I get you?"

"Turkish coffee, no sugar, please."

He bowed with a smile and walked away. Another waiter dressed the same came out of the bar, nodded to Yasmin, and stood in the corner behind a table full of wineglasses and started folding napkins.

To Yasmin's left, white poplars rustled in the soft breeze, and behind her on the limestone wall hung some potted geraniums.

Yasmin looked at her watch and then looked around. Other than the waiter who was folding napkins, there was no one on the terrace, but she could see a few couples in the bar through the glass doors. As she had done since Mahir had called her, she kept wondering what he was going to say. She had continued to fantasize about him bringing Sami and Mira with him, and in that same scenario, she made Mahir apologize and ask her to forgive him.

The waiter set her coffee on the table, stood back, and asked, "Anything else, madam?"

"Not now. Thank you."

He bowed and stepped to the corner, joining the other waiter. He picked up a wineglass and started wiping it with a napkin.

While Yasmin sipped her coffee, she kept glancing at her watch. When about twenty minutes had passed, she went inside to Carole's office. She hugged Carole, and then they both kissed on the cheeks.

"Call Mama and see if Mahir called," Yasmin told Fatin. "It shouldn't take him more than forty-five minutes to get here from Irbid if he left on time."

"Wait a few more minutes," Carole said.

Fatin took her cell phone out of her purse, called the house, and spoke to Yasmin's mother. After she hung up, she said, "He didn't call."

"I wonder what he's up to," Yasmin looked at Carole. "He said it concerned the children."

"Why don't you call him?"

"I should. I hope he answers. Not one of his parents."

"You're not afraid of them, are you?"

"It's not that. I just don't think they'll let me talk to him if they answer." Yasmin took her address book out of her purse.

"That's true," Fatin said. "Try. See what happens."

"We'll wait for you outside." Carole and Fatin closed the door behind them.

Yasmin dialed the number. Carole's office was small but tidy and clean. It had a big french door that overlooked parts of the terrace. Yasmin looked out at a couple that just walked in and sat at one of the tables. They held the menus and began talking to one of the waiters. The phone rang three times before Mahir answered.

"What's going on?"

"I got tied up," he said.

"Excuse me? Couldn't you call and say you're not coming?"

"Spare me the attitude, please."

"Attitude? Why did you do this to me and to our children, Mahir?"

He said nothing.

"You didn't have the guts to face me, did you? Look, it's not too late. We can still work things out."

She could hear him breathing. She stared ahead at a photo of two ponies standing in a green pasture. "Let me talk to Sami and Mira."

"They're out with my mother."

Yasmin looked away from the photo. "Of course they're out. What did you want to talk about?"

"I'm going on a trip to Germany with my mother. We're going to visit my aunt, and I wanted to ask you for the children's American passports. I want to take them with me."

Yasmin snatched a cigarette out of her purse and lit it. She moved a crystal ashtray sitting on the side of Carole's desk closer to her.

"Look, you know I could go issue new passports at the embassy now," he said.

"So? Go do it. Why are you even bothering to call?"

"I need your Jordanian passport too. I need to get the children off and issue separate passports for them."

Yasmin could not stop her trembling. "You must be kidding. I'll never give you my passport."

"That's fine. My father's cousin works at the passport agency. He can take care of it."

"Oh, I'm sure he could…I want to see the children. You have no right keeping them away from me like that. What's your point, or should I ask, what's your father's point?"

"My father has nothing to do with this."

"Never mind. How long are you planning to hold the children hostage? School starts in two weeks."

"They're not going back."

As if his intentions had not been clear from the beginning, Yasmin jumped out of the chair. "What do you mean not going back?"

"I quit my job at the firm. I'm not going back to Arizona: that's what I mean."

"Are you out of your mind? The house, the bills…"

He did not utter a word.

Yasmin sat down and put out her cigarette. "You can't just leave like that, damn it. Our stuff—"

"That's your problem. I've had nothing to do with that house since you kicked me out."

"That's a lie, and you know it. Enough drama, Mahir. Save it for someone who believes your crap."

He sighed.

"I'm going back," she shouted, looking out the window. The couple were now drinking wine and laughing.

"Do whatever you want. The children are staying here."

"If I go to court, I will get custody, you know, and then you can really make use of your visitations order. You can arrange to see Sami and Mira twice a month at a police station."

"Do it, and I'll kill you."

Yasmin could hear his teeth gritting as he said that. She pictured his face turning red, sweat covering his wrinkled forehead. "What? Are you threatening me? Go ahead and do it, Mahir. You'll have a lifetime in prison, figuring out how to explain to our children why they shouldn't hate you."

"Whatever," he said. "Can you please send the passports?"

"Not a chance."

"Keep the passports, and you'll never even get a glimpse of them."

"Yes, I will, Mahir. It's called a custody case." She hung up, walked out to Carole and Fatin, and gave them the details of her conversation with Mahir. "I can't believe this is happening." She slammed the table.

"Don't aggravate him, Yasmin," Fatin said. "You've seen what he's capable of so far. All you can achieve from not giving him the passports is delaying his trip a little."

"Fine, then that's what I will do, Fatin. I'm going to call a lawyer first thing tomorrow."

CHAPTER TWENTY-FIVE

At eight in the morning, Yasmin called the lawyer Mahmoud Saleem. She had thought about hiring him all night. Aside from knowing all the ins and outs of the law due to his long practice, he seemed to know how to manipulate it to someone's favor. During the consultation when he discussed Mahir's court order to prevent the children from leaving the country, he had mentioned how a bribe could make her departure from the airport or other borders hassle-free.

"Good morning," she greeted the secretary in a cheerful voice. "My name is Yasmin Nabeel. I've already been to your office once, and I was wondering if I could make an appointment for today. I decided to sue for custody."

"Not for today," the secretary said. "I can put you down for the first week of next month, September."

"No, no. That's too far. Can you get me in anytime sooner?"

"No, I'm sorry. I can't. The lawyer is not taking any new cases this month. Lawyer's holiday, you know. He's only finishing processing old cases for now."

Yasmin was shocked and couldn't utter a word for a few moments. Not only had she never heard of such a holiday before in her life, but did it have to be at this time? "OK, I understand. Thank you," she finally said.

Yasmin had the urge to pick up the phone and throw it out the window. She left the study and hurried to the backyard sobbing. She cursed the unfairness of all she had been through and felt colossal anger and resentment for wasting so much time chasing mirages and waiting for her father's consent. Why did her parents care so much about what other people thought of them? It was not like Yasmin was committing a crime by merely demanding her given rights. Yasmin took a few deep breaths and thought hard about her next step. Giving up was not an option and would never be. What would happen if she ignored her parents and the whole country for that matter, took matters into her own hands, and gave herself the justice they all seemed intent on denying her? An old proverb said, "Wed your son to your daughter, and the scandal lasts three days." But whatever Yasmin had in mind was nowhere near that. She had to do whatever it took to get Sami and Mira back. With that determination, she stood up and returned to the study.

Yasmin picked up the phone and called Fatin. "Fatin, I need to ask you a favor."

"What's wrong? Have you been crying?"

She cleared her throat. "Can you come now?"

"Yasmin, you're scaring me. Please tell me what's wrong."

"I called a lawyer about suing for custody. Lawyers don't take any new cases until next month."

Fatin was silent for a moment. "What do you have in mind, Yasmin? I'll do anything to help."

"I want you to drive me to Irbid."

"To get the children?"

"I have to try, Fatin. I've wasted too much time already."

"Oh, God."

"Will you take me, Fatin? Please."

"Look, Majid and your parents will not approve of this. They're not even in favor of you suing for custody because they think it will do nothing but aggravate Mahir and cause him to take more crazy actions." Fatin sighed. "Majid is not coming home for lunch today. He's spending the whole day at the farm. Tell your mother that I invited you to have lunch with a friend of mine, and wait for me outside, around one o'clock."

"Thank you, Fatin."

Four hours later, Yasmin stood on the balcony under the searing one o'clock sun, going over the many scenarios she had created in her head since that morning. She felt torn between her fear of Mahir and his father and her yearning for Sami and Mira. She could not help but expect the worst from her attempt, but no matter how frightened she was, she was not going to back down.

At the sound of a harmonica replaying the same tune, Yasmin leaned over the edge of the balcony. The walking musician who sold cotton candy was wiping his forehead with his sleeve. He carried a stick over his shoulder that had a stack of plastic bags full of pink lumps hooked at the end. Children suddenly appeared out of nowhere and swarmed like ants in the direction of his sweets. Mira loved cotton candy. She would have heard the faint sounds of the harmonica two blocks away and started jumping up and down before getting that sugar rush in her mouth. Yasmin felt a flutter inside her chest at the thought.

Fatin arrived at the promised time.

After Yasmin buckled her seat belt, she looked at Fatin. They both took deep breaths and laughed.

Fatin drove down the hill. "I'm nervous."

"Me too." Fatin honked a few times at the motionless cars that blocked the way by the bakery.

Yasmin turned around. "Back up quickly; there's no one behind you. Let's take another street."

After driving for five minutes on the main road, passing furniture and carpet stores, banks, and produce and grocery stores, they were stuck in another traffic jam. Shortly after, they were on their way, avoiding collisions with racing yellow cabs and microbuses. Before they reached the outskirts of the city, Yasmin peered at the big sign that read *Markiz Shurtah* (Police Station). The building was old; every stone among its walls bore the proof of weather abuse over decades. Police officers in blue uniforms, armed with guns in white holsters, stood around the entrance; the one guarding the gate winked at Yasmin.

"Did you see that? The sorry excuse for a cop winked at me."

"So, what's new?"

"I'm much older than him, and I look terrible."

Fatin moved to the left lane. "You're still a woman."

Yasmin shook her head. "They're supposed to be the ones looking after us."

"You know that saying, 'Guarded by its thieves.'"

"Is that where Mahir would see the children if I got custody?"

"If not this one, something similar."

"No kidding?"

"What did you expect? A station like the ones you see in American movies?"

"I don't know what to expect anymore. I guess I have to start taking everything as is."

Driving out of the capital, Fatin swirled her way down a narrow road lined with ancient eucalypti and junipers. When the road straightened, nurseries and pottery stands appeared on both sides. After they passed through a brown cloud at a construction site, the road turned into a freeway. In the far distance to the right, small towns were scattered over some hilltops. Mosque minarets rose in the middle of each cluster, and the golden crescents on their tops glistened like stars in midday. Rows of stone walls sectioned the land around the houses on the slopes, making the farming spaces in between look like steps for a giant. Some of the other mountains they passed had forests of pine and juniper, and some yielded nothing but dirt, thorns, and massive boulders.

Looking out the window, Yasmin said, "Wonder what happened to my plants."

"I thought your friend Dina was taking care of them and the pool, too."

"Yeah, and my neighbor Beth is taking care of my mail. I hope they didn't both give up on me coming back. I wonder what's going on with my bills. Mahir was still taking care of the payments when we left."

The freeway ended, and a dirt diversion led the car back to the old road. Traffic slowed as they reached the Palestinian refugee camp in the town of Baqaa, where cars double-parked and blocked the streets and a mass of pedestrians paced up and down the sidewalks. Strips of small shops lined both sides of the road. They were mainly car-repair shops, grocery stores, and butcheries with headless, skinned lambs hanging behind their glass fronts. Outside one of the shops, a slaughtered cow hung upside down with a bouquet of plastic red carnations stuck down its backside.

As they approached another detour, a worn-out white Suzuki truck inched its way in front of them while blurring their vision with smoke of burning diesel. An old woman dressed in black sat in the back of the truck next to a dead donkey that lay on its side, its four legs separated and stiff and an army of flies nibbling on its wide-open eyes.

Yasmin laughed. "What in the world is this?"

"That's disgusting. Wonder what she's going to do with it. Eat it maybe."

"I don't think so. I bet you if my friend Dina saw that, she would say the woman was going to use the donkey's brain for magic."

The street curved by the Radio Telescope Station, where massive dishes stared at the sky like curious eyes seeking all the knowledge they could grasp from the universe. Yasmin yelled and rolled the window up as they passed the sewage treatment plant. "Same old refinery?"

Fatin laughed. "They use it to irrigate farms." She drove through another twenty minutes of highway, speeding by fruit and lettuce stands, coffee vendors, and young men selling live partridges locked up in cages. How terrible they must feel, crammed on top of one another, their wings fluttering but taking them nowhere. When they reached the blue and white sign that indicated the exit to Irbid, Yasmin put her palm on her chest and took a deep breath. They passed a few miles of wheat plains, and then the roadsides gave way to residential areas that spread all the way to the horizon.

"We're almost there," Fatin said.

"Do you know how to get to their house?"

"Yeah, I still remember." Fatin passed Irbid's Safeway supermarket and turned left. By the end of that street, she turned right and entered a tidy neighborhood of limestone houses.

Yasmin looked around. "Don't park by the house. Let's watch from a distance first."

"OK, that's a good idea. They might not open the door if they see us." Fatin kept the engine running. The neighborhood was quiet; it smelled of cooked chicken and onions.

Yasmin lit a cigarette and stared at the two-story house of Mahir's parents with all the hatred she could gather at that moment. A bearded man wearing a caftan and holding grocery bags in his hands gave them no attention as he passed by and proceeded to the small mosque at the end of the street. After a few moments, Yasmin said, "Pass by the garage quickly. Let's see who's home and who's not."

Fatin drove forward.

"Stop! Mahir's father is not here." Yasmin threw the cigarette out. "Wait for me here."

"I'm coming with you." Fatin turned off the engine and un-buckled herself.

Yasmin paced ahead of Fatin, climbed the curvy steps that had jasmine interlacing their rails, and reached for the doorbell. She felt her head pulsing and heard a loud whoosh in her ears. Mahir's mother opened the door and stayed behind it. She pressed her thin lips and swallowed. All Yasmin could see of her was her pro-testing yellow face, the strap of her revealing dress, and the aging skin of her shoulder. Yasmin had no doubt her presence was not expected or welcomed. She did not even bother with a greeting. "I want to see the children."

"They're not here," she snapped. "They went with Mahir to buy yogurt."

Yasmin did not acknowledge the resentment in her squinting eyes. "Which way did he go?"

Mahir's mother stammered.

Yasmin asked again, "Which way?"

Fatin intervened. "Good afternoon. We came to see the chil-dren. We can wait for them outside if you don't want to tell us which way."

Mahir's mother opened the door wider. Behind the transparent skin of her face, her thin veins were darkening and the one on her neck fattening. She made an effort to smile back at Fatin. "Good af-ternoon." She pointed to the corner. "It's down this way to the left."

Yasmin turned around and ran down the steps. She heard Fatin say good-bye before the door slammed. The moment she set her foot on the sidewalk, Mira's voice came from the street corner. "Mama, Mama."

Yasmin ran in her direction, gasping, reaching out, and in a shaky voice shouting Mira's name and then Sami's. Mahir turned around, but his attempt to walk away failed as Sami stiffened and rooted his shoes into the sidewalk. When Yasmin reached them, she knelt down and wrapped Sami and Mira in one hug. She kissed their foreheads and their faces.

"What do you think you're doing?" Mahir screamed. He dropped a plastic bag from his hand and wiped his forehead.

"I want my children. You have no right keeping them with you." She stood up shaking, still holding Sami's and Mira's hands.

He gritted his teeth. "I'll kill you here before you even think of taking them with you."

"Go ahead. Do it." She started backing up.

Mahir took a step forward.

"If I ever see you here again, I'll break your legs." Abu Mahir's voice suddenly came from behind, followed by Fatin's scream of no.

Yasmin turned around and saw Fatin standing between her and Mahir's father, who was holding a *ganweh*, a wooden bat, in his hand. From the look in his eyes, she knew he meant every word that came out of his ruthless mouth.

Fatin's face turned white. She wrapped both hands in fists under her chin and looked back and forth at Yasmin and Abu Mahir. Yasmin did not move. From the corner of her eye, she could see two figures standing between opened curtains, watching from the next-door house, and some people gathering on a balcony. She had never thought humans could hear the rush of their blood or feel their frantic and irregular pulse, but she found herself aware of both at that moment. She stepped back, still holding Sami and Mira, both of them crying.

Abu Mahir took a step in her direction and lifted his stick. Fatin screamed, and so did Mira and Sami. Yasmin looked down at them; Mira was standing in a pool of her urine, and Sami's body rippled with fear.

Mahir grabbed Sami's and Mira's hands and yanked them away from Yasmin. They both screamed with their free hands, reaching out for Yasmin.

"Now get the hell out of here," Mahir shouted.

Yasmin stood still. "If either of you touches me, I'm calling the police."

Abu Mahir forced out a sarcastic laugh. "Shut your mouth, and do as he says."

Yasmin had the urge to lash at him, to scratch his face, or even to pluck his eyes out. She looked again at Sami and Mira. Their crying continued to pierce her ears and rip deep in her chest. If Abu Mahir beat her in front of them, the scenes would be engraved in their heads forever. Without uttering a word, she walked away, and Fatin followed her to the car. When Fatin started the engine, Abu Mahir came to Yasmin's side and spit on the glass.

Yasmin flinched. "Animal," she screamed, her voice full of anger and grief. "I hope you die." She pointed at Mahir, who stood watching as they drove away. She turned to Fatin. "Maybe that snake and her buffalo for a husband will get a taste of what they're doing to me."

Fatin wiped her eyes. "That was scary. I can't believe Abu Mahir did all that."

Yasmin did not comment. She leaned back and closed her eyes most of the way back, continuously picturing the frightened and pleading faces of Sami and Mira. How could Mahir stand there and watch his father's craziness and not say a word? For Sami and Mira's sake at least. Yasmin understood her culture well enough to know that, regardless of what the law and the Koran stated, men still considered that children belonged first and foremost to their fathers. They carried his last name and inherited the family assets and fortunes. Maybe Mahir was under that kind of pressure. He was feeling obliged to show the manly attitude expected from him. Still, as an educated and supposedly civilized person, he had no excuse for submitting to that kind of outdated thinking. He should never have consented to the idea of tricking her and following her to Jordan to take away Sami and Mira in the first place.

Halfway through the drive, she looked out the window at the sky and found it still colorless and depressing. The sky of Arizona had never seemed so appealing and inviting. Maybe she could do something there. See a lawyer or file a lawsuit…find a solution. Her mind was racing. She needed to calm down and think straight and take some action instead of accepting this enormous defeat. Who was she kidding? There was no use staying in Jordan any-more, weak and helpless, without her children. Mahir would never let her see them again, let alone allow her to live with them.

Fatin put her hand on Yasmin's shoulder. "Are you OK?"

"I can't believe what happened, Fatin. I expected a crazy reac-tion, but not like this. This was savagery." She looked out again. "I haven't done anything to deserve this."

"What are you going to do now?"

"I want to go back to Scottsdale. There's no use in me staying here." Yasmin did not feel like mentioning seeing a lawyer at that point. She had a good idea on how her family was going to react by now. "I have to go back at some point anyway to take care of my house, the bills, and my car—"

"Can't you take care of it from here?"

"I could take care of the bills if I had my checkbook and enough money, but I don't have either."

"Don't worry about the money. I'm sure your father will help."

"I know he would, Fatin, but I still eventually have to go."

When Fatin and Yasmin arrived at the house, the whole family was on the front balcony. Yasmin could see anger and frustration on their faces.

"The creep must've called Fadi." She could see her mother's eyes overflowing with unspoken words. "I'm not talking to any-one," she told Fatin.

"Just walk right in. I'll take care of them. It's about time they stopped their moral nonsense."

Yasmin pushed open the gate.

Her mother said, "Fadi—"

"Can go to hell," Yasmin cut her off and entered the house, leaving Fatin behind to take care of the explanations. She walked straight to the study, called a travel agency, and inquired the status of her unused return ticket. The employee said she could validate her ticket by paying one hundred dinars, about $130, so she arranged to stop by the next day, pay the fee, and make new reservations.

CHAPTER TWENTY-SIX

The next day at dawn, Yasmin slipped out of bed, made a cup of coffee, and sat in the backyard. She had been awake for quite some time but wasn't sure how long. All she knew was that she did not stop thinking of the sidewalk events, and at some point there was no telling what was real and what was dream. After her second cup of coffee, she turned the water on and started watering the plants. She stared at the geraniums and inhaled their strong scent absentmindedly. Her head thudded with pain.

"Yasmin," her mother called from the kitchen door.

Startled, Yasmin moved the hose from the overflowing planter to the one next to it.

Her mother tied the belt of the robe she wore over her night-gown. "Mahir's relative just called your father," her mother said. "He's that old lawyer their whole family consults with."

"What does he want?"

"He wants to see you. Your father is waiting for you inside to talk about it. He said that Abu Mahir had contacted him and asked him to find a solution because of the children."

"Solution, my ass," Yasmin muttered.

"What?"

"If they wanted a solution, they wouldn't have acted like barbarians yesterday. I doubt they've had an awakening since then, but even if they did, they would've called me or Baba."

Yasmin's mother stood silent and puzzled.

Yasmin turned the water off and went inside to talk to her father. She remembered her cousin Lina mentioning the man's name during one of her phone conversations. Lina had told Yasmin that he was an old relative of Abu Mahir's, very cherished for being a supporter who never missed any of the meetings they held for the purpose of trashing her and plotting against her. He was a business lawyer and an international referee who thought highly of himself and expected respect and appreciation not only from the family but from the whole world.

"He said he was working on some type of agreement and insisted on your presence," Yasmin's father said.

Yasmin knew that was not the case. "I don't know what to say, Baba. Even if Mahir didn't approve of his father's behavior yesterday and realized how much he traumatized the children, wouldn't he have called me or you?"

Her father squinted. "Maybe he's embarrassed to come forward on his own."

Yasmin shook her head. "Mahir embarrassed?"

Around noon, Yasmin buckled herself in her father's old Volvo and rolled down the window. The air was hot and damp. Her father put his glasses on, tightened his grip on the steering wheel, and eased his way out of the neighborhood. Cars sped past them and honked the moment they reached the main road. They stopped a few times behind a microbus picking up passengers or dropping them off. When a car ahead of them made a sudden stop by a watermelon tent, Yasmin lost her temper and slammed the dashboard with a fist.

"I can't get over how they just stop for watermelons like that and block the first lane."

"Calm down, Yasmin." Her father finally moved to the middle lane. "The referee sounded optimistic over the phone. I hope my poor hearing didn't betray me." He reached in his pocket, took out a handkerchief, and wiped his forehead.

"You really think so?"

They passed the ramp in silence, reached the end of the road, made a U-turn, and drove to the sixth roundabout. In the distance, Yasmin noticed a few men standing on the side of the road looking both ways, checking traffic before they crossed. She closed her eyes. When her father stopped at the red light, she opened her eyes and took a deep breath.

The office was on the third floor of an elaborate new building that had a reflective bluish glass front. The shiny marble floors of the entrance looked wet with heavy layers of wax. Once Yasmin and her father stepped inside the spacious elevator, a recording of a man's voice alerted them that the door was about to close and announced the floor number once they stopped. When they entered the office, a secretary escorted them to a room where they both declined her offer for coffee.

Minutes later, the referee/lawyer entered the room in very slow steps, carrying a stack of papers. The man was probably in his late seventies and had a frail figure and a crescent of white hair on the back of his head. Yasmin did not like the half-dumb, half-mean look in his eyes, because both looks augured disaster.

Yasmin's father stood up.

The man shook his hand. "*Alan wa sahlan* (welcome)," he said in a tone that sounded insincere to Yasmin. He nodded to Yasmin and then motioned to her father to sit down, sat next to him, and tossed a small stack of papers on the coffee table.

Yasmin's father adjusted in the big seat. "How are you, sir? In great health, inshallah?"

He forced a smile. "*Nahmid-u-llah* (we thank God)," he said.

We? Obviously one of those megalomaniacs who spoke of themselves in the plural. Mahir's father used that same term, so Yasmin figured that the conviction of being great must be something that ran in the whole family. She hated the man even more.

The secretary entered the room with a glass of milk in hand and set it in front of him. He took a sip and then removed his shoes and placed them next to his seat. The shoes kept the dome shape of his bony feet. Yasmin thought of his action as disrespectful.

"Pardon me. I had a long day at court today," he told Yasmin's father and then reached for the stack of papers. "Mahir said Yasmin had been very negligent of him and the children. She never even bothered to cook a decent meal since the day they got married."

Yasmin slipped out a laugh. The referee looked at her like a principal who despised a student. He then turned to her father, expecting an explanation from him, not from Yasmin.

It was very hard for Yasmin to believe that a lawyer/whatever with a supposedly big stature would even mention such a ridiculous accusation. She knew Mahir had started this silly rumor about her, because back at that meeting they had at her parents' house a few days after he took Sami and Mira, he had accused her of feeding them canned foods. Yasmin had heard that same accusation many times in the past from men divorcing in Jordan but never thought Mahir would so lack creativity to use it.

"Tell him the real reason for the dispute," her father said.

Yasmin could tell that the referee already disliked her. He barely acknowledged her presence and did not bother to shake her hand when he entered the room. Now he probably detested her more for the lack of humility she was displaying and for laughing at his statement. She knew that nothing she would say was going to make a difference, because he was already holding the printed agreement in his hand.

"I don't know what's exactly wrong with him, but back in Scottsdale he started sleeping on the couch, and after that—"

"This is nonsense," he shouted and flung the papers across the table in her direction. "Sign these papers." He handed her father a copy. The referee's reaction to Yasmin's half sentence resembled that of Mahir's father. She knew her honesty and her boldness outraged both of them. A man should never be accused of not sleeping with his wife, and a decent woman should never even think about mentioning it. It challenges a man's masculinity!

Yasmin held the document and read.

The first line declared that, by signing, Yasmin agreed to the following: She would hand her Jordanian passport and the children's American passports to the referee on that same day. She would never return to Arizona without Mahir's permission. She would never file for divorce in America, and when and if divorce took place in Jordan, Mahir would be the sole rightful guardian of both children. The only settlement Yasmin would receive would be the five thousand dinars identified in her marriage certificate as her postponed dowry.

When Yasmin's father finished reading his copy, he looked disturbed. "Pardon me, sir, but this is outrageous. It defies every law in this country."

"I think we should leave now." Yasmin stood up and threw the papers on the table. "I'm not signing."

"I've been doing this all my life," the referee shouted.

"I'll wait for you outside, Baba."

"Are you going to let your daughter disrespect me and talk to me like this?"

"I think you disrespected both of us, sir. I'm afraid we're not the dumb goats you expect us to be. We are both aware of the law and know Yasmin's rights."

Yasmin left the office. Seconds later, her father followed and stood next to her by the elevator with a copy of the agreement in his hand.

"I'm not signing."

He shook his head. "I can't believe this…an old friend of mine is a retired judge. I'm going to call him and see what he makes of this."

Yasmin did not comment.

The moment they sat in the car, Yasmin turned to her father and said, "Baba, I want to go back to Arizona, to my house. I can't just leave it like that. I have to go take care of things, pay bills, bring my stuff…you know."

He took his glasses off and bit on one of its handles, squinted, and stared ahead. "I think Majid should go with you." He put his glasses back on, started the car, and drove ahead.

"Majid? What for? He has his work, his family—"

"I don't think it's appropriate for you to go by yourself. People will talk."

"Why do you care so much about people, Baba? People with their stupid gossip ruined my life, and by now they've forgotten all about me. Look, Baba, I've been living in Arizona for ten years. I know how to take care of things without Majid's help." She looked at her father with begging eyes. "I'll go crazy if I stay here like this. I have to do something."

He released a long sigh. "If you promise to stay with a friend—"

"I will. I'll ask my friend Ellen or Dina to stay with me."

Her father's overprotection came as no surprise to Yasmin. She still remembered her conversation with her father when Mahir moved out. The first thing he said was that he did not think the living arrangement was safe for her or the children. According to her culture, age did not matter when a woman did not live under the shadow of a man, any man. She could be fifty or even older and still be regarded as a helpless creature who was not capable of being on her own.

As soon as they entered the house, Yasmin called Fatin and asked her to stop at the travel agency. That afternoon, Fatin came home with Yasmin's ticket and her confirmed reservations for the same night. Yasmin packed only some turkish coffee and her toiletries in one suitcase and some clothes in the other, leaving enough room for whatever she might bring back. She put Mira's blanket and Sami's bear in a duffel bag with the rest of their clothes and toys and set it aside.

When Fatin entered the room, Yasmin pointed to the duffel. "Just in case Mahir decides to get their things. He knows Sami is very attached to his bear and Mira to her blanket."

Fatin stared at it. "You are coming back, Yasmin, right?"

Though the idea of never coming back had crossed Yasmin's mind when she and Fatin were driving back from Irbid, she did not admit it. "What makes you say that?"

"I don't know. Just a feeling I guess. I wouldn't blame you if you didn't, but the children…"

Yasmin smiled. "I'm not leaving my children, Fatin. There's nothing more I can do now." She opened the drawer of her nightstand and took out Sami's and Mira's passports. "Give them to Mahir."

Fatin gasped. "Are you serious? I though you said—"

"I have no use for them with that court order to prevent them from leaving the country. Actually a trip might be good for both of them after all they've been through."

Fatin took the passports.

Before Majid drove Yasmin to the airport, her father handed her a sealed envelope. "Let me know if you need more after you pay your bills. I'll transfer it to your account."

Yasmin kissed her father on the cheeks and hand. "Thank you, Baba."

While Majid put her suitcases in the trunk of his car, her parents and Fatin stood by the door to say good-bye.

"Call us as soon as you get there. Keep e-mailing Fatin. Don't sleep alone at the house." Her mother hugged and kissed her.

"OK, Mama." Yasmin knew it was mean on her part to think that her mother's worry was more about what people might say if they found out that Yasmin was in Scottsdale on her own. But she could not help it. From the way her whole ordeal was handled by her family, she had every reason to believe her well-being came last.

Yasmin hugged and kissed Fatin.

The night was peaceful with the abandoned streets. A nice breeze came to the city after a hot and humid wave had lingered over the country for weeks. Pained to leave Sami and Mira behind, Yasmin could not cherish the relief of finally returning to her home. Majid chatted a little about the weather and his work, and when Yasmin only responded with nods and dazed eyes, he let her grieve in silence for the rest of the drive.

Inside the terminal, Majid stood behind a partition while Yasmin moved on the other side from counter to counter. She checked her suitcases, paid the airport tax, and finally tailed a line of passengers holding passports. After she finished all procedures, she glided up the escalator, looking down and waving back at Majid. When the glass door slid shut behind him, she paced toward the terminal, already packed with hundreds of boarding passengers.

Yasmin found her seat, buckled herself, and closed her eyes. The overhead compartments opened and slammed. A baby's cry faded behind the humming engine, and as the pilot's voice greeted the passengers, Yasmin drifted away.

CHAPTER TWENTY-SEVEN

Yasmin dragged her suitcases and walked out of the Sky Harbor terminal into the flaming August noon that felt strangely comforting. She was home. She took a deep breath, filled her lungs with hot air, and then proceeded to the first car in the cab line. As she approached the driver, standing beside his shiny town car, he nodded and smiled.

Yasmin smiled back. "I'm going to south Scottsdale." She then gave him the address.

He placed her luggage in the trunk while she sat inside the clean car that smelled of a freshener, not tobacco, food, or sweat. It felt unusual to be in a cab that had no glittering stickers of verses or postcards of winking oriental women. No rosaries or miniature Korans hung from the rearview mirror, either. Other than the whoosh of the cold air, there were no other sounds. The driver did not start a conversation or turn up the volume to the voice of a singer moaning about his or her lonesomeness without his or her beloved.

The sky was as blue and dazzling as Yasmin had imagined it back in Jordan. She stared out the window, passing familiar places, giant palms, paloverde trees, and colorful billboards. When they neared Hayden Road, she felt her chest hollowing. Her eyes stayed fixed ahead, anticipating the moment of arrival that felt surreal. She smiled with sadness at the McDonald's as they passed it, at the dry cleaner's, at the pet shop, at every building and street corner that had been a part of a ruined life. She reached in her purse, tore the side of the envelope that her father had given her, and pulled out two twenty-dollar bills from the thick stack. When the driver parked by her house, she handed him the bills, and he handed her back some change. He stepped out of the car, set her bags on the sidewalk, and then drove away.

The neighborhood was as still as a painting, its immense silence disturbed only by the sounds of her dragging suitcases. Her house was beginning to show signs of neglect. Weed tops were knee-high. Heaps of crunchy leaves gathered by the front door, the carport, and under her car. Monsoon rain had fed the thorny branches of the mesquite tree and caused them to extend past the front door, curving like the swords of a sultan's guard.

The long weeks of heat had turned the house into a hot and musty space, housing nothing but abandoned memories and dead plants. When Yasmin saw Sami's miniature cars and Mira's one-eyed doll under the coffee table, she collapsed on the couch, tears streaming down her face. Holograms of her children appeared before her wherever she turned her eyes; she could hear their voices and smell their scents. Every wall, every corner, every inch of the house reflected flashes of the past, home movies her subconscious had stored for this moment.

She reached under the coffee table and grabbed the toys, her sobbing turning to screaming that after a while no longer made a sound. She wiped her face, feeling claws scratching down her throat every time she swallowed. She dragged herself to the thermostat and turned the AC on. It was going to be a long time before the cold air replaced the heat that she could feel radiating from the walls. Her neighbor Beth had placed her past-due mail on the dining table in neat stacks. Beth had taken care of Yasmin's and Mahir's mail whenever they traveled, but Yasmin had never returned to such an overwhelming pile of envelopes.

Through the french door, Yasmin looked at the pool, full of green water and leaves. She could tell that a storm had ravished it beyond Dina's control. It had happened many times in the past years during the monsoon season. Her eyes began to water again at the sight of Sami's goggles and Mira's arm floats lying on the patio floor next to their pool noodles and fins. More evidence of a lost past lingered in every room of the house: Sami's and Mira's pajamas over their unmade beds, rubber ducks by the tub in the bathroom, drawings on the fridge door, and boxes of mac and cheese and Teddy Graham crackers in the pantry.

After showering and unpacking, and not having an appetite for food or drinks, Yasmin sat behind the dining table and sorted out her mail. Mahir had stopped making payments the day she and the children left. The mortgage was one month behind, and so were the utility bills. A letter from her health insurance stated her benefits had been canceled upon her request, which was not true. Mahir must have done that, and now she could no longer get a re-fill on her allergy medication. Mahir had also paid all their credit cards in full and closed them, and that was going to make her stay more difficult than she had anticipated.

When Yasmin was done, she called Ellen and left her a voice mail asking her to call back or just stop by around six if she was in town. Yasmin then drove to the bank, passing the golf course she used to pass every morning on her way to Sami and Mira's school. She ached for them every moment of the way. After making a deposit at the window teller, she drove across the street to the post office and mailed her payments. Driving back, she wondered how long the $600 she had left in the envelope was going to last. Other than bringing her payments up to date, she had no definite plans, but the idea of throwing everything away and heading back to Jordan immediately did not make sense. She thought about selling some of her belongings in order to prolong her stay and figure out what to do with the house and a lifetime of possessions.

When Yasmin returned, she picked up the phone and called Dina.

"Yasmin, thank God you're back," Dina said. "What happened? I've been going crazy since your friend Ellen called."

Yasmin told Dina what had happened in detail, and as Dina commented every now and then, Yasmin sensed her genuine sadness and concern. When Yasmin spoke about her sidewalk encounter and told Dina how horrified both Mira and Sami were, Dina cried.

"I expected trouble, but nothing like this," she said and sniffled.

Before they hung up, Yasmin explained to Dina that though she did not have any definite plans so far, she had decided to have a garage sale and asked her to stop by.

"Sure," Dina said. "Look, I want you to know that I did my best taking care of the pool—"

"Don't worry about it," Yasmin said. "I could tell there had been a sandstorm."

"I watered your plants on time, but I think they died from the heat. I didn't know when you were coming back, so I didn't turn on the air."

"That's OK, Dina. No big deal. You think after being deprived of my children I'm going to worry about a couple of plants?"

When Ellen called back that evening, Yasmin gave her the details of her horrendous ordeal as she had with Dina, starting from the moment Mahir had taken Sami and Mira and ending with the moment she had left them crying on the sidewalk.

Ellen did not interrupt. Once in a while, she whispered, "Oh dear."

Yasmin told Ellen how she dreaded waking up every morning. How she shut her eyes and tried to force herself back to sleep so she did not realize who she was and where she was and what had happened. She explained to Ellen how the way she felt upon waking up every day reminded her of a horrifying scene from an old movie in which a woman opens her eyes inside a dark coffin made from thin shards of wood. She knows by the taste of soft dirt sprinkling on her lips that somebody has entombed her alive and knows that screaming and kicking will prove useless within a few short breaths. The idea of digging her way out crosses her mind for an instant, and then it's lost as her lungs begin to collapse in horror and despair.

"I'm so sorry you had to go through all this, Yasmin," Ellen said. "I'm so shocked because, from what you've always told me, I thought of Jordan as a civilized country."

Yasmin could not tell if Ellen's tone was full of pity or disgust. Either way, she could not blame her.

"What are your plans now?"

"I can't concentrate long enough to know what I want or should do. I have many things in mind. I know this doesn't make sense, but I thought a lot about seeing a lawyer here. I know I probably don't stand much chance, but I don't want to have any regrets later. Maybe I'll do it after I sell a few things and have enough money."

Ellen talked Yasmin out of selling anything and offered help, which came as no surprise to Yasmin. Before they hung up, Ellen told Yasmin that she had a cousin in Ohio who was a lawyer and promised Yasmin to get her a consultation in a few days. She was traveling to Ohio to see her aunt anyway.

After they hung up, Yasmin thought long and hard about what she should be doing next. Could she sell the house without Mahir's signature if she wanted or had to? Should she look for a job and seriously consider never returning to Jordan? Maybe she should just take it easy for now and wait until she could think straight. But she still wanted to get rid of some stuff she never used and never would. Nothing wrong with having extra money as a backup since she no longer owned a credit card.

That night, Yasmin went through another stack of her mail and found some with Mahir's name on them. She was not sure why he would be using the house address after moving out, but she decided to check them out later. Right now, she could not tolerate anything related to him.

Before she went to bed that night, she checked her e-mail and then e-mailed Fatin.

To: Fatin@jomail.com
From: Yasmin@azmail.com
Subject:

Dear Fatin,
    Please let everyone know I arrived safely. The house is a mess. I found all my plants dead and my pool turned into a swamp. Mahir had stopped making payments since we left, so I took care of that. Please write as soon as you hear any-thing about Sami and Mira. Check with Lina; she should be able to find out from Fadi since he's constantly in touch with Mahir.

Yasmin.

When Yasmin went to bed that night, she held Sami's and Mira's pajamas to her nose and kept inhaling their scents until she fell asleep.

CHAPTER TWENTY-EIGHT

Early Friday morning, Yasmin piled clothes, shoes, linens, toys, and the books she decided to keep on Sami's bed. She filled one of the two large plastic containers she set on the floor with photo albums, framed pictures, home movies, Sami's and Mira's preschool art, their one-year picture outfits, their first baby shoes, and their baby books. In the second container, she placed her embroidered cushion covers and the oil paintings she had taken out of their frames, some letters, and postcards.

The night before, Yasmin had moved some of the furniture around and placed price stickers on everything she had decided to sell. The big television Mahir had bought the previous year had never appealed to Yasmin, but when she noticed her children's little fingerprints on the dusty screen, she had second thoughts. Until that moment, she had only thought of her belongings as things, but now that she was about to sell them, they became precious memories.

When Dina pulled into the driveway around six thirty that morning, Yasmin was taping the last garage-sale sign on the light pole by her house. She had placed one on the corner of her street and Hayden and a few by other street crossings around the neighborhood. Though Yasmin had already explained to Dina that she had no specific plans, when Dina stepped out of the car, she still looked around and asked, "You're not going back?"

They kissed and hugged. "I don't know yet." Yasmin locked the door and walked ahead of Dina to the kitchen. "You want coffee?"

"Sure." Dina took her seat behind the island, while Yasmin filled the coffeepot and set it over the jittering blue tongues of the fire.

"How come you lost so much weight, Yasmin?"

"Why do you think, Dina? From spending my summer at a Swiss spa?"

Dina laughed. "At least you still have your sense of humor in the middle of all this."

Yasmin wanted to change the subject. "How is Mahmoud doing?"

"Not too good. He was laid off. He has two more weeks at his job and is looking for something else right now. It's not looking good though."

"Oh, I'm so sorry to hear that."

"He's going to work as a temp for an Arab store owner in Scottsdale until he finds a full-time job. He won't be selling Indian jewelry but running errands, doing the packaging for UPS shipping, stuff like that."

"That's good. At least you can pay your bills."

When Yasmin finished boiling the coffee, she poured it in cups, took her seat, and lit a cigarette.

Dina took a sip of her coffee. "Mahmoud said I might have to go back to Jordan if he doesn't find a job soon enough. Just until the economy picks up and things get better. Almost no one is hiring right now because of the 9/11 anniversary. It's easier for him to be on his own and look for a job, maybe in another state."

"Ah." Yasmin looked down and smiled. Dina had once criticized a few Arabic men who sent their wives and their children back to their countries, all using the same excuse. Other than suddenly realizing that living costs were cheaper overseas, they had insisted on the importance of teaching their children their language and their religion. The husbands had stayed behind, earned more money, and enjoyed the privileges of being single in America.

"I know what you're thinking," Dina said. "I don't mind going home. When things get better, I'll come back."

"Hey, I'm not thinking anything. You're the one who always laughed at the Arabic men who sent their wives and their children back home. You know I wish you the best, Dina, and if you're OK with this arrangement, then it's perfectly fine."

"I know." Dina smiled.

When they finished their coffee, Yasmin taped a sale sign on the family-room window and placed only a few old items outside by the door.

"It's too hot to drag everything outside or even leave the door open," she told Dina as she followed her into Sami's room. Yasmin sat on Sami's Mickey Mouse chair and stared at the containers she had filled earlier, trying very hard not to fall apart or go crazy.

"I can't believe this is happening. I mean…" She held her head in her hands. "…I know it is, but it's too much to take in."

Dina sat next to her on the floor. "One day you will have everything new. Money comes and goes."

"Who cares about money and things? You see these containers?" She pointed her index finger. "This is what my whole life is worth. I think everything else was nothing but costly delusions."

"Look, sometimes what seems like a bad situation is nothing but a change for the better. Maybe something good is going to come your way after all this."

Yasmin laughed. "Good?"

"I don't mean it in a bad way, but maybe you're fulfilling a fate. Maybe it's better for you to move to Jordan, have a new home—"

"Oh, please, Dina. I'll never have a home. This is my home, and I love it. It took me years to make it a home. Sometimes in the past I'd still think of myself as homeless, the way I felt when I left Jordan the first time. The more time I spent here, the more estranged I became from my own country and my own people. I'm going to be a foreigner wherever I go now." She placed a hand on Dina's arm. "Do you understand what I'm saying?"

Dina nodded.

The doorbell rang. Yasmin stood up and looked out the window. A few cars had parked by the sidewalk, and a group of people stood in the driveway. She walked to the front door, and Dina followed.

Yasmin had a hard time allowing into her house people she had never seen before in her life. Strangers wandered around, touched her things, sat on her couch, and haggled over prices. She completely lost it and snapped at a pregnant woman who offered seven dollars for Mira's Barbie_tricycle. When the woman held her stomach and started walking out of the house making faces, Dina intervened, took the woman aside, and finished the sale.

"I've never sold a memory before," Yasmin said in a mourning tone afterward. "I didn't imagine it was going to be this hard. You know what I mean?"

Dina banged the kitchen island. "Damn that Mahir, wherever he is."

Half an hour later, the doorbell rang again. Assuming it was another rush of bargain hunters, Yasmin let Dina open the door, but it was her neighbor Beth.

Yasmin hugged Beth. Her petite figure felt fragile in Yasmin's arms, and her auburn hair smelled of apples. She handed Yasmin her key and sat down.

"I just returned from visiting with my grandchildren in Omaha," Beth said. "When I saw the sale signs, I came right away to give you back your key. I got worried when you didn't return on time. I hope everyone is OK back there."

Yasmin briefed Beth on what had happened since she started fighting with Mahir until she saw him last. Beth's face took on different expressions of shock, sadness, and sometimes disbelief while Yasmin spoke.

"You rocked his boat," Beth finally said. "Men don't like that."

Yasmin nodded. There was regret in her nod. She did rock Mahir's boat but had never expected him to react like a tsunami. She even wondered if confronting him was worth it in the first place.

That afternoon, more people walked in and carried things out of Yasmin's house, and Dina handled most of them. As much as Yasmin tried, letting go of her possessions did not get any easier as the day went by. She snapped again at a man that bargained in Spanish over her children's movies. Yasmin not only did not understand what he was saying but also ached for Sami and Mira at that moment. She could hear them giggling, and she could picture them rolling on their backs on the couch, as they did for years when watching their favorite cartoons. Dina intervened again and handled the situation.

Yasmin kept Sami's television and his Nintendo but sold the big television, the entertainment center, and the VCR. She got rid of some small kitchen appliances, a vacuum cleaner, a carpet steamer, a sewing machine, an old computer, books, rugs, toys her children had outgrown, strollers, high chairs, and car seats. By the end of the day, most of her belongings had become the property of strangers, and she had around $1,200 stacked in front of her.

She counted the money for the last time. "I have enough for September's payments."

"I have a feeling you're not going back," Dina said.

Yasmin looked down for a few seconds and then said, "Honestly? I don't really feel like going back. Just thinking about it makes me shiver. I keep asking myself over and over…go back to what? To living with my parents without my children? To being penniless and helpless, not having a say over my own life and my future? You have no idea what it feels like to be let down by your family, to be betrayed by your relatives, to be taken advantage of by every stranger who thinks of your misfortune as an opportunity."

"But the children, Yasmin!"

"The children are with Mahir, Dina. He wouldn't even let me see them. If I get them through court without being killed by him or his father, I still can't afford to feed them."

Dina pressed her lips and nodded.

"Let me tell you something, Dina. As hard and painful as it is for me being here without my children, I'm so damn happy for feeling like a free and dignified human again. Does that make any sense to you?"

Dina nodded again, but Yasmin could tell that Dina did not relate to what she was saying. In a way, she envied her.

"How are you going to manage here? You sold most of the expensive things you have today."

"I'm going to look for a job. If I can't sell the house without Mahir's signature, I'll find roommates. Whatever works."

Yasmin reached for Mahir's unopened mail, sitting on the counter next to the phone. She stacked the envelopes on top of the big off-white manila, leaned over the recycling bin, reconsidered, and threw the stack back on the kitchen counter. She lit a cigarette, walked to the stove, and started making coffee.

"I'm afraid of going back, Dina. Every time I think about it, I remember all the helpless feelings, like it's happening all over again." She let the coffee boil three times before she poured it in cups. "The day Mahir took Sami and Mira, I had a nightmare. It was more like a movie." She took the coffee to the kitchen island.

Dina sat up. "What was it? Tell me."

Yasmin took a sip of coffee. "I only remember it vaguely now. I was hanging in the sky, looking down at a primitive battle. The horsemen dressed like Bedouins and had ugly and cruel faces. They held swords and charged after women and children who screamed in terror. I remember being horrified when I realized that I was descending through a cloud of dust with my hands tied behind my back. In the dream, I told myself that my only chance of outwitting that war was to let my slow-motion run take me behind the large stones that had all of a sudden piled in front of me. I knew I had to stay there until the warriors were gone and I was able to untie my hands."

"That's actually not a nightmare." Dina smiled and sat forward. "Being tied and lowered down means something happening against your will or contrary to your liking. The ancient war is something you consider old or outdated. In general, and according to your situation, it means you should stay away from confronting anybody for the time being. This way you'll stand a better chance of surviving your dilemma or even winning in the end."

Yasmin released a long sigh.

"You know what they say. 'Nothing stays the same.'" Dina peered into Yasmin's cup.

Yasmin smiled. "Go ahead, be crazy and read my cup if you want, Dina. It's OK, really." She took a few more sips from her coffee and then turned her cup on its saucer. "I'm tired of being miserable."

Dina waited a few moments before she took Yasmin's cup and looked inside it. She smiled. "It's good."

Yasmin shook her head.

"You'll see. I'm not going to tell you anything because, as usual, you're going to make fun of me. But mark my words. I don't know how or when, but you're going to make up with Mahir and come back here."

Yasmin and Dina spent most of that night in the study, going through boxes of old documents, bank statements, and receipts. Before Yasmin went to bed that night, she checked her e-mail, but she had no mail from Fatin relating to Sami and Mira. Nothing else was worth reading.

CHAPTER TWENTY-NINE

On Monday morning Ellen called, and from the sound of her voice, Yasmin sensed the disappointing outcome of her conversation with her cousin Anne, the lawyer.

"Yasmin, I'm sorry I don't have encouraging news for you. Anne said that you don't really have a case, so there is nothing you could do about the situation legally."

Yasmin released a long exhale and stared out the window at a black crow trying to drink from the pool. "Did she give any details or explain why?"

"She said it's because you traveled with the children to Jordan by choice and you don't have any legal documents to prove separation or divorce," Ellen said. "What's more important is the fact that you left Sami and Mira in Jordan does not work in your favor."

Yasmin closed her eyes and pressed her lips. Her legs felt weak. She slowly lowered herself and sat down. "I see. Thanks for asking Anne anyway, Ellen. I hope it wasn't too much trouble."

"Not at all. Don't say that. I told you I would do anything to help. So, tell me. Did you figure out what you're going to do?"

"I really hate being here without the children, but the thought of going back frightens me to death. I'm going to examine my possibilities for staying here. I know it sounds stupid, but maybe this way I will force Mahir to reconsider his decision."

Yasmin thought seriously all day and all night about never returning to Jordan. She pondered over different scenarios of what her life would be like if she did. Mahir and his father would never let her have Sami and Mira even if she gained legal custody. Living alone back in Jordan was out of the question; her parents would never allow it, and she could never make enough money to support herself. Finally, and after three days of contemplating possibilities, she arrived at the conclusion that staying in Scottsdale seemed like her best choice. She called Dina early one morning and asked her if she could help with another garage sale on the coming Friday. Dina agreed.

When Dina arrived Friday morning, Yasmin had already finished taking apart Mira's bed and her dresser and was ready to go into Sami's room.

Dina looked at Yasmin's face for a few moments before she looked down and sighed. "You look worn-out."

"I am," Yasmin said, her voice barely audible.

"Sit down. I'll do it." She reached for the screwdriver in Yasmin's hand.

"No, that's OK, Dina. I'm not tired from the work. I feel like a piece of me is being ripped out with every screw I take out." She looked up at Dina and caught her wiping a tear before it got a chance to leave her eye.

Dina helped Yasmin take the small mattress out of the bed frame and set it aside. Yasmin traced a dark spot on the mattress with her fingers and then turned to Dina.

"Sami used to get nosebleeds all the time when he was younger." Dina's eyes welled up again. She hugged Yasmin.

Yasmin let herself go in Dina's embrace. "I was erasing their scribbles from their furniture before you came. This is hard, too hard…I will never forget the way I feel right now. Not in a million years."

Dina stayed on her feet all morning, dealing with a mix of people who were only looking and bargain hunters. She sold Sami's and Mira's bedroom furniture, their little desks, Sami's wagon, and Sami's television to one couple. While sitting behind the kitchen island, Yasmin could see and hear Dina talking the buyers into taking the furniture of both rooms along with Sami's and Mira's other belongings as a package deal. Yasmin knew what Dina had in mind the moment she approached the woman who inspected Sami's bed and asked if she could get a better price. She wanted to rid yasmine of as many memories as she could and spare her the agony of looking at their things and crying. Yasmin appreciated that gesture on Dina's behalf.

Dina helped the woman and her husband carry everything to their truck as fast as she could, while Yasmin stood behind the family-room window and watched the most precious years of her life drive away. She felt like running after the truck, screaming, begging them to let her have her children's childhood back. Dina closed the door behind her, put her arm around Yasmin, and walked her back to the kitchen. They sat in miserable silence until the doorbell rang again.

A few more people came and bought whatever Yasmin agreed to sell for half the price marked. By late afternoon, she became sickened by the process of selling her past. She took off all the sale signs she had placed. Dina helped her put whatever she had left and did not want to keep in bags and boxes.

"We'll pack both cars and make one trip to the thrift store," Yasmin said.

As soon as they finished loading the cars with bags and boxes and a few toys, Yasmin and Dina were on their way. When they arrived at the thrift store a few blocks down, they drove to the back of it and parked next to each other. They were unloading on the sidewalk by a small door when an employee, a man in his midthirties, came out, talked to Dina for a few seconds, and left. Dina carried a bag and followed him inside. When Dina came back, Yasmin was sitting on the sidewalk next to Sami's Mickey Mouse chair, holding her head in her hands.

Dina patted her on the back. "I'll be right back." She carried more bags inside the store and then came back after a couple of minutes and said, "Let's go, Yasmin. We can leave everything here. Can you drive?"

Yasmin nodded and walked to her car.

When they returned around six o'clock in the evening, the house echoed to their voices.

"Are you sure you don't want me to stay?"

"Very sure. Thank you for everything, Dina." Yasmin gave her a hug. When Dina left, Yasmin went to her room, took Sami's and Mira's pajamas from under her pillow, and held them close to her chest for a long time, rocking back and forth.

CHAPTER THIRTY

It took Yasmin more time than she had estimated to get the house ready for market. She did her best trimming a few of the mesquite branches and some of the bushes in the backyard. Cleaning the pool turned out to be a never-ending process of backwashing, taking the filter apart, washing it, and then backwashing again. When the house looked good enough inside and out, she called her realtor, Lindsey, and left a message on her voice mail. She briefed her on the situation and asked if she could sell the house without Mahir's signature. A few days later, Lindsey called back and told Yasmin that she could not sell the house without Mahir's signature. She also added that even if Mahir signed, it was not a good idea for them to sell the house.

"Look, Yasmin. Legally I'm not supposed to be telling you this. But as a friend, I know whatever I say will stay between us."

"Sure."

"You won't make any money if you did," Lindsey said.

Yasmin related Lindsey's advice to the approaching anniversary of 9/11. "Why not? Is it the timing?"

"No, Yasmin, it's not the market. When you guys refinanced, you cashed out the last penny, so there's no equity in the house."

"What? That's impossible. I know we refinanced back in January, but I don't remember taking out a loan."

"That never went through, Yasmin. Mahir changed his mind last minute. The refinance took place sometime in March. Mahir called me at the time, and I recommended the mortgage company for him. The employee who took care of your file is a friend of mine. I checked with him again after I heard your message, and he still confirmed the fact that you did."

"This is confusing. Lindsey, let me try to find out what you're talking about and call you back."

Yasmin knew something was not right. She remembered that night in March when Mahir asked her to sign a few of the refinancing papers because her signature was missing. But according to Lindsey, Mahir had refinanced a second time, cashing out every penny he could get his hands on without informing her.

Yasmin reached for the stack of mail she had kept aside and shuffled through the envelopes again. She opened an envelope from ASU that had a copy of Mahir's transcripts. She reduced it to shreds and tossed it in the recycling bin. Nothing else in the stack was of any importance. There was an invitation to a conference, a couple of letters from a car dealership, and one from a bank with a credit-card offer. She rushed to the study, went through the file cabinet, and took out the mortgage file. One of the two thick stacks was the original contract they signed when they first bought the house. Flipping through the pages of the other stack, Yasmin realized that Lindsey was right, but Yasmin found no trace of her signature on any of the pages, and that baffled her.

After putting the papers aside, she continued to go through the other papers in the file. An envelope addresses to Mahir's work caught her attention. He had never used the firm address for personal mail, but when she read "Quitclaim deed" on the top of the letter, she figured out why he had done it. That was what he made her sign back in March when she thought it was the refinancing papers.

"Damn. I'm so stupid." She banged her forehead with her palm.

After Yasmin calmed down, she sat by the kitchen window and smoked. Now that selling the house was not an option, she had no other way of staying unless she managed to find roommates. That could help with the mortgage and the bills. Although she no longer owned the house, she could still make payments and live there until she had something figured out. An hour later, she put on a button-up shirt and dress pants and decided to go out and look for a job. Before reaching the door on her way out, the phone rang. She ran back to the kitchen, looked at the caller ID, and read her parents' number. She snatched the handle. It was her mother.

"Hi, Mama, How are you?"

"What are you still doing there?" Her mother sounded upset.

"I'm waiting to sell my car."

"You couldn't sell it in three weeks? Leave it with a friend and come back. People are starting to talk."

Yasmin felt sick. The damn stupid people...again. "I can't; it's too complicated. I have to sell it in person." There was silence. "Mama, did you hear anything about Sami and Mira?"

"Lina called ten minutes ago and said they left with Mahir for Germany."

Yasmin immediately wondered if getting Sami and Mira back from Germany was an option and thought that maybe an international lawyer would know. "Did she say where in Germany or how long they're staying?"

"No, she didn't. I don't think she knows. Why do you want to know, anyway? Just finish up and come back."

"OK, I'll e-mail Fatin as soon as I know when I'm coming back."

Yasmin ended the conversation at that. She knew if she stayed on the line any longer, her mother was going to open like a broken dam.

Yasmin opened the yellow pages and looked under *attorney* for an international lawyer but found none listed in Arizona. As tempting as the idea of taking back her children from Germany seemed, Yasmin had to drop the idea that same moment. She figured by the time she found a lawyer who would agree to represent her from somewhere in the States, Mahir and the children would probably be back. She put the yellow pages back on the counter and left the house.

In the 110-degree heat, Yasmin drove north on Hayden Road, passing condominiums overlooking a golf course. As she had been doing the past three weeks, she wondered again if she were doing the right thing by staying in Scottsdale. But when she passed by the deserted park on Chaparral, she winced at the memory of Sami and Mira spending many afternoons there. She wondered again, if she actually found a job, would she really stay in Scottsdale, start a new life, and never return to Jordan and to her children? God. Why does every solution have to be more difficult than the next? Yasmin felt that no matter what she decided there was a big sacrifice involved. Putting her children first made it such an impossible task for her to gain any amount of control over her life.

Yasmin continued on her way through mild traffic until she reached the shopping center on Indian Bend. She drove around, passing stores and looking for Help Wanted or Now Hiring signs, but she saw none. It was obvious that the anticipation of the first anniversary of September 11 had placed every aspect of the economy on hold, except for the flourishing business of flags. They were everywhere. Stickers on some storefronts read Flags Sold Here, and in the parking lot, a man sold flags of every shape and size from the back of his van.

Yasmin passed him, parked her car, and walked into a craft store. She approached an employee, who was chewing gum and leaning on the counter next to a cash register, and asked her for an application. The woman took out a paper from under the counter and handed it to Yasmin.

"They're not hiring at this time," she said while chewing. "Fill it out and bring it back if you like. You never know."

Her tone did not sound friendly to Yasmin, but she took the application anyway and walked out. She sat in her car and filled it out. When she was done, she took it back to the store and handed it to the clerk.

From there, Yasmin drove to the mall. There were only a few other cars in the vast parking lot. She took the elevator to the Human Resources office of a department store on the third floor. The red-haired woman sitting behind the desk told her that the department store was not hiring at that time but she was welcome to apply. Yasmin filled out the application. The part that asked for her race was marked optional, so Yasmin left it empty. She did not think it was a good idea to specify her origins at a time when the whole world was looking at her culture as one of terror. She walked back to the desk and handed her application to the woman, who flipped through the pages and stopped at the section Yasmin left unanswered.

"You didn't complete this part, honey." Her makeup-buried face cracked a little and produced a challenging smile.

Yasmin immediately sensed the attitude. "It's not mandatory."

The woman scanned Yasmin from head to toe as she was getting up. "We will call you when we start hiring." She moved to the filing cabinet behind her.

Yasmin turned her back and walked away, angry. If anybody stood a slight chance at finding a job in such difficult times, it was not going to be her. During her ten years in Arizona, she had met many people who did not understand the difference between Arabic and Muslim. Many failed to distinguish one race from another, and whenever a conflict arose around the Middle East, they held anyone from that part of the world responsible.

Ever since she realized her marriage was shaky, the regret of never pursuing a career in America haunted her. The reality hit her in the face when she applied for several schools hoping to get an office job or even a classroom-assistant position but never heard back. Ellen had helped her write her résumé, but there was not much to show for. No experience and no recent schooling or training. What was she thinking ten years ago when she gladly took Mahir's advice and stayed home? That she had found her prince and was going to live happily ever after? Who could she blame now for not giving her advice, for not warning her, for not telling her the truth about the simple facts of life and love? Who was supposed to tell her that all relationships expired at some point? That nothing is forever and that having a career and a job is the only power.

Yasmin repeated her job hunt in different areas over the following days but to no avail. Not even the candy store or the neighborhood dry cleaner called back. After making September payments and having enough money left to get by, she knew that the countdown had started and that staying in Arizona pretty much required a miracle. Even though the anniversary of 9/11 passed in peace, the president started talking about deploying troops to the Middle East, which did not promise a change in the economy anytime soon.

Unsure if by staying in Scottsdale she was biding time or just killing it, Yasmin continued to live in an empty house that she did not own. She knew once she ran out of money, she had to go back, but she did not look forward to returning now, especially since Sami and Mira were in Germany with Mahir.

A job interview that did not go well dashed a droplet of hope she had still held on to. When Yasmin had stepped into the Western-clothing store, she thought that she might stand a chance at getting the job. But after the young lady who interviewed her asked about her nationality, Yasmin lost control over the smile she had kept on her face. It slowly faded away. The young lady had lost her welcoming expression too.

"Oh," she said with a bit of a shock. "I thought you were South American or something. But you could still pass as Hispanic."

One day Yasmin called Ellen and asked her to help sell her car. Ellen called two days later and said that she was going to buy the car on behalf of an old friend who was moving to Scottsdale within the next few weeks. Yasmin did not know if Ellen was telling the truth or just going out of her way to help. Either way, Yasmin was overwhelmed with appreciation and relief, especially since Ellen offered a little more than the blue-book price.

On the morning of Sami's birthday, September 28, Yasmin awoke with a painful lump in her throat. She could not call him and wish him a happy birthday. She wondered if he had a party, if he received gifts, and if he thought about her and missed her. That afternoon, she moved her easel by the french door in the dining area and started a new painting of a camel floating like a ship in a dark sea toward the east. The woman riding it had her gaze set on a saguaro cactus standing tall on the other shore, but a barbed-wire fence stretched across that sea, preventing her from reaching her destination.

Ellen stopped by one morning and gave Yasmin a check for $2,600. "You can give me the key when you decide to leave," she said and hugged Yasmin. She called Yasmin a few days later before leaving on a three-day trip to San Francisco and promised Yasmin to stop by as soon as she returned. Dina stopped by one afternoon to say good-bye to Yasmin, too. She and her husband, Mahmoud, had decided to visit with a relative of his in Los Angeles. The man had offered Mahmoud a job at his grocery store, and Dina told Yasmin they were going to check things out before they made a decision to move there.

Yasmin's mother did not stop calling, but Yasmin stopped answering the phone. She e-mailed Fatin every other day and told her she was still waiting to sell her car.

On the third week of September, a little after midnight, Yasmin's cell phone rang and awakened her. Jordan's area code appeared on the screen, followed by a number she did not recognize. She hesitated a little and then answered.

When she heard Sami's voice, she jumped out of her bed. "How are you, habibi? I miss you and Mira very much."

"When are you coming to get us, Mama? We are back from the trip."

"Soon," she said. "Did Baba ask you to call me?"

"No, I took his phone to the kitchen. Your name is on it. I know how to call."

"Let me talk to Mira." Yasmin could hear Mahir calling Sami. His voice was getting closer and closer.

"Come and get us, Mama," Mira said. There was silence after that. The screen no longer displayed the number.

Yasmin kept her gaze on the phone, smiling as if reacting to a beautiful dream right after waking. She just had a few happy moments, the first in months. She lay in bed with Sami's and Mira's pajamas, holding them tight. As much as she had dreaded going back before, now she decided to leave as soon as she could.

CHAPTER THIRTY-ONE

Though Yasmin was looking forward to seeing Sami and Mira, leaving Arizona with a one-way ticket was very disconcerting. Not that it meant she would never be back, but given what she had been through and how she had little or no control over it, fear overpowered any other emotion and impaired judgment. The ticket had arrived by mail four days earlier. Not certain if opening a savings account that week was a good decision as opposed to holding on to her money, she did it anyway. Mostly because she needed to remain attached, have a constant connection. When Ellen had given her the money for the car, Yasmin set aside $600, and the remaining $2,000 went into her new savings.

Looking around the house one more time before leaving that morning felt almost as painful as arriving without Sami and Mira. When Yasmin dragged her suitcases to the driveway and locked the door behind her, she took a last look at her house, her front yard, and her neighborhood. The night before, her neighbor Beth had come over and said her good-byes, and they had exchanged addresses and phone numbers. While she waited for Ellen to pick her up and drive her to the airport, she remembered a verse from the Koran that her mother had made her write on their door in Amman, on the day that Yasmin had traveled with Mahir to America. "It will always bring you back," her mother had assured.

Yasmin took out a pencil from her purse and wrote on the dark wooden door, "He who has given you the Koran will surely bring you back to a place of return."

Soon after, Ellen pulled into the driveway. She helped Yasmin put her suitcases in the trunk, and then they were on their way. As they drove south on Hayden, heading toward the freeway, Yasmin gave her neighborhood a sad farewell look. She lifted her eyes to the sky and held her gaze for a long time, as if trying to memorize it. Ellen patted her on the knee.

"Look, Yasmin, as much as I'm happy for you because you're going to be back in the same country as your children, I'm very worried about you."

Yasmin turned and looked at Ellen. "In what way?"

Ellen released a long sigh. "Promise me you'll look after yourself. I can't help but expect the worse from Mahir and his father."

"I know what you mean. Don't worry. I'll be careful." Yasmin reached inside her purse and took out two keys and a piece of paper. She held them out. "Before I forget. Here are the keys to the house and the car and my parents' address and phone number."

Still looking ahead, Ellen said, "Oh, perfect. Put them in the glove compartment please." Airplanes flew overhead, getting bigger as they descended toward the airport that became visible from the freeway. Ellen drove past the terminal twice before she finally spotted a car leaving. She pulled over into the empty space, stepped out of the car, and helped Yasmin with her luggage.

"E-mail me as much as you can." Ellen gave Yasmin a long embrace.

"I will."

Yasmin dragged her suitcases through the sliding door and proceeded to the airline counter. Her suitcases were filled to their maximum with clothes, shoes, and toys. Despite her long hours of packing and unpacking and then donating again, she still had too much baggage. Shipping her paintings, paint, brushes, her easel, and the contents of the two plastic containers she had packed on the day she had a garage sale was definitely a good idea.

Security procedures were obviously causing delays. A long and snaky line of travelers preceded her, passports and tickets clutched in hands, anger and frustration deforming every face. She stood in line for over half an hour before she finally received her boarding pass.

At the security check, she took off her shoes and followed directions like some of the other passengers. At the boarding gate, however, a security officer pulled her out of the line and escorted her to a side room. As she was entering, a young Caucasian man was about to leave, dragging behind him a carry-on. He stopped and talked to the officer who had just finished instructing Yasmin on where to stand. Yasmin only caught the words *sue you*, as the man shouted with an angry Irish accent. After the officer mumbled something to him, the man said, "Fuck you," and walked away still cussing. At the sound of his words, a woman who sat on the floor by her scattered belongings looked up. She looked Middle Eastern to Yasmin; they exchanged a smile.

Six gloved hands performed their fifteen-minute excavations of Yasmin's purse and her handbag, while she stood separated from the three security officers by a long table. A male officer mentioned the Nintendo she had packed in her suitcase.

Yasmin shrugged. "Yes, I have one."

He then asked her why she was traveling with a one-way ticket. After Yasmin told him that she was moving back to Jordan, he nodded and continued his search. When it turned out that she was not a risk, she gathered her mess and stepped aside to make room for the next suspect. While bent over her handbag on the floor, trying to repack as fast as she could, the female of the security trio approached her.

"Do you speak the language of bin Laden and the Taliban?"

Yasmin kept her eyes down, tidying her things.

"Is the language difficult to learn?"

"I don't know." Yasmin wiped her forehead with the back of her hand. It was getting unbearably hot inside that little room. "To be honest with you, Miss, I had no interest in researching his background. Why don't you Google him and his friends on your break?"

"I want to join the CIA and fight the terrorism of that culture."

Yasmin turned her back and started walking out of the room, wondering what the CIA would do with a brain like that. Even if pure luck played a factor in getting this woman's application processed in the first place, Yasmin doubted she would ever make it beyond a first interview.

An airline employee outside the door instructed Yasmin to go directly to the nearby boarding gate. Yasmin nodded and continued on her way without making eye contact with anyone. Once she entered the plane, she ignored all the eyes that examined her, speculating on her origins and religion, and walked to her seat at the back of the plane. She wished at that moment like she had many times in the past that she could gather all the uneducated people of the world, sit them in front of a gigantic map of the world, and explain the following: There are twenty-five Arab countries in the world, and what unites them is the Arabic language. You don't have to be Muslim to be an Arab; you could be Christian too. Furthermore, Iran, Turkey, and Afghanistan are not Arab countries, but the majority of their populations are Muslim, and so are the majority of the populations of forty-four other non-Arab countries around the world.

Thirty minutes passed while Yasmin was lost in her thoughts. When the last passenger delayed by airport security boarded, the plane took off.

Fatin met Yasmin at the airport and immediately updated her on whatever she knew about Mahir and the children. They had settled at his parents' house in Irbid after returning from Germany. Mahir had enrolled Sami and Mira in a private elementary school and started his new job teaching at the Jordan University of Science and Technology. Fatin also told Yasmin about her father's car accident three weeks ago. She said it was minor enough to keep from Yasmin, especially since Yasmin already had too much to take care of and worry about. Though he only suffered a minor pain in the neck as a result, her mother and Majid had convinced him never to drive again. They feared for his safety and thought it was about time for him to let Majid help him run his errands. They had talked him into selling both cars, the old and the new, and he had agreed.

"People in America get to be ninety or even older but still depend on themselves if they are in good health," Yasmin told Fatin.

"I know, but this is Jordan. There is nothing wrong with having a son take care of his father in his old age. It's what's expected from him."

Yasmin and Fatin chatted on the way about Yasmin's difficult experience in Scottsdale and about how much she had missed Sami and Mira. When they arrived at the house, and after Yasmin hugged and kissed everyone, she pretty much repeated to all of them what she had told Fatin on the way. And, of course, listened to her parents repeat what Fatin had already told her about her father and about Mahir and the children.

That evening Lina telephoned Yasmin and told her how Sami's and Mira's constant nagging and crying had denied Mahir and his parents any signs of a calm or normal life ahead.

The news delighted Yasmin. "What did Mahir and his parents expect? Sami and Mira would forget all about me because they took them on a trip?"

After Yasmin hung up with Lina, she took out her phone book and called Mahir. Ellen's warnings were still ringing in her head, but that did not lessen her longing for Sami and Mira. The phone had barely finished the first ring when the voice of Mahir's mother came through.

Yasmin skipped the greeting. "Can I talk to Mahir?" After the sidewalk encounter, showing courtesy to Mahir or any member of his family was the least of her concerns.

"Yes, one moment."

Yasmin was surprised. She expected Mahir's mother to claim he was out like she always did. Maybe she did not recognize her voice.

Mahir came to the phone by the time she finished her thought.

"I want to talk to the children, Mahir." She sounded like she was giving an order, not asking for a favor.

"Sure," he said in a calm tone, without a trace of his usual attitude.

Yasmin could hear him put the phone receiver down and then call out for Sami and Mira.

"Mama, are you back from Arazona?"

"Yes, I am, Mira."

"Did you bring all my toys?"

"Some of them. Did you have a good time in Germany?"

Mira began to cry, and Yasmin heard Mahir trying to calm her down.

Sami's voice came to the phone. "Mama, when are you going to take us home?"

"As soon as I can, Sami. Let me talk to Baba now." She gathered her strength and took a deep breath. "Mahir, I want to see them. We also need to talk."

Mahir promised to call back to schedule a meeting.

While Yasmin waited to hear back from him, Lina called her every day with a rumor that either confirmed the reunion or vowed it would never take place. Lina said that when Abu Mahir found out from Mira about the meeting, he was enraged and very disappointed. He and Mahir's mother started indulging Sami and Mira with toys and candy the following days, hoping their gifts might help their grandchildren forget their mother for a while. Sami and Mira ignored all the bribes and never stopped talking about Yasmin as they looked forward to seeing her.

Four days later, Mahir finally called back and set the date for Friday at noon at Irbid's McDonald's.

Yasmin agreed. The restaurant was a public place, and if Mahir lost his temper and acted crazy for some reason, she could handle the situation.

A few hours after Mahir called, Yasmin's aunts came to the house dressed in their athletic uniforms, loaded with enthusiasm and optimism.

"This time you have to play your cards right," Nihad said as she walked toward the family room. "When you go see him and the children, don't look like a coal sack. You never wear anything that isn't black." She shook her head a few times in disapproval and then sat down next to Yasmin's mother.

"I don't care what he thinks of my looks, Khalto Nihad," Yasmin smiled. "I don't care what anybody thinks anymore. If he doesn't agree to let me have the children this time, I'm suing for custody."

"Why go to court if you can solve the problem between the two of you?" Yasmin's mother sat forward in her seat. She picked up the remote, turned the television off, and looked around searching for anyone to back her up.

Yasmin did not reply, and neither did Fatin or her aunts.

Since Fatin and Majid had to attend a soccer game at their children's school on Friday, Yasmin's mother decided to arrange with a cabdriver and go with Yasmin to Irbid. Nihad and Samira volunteered to join.

Friday morning Yasmin's aunts approved her makeup but agreed that she could have looked better if she had plucked her eyebrows thinner. They loved the pink top they talked her into wearing but said she should have worn a skirt instead of jeans. Nihad sat next to Yasmin in the backseat and on the way gave her advice on winning Mahir back. Yasmin knew her mother had put Nihad in charge of that task, so she replied to Nihad's whispering with polite nods. Halfway through the drive to Irbid, her mother and her aunts stopped the driver a few times to buy lettuce and cucumbers from the farmers scattered on the side of the freeway and said on the way back that they would pick up some walnuts and pine nuts from the vendors they saw on the other side.

When they dropped Yasmin off at the sidewalk of McDonald's, her mother mentioned the restaurant that would be their rendez-vous later and then handed Yasmin her cell phone.

"Keep it with you just in case. Call Nihad if you need directions."

Yasmin rushed toward the entrance, pulled the glass door open, and slid inside. At first glance, the place looked like any McDonald's in America. The smell of frying mixed with cigarette smoke was overwhelming though, probably due to a lack of proper ventilation. Sami and Mira ran and collided with her, as she knelt on the floor with open arms. They rested their heads on her chest and surrendered to her random kisses and her pressing arms. Mahir stared at her from a booth, and so did a group of college students sitting in the far corner and the three employees standing behind the counter. The woman who appeared to be in her midthirties and had her hair pulled into a tight bun went back to putting together an order. An older man turned and started talking to the young employee, a handsome teenager with dark and curious eyes.

Yasmin took Sami and Mira back to their Happy Meals.

"Hi, Yasmin." Mahir looked her over. "You look good." He held a cup of coffee in one hand and a cigarette in the other. The disposable aluminum ashtray he had placed next to the napkin holder was already full of cigarette ends.

"Thank you…how are you?"

Mahir shrugged. "Fine, I guess."

She turned to Sami and Mira; they both had their eyes on her as if examining some phenomenon. She kissed both of them again. "Go ahead and finish your food."

"Mira, come back here and sit next to me," Mahir said. "It's too crowded on the other side."

Mira slipped under the table and came out from Mahir's side. She held a fry between her fingers and dipped it in a small cup of ketchup.

"Watch it! You see what you did?" Mahir snapped. "You have ketchup all over your fingers. Now you're going to get it on your clothes."

"Calm down. It's OK; that's what children do. They get dirty, and then you clean them up."

"Well, I'm tired of doing it. It's never-ending."

"You finally figured that out?"

Mahir began to sweat. His nervous fingers traced his mustache. He lit a cigarette while one was still alive in the little ashtray. "I work till six. The children return from school at two thirty. It's too much work for my parents."

"Well, I don't know what to say. You're the one who took them."

"You should've been here sooner."

"What for? So you could trash me every time I tried to see them?"

"I can't work and take care of them. They have too much homework. They're learning a new language."

"What are you getting at? Last time I saw you, you made it very clear that you didn't want me anywhere near you or them."

"You know what I'm getting at." Mahir looked down. He cleared his throat a few times, and then without looking at Yasmin he continued, "I think we should reconcile."

"Really? Just like that? I just came back from Scottsdale, Mahir. I not only went through hell while throwing away our past but also know everything you did behind my back."

Mahir looked down.

"You obviously want me back because I serve a purpose, which is fine. I want nothing more than to be with my children and take care of them. But you…I don't know if I ever want to be with you. I can't trust you anymore. You cheated on me and then tricked me. You took away my children and the house and wrecked our lives."

Mahir continued to look down.

"You left me helpless weeping over my ruin, and to this day, you face me with this despicable attitude as if it were all my fault while we both know very well what went on back in Scottsdale."

"Watch that damn ketchup! Use a fork for God's sake!" Mahir yelled at Mira.

Mira flinched, and Sami shifted in his seat and then reached for his fork.

Yasmin ran her fingers through Sami's hair. "It's OK." Her eyes shifted between him and Mira.

"Look, I did what I did because I love you—"

Yasmin laughed. "Sorry, go on."

He gave her a look. "I had no choice. I thought if I let you and the children return, then we would have divorced and never had a chance to patch things up. The house and the credit cards… well, I didn't want to make it easy for you to live without me. I just couldn't imagine us not being a family anymore."

"Really, Mahir? Is this the best you can do to justify everything you did? I wish you'd stop treating me like I was five years old. I know there's more to what happened than you are willing to admit. Nothing you said or did since it all started has made sense. So I don't understand why you expect me to put all that hell behind me now and act as if none of it ever took place. The children? I have the right to custody, and you know that. If you want to punish me any further for your own mistakes, you can always make our lives miserable and not give me or the children a penny."

Mahir turned to Mira and slapped her hand. "You see what you did now?" He held her hand up, soaking in ketchup.

"God, Mahir. When do you ever stop? It's not the children's fault, so don't vent on them." She reached across the table with a napkin and wiped Mira's hand. "What does it take for you to admit your wrongdoing for once in your life? I can't believe you still have the nerve to act this way."

Mahir's face reddened. He rubbed his temples. "Sami, Mira," he said. "Go play. I want to talk to Mama."

Sami and Mira both shrugged.

"Let them finish their food."

Mahir ignored her. "*Now!*"

Mira slipped under the table, and Yasmin let Sami out of the booth. They stood next to each other and held hands.

"It seems to me that you don't give a damn about anything anymore. I think you're looking for a new husband."

Yasmin did not deny or confirm. "You know what? I don't just feel like I don't know who you are anymore: I don't want to figure you out. I've seen wild animals with more conscience than you—"

"Shut your mouth!" He banged the table.

Still holding hands, Sami and Mira flinched and took a step closer to Yasmin.

"Keep your voice down; you're scaring the children."

"You don't tell me what to do, *sharmuta*!" Mahir shouted. He placed his hands on the table and tried to turn it over. The table did not move. It was bolted to the floor. When he stood up, Yasmin slid out of the booth and moved a few steps back. The three employees stood still and stared, and so did the students. Sami and Mira screamed when Mahir made a fist and raised his hand. One of the students came running and stood next to Yasmin. He wore faded jeans and had spiked hair.

"Do you need any help?…Would you like me to call the police?"

"She's my wife." Mahir took a step forward.

"I didn't ask you."

"Get the hell out of my face. This is none of your business. This is a private matter."

"Yeah, and this is a public place." The student looked at Yasmin again. "Shall I call the police?"

"I'm OK, thank you." She looked at Mahir. "You had to screw it up for the children, didn't you? I should've expected. You screwed up our lives without blinking. I'm getting out of here before this turns into a disaster. You will hear from my lawyer." Yasmin kissed and hugged Sami and Mira. "Mama has to go now."

They both started crying and clung to her legs.

"You will come and live with me soon. I promise." She patted their backs, wiped their tears, and turned to Mahir. "You know I'm going to take them through court anyway, so let me take them now." Holding their hands, she started to walk away.

"Like hell you will!" Mahir shouted and moved forward.

The student blocked him with his body.

Mahir shoved him with both hands.

He returned Mahir's shove.

Mahir scrunched up his face in disgust. "This is none of your damn business, you punk. Get the hell out of my face before I kill you."

"Kill me?" The student narrowed his eyes and pointed at his chest. "Who the hell do you think you are? If it weren't for the little children, I would've trashed you a long time ago. Besides, this is not a jungle; my friends can always call the police."

Mahir took a step forward. "Yeah? I'll tell them you're helping in a kidnapping."

The student did not move. He looked at Mahir as if he were eying an insect. "Nonsense."

The older man came out from behind the counter, said he was the manager and stood between Mahir and the student.

"let's not creat a sceen here," he said and placed his hand on Mahir's shoulder.

"Take your hand off me." Mahir looked down at the manager's hand.

The manager removed his hand. "I'm going to ask you nicely to keep your voice down and to let the Lady leave with the children. You all can go outside and settle this, otherwise I have no choice but to call the police."

"And accuse me of what?"

"Of creating chaos in a public place and attempting to hit a woman infront of children."

"Move out of my way. You are threatening an Ahmad who is trying to leave with the children he came in with. She is the one who should be escorted out by the police."

The older man and the student shook their heads. They both had a disgusted look all over their faces.

Yasmin had enough. She let go of Sami and Mira.

Mahir grabbed their hands and proceeded to walk out. Yasmin followed them to the parking lot and watched as Mahir put them in the car and then drove away.

"Are you OK? Can I do anything for you? Stop a taxi?" th student asked.

Yasmin shook her head. "That's very kind of you, but I'm fine. Thanks for everything."

"Allahu Akbar" echoed from the mosque across the street and the others nearby, calling for noon prayer. Since the cars of Friday worshippers had already blocked most of that street, Yasmin walked all the way down to the corner, shaking.

CHAPTER THIRTY-TWO

As soon as they returned from Irbid, Yasmin's mother called Hala in Cairo and gave her a briefing on Yasmin's meeting with Mahir and the children and then handed the phone to Yasmin. While Yasmin gave Hala the details of Mahir's outburst, her father, Majid, and Fatin listened with anger and contempt to Mahir. Though her mother and aunts had heard the story on their way back from Irbid, they still listened attentively, shook their heads, and repeatedly tsked their tongues. When an hour later Carole called and Yasmin repeated the story to her, every neck in the room craned in her direction, as if they were hearing the story for the first time.

Nihad cussed Mahir, opened her eyes wide, and waved both arms in the air. "No, no, no, no. This time, he has gone too far."

Her declaration sounded as if it were a new revelation, not that she hadn't already said it when Mahir took Sami and Mira, when he came to Yasmin's house and insulted her father, when he sued her, and when the sidewalk incident took place.

Lina called Yasmin the next day and told her that Mahir had visited with her family right after the McDonald's encounter. She said that her parents and even Fadi spoke of Yasmin with sympathy when they met with Mahir.

"Too late for that," Yasmin said. "I could've used their sympathy when they all sided with him and conspired against me."

Lina told Yasmin that Mahir was desperate to find a solution. He said that his father's temper had been unbearable since Friday, and that his mother complained even more about the children. They made too much noise and were too much work and too much responsibility, and on top of all that, they cried for Yasmin all the time.

Lina continued: Mahir also said that before he drove to Amman, his father had visited with some of his relatives and some of his old friends to gather opinions on how to handle the situation without bringing Yasmin into the picture. Most of his supporters thought that Mahir should take a second wife. Happy with their suggestion, Mahir's father had sworn on his father's grave that if Mahir agreed, he would find him a wife in less than a week.

"Mahir said they were miserable. Sami has severe diarrhea and has not spoken to anyone since Friday morning. Mira is spending most of her time clutching her blanket, staring, and crying."

"Oh God."

"Look, Mahir asked my dad if he could convince you to reconcile because otherwise he would have no choice but to rent a small place and hire a maid to take care of the children."

Yasmin thought for a few seconds. "Tell your father this, Lina. If Mahir agrees to transfer the children to a school in Amman and take care of all their expenses, he can go get married if he wants. But he will not bring a stepmother to Sami and Mira or even think about having them raised by a maid."

⊫⊪

Suka the maid handed Yasmin the phone. "It's your khalo. He wants to talk to you, madam." Yasmin stared at the receiver for a few moments while her mother stood beside her. She had not seen her uncle or even spoken to him in years. When he and his family moved to Amman and made up with her parents, she had already moved to Arizona. After she found out how her uncle and Fadi had sided with Mahir and his father, she knew she had done the right thing by not calling him when she had arrived in the country to attend Hala's wedding.

Her uncle repeated what Lina had already told her about the last meeting with Mahir and then asked, "Can you please come over so we can discuss this further?"

Yasmin figured that Lina must have given her uncle the message she intended for Mahir, and now her uncle was going to discuss Mahir's reply.

"Khalo…why should I come? You can go ahead and tell me Mahir's decision over the phone. I don't really want to come to your house. I'm very hurt by the way you all treated me."

"Will you ever forgive your khalo for misunderstanding the truth?" His tone was slow and gentle. Yasmin could not decide if it was real or fake remorse she was sensing in his voice.

"Come, Yasmin. I promise you'll leave this house happy."

Yasmin sighed. "OK, fine. I'll come."

Even though Yasmin's mother was still on bad terms with her brother, she seemed optimistic about his call and urged Yasmin to leave the house at once.

"I hope you come back with good news." She lifted her palms to the sky and muttered a prayer.

A nice breeze played around the neighborhood that afternoon, so Yasmin strolled the short distance to her uncle's house. She passed neighbors sitting on their front porches or in their carports under grapevines, children playing in front yards, and some riding their bikes out on the streets. A vendor pushed a cart stacked with tied bunches of roasted green garbanzo and shouted, "*Hamleh!*" going up the hill, losing momentum with every step. He stopped when children gathered around him, and his face reddened from supporting the weight of his cart with his small, thin body.

Lina was waiting for Yasmin on the sidewalk by her house under a big olive tree. She took her hands out of her jeans pockets when Yasmin approached, and tossed her long braid behind her back. She gave Yasmin a long hug.

"Good to see you, Yasmin. Please listen to my father to the end before you react." She pointed to the door where he was standing.

"I wouldn't be here if I had any other intentions."

Yasmin's uncle hugged and kissed her, patted her on the back, and walked her to the family room. She immediately noticed that he had colored his white hair brown, but his skin and his posture still gave away his old age. He wore a wrinkled beige caftan and looked like he had just awakened from his afternoon nap. The small family room had a coffee table in the middle and a couch on each side. Yasmin and her uncle sat on one to the left. On the wall above it hung a framed print of a big fruit bowl.

Lina entered the room shortly after, carrying a tray of coffee cups. Her mother followed right after, wearing a pink short-sleeved caftan and with her hair pulled back in a bleached bun. The parting through her black roots stood out like a runway in a desert. She greeted Yasmin and sat on the opposite couch. When Fadi entered the room, he said hello and sat next to his mother facing Yasmin. Yasmin did not greet him back. He sipped his coffee while glancing at her. His glances were more like quick snapshots. Yasmin knew he was waiting for the right moment to start his usual interference, but she was determined not to give him a chance.

"I love you very much," Yasmin's uncle said in a quivering voice, his eyes watering. "I want you to know that I was misled to believe—" His throat trapped the rest of his sentence. His shoulders shook up and down as he covered his eyes with a tissue.

Yasmin did not know what to make of his sudden burst of emotions. She looked at his wife.

"We want to do whatever it takes to fix the situation," his wife said.

Fadi attempted to speak. "I think—"

"If you don't stay out of it, I'll leave now." Yasmin took a cigarette out of her purse and lit it.

Fadi did not attempt to speak after the look his father gave him.

"I had a long talk with Mahir." Her uncle sniffled and wiped his nose. "The children are in very bad shape. We want to help you and Mahir reconcile for their sake."

"How is this going to be possible after all he did?"

"Look, we now realize that Mahir had twisted some facts and overreacted. He wanted to keep you, and keep the family intact, but I guess he panicked, took some bad advice, and did not know how to fix the situation after taking the children and making it financially impossible for you to be on your own. So apparently he meant well."

"He meant well? Is that how you all justify what he did?" She looked around the room. "Honestly, I find all this hard to believe."

"I understand how you feel, but it seems that we have no other way to deal with the problem without jeopardizing the best interests of the children."

"Oh? Finally everybody realized the importance of the children's well-being?"

"Look, I know you can get custody, but think of the consequences for the children. They are hurting enough now. Don't you think they will hurt even more if they were to live without their father? That's what I mean by doing what's best for them. They need both of you."

Her uncle's concern for Sami and Mira made sense. Yasmin still remembered how they cried themselves to sleep for weeks after Mahir had moved out. "So what is expected from me now?"

"I think both of you should take responsibility for what happened, and I also think you should both start over without rehashing the past."

"No." Yasmin shook her head. "This isn't fair."

"I agree." He pressed his lips. "But it's up to you to decide if your children are worth the sacrifice."

If Yasmin had read her own story from the beginning until this moment as a work of fiction, this would be the time for her to toss the book aside because of how unconvincing it had become. She would have turned off the television if she had been watching all the unbelievable and sickening details of her own melodrama unfold in a movie. Yasmin's long months of humiliation, her agony over the loss of children and her ruined life, obviously did not weigh much on anybody's justice scale. But why should that surprise her? Mahir was not just a man to all of them after all; he was an Ahmad.

"There's one more thing." Her uncle rubbed his hands, as if applying lotion.

Yasmin had a feeling he was about to mention the agreement the referee wrote on behalf of Mahir. She knew it was a matter of time before somebody brought that subject up. Now that she had made her intentions for retaining custody clear, Mahir was probably thinking his stupid agreement was actually some kind of insurance he would hold in his hand.

"The agreement?" she asked.

"Yes." Her uncle looked half-relieved.

Yasmin stared at the ashtray long enough to feel everyone in the room inflate with anxiety. Her father had actually remembered to call and consult his old friend, the retired judge, about the agreement. His friend had told him back then that the agreement not only read as if it were written by a law-school trainee but was a waste of ink and paper. It could not stand before any judge in the world and pass as legal. A woman did not need her husband's permission to leave the country according to the Jordanian law. Furthermore, denying Yasmin the custody of her children for no legitimate reason was unfounded.

She finally spoke. "OK. I'll sign it." Yasmin made it sound like she was doing them all a favor. She could feel their bodies deflate as they all sighed.

"Believe me, one day you will look back and laugh at all this. If anyone ever tells you that what happened to you does not interrupt almost every marriage, don't you dare trust them." He put his arm around her and patted.

Laugh? Trust? Yasmin did not comment.

"Shall I call Mahir now?" her uncle asked. "He's waiting for my call somewhere nearby."

"That's fine. Go ahead."

Yasmin's eyes had always given her away no matter how hard she tried to hide her feelings. Mahir always claimed that she had a certain look that made people feel small, transparent, and defenseless. Now to prove her good intentions, for the sake of Sami and Mira, she had to make sure not to look Mahir in the eye. She even had to fake a smile during the meeting, had to act, be a part of the big production everybody was directing horribly: her life.

When Mahir arrived, her uncle made him shake hands with her. "The kiss afterward."

Everybody faked a swift laugh.

Mahir looked tired; his beard was a couple of days old, and he had his old and worn-out jogging suit on. He did smell of cologne, but knowing Mahir, Yasmin figured it must have been a last-minute touch before getting out of his car. He always kept a bottle in the glove compartment. He set a dossier on the coffee table and sat next to Fadi. Lina and her mother gathered the empty cups and left the room. The silence that followed, although just a moment, felt awkward to Yasmin. She lit a cigarette.

Mahir leaned back and crossed his legs. When Yasmin noticed how fast his foot vibrated, a dose of power settled in her.

"I think we should follow a new life order," Mahir said without looking at her. "You will concentrate on the children, and we will both work hard to prevent our family from shattering again."

Yasmin nodded, pondering his ludicrous statement. He made it sound like he was giving her a new task, as if she had ever done anything other than take care of her children.

Lina and her mother came back a few minutes later with a new round of turkish coffee. After they served it, Lina sat next to Yasmin, and her mother sat next to Fadi and Mahir.

Mahir took a sip of his coffee. "We are going to start a new page now."

Yasmin resumed acting her part with convincing talent; she nodded again, hoping his new page was not going to be on his same old notebook.

"I will pick you up as soon as I find a place in Irbid," Mahir continued. "It's going to be furnished, of course. This will be our trial period. When things between us go back to normal, we will both discuss other options and further plans."

"That's fine."

"Now it's time for the kiss," her uncle said.

Laughter and applause filled the room.

Mahir held his dossier and walked to Yasmin while Lina got up to make room for him. He leaned over and kissed her on the cheeks before he sat down. After she signed the agreement, Mahir and Fadi talked about the changing weather and the rain predictions broadcast that morning. Then they talked a little about the situation in Iraq and the Iraqis who were flooding the country. And of course, as Yasmin expected, Fadi blamed the greedy Americans for the suffering of the Iraqi people. Yasmin's uncle nodded, but Mahir did not comment.

When Yasmin stood up to leave, Mahir insisted on driving her to her parents' house in his new red Mitsubishi hatchback. On the way, Mahir held her hand like he had when they dated, during their engagement, and in the first few months of their marriage. Yasmin pretended to need her hand to light a cigarette even though she was almost home. The swift reconciliation meeting only guaranteed her reunion with her children, but it did not eliminate Mahir's deception or his ability to lie and humiliate her, even in public. Trusting him was a mistake of the past.

CHAPTER THIRTY-THREE

"Yasmin." Her mother stood behind her, holding a mug in her hand. "Did I ever tell you how my mother, God rest her soul, made me go back to your father in the same cab when I tried to leave him once?"

Yasmin dragged the hose to the other planter full of geraniums. "Six hundred million times, Mama."

"Life has to go on. Be smart when dealing with your husband."

"Be smart how? By looking the other away and pretending everything was perfect or maybe by looking behind my back this time, Mama?" She immediately regretted saying that.

"You see, I was right." Her mother wagged her index finger. "You haven't learned a thing from your ordeal, Yasmin, and that worries me to death."

"Don't worry, Mama. I learned more than you can imagine."

"Good. Then you won't go through that hell all over again and drag us all with you?"

"I didn't drag anybody, Mama. I'm the one who got burned. The rest of you only felt the heat from the distance you kept." She could see confusion on her mother's face.

"What in God's name are you saying? You're not making sense anymore."

"I don't know if anything makes sense around here. I'm surprised I still have some of my sanity left."

"Oh, stop it. Your father is very happy for you."

"I'm sure he is."

"For the first time in months, he slept through the night."

"Thank God for that, Mama."

Her mother called Hala in Cairo that day and gave her the great news, and as she always did when she was done with her part, she handed the phone receiver to Yasmin. Hala congratulated Yasmin and wished that soon enough Mahir would reconsider this arrangement and all of them would move back to Arizona.

Yasmin's aunts called that evening to congratulate her, too, and promised to come over soon and celebrate her reconciliation.

When Yasmin hung up with them, she called Carole and gave her the news.

"Congratulations. I knew it was going to end like this from the beginning. It was just a matter of time."

"How did you know?"

"That's how things work in Jordan. I've seen it a million times. Now that you're going to live here for a while, you'll understand." Before they hung up, Carole urged Yasmin to be cautious and look after herself, and then they hung up.

Before Yasmin went to bed that night, she borrowed Fatin's laptop and e-mailed Ellen with the news.

To: Pat34@azmail.com
From: Yasmin@jomail.com
Subject: The new developments

Dear Ellen,

I know this may come as a shock to you, but Mahir and I made up. I don't know where to start. Whatever I say would not make sense to you and would probably leave you confused. I'm moving to Irbid, Mahir's hometown, and I can't wait to see the children. It might be a while before I can check my mail, so don't worry if you don't hear from me for a while. Please send my regards to Dina and update her on my news.

Take care,
Yasmin x o x o x

Two days later Mahir called Yasmin and said that he had found a furnished apartment and he and the children would pick her up the next evening. Majid came to her room that night and gave her a cell phone as a gift, along with three hundred dinars.

"Thank you so much, Majid. I really appreciate it."

"Don't hesitate to call, especially if, God forbid, something goes wrong. I don't care if it's in the middle of the night," Majid said.

"Something like what?"

"Calm down. I didn't mean anything bad. I'm just trying to tell you that whenever you need me, I'm here for you."

The next evening Yasmin said her good-byes to her family and stepped out to the front balcony to wait for Mahir and the children. She dragged her bags to the gate, opened her purse and checked whatever she had left of her allergy medicine, and made sure she did not forget the cell phone Majid had given her. She opened her duffel and made sure she had not forgotten to pack the sheets, pillowcases, towels, and the blanket she had taken from her mother, because she was certain that Mahir would not think of buying new ones before they moved into that furnished apartment.

The gradual descent of the sun had left parts of the sky stained with an orange hue. The distant streetlights flickered, and the ones that lit the mosque minarets were green. "Allahu Akbar" reverberated from a mosque nearby, and in seconds, a temporary silence fell over the city. The setting filled Yasmin with both fear and anticipation. When the call for prayer ended, Mahir's red car appeared, making its way up the hill.

The moment he stopped, she opened the back door and leaped at Sami and Mira, kissing and hugging them. Mahir kept the car running, while he placed her suitcases in the trunk.

When he came back, he had a smile on his face, a smile that Yasmin had seen before and immediately recognized as fake.

Still sitting between Sami and Mira, her arms tight around them, she said, "I hope you don't mind, but I'm staying in the back with the children."

"That's fine." Mahir lit a cigarette and drove down the street. "Tomorrow morning when I drive the children to school, I'll give our address to the principal's office so the children can return by bus." He looked at her in the rearview mirror. "Make sure you wait outside at two thirty for them, not just tomorrow but every day."

"OK." Yasmin looked at Sami and Mira. "Do you like your new school?"

"Yes," Mahir said.

Sami and Mira nodded, but their eyes said otherwise.

The night had blackened everything by the time Mahir reached the freeway. Lights appeared in pairs every now and then and flashed inside the car before they disappeared. Mahir turned the radio on and rotated the dial back and forth until he found the news. The news anchor said that, according to Reuters, the war was no longer a subject for speculation and the American and allied troops were expected to arrive in the region any day.

Sami and Mira melted in Yasmin's arms. Halfway through the forty-five-minute drive, they fell asleep. She closed her eyes and tried to imagine what her life with Mahir would be like now, but no scenarios came to her mind. She did not know what to expect anymore, and all she could think of was how Mahir turned out to be capable of deception and cruelty. She pressed Sami's and Mira's bodies close to hers.

A while later Yasmin opened her eyes, awakened by the sounds of a busy street. They passed Irbid's Safeway, and then Mahir turned right and drove by a *bus station* and *taxi station*.

"We're almost there," he said.

Yasmin looked around. Only a few parts of that area were visible under the dim streetlights; everything else was black shapes against the night sky. Mahir drove two more miles and then pulled over by a small garage that had a corrugated-iron gate secured in place with a big brass lock. The sign over it read Paradise Mini Market. A group of women that had just passed by the store turned around and stared at Mahir's car for a few seconds before they continued to stroll and munch on whatever they had in small paper bags.

"Wait here." Mahir took his cell phone out. "I have to go get the key."

"From where?"

"From Basim."

"Basim who?"

"My father's driver." He turned the light on and scrolled down his list of contacts.

"Why does he have the key?"

"Because he owns the place." He looked back. "Any more questions?"

"Don't snap at me like that. I'm just asking."

When Mahir stepped out of the car, Yasmin looked across the street. Black garbage bags shone under a beam of glow falling from a pole. The more she stared, the more objects around the bags that became visible. There was an empty gallon of corn oil, newspapers, and a broken stroller. Two or three houses on the street were lime-stone. Most of the other houses and buildings were block covered with gray stucco, and old and shabby-looking cars were parked on both sides of the street.

Mahir came back and knocked on the window. A man about his height, maybe his age, stood behind him, smiling.

Yasmin rolled the window down.

"Let's go," Mahir said. "They can't find the front-door key. We have to use the kitchen door for a while."

Yasmin opened the door and let Sami out first.

"*Masa'-el-Kheir* (good evening)," the man said, still smiling.

"This is Basim," Mahir said.

Now that she was outside the car, Yasmin remembered seeing him once, a long time ago. He had the same irritating smile, rude and bulging eyes, thick black mustache, and head full of hair combed back. He wore a blue T-shirt, black sweatpants, and thick-heeled slippers.

Basim led them through a sliding iron gate, swaying a little as he walked. He stopped in the middle of a small paved area and pointed to the building of plastered and whitewashed blocks.

"This is it. The one with the balcony," he said.

Yasmin noticed that he made an effort to stand still before he walked again.

They passed under a canopy of grapevines, growing on a pergola of thin welded water pipes and wires. A narrow concrete path led them to the back of the building.

"This is the staircase." Basim pointed. "This is the water-pump switch. When your tank on the roof gets empty, you pump water from the well," he said as he stepped closer to Yasmin.

Yasmin flinched and turned her head away. His breath smelled of alcohol. His clothes smelled like they had been sitting in a hamper with other dirty clothes for days if not weeks. Basim turned the key and opened the kitchen door, a metal door painted white with a small glass window on each side. Yasmin entered last. To her left, a rusted green refrigerator balanced on wood planks, and behind it, a covered table surrounded by three patio chairs leaned against the wall. Over the sink that separated the yellow cabinets from the stove was a big and undressed window. The kitchen walls were tiled from floor to ceiling, and though they were all one color, the tiles on each wall had different shapes and sizes. Surrounding the light switch, there were six rectangular tiles that consummated a peacock. Yasmin assumed they were a recent addition since the caulking was white and clean. A bulb hung on a black cord and dangled from the ceiling, close to an opening that functioned as a storage area. From where Yasmin was standing, she could see pots, plastic containers, and a baby walker.

Outside the kitchen, Basim pointed to the right. "This is the guest bathroom." He turned his head to look at Yasmin and Mahir, his silly smile still attached to his face. He then proceeded to a small foyer and pointed to an old Japanese washing machine that had two tubs. The faucets above it were soldered shut. Basim said the washing machine had to be filled with a bucket and drained through the hose sticking out from the side. He continued down the hallway and pointed left.

"This is the family room. It has four points of entry. Two doors you can acces from the hallway, one you can acces from the master bedroom and of course the main door.

The room was big, lit by five neon tubes mounted above each door Basim had pointed out. A huge chandelier hung from the center, missing all bulbs. The main door was metal too, double the size of the kitchen door, with bigger and longer glass windows, panes painted white. On the right side of the room lay an old gray couch and four matching seats. Disgusted from that sight, Yasmin turned and looked at the big dining table that was surrounded by scraped, torn, and squatting chairs. She felt nauseous. She took a deep breath.

Basim walked ahead and pointed to the right. "This is one of the bedrooms."

Yasmin glanced inside at the complete brown Formica bedroom set and said nothing. She glanced inside the other bedroom Basim was showing Mahir. It was the one Basim had pointed out when they were outside, and it had a door leading to the balcony.

The door did not have a key. Mahir pushed the handle down, and the door opened.

"We can lock it with a chair for now," Basim said. "I'll look for the key."

Mahir did not comment. He seemed very much at ease.

By the end of the hall, there was a sink. Basim opened the door to its right. "This is the master bathroom."

The big hole in the ground was the toilet, a showerhead had no tub underneath it, and the space he called a bathroom was not accessible from the room he called the master bedroom. The furniture of that room was of dark wood. Pairs of carved peacocks faced one another on the headboard, the cupboard doors, and the broken frame of the mirror, held together by duct tape and hammered to the dresser with big nails.

Water pipes snaked their way around the apartment, passing from room to room through holes in the walls. Basim explained how they had added central heating to the apartment years after his father had built it because they could not rent it in the winter. Naked wires stuck out of many uncovered sockets. Clusters of old and dried glue stained the hallway and the bedroom floors where there used to be wall-to-wall carpet a long time ago.

Yasmin held Sami's and Mira's hands while something sharp formed in her throat. It felt like razors when she swallowed. Sami and Mira lifted their heads and looked into her eyes. Their little palms still in her hands, she gave them an assuring tug. She then looked at Mahir and waited for his reaction. Mahir and Basim started a conversation that Yasmin tuned out. Flashes of her house back in Scottsdale passed like arrows through her head. Looking down at the floor, streaked with crusted old glue, she remembered complaining so many times about the broken tiles under the sink. She never imagined that one day she would actually regret ever complaining or getting frustrated over such a simple thing. Now she felt how much her house with all its unremarkable glitches was a blessing that she did not appreciate. She felt a twitch in her heart. Her house back in Scottsdale was not extravagant, yet everything in it was tidy and clean. It was so inviting and comforting, so full of sweet memories of her own, not an accumulation of the memories of the many strangers that had occupied it over the years.

"It isn't much," Basim said, bringing Yasmin back to reality.

Yasmin stared at him as he smiled and shifted his eyes between her and Mahir, waiting for a reply.

"No, it's perfect," Mahir said. "We'll take it."

Yasmin felt her heart stop. She pressed harder on Sami's and Mira's hands. Why was Mahir pretending to like the apartment when he could have easily afforded a place ten times better?

As soon as Basim left, Mahir said he was going to bring their suitcases from the car.

Yasmin stared at him. "Perfect? I'm not spending the night here with a broken door." She trembled. "Unless of course you're planning on getting one of us killed tonight…me for example."

Mahir stammered. He looked nervous. "What are you saying? Look, this is the best I could do in such short time. I'll go ask Basim for the key right now."

"You could've looked for a few more days."

"No, I couldn't, OK?" he snapped.

She flinched, and so did Sami and Mira.

"Calm down. This town is very safe. No need to make a big deal because of a missing key."

Sami and Mira moved closer to Yasmin. "It's OK," she whispered and walked them to the family room. She turned the television on manually and clicked the knob around until a picture appeared on the screen. Pikachu was rolling in the air, saying something in Arabic. She sat on the couch between them with her arms wrapped around them. "Everything will be OK."

When Mahir came back, he set her suitcases on the family-room floor. "I'm going to get our suitcases from my parents' house.

I left them there to make sure there was enough room for yours in the trunk. On the way back, I'm going to stop somewhere and get sandwiches or something to eat. Do you need anything else?"

"Don't forget the key."

"I won't. I'm going to see Basim right now."

After Mahir left, she dragged the suitcases to the Formica room and started unpacking.

CHAPTER THIRTY-FOUR

The next day, Sami and Mira drank their milk while staring at Yasmin and smiling.

"Can we stay with you today?" Sami asked.

"I would love that, but I don't think it's a good idea," Yasmin whispered to both of them. "Let's not make Baba angry. We will have all afternoon and all night together."

They looked disappointed, but they still nodded in agreement.

Both held her hand and walked to the bedroom to get dressed. Their uniforms were wrinkled and full of stains. "I'll wash them today."

It was so hard for Yasmin to see the looks on their faces when she said that. She could tell they were embarrassed. Both tried to wipe away the stains with their hands as if that would make them disappear. It broke her heart to see her children so vulnerable.

They had changed so much since she had last seen them, and it was not just the little signs of neglect on Mahir's part like wearing mismatched and untidy clothes or the obvious fact that they had not gotten a haircut since they had left Arizona. It was almost as if their souls had aged beyond their little sizes. She held their faces in her hands and said, "No one will ever take you away from me again."

They threw themselves in her arms.

Even though Mahir had brought the key to the door of the balcony room from Basim the night before, they had all slept in the Formica room, Yasmin and Mahir on the far sides of the king bed and Sami and Mira between them. Mira had awakened startled during the night, but when Yasmin pulled her close to her chest, she closed her eyes and went back to sleep.

When Yasmin finished dressing them, they walked together to the family room. Mahir was standing with his back to door, knotting his tie and watching the news.

"Should I pack lunches for Sami and Mira?"

"No, they have a canteen at school. I'll give them money," Mahir said without turning.

"Can you leave me some money? I need to buy more food, cleaners, and some other things."

He took out his wallet. "Here's a hundred dinars. That's all I have." He threw the money on the coffee table. "Let's go," he told Sami and Mira.

Yasmin picked up the money. If she spent it wisely, $130 would go a long way in Jordan.

Sami and Mira held each other's hands and followed him to the kitchen. Yasmin kissed them, handed them their backpacks, and then locked the door behind them. She walked to the bedroom and took out from her handbag a bag of turkish coffee, a notebook, and a pen. On her way back to the kitchen, she turned the water heater on.

She opened the upper cabinets and took out a turkish-coffee *doleh*. While she waited for the water to boil, she started her inspection of the kitchen. She found some plates, a few glasses, and coffee cups. Everything shy of half a dozen and most of it chipped and stained. Some coffee cups were missing their handles. In the drawers, she found wooden spoons, some rusted spatulas, screwdrivers, a wrench, a few stainless-steel spoons, and a couple of knives. Two aluminum pots, large enough to cook for an army or even a prison, were in the lower cabinets. She took them out and took out everything that she found broken, chipped, or rusted and placed them on the side of the kitchen table. When she finished making her coffee, she started writing a long list.

Half an hour later, she stepped out the kitchen door, dressed in jeans, a black top, and a denim shirt, buttoned up halfway. On a soil patch near the door, a boy around the age of five was supervising two younger girls while they filled the back of his plastic truck with weeds and rocks. When they finished, he dragged the truck by a rope tied to its front a few feet down and then asked the girls to come and empty the load onto a pile. When Yasmin shut the door behind her and locked it, they all stopped and stared at her.

The boy walked in her direction, and then the two girls followed him with reluctance. Yasmin's cell phone chanted the tune of an old folk song at that moment. She took it out of her pocket and stopped. So did the children.

"Good morning, Mama."

"Is everything OK?"

"Yes, everything is fine since last night, Mama." She took a few steps forward. "Say hello to everyone and tell them I'm fine."

Yasmin had not taken notice the night before of the olive trees that lined the front fence and the other three that grew in basins on the sidewalk. A laundry line zigzagged between the trees and the wrought iron of two thin windows of what looked like a basement under her apartment. Farther down from the windows, there was a door that she assumed led to a basement. She stepped out of the building and noticed that the garbage pile across the street had doubled since the night before.

Inside the Paradise Mini Market, a young woman sat behind a desk, wearing a hijab, a scarf that gave her tanned face a perfect roundness. When she smiled at Yasmin, her eyes glowed with kindness.

"You must be Yasmin, Mahir's wife."

"Yes, I am, and you?" Yasmin extended her hand.

"Tahani. Waleed's wife." She stood up and shook hands with Yasmin. "My husband and his brother Basim are distant relatives of Mahir. Did you know that?"

"No, I didn't." That explained why Mahir chose their apartment. It had nothing to do with being pressed for time. He probably wanted to do them a favor, besides having other motives in mind.

Tahani smiled again. "Waleed is home, taking a bath. I'm sitting in for him."

"I see." Yasmin heard a sound and looked behind her. There was a man dragging himself along the sidewalk. He looked young, in his early or mid thirties, and smelled of soap and aftershave. He wore brown plastic pants like the ones worn by men fishing in ponds or lakes.

"That's him." Tahani giggled.

Yasmin stepped back and made a passage for him. The children that had followed her stood behind him and stared at her.

"*Ahlan*," he welcomed Yasmin. "You must be Um Sami."

"Yes, I am."

"Welcome to Irbid." He slid behind the desk, pulled himself up, and sat on the revolving desk chair. He then slipped down the brown pants he wore over his jeans.

"Ah…I need to buy some things," Yasmin said. "Actually a lot of things." She looked around the small store.

"Go ahead, Um Sami. Just bring whatever you need here for me to add up." Waleed cleared his desk.

Yasmin nodded and started grabbing items from the shelves. Olive oil, thyme, rice, spices, beans, pasta, tuna cans, pickles, cereal, laundry detergent, and cleaners. She then moved to a big fridge with glass doors and again covered the desk with cheese, butter, eggs, milk, cold cuts, and chicken nuggets. Tahani stood next to Waleed and filled up bags with the things he had already added up and pushed aside. There was no cash register or even a calculator in front of him. He just added figures in his head and scribbled totals on a small piece of paper.

Yasmin placed a bag of flour and a bag of sugar in front of Waleed and Tahani and then scanned the candy shelf behind her, looking for chocolate chips. All she could see were candy bars with either Arabic or Turkish names. "Do you have M&M's?"

"No." Waleed shook his head. He scribbled a number and looked up. "I don't get them because they're too expensive, half a dinar each. Nobody buys them in this neighborhood. I can get them for you by the box, though."

"Great. Get me a box, please." Yasmin turned around and grabbed a few milk-chocolate candy bars and set them on the desk. "Do you know of a place that sells kitchenware, small appliances… that kind of stuff?"

"*Al-Mumtaz*," Tahani said. "It's very close, just around the corner." She pointed her finger in the direction.

"OK, that's good to know." Yasmin took the list from her pocket and gave it a quick check. She then stared at the cigarette case behind the desk.

"You smoke?" Tahani asked.

"Yes. What do you have in foreign?"

"Kent!"

"I didn't know they still made them," Yasmin joked. "I'll take a carton."

Yasmin paid forty-seven dinars for her groceries and lifted two bags off the floor.

"I'll help you," Tahani said and picked up a few.

"Thank you. That's very kind of you. Let's set them on the edge of the balcony for now, and then I can take them in when I go back inside."

A man in orange overalls, pushing a wheelbarrow, stopped by the garbage pile and started loading it.

"That's our garbageman," Tahani said. "If you pay him one dinar, he'll hose the balcony for you."

The children were still on the sidewalk staring. Yasmin and Tahani passed them a few times as they went back and forth.

Yasmin pointed to the children after she put down the last bag. "Yours?"

"No, these are Basim's children. Mine go to school." Tahani frowned at the children. "Go home."

"Would you like to come in and have coffee with me?" Yasmin asked.

Tahani's tanned face took on a pink glow, and her eyes widened in disbelief. "Really?"

"Yeah, really." They walked to the back of the building.

While the water boiled on the stove, Tahani helped Yasmin bring her groceries to the kitchen and put them away. She took her scarf off and sat down while Yasmin made the coffee.

"How old are your children, Tahani?"

"Murad is ten, Ferah is six, and Suha is four."

"Beautiful names."

Tahani looked around. "Do you like the apartment?"

"No, I don't." She poured the coffee in cups and sat facing Tahani.

Tahani smiled. "I didn't think you would."

"How come? You've never met me before."

"You know…from the things they said about you."

"Oh, I'm already popular?"

"Mahir's parents have been saying things about you…some of it not nice." Tahani looked down at her cup. "I don't believe any of it. I've been through a similar situation myself, so I know how it goes."

"No way."

Tahani nodded.

"So, you're not friends with your in-laws, Tahani?"

Tahani thought for a moment. She smiled. "Now we're OK. Each of them minds their own business. When I first married Waleed, we lived with his mother, Um Basim. She drowned me in housework. She and Basim's wife, Faridah, continuously taunted me because I came from a small and unknown family and because my father was not rich."

"How did Waleed react to that?"

"Well, at the beginning he used to get upset but kept telling me to let go and not to make a big deal out of it, until one day Um Basim asked me to clean Faridah's apartment because she was not feeling well, and I refused. She got furious and told Waleed that he should hit me. She pulled me by my hair and took me to him, and when he yelled at her and asked her to let go of me, she called him a wimp and a worthless cripple. Waleed got so upset that night that we took him to the hospital. He's had diabetes since then."

"God, Tahani. I can't believe she did this to both of you. It sounds like she's one of those controlling woman."

"Not as bad as she used to be. She still tries to get things her way sometimes, though. Like she actually told Waleed that our son Murad should quit school and help at the store. She tried a few times to make Ferah help her clean, and when I protested, she got mad and told me I should be grateful that someone like me had the honor of marrying into their family."

"What? You're kidding me. This family never ceases to amaze me. Is Um Basim's family also Ahmad?"

"Yeah."

"So, what did you tell her?"

"Oh, I got so mad and told her she's the one who should be thankful I married her son. You know one of their distant relatives is in prison for raping his cousin, and another for counterfeiting. Their last scandal came from a close cousin who fled to Syria after he had stolen fifteen thousand dinars from the bank he worked at."

"So why are they all so arrogant and full of themselves, especially Mahir's father?"

"They all still live in the shadow of their relative who was a general in the army and a few years before his death was awarded a medal for his achievements."

"Oh, I know about him, but the man died over twenty years ago."

"Correct. And not one member of their so-called important and influential family has lived up to his name."

Yasmin shook her head. "That is so ridiculous, you know. I mean, look what we both went through because of a name. It's not fair. So what did Waleed think of your confrontation with his mother? Was he upset over you mentioning his family's dirty past?"

"No, he wasn't. He told her that I was right, and since that day she kept her distance."

Yasmin offered Tahani a cigarette and lit it for her. "What happened to Waleed? I hope you don't mind me asking."

"*Shalal atfal* (infantile paralysis)," she said. "He used crutches before, but he doesn't anymore. It's easier for him to go up and down the stairs like that. Our apartment is the one underneath yours, the basement."

"I see. I guess he never got his immunizations?"

"I was told that when his father was alive, he was a merchant. He traveled a lot, and Waleed's mother traveled with him most of the time, so I guess that's why he never got his shots."

Yasmin and Tahani turned to the door at the sound of the handle being pressed down. "Mahir must be back for some reason."

The handle continued to go up and down. "No. That's probably Um Basim; she never knocks." Tahani put out her cigarette.

"Not anymore." Yasmin put out her cigarette too and then opened the small glass window on the door. "Yes?"

"I came to see you, welcome you to the neighborhood," the woman said.

Yasmin unlocked the door.

Um Basim pushed herself in, holding a yellow cake in her hand. She was in her late fifties, light skinned with dark eyes, wearing a long black dress and a white hijab. "You're here?" She squinted at Tahani.

Yasmin sensed resentment in her voice, as if implying that Tahani overstepped her by visiting Yasmin first.

"I was just leaving," Tahani said.

Yasmin held her hand up. "Wait, I'm leaving in ten minutes, too."

"Faridah made this cake for you. She couldn't come with me. She'll stop by some other time." Um Basim placed the cake on the table, pulled out a chair, and sat down looking around, inspecting. "Why do you have all these pots, plates, and glasses out?"

"You can have them if you want them. I have no use for them. I'm going to buy some new ones today."

Um Basim frowned, as if Yasmin had insulted her and failed to treat her old junk like the china of the Ming dynasty. "We cleaned everything," she said.

"I could tell." Yasmin poured coffee in a cup and placed it in front of Um Basim, who began to speak of the apartment like it was her inherited British castle. She told Yasmin how her late husband had built it with his own hands. How they all lived in the basement first and rented this one for years until they saved enough to build a smaller one above it for Basim and, above that, a studio for her. Then she went on explaining the history of the old furniture in the bedrooms and the living room while Yasmin and Tahani drank their coffee.

"The carpet in the family room is in four sections," she said. "We had to cut it up when we took it outside to wash it."

Yasmin nodded. "Yes. I noticed that. I wondered why you couldn't shampoo it in its place."

Um Basim seemed confused.

"I was wondering if someone could cover the exposed outlets," Yasmin said. "That's dangerous, you know."

"Yeah, that was on the list, but we didn't get to it. I'll have Basim take care of it," she said. "I have a bucket full of bulbs for the family-room chandelier. I'll have him take care of that, too."

Yasmin lit a cigarette. "How come the glass on the main door is painted white?"

"We did it because the neighbors complained about the tenants looking at them. Sometimes we rent for students, bachelors… you know."

Yasmin nodded again. They sat in silence for the next few minutes, and then Tahani said, "Thank you for the coffee." She reached for her scarf and started putting it on while she was getting up.

"You're welcome."

Um Basim stood up. "I have to go too. Come and visit sometime."

"I will," Yasmin lied. She opened the door for Um Basim. She then smiled and winked at Tahani. "I'll see you later if you want to go shopping with me," she whispered.

Tahani confirmed with a quick nod.

After she locked the door, she stared at Um Basim's cake for less than a second and without hesitating dumped it in the trash can.

A little after two thirty, Sami and Mira stepped out of a yellow bus full of children their age. Basim pulled over at the same moment and honked. His silly smile was all over his face.

Yasmin ignored him. "Hurry up. I'll meet you at the door," she told Sami and Mira from the balcony.

The chicken nuggets and french fries she had set on the kitchen table made Sami and Mira give her thank-you smiles like the ones little children would give to a kind and loving stranger. They both remained quiet as they ate and looked at her with shyness in their eyes. After their long separation, Yasmin felt like some ice had formed between her and her children, but it was no more than a sliver that she would easily break or melt away in one afternoon.

"You can eat your fries with your hand if you want." Yasmin smiled at Mira. "What did you do at school today?"

"We watched TV and wrote some letters, and then we made a drawing."

"Oh, that's nice. What did you watch on TV?"

"Songs."

Yasmin raised her eyebrows. "Really?" Yasmin was not sure if Mira was telling the whole truth. Maybe Yasmin needed to look into what Mira was saying and have a talk with Mahir about it. She then turned to Sami. "Do you have homework?"

"Yeah. Arabic is hard."

"Don't worry about it. I'll help you. When we finish studying, we can play a game or do something fun. Sound good?"

He smiled.

"Mira, you can watch TV or play with your dolls while Sami studies. OK?"

Mira nodded.

Mahir had enrolled Sami in first grade again as the school's principal had recommended, since Sami had no previous knowledge of the Arabic language. For that same reason, Sami's religion teacher had temporarily excused him from memorizing verses from the Koran; he pronounced the words in a way that made his classmates laugh, and she thought that was very disrespectful to God's words.

The first lesson in Sami's Arabic book was about the first five letters of the alphabet. When he finished reading them aloud to Yasmin, he repeated the words *Mama, Baba, dar* (house), and *door* (houses). He then tried unsuccessfully to read the few sentences under a small illustration of a family on the beach: A bearded father and his son were splashing around in the blue water. A mother wearing a scarf on her head sat under an umbrella. A little girl in braids drawing a picture sat on the other side.

An hour later when Sami finished his homework, Yasmin took out from her dresser a bag of beads she had brought back from

Scottsdale with her. She sat with Sami and Mira on the family-room floor and strung necklaces and bracelets like they had some-times back in Scottsdale. She surprised both of them later with the cookies she had baked that morning using crushed candy bars instead of chocolate morsels. The three of them were cuddling and giggling on the couch when, a little before five, Mahir called Yasmin from his cell.

"Let Sami and Mira meet me outside by the gate," he said. "I'm taking them with me to my parents' house."

"Why?"

"I need to pick up a few things I left there. We'll be back in minutes."

She looked at Sami and Mira as they both stared at her. This was not a good time to start an argument with Mahir. "Fine," she said and then hung up. "Baba is waiting for you outside."

They continued to stare at her.

"You'll be back in a few minutes," she said. She then walked them to the kitchen, kissed both of them, and let them out. They held each other's hands and stepped out, took a few steps, and then turned around.

"It's OK," she said in a soft tone. "I'll see you soon."

After the long months of separation from her children, Yasmin was hoping to spend every moment of their first day together, and obviously they were thinking the same.

When an hour passed and they were not back yet, Yasmin knew she was going to spend her first evening alone at the apartment. As much as she resented that, she kept herself busy by unpack-ing more of her things and rearranging some of the kitchen cabi-nets. Around nine thirty that night, Mahir and the children finally came back. Yasmin was about to get out of the bed when Sami and Mira stormed into the room, each carrying a plastic bag. They both opened their bags and brought them closer to her so she could see their new crayons and coloring books.

"Very nice." She gave each a kiss. "Let's get ready for bed. We can color tomorrow after school."

Mahir walked in and said hi. He turned his back and changed into his pajamas, while Yasmin helped Sami and Mira get into theirs. Seconds after he left the room, Yasmin heard him turn the television on, and then a little after that she heard his laptop start. She put Sami and Mira in bed and started reading *A Bug's Life*.

CHAPTER THIRTY-FIVE

B y the end of their first week in Irbid, Yasmin realized that the events of her first day had basically become the daily routine.

At seven thirty every morning, Mahir carried his laptop and his briefcase and went to work. After Yasmin and Tahani put their children on their school buses, they had their coffee in Yasmin's kitchen. Later on, Yasmin did a bit of cleaning and tidying, sometimes called either Carole, her mother, or Fatin, and then prepared lunch. When and if she had enough time, she sketched on her drawing pad.

Afternoons kept Yasmin busy with Sami's homework, watching cartoons with Mira, or doing some kind of craft. She gave both of them a bath in the late afternoon since there wasn't enough time in the mornings or in the evenings because of their daily visits with their grandparents. No matter how many strong urges Yasmin had to protest this routine, she never did. Who was she kidding? Just because they reconciled and were living together now did not eliminate the chance of Mahir snapping again and doing something crazy to further traumatize Sami and Mira. She would have loved to accompany them everywhere they went, but she was obviously not welcomed by Mahir's parents. And that suited her just fine. She had no desire to see her in-laws anymore either. Every night after Mahir returned with Sami and Mira, Yasmin read them a bedtime story while Mahir watched the news and worked on his laptop.

On their first Friday in Irbid, Mahir got dressed after drinking a cup of coffee in the morning and asked Sami and Mira to get ready. Yasmin felt that was the straw that was about to break the camel's back, but again, she restrained herself. She had no doubt Mahir was avoiding her with the schedule he had set for himself from the first day. But since giving Sami and Mira a sense of security was still her priority, she helped both of them get dressed and gave each a kiss before they walked out the door with Mahir.

It saddened Yasmin that their lives had amounted to this. And it saddened her even more that she could not prevent it from happening in the first place and that she could not reverse it or change any of it now. She had explored every avenue and found no support or a tangible solution. Returning with her children to their home in Scottsdale would take patience, perseverance, and of course the right circumstances while moving forward one day at a time.

By their second week in Irbid, autumn started hinting at the harshness of the fast-approaching winter. The sky became moody and did not allow the sun to shine on many gloomy days. Grapevines continued to undress, exposing snaky brown vines, and when the chilly winds came and shook the half-naked trees, it saturated the air with melancholy.

One morning after putting their children on their school buses, Yasmin and Tahani started their morning ritual in Yasmin's kitchen. Tahani took off her hijab and lit a cigarette while Yasmin boiled the coffee.

"Tahani, I'm switching the family-room furniture with the living-room furniture today. It's so dirty. The backs and armrests shine."

"They bought it used from one of the neighbors. They didn't have enough time to clean it."

"No kidding. I'm glad you told me. Will you help me after coffee? I need to make a space in the living room for my easel. I was thinking if we pushed the dirty gray set to the wall, I'll be able to set up my easel and a small table for my paint and brushes."

"You paint?"

"Uh-huh." Yasmin stirred the coffee. "What do you do for fun, Tahani?"

"Nothing since I had my children. I used to like embroidery…I read a few books, but now I only help my children with homework, cook, clean…you know."

"What do you like to read?"

Tahani shrugged. "I don't know. I read a couple of books about herbs and natural medicine a long time ago."

"Interesting." Yasmin finished making the coffee. She poured it in cups and placed them on the table. She sat down and lit a cigarette.

"Do you know where I can buy art supplies?"

"*Share'-el-jama'* (the University Street)." Tahani picked up her cup and took a sip. "I can go with you later if you want."

"I'd love that."

A dark shadow came to the kitchen door, and a loud banging followed. Yasmin looked at Tahani and then at her watch before she moved to the door. "I hope it's not Um Basim," she said. She opened the small window and saw Basim's face. "Just a minute," she said and closed the window. "It's Basim," she whispered to Tahani and rolled her eyes. She waited for Tahani to slip her hijab back on her head before she opened the door.

Basim was holding a plastic bucket full of candle-shaped bulbs. "Good morning." He smiled and stared at her breasts. "I brought the light bulbs."

Yasmin folded her arms. "What about the outlets? When are you taking care of that?"

Basim stammered. "I have to get the parts and the tools first."

"Fine, you can set the bucket here." She pointed to the kitchen floor.

"No, no, I'll do it. I still have half an hour before I go to work." His smile faded away when he stepped in uninvited and saw Tahani.

He smelled so bad that Yasmin gagged and held her hand to her mouth. She could not define that smell but guessed it was a mixture of dirty clothes worn over a sweaty, unwashed body for a while.

Basim proceeded to the family room.

Yasmin looked at Tahani and made a face. "What in the world is he thinking?" she whispered. "What does he do besides drive Mahir's father around anyway?"

Tahani came closer to Yasmin. "He works for the city. He reads water meters."

"He smells terrible." She suppressed a laugh.

Tahani laughed. "He probably bathes once a week to save water."

They followed Basim to the family room, stood by the door, and watched him. He was standing on the coffee table, screwing the light bulbs in place.

When he noticed them standing there, he looked at Yasmin. "You should visit with Faridah sometime. Nice lady, my wife. You'll like her."

"Should? Is that an order?" Yasmin squinted at him.

"No, no, I didn't mean it that way. You know, we're family, and you women should get to know each other."

"Mmm…I see. Maybe one day when I have time." Yasmin looked at Tahani and gestured for her to follow. "What was that all about?"

"He is always rude like that, but I don't know what makes him think he can act so casual with you."

"I think it's that sorry excuse for a father in-law I have. After going around the country for months and saying all kinds of bad things about me, I'm sure he gave Basim and others the impression that anyone can step all over me."

Tahani thought for a moment. "Mahir's father probably asked them to be close to you so he could get reports. You know what I mean?"

"Yeah, in their dreams. I think there's much more to it than that, Tahani."

They stopped talking when they heard Basim's footsteps in the hallway.

"I'm done," he said on his way to the door.

Yasmin stayed in her chair. "Thank you. Make sure you call when you come to fix the outlets, please."

Basim held the door handle and looked back. "I'm going to be honest. I can't do anything before Abu Mahir gives me the OK." His silly smile came back to his face.

"Never mind then. I can always hire someone else."

His smile faded away. He opened his mouth to say something, but Yasmin did not give him a chance. "Close the door behind you, please." She turned to Tahani and started talking.

Basim closed the door with a bang.

"I'm going to have a talk with Mahir about this. It's dangerous for the children to have exposed wires like that all over the place, you know. I guess asking them to connect the washing machine to a source of water is out of the question."

"Did you use it?"

"I had to fill it with a bucket and drain it after each cycle. I'm going to be spending weekends at my parents' house in Amman, so I guess I'll just do my laundry there. Mahir dry-cleans his clothes anyway."

An hour later, Yasmin and Tahani strolled out of their building toward the main street so they could find a yellow cab. After they walked by a limestone house that had a front yard full of rosebushes in every color, they crossed to the other side and continued on their way, passing a few blockhouses that were covered with a grayish plaster. On one of the rooftops, Yasmin saw a young girl hanging laundry on lines, and on an opposite roof, a young boy smoked and stared at her. Before they reached the main street, Yasmin noticed a car driving slowly by them. Behind the steering wheel sat an ugly man with his head turned in their direction. He honked and then winked at them. The woman sitting beside him with her hair covered looked straight ahead and took no notice of them.

"What in God's name was that?" Yasmin looked at Tahani.

Tahani squinted at the car. "That's the new bride and groom."

"You know them?"

"Not really. I see the man at the store sometimes. He buys stuff from Waleed."

"Why did he honk and look at us then?"

"No manners. I'll mention it to Waleed. He'll have a talk with him. I don't think he recognized me, or else he wouldn't have done such a stupid thing."

Yasmin thought back to when she was growing up how men whispering profanities followed women and young girls on the sidewalks in the hope of brushing against them or even touching them. Too bad sick and outdated mentalities did not disappear with all the great and modern changes to the country that were outwardly visible.

Tahani waved down a cab and told the driver of their destination as she was getting in. The driver continued on the main street for a while and then turned into a side road. He passed through neighborhoods of pink and white limestone houses and many of plastered but unpainted blocks. As they drove by a house that had two stone palms arching over a gate, Yasmin remembered what Mahir had once said. Very few people in Irbid believed in architects, and as a result, the city had become a good example of what he considered an architectural disaster. People built their houses on Irbid's very fertile farming land without even bothering with a blueprint. Houses sunk down with time, and ants and humidity always challenged homeowners by creeping through the walls.

Share'-el-jama' was bustling with pedestrians, honking cars, and screaming vendors. Yasmin and Tahani paid the driver, stepped out, and pushed their way among the crowds. Yasmin immediately noticed how women dressed more conservatively than they did in Amman. Hijabs covered almost every female head on that street, including the heads of the younger girls, who sported low-waist jeans and stretchy tops. Caftans and slippers were obviously the trend preferred by many men.

Almost every other store on each side of the street sold cell phones or computers. In between, there were bookstores, pharmacies, falafel and shawarma shops, and American fast-food restaurants. Most shop owners and employees stood at the store entrances, leaning against walls, smoking, and watching people go by while the Koran blasted from the speakers inside. Just about every sign on the upper floors of the tall and interconnected buildings ended with the words *Internet café*. Tahani told Yasmin how it had all started when a man returned to Irbid after years of living abroad and established the first café. He had remodeled a vacant shop between the butchery and a produce shop and rented each of his ten computers for five dinars an hour. The butcher and the produce merchant, who had never ceased to inquire about his daily income, had switched their businesses to Internet rental before the end of that year.

Months after the three cafés had stolen each other's customers and competed by lowering their fees down to one dinar an hour, many shops along the street had also converted. Building owners started designing their new upper floors to accommodate that same purpose. When the whole street had become hundreds of Internet cafés providing the same services, the owners had begun offering food and drinks in order to survive the competition.

Yasmin bought canvases and paint from Dar-el-Funoon, the house of arts. The two men who sat on the other side of the glass counter talked about the changing weather and speculated on the first rain. After they chatted about Iraq and the expected war, they concluded their conversation by cussing America and Americans. Yasmin felt insulted but said nothing. When she and Tahani walked out, they were approached by men and young boys who sold Korean watches, sunglasses, socks, calculators, fake Nike hats, and imported cigarettes, all displayed over cardboard boxes turned upside down. A man held sunglasses and offered Yasmin and Tahani to take a look.

"One dinar," he said. "It's real, not Chinese."

Yasmin and Tahani crossed the street running between cars, forcing them to stop. "If we don't do this, we'll never get to the other side," Tahani said.

"I noticed. Is there a pharmacy nearby? I need allergy medicine. I ran out yesterday." They passed under a huge glass-encased poster of Bruce Willis in dark shades, grinning. The neon-lit advertisement protruded from the wall of the sunglasses shop next to Saydalyet-el-shifaa, the "pharmacy of cure."

"Do you recognize this actor?" Yasmin pointed at Bruce.

"No."

"He's American, very famous."

Tahani shrugged and smiled and then stepped inside the pharmacy with Yasmin.

Yasmin bought the allergy pills recommended by the pharmacist in a white coat. A small television behind him revealed a news channel. The voice of the anchor was muted, but from the pictures on the screen, Yasmin knew it had to do with Iraq. She paid three dinars for her medicine, and then both she and Tahani stepped out. They waved down a cab, and Tahani gave him directions to their neighborhood. Halfway through the drive, Tahani whispered to Yasmin, "Do you mind if we make a quick stop downtown? I just remembered that I have an order at the spice market I need to pick up."

"Sure. Go ahead."

Tahani gave the driver new directions.

Every street they passed had tall buildings standing over stores with huge signs that looked more like posters. They drove by a clothing store that had the singer Shakira as the centerpiece of its sign, and a tobacco shop that Humphrey Bogart held a cigarette over. Further down, just before they reached the downtown, a big sign that covered almost half a building had a panorama of Window Rock. Reminders of Yasmin's homesickness seemed to be at every street corner, but the latter picture hit home the most. She closed her eyes and let her imagination take her to the rock, fly above and under it while the sun warmed her face and calmed her anguish.

The driver squeezed his way through the downtown traffic, pulled over, and parked under a No Parking sign. Tahani stepped out and said she would be back in a minute. She entered a store that displayed jute bags full of herbs and spices on the sidewalk. Turtle shells, claws, mummified animal heads, and other objects Yasmin did not recognize dangled from the ceiling by the entrance.

After a few minutes, Tahani came out of the store holding a bag. She stood by the car and squinted ahead. Yasmin turned in that direction and saw Basim looking back at her as he drove by. Next to him sat a stranger who turned in his seat and kept looking at Yasmin until they disappeared.

Tahani slipped into the car. "Did you see that?"

Yasmin nodded. She did not know what to make of it but had a strong feeling it was no coincidence. Everything about Basim made her cringe: the way he stared, the way he talked informally to her, and the sleazy way he smiled. And now she suspected that he was following her, and though she could not quite decide why, the thought of it really frightened her.

The cabdriver struggled to avoid a jam down the street. With his head stuck out of the window, honking and yelling, he tried to maneuver his way through. On the right side of the street, a crowd of young men gathered by the cinema entrance and stared up at the advertisement of a kung-fu movie. When the driver passed them, he tried to make a right but found no outlet to the main street. He drove further down looking for a clear passage and made a few left and right turns before the main street came in view. As he drove toward it, he passed an old and deserted building. Whatever was left of the sign above the gate read Arizona Café. Yasmin grabbed Tahani's arm.

"Look. I can't believe this."

Tahani smiled. "They closed down a long time ago."

"Arizona is my state, Tahani; that's where I lived."

The wide wrought-iron gate revealed the shredded canvas canopies hanging over a pile of broken chairs and tables. A small ruined building in the far corner of that garden had bolted doors and broken windows. It was a sad sight, but Yasmin refused to link the ruins to her life even if it was just metaphorically.

CHAPTER THIRTY-SIX

On a quiet afternoon a few days later, Yasmin sat behind her easel and worked on her new painting. She had painted a mermaid standing on her tail facing a shore. The unrealistic image captured parts of how she had been feeling, out of her element, in an awkward position yet still standing. Yasmin painted a sand trail in front of the mermaid and split the sea. No matter how difficult and seemingly impossible it felt at this point for Yasmin to return to Arizona with her children, she could not give up her dream. Deep down inside, she believed it was going to happen, but she had no idea when or how. Sometimes she regretted giving Mahir Sami's and Mira's passports, only to remember right away that she could never depart the country with the court order Mahir had obtained to prevent Sami and Mira from doing so without his permission.

When her cell phone rang, she looked down at the screen. It was Majid. She wiped her hands and picked up the phone.

"Hey, what's going on?"

"I'm in Irbid."

"You're kidding. Did Mama send you to check on me?"

Majid laughed. "No, she just wanted me to bring some home-made pickles for you."

"Yeah, right. Do you know how to get here?"

"I'm parked outside. Which way is the door to your apartment?"

Yasmin stepped out onto the balcony and pointed the way to Majid before letting him in through the kitchen door. He set down the pickles on the kitchen counter and gave her a hug. When he looked around the kitchen, his smile disappeared, and he frowned.

"Let's go to the family room." Yasmin walked ahead of him.

Once Majid sat down, she said, "I'll go make coffee."

"No, don't. I can't stay that long." Majid smiled. "Next time." He lit a cigarette and looked around.

"I know what you're thinking. It's OK, Majid. It's a temporary situation. I'm fine, the kids are fine, and that's all that matters right now."

Majid smiled with effort and nodded.

After twenty minutes of catching up, they said their good-byes, and Majid was on his way back to Amman. Minutes after he left, he called Yasmin.

"You're not going to believe this," he said. "That guy Basim raced me all the way to the bus station."

"What? How do you know it's him?"

"After he closed in on me and forced me to stop, he walked up to my side and started talking to me. He asked me what my name was. Then he said, 'Ah, you're Yasmin's brother.' Then he apologized and said that he mistook me for someone else."

"What an idiot. What was he thinking? That you were my boyfriend?"

"I guess so. Never mind. I have to get going. I will call you soon."

Yasmin had no doubt by now that Basim was seriously watching her, and that made her feel very uneasy, so she decided to have a serious talk with Mahir. A loud knock on the kitchen door snapped her out of her thoughts. Another knock followed before she reached the kitchen and opened the door. Standing outside was a young woman wearing a loose scarf over her head, smiling so hard her eyes looked like belly buttons in her face. She held a thermos in one hand and extended the other to Yasmin.

"*Marhaba* (hello)," she said. "I'm Faridah, Basim's wife."

Yasmin just stared.

Faridah pushed her way in anyway, tailed by her three children who walked behind her to the family room.

Yasmin walked behind them.

Faridah turned around and faked a laugh. "Basim didn't recognize your brother." She set the thermos on the coffee table. "I brought you some of my famous cinnamon drink."

Although angry, Yasmin spoke with a calm tone. "I don't really care what Basim or anyone in this town thinks." She folded her arms. "Thanks for the drink, but I'm allergic to cinnamon."

Faridah took a seat, and her children gathered around her.

Yasmin sat on the opposite seat and stared at Faridah's bangs, her bright-blue eye shadow, and her tight red sweater that stretched with every fold of her sagging stomach.

"I've wanted to come welcome you for a long time, but you always seem busy or distracted by Tahani."

"Tahani doesn't distract me. She's my friend, and yes, I'm always busy."

"Did you like my cake?"

"I accidentally dropped it in the sink."

Faridah looked disappointed for a split second and then continued, "Mahir and Basim are related. Did you know that?"

Yasmin shrugged. "And?"

Faridah shifted in her seat. "You changed the seats."

Yasmin nodded.

"Did you hear about the baby that was born with a black split tongue?"

"No."

"Everybody is talking about it; it's a true story. Because the doctors were puzzled, they let his mother breastfeed him. The baby bit her, and she died."

Yasmin did not even blink.

Faridah looked around. "Is that a Koran over there?" she pointed to a side table.

"Yes."

"You don't look religious."

"And you do, I suppose?" Yasmin looked at her watch.

"The imam of the masjid said—"

Yasmin stood up. "I don't mean to be rude, Faridah. I would offer you coffee or tea, but I have to leave right now."

"No problem." Faridah hid her embarrassment behind a fake smile. "Basim said we are coming to visit with you and Mahir one night soon."

Yasmin walked ahead of Faridah and her children to the kitchen. She handed Faridah her empty plate and then opened the door and let them out.

"By the way, I want Basim to connect the heater for me. I tried to turn the heat on, and it seems to be disconnected."

"It's too soon for the heater; it's only October."

Yasmin was very tempted to tell Faridah that the decision was none of her business. "I would like it turned on anyway. Please." She closed the door and went back to her painting.

⊷⊷ ⊶⊷

Later that evening after Sami and Mira fell asleep, Yasmin walked to the family room, where Mahir was hunched over his laptop. Though she decided to avoid conflict with Mahir at any cost to ensure a peaceful start to their new life as he called it, she was not willing to put up with crazy attitudes from anyone, whether they were actually Mahir's relatives or not.

Yasmin stood behind him. "We need to talk."

289

Startled, he snapped his laptop shut and looked up.

"Don't worry, Mahir. I didn't get a glimpse of your secrets."

"I wanted to talk to you too. Why did you treat Faridah like that today? She's trying to be your friend."

"I'll get to Faridah in a minute, but first I want to discuss something more important. Look, Mahir, you have been avoiding any kind of communication with me since the day we came here. In the past I saw you temporarily into someone I didn't recognize once we landed in this country, but this time, since we're staying, especially under such difficult circumstances, I feel I need to give you a wake-up call."

"I—"

"Let me finish, please. From the moment we started having problems, I made no decisions. You started sleeping on the couch, you moved out, you moved to Jordan, you took the children, you sued me, you began the reconciliation, and you picked this apartment. And to this very moment, I don't know how you can justify what you did to all of us. Are you ready to help me understand?"

Mahir rubbed his temples.

"Is this really the quality of life you want for our children and for us? You know as well as I that we are all losing so much by being away from our home in Scottsdale. Why are we really here, Mahir?"

Mahir looked perplexed, as if he were digesting what Yasmin was saying, but still did not reply.

"Am I ever going to know the truth, Mahir? You said we were going to give ourselves a second chance, a new beginning, but all I see happening is a reincarnation of our last unbearable months in Scottsdale. You are still carrying on with the silence, excluding me from everything as if I don't exist, and that is not right. Why are we back together, Mahir?"

Mahir sighed.

"Look, if you asked me back just to take care of our children, then I can understand that, but if you asked me back so Basim could help you find a good excuse to get rid of me somehow, then you need to reconsider your plans and come up with something more creative—"

"What are you talking about?"

"When he called to complain about the way I treated his wife, did he tell you that he's been following me around? Did he tell you he chased Majid, thinking he's my boyfriend or something?"

Mahir frowned. "No. I know nothing about it."

"Well, now you do. Furthermore, I think you should know Basim talks to me with such informality that it's as if we were pals. He gives me dirty looks with his bulging, rude eyes as if he were given the impression it was OK. So, he's the one you should be watching, not me, Mahir."

"I didn't ask him to watch you. Could you stop accusing me of that?"

"Who did then? Your father?"

"No way."

Yasmin shook her head. "Think about everything I said, Mahir, please. You need to wake up and consider the well-being of Sami and Mira. For their sake, I can get over the past. I can pretend to forgive and forget everything you did. I can even pressure myself into starting over if I feel you're being honest with me. But if you remain like a remote control in your father's hand, pleasing him as you put up this ridiculous Jordanian macho act, then I can't be with you. Now, as for Faridah, we have nothing in common, and I don't want to be friends with her. So, if she and Basim ever come to socialize, I'm not going to oblige them."

Yasmin left the room. She lay in bed next to Sami and Mira still trembling. More than ever she felt lost in a maze. Not just a massive one but one that seemed to leave her breathless after a long run only to find herself back where she had started. She closed her eyes. Once she had read that timing was a thing of the universe, and now she wanted so badly to trust in its wisdom for withholding the missing links in the chain of events that brought her to this moment. A moment she had relived so many times over the past months with Mahir and his torturing silence. She was not sure what to make of his facial expressions anymore. Was Basim really acting on his own? Was Mahir's denial of having anything to do with Basim just another lie? Even if Mahir had insisted on reconciling just so he could stop her from suing for custody, why would he have her tailed by a creep? Was he looking for a way to help him discredit her as a mother once and for all so she could never gain custody of Sami and Mira?

The thought of it sent Yasmin's heart racing. Was Mahir truly so desperate to get her out of his life one way or another? She tried to picture Mahir's face while she was talking to him. He did look confused as he listened, and when he asked her what she was talking about, he did not sound like he was faking his surprise. There was always the possibility that Mahir's father was the one directing Basim. He threatened her one time that she would pay a high price for scandalizing his son.

The sun never shone the next day. It could not melt its way through the gray clouds that plastered the sky. Yasmin could not find a better word to describe the air than *cruel*. It was cold and penetrating. Unmerciful to the skin, flesh, bones, and even marrow. When the sky darkened further that afternoon, rain fell in the form of millions of miniature needles. Not in bubbles like the ones Yasmin got used to seeing in Arizona, where the sun had no problem appearing in the midst of a storm to help create a double rainbow. She remembered how after storms the clouds opened up like curtains to reveal a blue screen and how the warm sun made everything underneath it gleaming and clean.

Tahani came to visit with Yasmin that evening. They sat in the family room as close as they could get to the central heating unit, sipping hot tea flavored with the sage leaves Yasmin left floating inside the kettle. The television, on the news channel, was muted.

Tahani took a sip from her tea. "Why do you always have the TV turned on to the news?"

"I'm worried because of the war. Aren't you?"

Tahani shrugged. "No, it's going to be in Iraq, isn't it?"

"Yeah, but what if something happens and we get dragged into it? They say Iraq has all these weapons and their president is angry with everybody. It's scary."

Tahani turned her lip. "If it's written, then we can't do anything about it. Nobody dies before his or her time."

"I hear you." Yasmin laughed.

"I hope it stops raining."

"What? You guys never stop talking about the rain, and now you want it to stop?"

"I know. It's good for the olives; they ripen. I worry because my guest bathroom overflows sometimes when it rains too long."

Yasmin widened her eyes. "Why?"

Tahani pointed her finger to the ceiling. "Because Basim and Faridah forget to have the septic tank cleaned when it's their turn."

"I'm sorry, Tahani. That sounds terrible. I would be worried too."

Yasmin put her teacup down, picked up the remote, and gave the news anchor his voice back. He spoke of the American and allied troops for a few moments before his face disappeared from the screen that went all over the world, showing people marching in protest, in some countries finishing up with burning the American and Israeli flags.

"Do you like Americans?"

Yasmin turned the television off. "I don't know all three hundred million of them, but the ones I know, yes."

Tahani fell back in her seat laughing, her feet lifted off the floor. "What are they like? Are they really mean?"

Yasmin thought for a moment. "Look, Tahani, you can't just label the citizens of one country or one continent, a race, or the followers of a certain religion with one word. You know how Jordan is a mix of Jordanians, Palestinians, Armenians, Circassians, Chechens, and some other Arab nationalities? America is the same. Americans are a mix from all over the world, and just like us, they have every kind among them."

"I didn't know you for a long time, but I can feel how sad you are because you no longer live there. Sometimes I wonder what it would be like to live in another country."

"Tahani, I love Jordan, but there are some very important things to me that I miss there. Aside from all the freedoms in America and the fact that no one interferes in anybody's life, the majority of people are not judgmental. Women work, and young girls and boys work. They don't sit around in their homes gossiping and complaining. People there respect each other and don't look down on one another. They're all protected by the law regardless of their family name, race, or gender, especially women and children. Did you know that child abuse is against the law in America and that if it's reported, the government places the abused children with foster parents?"

Tahani gasped.

"The same goes for women. In some cases they are provided shelter and the abusing husbands are prosecuted."

Tahani's bafflement increased.

"In divorce cases, the law is as clear and doesn't only serve men. Men can't do the things they get away with here. The courts decide on the custody, child support, and alimony and also divide assets."

"In that case I ask God to take you back." Tahani lifted her hands to the ceiling and muttered a prayer.

"Thank you, Tahani. Listen, next time we go out, we'll buy you a bunch of books, my treat."

"Why? What kind of books?"

"Whatever we find interesting. It's good to read, Tahani. It's entertaining and gives you knowledge. When you read, you find the truth and learn how to form your own opinion. You don't ever say 'he said' or 'she said' like Faridah and many other people I come across."

Tahani nodded, but there was worry in her eyes. "What if somebody finds out? Faridah once said that only women who are interested in learning magic bother with books."

"What? Tahani, don't ever say that. Who is Faridah to judge or even have an opinion? Look, from the two minutes I spent with her yesterday, I knew she was a nut. With a face colored like that of a clown, a scarf that's barely covering half of her hair, wearing repulsively revealing clothes, she tried to imply that I was not religious. So please, don't ever let her or anyone tell you what's right and what's wrong."

Tahani laughed. "You are absolutely right. I know Faridah is not religious by any means, but her big mouth scares me. She has the morals of…I don't even have an example to give. She and Basim would never hesitate to accuse anyone of anything, and people who don't know them as well as I do would easily take their words for granted."

"Why does she even bother with her stupid head cover then?"

"To give a wholesome impression." Tahani squinted at Yasmin for a moment. "I didn't want to mention this to you when we talked about Faridah and Basim this morning, but I think you should know that Basim was once arrested drunk, peeking at a half-naked relative of his."

Yasmin was not surprised.

CHAPTER THIRTY-SEVEN

Yasmin worked on her mermaid painting all afternoon. Facing her mermaid, there was a man and two children approaching the shore, riding in what looked like a huge turtle shell turned upside down. She was about to add a few touches to the parted waves when the sound of explosives disturbed that quiet November evening. Yasmin flinched, and her heart beat fast.

She could hear screams outside, what sounded like a machine gun, and then one big blast after another. She looked around in panic for her cell phone, but it was nowhere in sight. Then she remembered leaving it on the dresser of the peacock's room where she had hung her laundry on racks to dry.

The distant bangs seemed to go on without a pause, but the ones nearby stopped as she entered the room. After taking cautious steps toward the window, she held the side of the thick curtain in her hand and peeked out. She saw Tahani, her children, and other faces she could not recognize in the dark. They stood under the pole that had no light, the one Tahani once said that the city had given up on fixing because children kept breaking it with rocks. Yasmin could hear Tahani talking in a calm manner, the children around her not alarmed or frightened.

Yasmin slid the window open and called Tahani. "What is going on?"

"Tomorrow is the first day of Ramadan." Tahani moved closer to the window, smiling. "*Kul saneh w-enti salmeh,*" she said, wishing Yasmin well for all the years ahead.

"Same to you. What was that banging?"

"Fireworks. Firecrackers and rockets."

"Who did that?"

"Everybody. Right after they announced Ramadan on TV. You missed it."

Yasmin took a deep breath. "Well, thank God it was just celebrations."

"What did you think it was?"

"My TV was off. I didn't know what to think."

Tahani giggled. "Were you scared?"

"A little. This is my first Ramadan here in ten years. I don't remember Ramadan being celebrated with explosives in the past."

"Don't get scared when they announce Eid, the feast after," Tahani said.

"I'll remember that." Yasmin's phone started ringing. "OK, see you tomorrow." She closed the window, picked up her phone, and looked down at the screen; the number was of a house phone in Amman. She pressed the green key.

"Kul saneh w-enti salmeh," Lina said. "Everybody here says the same."

"Thank you, Lina. Tell them I wish them well, too."

"Baba wants to know how everything is going."

"Tell him everything is fine." She could hear Lina talking to her father.

"Hold on, I want to take the phone to my room," Lina whispered.

Yasmin waited a few moments before Lina's voice came back.

"Look, I want to tell you something, but you have to promise not to mention a word to Mahir. I don't know if it's good or bad, but I think you'll like it."

"I promise. What is it?"

"I caught my father and Fadi talking about Mahir half an hour ago. Fadi said that Mahir is not happy with his job. They refused to give him a teacher's title or even a salary of one, because he doesn't have a PhD. Even though he teaches five classes a day, he was assigned as a lab technician and gets only three hundred and fifty dinars a month."

With the way Mahir had been carrying on, it did not surprise Yasmin that he kept this information from her. It bothered her a great deal and actually frightened her to be so excluded, never knowing what was on his mind, what kind of plans he had, and whether she and the children were included in them.

"That's very odd. Did he say why he's not looking for another job?"

"Fadi said Mahir signed a contract for one year, so he can't break it, or else he has to pay a penalty. When Fadi noticed me standing behind him, he stopped talking, so that's all I can tell you."

"Well, I guess you can call this good news, Lina."

Lina laughed. "That's what I thought. I hope you guys go back to Arizona."

"I wish for nothing else, Lina."

Yasmin called Mahir as soon as she hung up and asked him if he could drive her and the children to Amman to spend the weekend with her parents, and he agreed.

As Mahir stopped the car by Yasmin's parents' house, the faint bang of the distant cannon permitted *iftar*, the major meal of the day after twelve hours of fasting. Once Yasmin and her children stepped out of the car, the call for dusk prayer started. Mahir said he would pick them up Saturday evening and then drove back to Irbid.

Yasmin and her children were hugged and kissed by everyone in the foyer. Then they all moved to the dining room and took their places at the table, where they broke their fast with apricot nectar and dates. Aside from comments on the cold weather, no discussions took place as they ate their vegetable soup and the okra-and-lamb stew. When they finished their meal, Sami and Mira ran downstairs to play with Omar and Zaid, and the rest of the family moved to the family room for their coffee.

Besides her previous and almost daily updates on her life in Irbid, Yasmin did not have much to add. She gave more descriptions of her apartment to Fatin and her mother and spoke a little about Tahani. When the coffee cups sat empty on their saucers, her father picked up his glasses and the second volume of his book and moved to the veranda. Nihad and Samira arrived shortly after, so Yasmin gave them an update as she sat hazed by their hookah smoke, drinking tea and nibbling on Ramadan's dessert, *qatayef*, which her mother had smothered with syrup and stuffed some of with sweetened goat cheese and some with walnuts and sugar.

Yasmin's mother told Nihad and Samira that she had already finished reading three parts of the Koran and then consulted with Fatin on what to cook for the next day.

"Let's make noodle soup and chicken-and-potato casserole for the main dish," Fatin said.

Yasmin's mother nodded and then blew a puff of hookah smoke toward the ceiling. It smelled like grapes with a hint of mint.

"That's a good idea," Nihad said. "I think I'll do the same and save myself a trip to the store tomorrow. Ever since a number of Iraqi families moved into the rental apartments in my building, the nearby grocery store has been running out of almost everything."

She took a long drag from her hookah and released it. "Now I have to take a chance and drive a longer distance to several stores, because it seems like the refugees are creating a shortage in every part of the city."

Samira nodded. "I know. It's the same wherever you go."

Fatin leaned toward Yasmin and asked, "Is school getting any easier for Sami?"

"A little. He still has trouble dealing with the children in his class. They make fun of his accent."

Fatin shook her head. "How is Mira doing?"

"She's doing OK. She never brings homework though."

"Poor kids. They had to make so many adjustments in a very short time. Did you and Mahir discuss future plans?"

Yasmin shook her head. "Not even once. Even though Mira keeps asking in front of him, 'When are we going back to Arazona?' like it's in the backyard or something."

"Any improvement on his attitude since we last spoke?"

Yasmin whispered, "Not really. Please don't say anything about it to anyone. I don't want my mother starting a lecture now."

"Don't worry. I understand," Fatin said. "Majid told me about Basim. What was that all about?"

"I told Mahir what he did. Hopefully he will have a talk with him."

Yasmin did not think it was a good idea to share her unsettling suspicions with Fatin at that point. Fatin was going to worry and eventually tell Majid, who in turn would tell her parents. If Basim acted in a similar manner again, confirming that Mahir or his father were up to something, then she would definitely call Majid.

Later that evening, Yasmin called Carole and asked her to stop by with the intention of discussing Basim's behavior with her in mind. Carole said she could not leave the restaurant because of the Ramadan tent. She told Yasmin how she had enclosed the patio at the restaurant with *seewan*, a red background of canvas decorated with colorful designs. She had also placed a few gas heaters between tables, hung lanterns on the walls, and hired a singer and a fortune-teller for entertainment.

"It's a new thing in the country. You should come sometime," Carole said. "We serve hookahs and munchies like boiled garbanzo and fava beans, coffee, tea, and other beverages."

"Sound great, but I can't this week. Maybe next time."

Yasmin did not bring up the subject of Basim to Carole over the phone. Carole sounded busy enough with her own issues, and it made no sense to bother her with speculations at that point.

That night, Yasmin used Fatin's computer to check her e-mail. There was a short one from Ellen, saying that she hoped everything would work out just fine. She also informed Yasmin that she had lost contact with Dina, who had not called Ellen since she and her husband had moved to California. She urged Yasmin to e-mail as much as she could and let her know she was fine. Yasmin wrote Ellen a few lines. She told her everything was OK, apologized for being in a hurry, and promised to write more details as soon as she could.

On the way back to Irbid, Mahir turned the radio down and asked Sami about his stay in Amman.

Since Sami had engaged all his senses on his Game Boy the moment he sat in the car, he just said, "Fine."

When Mahir asked Mira if she had a good time, she said, "A-huh." She then continued to undress her doll with the half-shaved head.

Without addressing anyone in particular, Mahir said that he had spent the weekend at his parents' house.

Yasmin did not comment. She looked out the window at nothing but darkness.

Mahir turned the radio up and listened to the news for the next forty minutes.

When they arrived at their neighborhood, Basim was standing on the sidewalk, smoking. He raised his hand in greeting when Mahir pulled over. Mahir waved back.

As they all stepped out of the car, Basim put his silly smile on his face and approached them.

He reached in his pocket. "We found the front-door key."

Mahir took the key and turned to Yasmin. "Let's use the front door, then."

Yasmin held Sami's and Mira's hands and walked in that direction. She looked back at Mahir. "Can you get the handbag?"

Basim was still standing there making Yasmin feel uneasy. There was something disturbing, more than usual, behind his smile.

Mahir opened the door and let himself in first. He turned the lights on as Sami and Mira were entering. The moment Yasmin set her foot in the door, she knew Basim had been in the apartment.

"What's this smell?" She closed the door behind her.

"What smell?" Mahir sniffed right and left. "I don't smell anything."

She stared at him. How could he not smell that repulsive human odor mixed with cigarettes and the musty scent of dirty clothes dampened by rain?

"It's probably humidity. The heater was turned off for two days." Mahir left the room. Seconds later the heater switch clicked.

The night took its usual course. Mahir changed his clothes and sat in the family room, watched television, and worked on his laptop. While Sami and Mira ate their peanut butter and jelly sandwiches, Yasmin sniffed every inch of the kitchen for a possible source for that smell that still lingered in her nose. The trash was empty as she had left it. There were no food leftovers anywhere. She leaned over the washing machine even though she had taken all their dirty clothes to wash at her parents' house. No smell there.

Late that night, as soon as she heard Mahir shutting down, she slipped out of bed and went to the living room. She turned the lights on and sat behind her easel, lit a cigarette, and stared at her painting. The bathroom door opened and closed. After the toilet flushed, she heard water coming down the faucet, and then the door opened. She listened to Mahir's footsteps turning to the bedroom. The bedspring squeaked a little, and then there was silence.

Sitting next to a palette full of paint did not muffle that persisting stench of an unwashed stranger that she could smell everywhere. Yasmin had no doubt that the stranger was none other than Basim. She could not mistake his smell if he were standing next to carrion. Nothing in the world could convince her that Basim had not entered the apartment before handing them back the key. Though Basim was the type of person that would not hesitate to violate people's privacy, the thing that really worried her was that Basim did not just pass through. She was very certain he had stayed long enough to leave his odor behind.

Basim risked being spotted by Tahani and her children and took his time doing whatever he wanted to do, or most likely was instructed to do. Things were adding up now. Basim had followed her around and watched her when she was home alone, but nothing came of it. Yasmin shuddered at the thought of Basim entering the apartment to plant something incriminating like a love note to get Yasmin in real trouble. Yasmin put out her cigarette, and like a forensic expert, she started an inspection of the place. She began with the living room and then moved to the bedrooms. She opened every closet and every drawer and looked under the mattresses in the peacock's room and the room that had a balcony. She then tiptoed to the Formica room where Mahir and the children slept and quietly looked through drawers and cupboards, not for something missing as much as for something new. Like a photo, a gift with a note, or even a love letter.

She searched the kitchen again and the bathrooms and found nothing. It suddenly struck her that if her suspicions were true, then whoever wanted to plant such evidence was not going to place it in an easy or obvious place. She remembered Um Basim talking about cutting up the wall-to-wall carpet in the family room into pieces in order to take it out and wash it. She went back to the family room and switched on the five neon tubes and the thirty-six bulbs of the chandelier.

She lifted the carpet behind the couch, the dining table, the opposite wall, and then the center of the room where all the pieces of the carpet overlapped. She finally moved to the front door, looking down for a split in the carpet she could lift up. When she noticed a dark spot right by the door, she took a step back. She moved to the side and let the light fall on a muddy footprint. She went to the bedroom and checked her shoes and then Mahir's. Their soles were clean. Not a trace of dirt or mud on any of them.

Yasmin's long search yielded nothing but a dirty footprint. As she lay in bed that night, she stared at Mahir, sleeping on the other end of the big bed. She watched him breathe, his chest going up and down, one of his arms wrapped around Sami. Would he ever stoop to the level of Basim and his conduct and ask him to do such a thing as hurt her, his wife? She did not know what to believe anymore. She left her question unanswered and planned to perform another more thorough inspection of the whole place in the morning. She also decided to put off her trips to the capital for a while and thought about ways to secure her apartment.

CHAPTER THIRTY-EIGHT

On a cloudy and rainy morning during the last week of Ramadan, the first week of December, Tahani and Yasmin put their children on their buses and rushed to Yasmin's kitchen. Tahani said that they should take a trip to Share'-el-jama' to buy clothes for themselves and for their children.

"It's a *Sunna* to wear new clothes for Eid," she said. "It's following the path of the Prophet."

Tahani's shopping venture did not appeal to Yasmin. "The children have a lot of new clothes they never got a chance to wear, Tahani. It's cold. I'm tired and don't have the energy to go around shops, Tahani."

Tahani persisted. "If you don't buy new clothes for Eid, then when do you do it?"

Yasmin released a long sigh. "I know, Tahani, but—"

"I understand your lack of enthusiasm because of what happened to you, and I know all your thoughts are about going back to Arizona, but you can't let it get the best of you all the time."

"It's not just that. Tahani, I want to tell you something, but I want it to stay between us."

"Of course."

"I think somebody entered my apartment when I went to visit with my parents. I think it's Basim."

Tahani looked at the kitchen door. "I can get in real trouble for what I'm about to tell you."

"Tahani, you know I would never tell a soul."

"I suspected he did the night you came back from Amman. I heard your front door open and close and thought it was you, but when I looked out, Mahir's car was not there. This isn't his first time, you know. He has a history of snooping around."

"I don't think it's about snooping, Tahani. He wouldn't take the risk of being caught and looking bad in front of Mahir and his father. I think one of them asked him to look for something or put something somewhere, if you know what I mean."

Tahani nodded. "If he ever does it again, I'll call your cell phone immediately. Is that why you don't want to go out? He wouldn't dare do it during the day."

"OK, but I need to stop at an Internet café and check my mail. Do you mind?"

"Not at all. I actually know a good café. I went once with my sister."

An hour later they sat in the backseat of the cab that Tahani had called from a nearby company. The color of the day was still grimy, and the sky continued to pour down, filling the ditches with soiled water and giving more speed to the muddy streams that formed on the sides of streets. Tahani told Yasmin that she did not tell her what happened at the store the night before because she did not want to scare her, but she could not hold off anymore. A man came late at night and stole a propane gas tank from the Paradise Mini Market when Waleed was alone. Waleed had crawled out of the store but not fast enough to get the license plate of the thief. She also told Yasmin that it had happened almost every year on the last week of Ramadan, probably by a desperate man who wanted to buy Eid clothes for his children. The propane tank sold for thirty dinars.

Share'-el-jama' was more crowded than Yasmin had expected for that time of the day. People normally were tired from fasting and so did their Eid shopping after their evening meals. Pedestrians with worn-out faces sped up and down the sidewalks, bumping into each other, trying to avoid getting splashed with muddy water by the passing cars. Shopkeepers stood outside their stores and in desperate tones invited people in. Beggars of all genders and ages were everywhere. Some of them followed people around, and some stood by traffic lights and fought over their spots. Cars never stopped honking, and drivers never stopped yelling at pedestrians and at each other.

"What is wrong with everybody?"

Tahani smiled. "They're fasting."

"And? They're going to kill each other."

"That's normal. It's always like this in Ramadan."

Yasmin shook her head. She had always thought of Ramadan as the serene time of the year when people withdrew from the chaos of life and made time for worship and meditation and for cleansing their bodies, minds, and souls. But apparently, that was not the case anymore.

After an hour of going in and out of stores, Yasmin bought a dress for Mira and a sweater for Sami. Tahani carried two large bags filled with everything on her list but still needed corduroy pants for her son. They entered a small shop that displayed children's clothes in the window, alongside sheets, towels, and small electronics. They greeted an old man, sitting behind a glass counter, wearing a white skullcap and a wool sweater over his gray caftan. He nodded and then looked down at the praying beads in his hand.

Tahani walked around the store for a few moments before she asked the man for the pants.

He shook his head.

When Yasmin and Tahani stepped out of the store, they were taken aback by the sudden and overwhelming commotion outside. They stood on the sidewalk and looked both ways. A crowd coming from the east had blocked the street and caused the stranded cars to honk continuously. As the mass of pedestrians moved closer, Yasmin realized they were marching against the United States for its intention of invading Iraq. Some of them held signs, and some moved their fists up and down as if punching an invisible enemy that hovered above them. A man yelled into a speaker, but Yasmin could not make out a word from that distance.

Yasmin and Tahani stepped back into the store and watched the march go by the glass storefront. Men and women of all ages marched behind a teenager holding a speaker and repeated after him, as he condemned America, Israel, and all the allied forces of evil. Some of the men were dressed in Muslim habits and had long beards; others wore jeans and Nike sneakers. Most of the women wore hijabs and had makeup coloring their faces, and they sported clothes defining their figures. The majority of the signs they held were in Arabic, and the few written in English were misspelled. Down Down Push, read one of the signs that Yasmin was certain was meant to say *Bush*. Another had *America* spelled with a *K*. Some held pictures of Saddam mounted on sticks, and a few waved the Iraqi and Jordanian flags.

When Basim appeared in the crowd, walking between two bearded men and repeating after the speaker, Yasmin looked at Tahani with her eyes opened wide. She wondered if those men knew the real Basim or if they were hypocrites like him or even worse. She questioned the integrity of the whole crowd, frowning like Basim to give the impression that they were people of principle, that they had values. She wondered how many of them had endured standing under

the searing sun outside the American embassy for hours, seeking
a visa. How many of them consumed alcohol in secret, cheated on
their spouses, or abused children.

Yasmin had noticed during Ramadan that some people
grasped at the opportunity to deposit good deeds in their heavenly
accounts, as if the rest of the year did not count. Basim for instance
went to the neighborhood mosque on Fridays during Ramadan,
and Faridah gave the garbageman leftovers tied in plastic bags
once a week. Um Basim bragged about the bit of change she dis-
pensed and the shabby garments she donated.

Yasmin also thought about Mahir. Was he one of those hypocrites? Was it possible that he had worked on that mosque addition
in Phoenix as a way of redeeming himself for something he had
done?

When the last protester passed the storefront, Yasmin and
Tahani slid out, and Tahani led the way to the Internet café she
had mentioned earlier to Yasmin. They discussed Basim's partici-
pation in the march as they walked, and Tahani said that such an
action by a disgusting person like Basim did not surprise her. He
was one of many who felt no shame or remorse for deceiving God
by drinking all year and praying once a week during Ramadan.

Half a mile down the road, they entered a building with a
three-story, open atrium. A woman clad in black leaned against a
wall with a baby in her lap. Over a newspaper section to her side,
she displayed a few packs of cigarettes, bobby pins, and gum.

"She's Iraqi," Tahani whispered to Yasmin. "I've been seeing
others all over town trying to make a living on the sidewalks."

Yasmin took out five dinars from her purse and thrust it into
the woman's palm.

The woman looked at the bill and then began to pray for
Yasmin, her tears streaming down her cheeks.

Yasmin and Tahani climbed the stairs to the second floor and
entered a café. A man greeted them at the front desk and then

escorted them to a long hall full of computers. Only a few students sat behind computers in the corner, and they did not pay attention to Yasmin and Tahani. Once they sat down, the man handed each of them a menu and left.

Yasmin found an e-mail from her realtor, Lindsey, who had never e-mailed her before. With much grief she assumed the e-mail was about foreclosure, but as she read the first two lines, she realized that Mahir had contacted Lindsey and asked for her phone number. He needed to discuss a matter that concerned the house, so Lindsey promised Yasmin to write again after talking to Mahir.

While Yasmin replied to the e-mail, she told Tahani what Lindsey wrote about. "I'll probably lose my mind before I hear back from her."

"You'll be sad if he sold the house, right?"

"No, Tahani." Yasmin turned. "I'll die if he did."

The other e-mail worth a reply was from Ellen. Yasmin wrote back that nothing had changed since she last contacted her. She also added that she and the children were fine and that she had just witnessed a march against the war she was not looking forward to.

That night, Yasmin did not mention Lindsey's e-mail to Mahir, but she stayed up most of the night, speculating on his intentions while she completed her painting. She drew the face of the mermaid on the sand next to where she stood. In Arabic calligraphy to the side, she wrote a small prayer; the mermaid was asking God for a miracle like that of Prophet Moses. The next day when she awakened, she remembered parts of a dream about her house in Scottsdale and a brown German shepherd sitting by the entrance.

CHAPTER THIRTY-NINE

The news anchor who greeted the viewers with a broad smile on the night of December 4 announced that the following day was the first day of Eid al-Fitr, the feast that follows the fasting month of Ramadan. He then proceeded with the daily news, and shortly after, firecrackers banged the sky of the quiet night, and Yasmin heard the laughs and screams of the neighborhood children. Late that night Mahir entered the apartment with a frown and told Yasmin that his father's cousin who worked at the passport agency had passed away two hours earlier.

He said that as a result he would not be driving Yasmin and the children to Amman the next day because celebrating Eid would be inappropriate on their behalf.

"Out of duty of course, I'm going to spend the next three days at the Ahmad's Madafah, the family's community center," he said.

"That's fine," Yasmin said, while helping Sami and Mira get into bed.

Though she had looked forward to spending Eid with her family, she was relieved that the apartment was not going to be unattended for three days. She could not imagine Basim or even Faridah entering in her absence, looking around, touching her things, or doing God knows what.

Mahir changed into his pajamas, and then before leaving the room he said, "I know you're disappointed, but I have a responsibility toward my family. I have to share their grief and show my support. And also help with the enormous flood of mourners that we normally receive on such occasions."

Yasmin did not have anything to say. She nodded and then grabbed *The Cat in the Hat*, opened it, and started reading to Sami and Mira.

The next day Yasmin's parents were disappointed when she informed them of the sudden change of plans, but she promised to do her best and visit as soon as possible.

There was rain and the temperatures continued to drop during the first two weeks of December. Every gray day was wet and thunderous, and on the few days that the sky turned blue, the air was icy. On the twentieth of the month, both Sami and Mira came down with severe colds, so Yasmin disappointed her family again by canceling a trip she had planned to the capital. Carole was let down too. She had invited Yasmin and the children to spend Christmas Eve with her, knowing how much Sami and Mira loved that time of the year in Arizona and looked forward to taking pictures with Santa.

On New Year's Eve, Mahir went to his parents' house and spent the night in the company of some of their close friends. Yasmin enjoyed the night at home with Sami and Mira, baking cookies with M&M's, watching television, and speculating on what the New Year had in store for them. Though Yasmin had much to celebrate with her children, she was filled with sadness at midnight as she thought about the pains and the losses of that year. She wondered when, if ever, she would return with Sami and Mira to their house in Scottsdale.

A snowstorm whitened most of the country in mid-January. It blocked major roads and isolated cities, villages, and even neighborhoods from one another and from the world. Schools, government departments, and most businesses closed down during the storm. Local channels dedicated all-day programming to monitoring rescue missions and interviewing citizens. Heavy rain persisted afterward as if the sky were determined to obey the thirst of every layer of earth down to its flaming center. So when the snow melted, it turned into brown rivers and ponds, causing parts of the country to remain inaccessible. Tahani had a minor overflow in her guest bathroom and told Yasmin that the man who had honked at them one time while driving by with his bride had to evacuate because his whole apartment drowned in a mix of dirty rainwater and sewage. Tahani also told Yasmin that, despite the challenging weather, Iraqi refugees who opposed their regime for various reasons continued to pour into the country. They had brought along very little of their belongings and many tales of horror to share. She also added that they had been shopping at the Paradise Mini Market and Waleed was barely keeping up with his orders.

A week after Sami's and Mira's midterms around mid-January, the school sent a letter to Yasmin with Sami and informed her that he had passed only two subjects, English and math. The letter also stated that Mira was incapable of writing or even recognizing her own name. The news devastated Yasmin. When Mahir came to pick up Sami and Mira that afternoon, she gave him the letter. From the way he scrunched his face while reading, Yasmin knew he was upset too.

Before he could utter a reaction, she said, "I did my best with Sami. If you were expecting a miracle, maybe you should've tutored him yourself or hired someone to do it." She then went to the bathroom and locked the door.

The first day of Eid al-Adha, the feast of sacrifice and the biggest feast in the Muslim calendar, fell on the eleventh day of

February along with another snowstorm that lasted a whole week. Of course, Yasmin had to disappoint her family again and not make it to Amman.

The sun started to come out more often by the end of February, and with the first signs of its warm rays, rugs dangled from every rooftop in Yasmin's neighborhood. Tahani elaborated on that phenomenon for Yasmin. It was warm enough to wash rugs and carpets, dry them on the roofs, and then roll them and put them away till next winter. She also told Yasmin that the use of gas furnaces had narrowed down to a few hours a day by almost everybody, but Yasmin's heater still growled in the boiler room day and night.

News channels no longer mentioned the weather and switched their complete attention to the American and allied troops, who by then were settled in their positions, ready to attack Iraq. Tahani told Yasmin that some of the neighbors who feared that the country would be dragged into that war were stocking up on tea and sugar. Some even asked Waleed if he could buy them rice and flour in wholesale quantities.

One afternoon as Yasmin worked on a new painting, Mahir and the children returned home only an hour after leaving. When they entered the living room, Sami and Mira gave her a kiss and then went to the family room and turned the television on. Yasmin did not like the expression on Mahir's face. She knew that look very well and what it meant. Mahir had something to tell her, and it was not of a pleasant nature. She turned her head and continued to paint. He stood next to her, and from the corner of her eye, she could see him staring at her painting. It was of a woman's face underwater, her eyes full of yearning and her mouth covered by a dark wave that looked like a triangular cloth. On the surface above the woman's head sailed a ship, and a big white moon lit the indigo sky of the night.

"Why is she under the ship?"

"She's not under the ship. She has travel on her mind."

"Ah…" Mahir laughed. "I need to talk to you."

The brush trembled in her hand. "What is it?"

Mahir pulled out one of the gray seats and sat down. "Things are not working out for me here. I mean at work."

"And?"

"I'm going back to Arizona when my contract expires, at the end of May."

She looked at him. "What? What about us?"

He looked down. "You'll follow next year."

"No," she shouted. "You're not leaving us behind."

"Calm down. It's just temporary. I need some time to start over, adjust, and buy furniture."

"We'll sleep on the floor," she said, getting up. She was certain that if she and the children did not board the same plane as Mahir, chances were they never would board one.

Mahir stood up. "Sit down." He put his hands on her shoulders. "Let me just finish. You and the children will stay with your parents. I'll take care of all the expenses."

"What? No!"

Sami and Mira walked in frightened. They held each other's hands and shifted their eyes between Yasmin and Mahir.

"Look at them for God's sake," Yasmin shouted again. "For once in your life, take a good look. Haven't they suffered enough? Do they always have to be without one of us? What in God's name are you thinking?"

Mahir reached out for Sami and Mira.

They stepped closer to him.

Without looking at Yasmin, he said, "Can you please calm down?"

"No, I can't. I've had it. I don't know where in the world you find your crazy ideas and solutions all the time. Am I ever going to understand what the hell has happened from the beginning till now?"

Mahir hugged Sami and Mira.

Yasmin glared at him.

Mahir ran his nervous fingers over his mustache. "My parents are worried. They don't want us to go through our fights and separation again. They just want to make sure things are back to normal when we return."

"*Your parents?*"

Mahir remained silent.

"What happened between us was not my fault, and you know it. I'm sure they think it is because of whatever you told them, so tell me straightforward, what do they want? Guarantees?"

"Look, when we separated back in Scottsdale, I thought that was the end of our marriage, so I hired a lawyer. He had written the divorce papers and mailed them to my parents' address because that was my forwarding address—"

"You moved out."

Mahir kept his eyes down and nodded. "My parents read the papers back then, and now they think we should sign them and remarry with a prenuptial agreement."

"What?" Yasmin squinted at him. "Prenuptial? It's all about money then?"

"No, no."

Yasmin slapped her thigh. "Then what?"

Mahir looked at her and then rubbed his hands and looked down. "It's too complicated. You wouldn't understand, and it will make things worse. Please trust me."

Yasmin could not suppress a laugh. "Really, Mahir? Trust you? Why don't you give it a try, and I promise you whatever you have to say is going to make more sense than keeping your silence."

He stared at Sami and Mira for a few moments.

"I'm waiting, Mahir."

He did not reply.

Yasmin held Sami's and Mira's hands. "Let's go wash up." She released a long sigh and turned to Mahir. "When I see our tickets and Sami's and Mira's passports, I'll sign the divorce papers for your parents. You are not leaving without us."

"Let's give the idea some time to settle. It's not as bad as it seems. We'll talk about it more later."

Yasmin disagreed by shaking her head. She walked Sami and Mira out of the living room.

Late that night, Yasmin was in bed reading, Sami and Mira fast asleep beside her, when Mahir came to the room.

"Let's go to the other room." He touched her hand gently. "I want to talk to you."

After Yasmin entered the peacpck's room behind Mahir, he tried to pull her next to him on the bed.

She pulled herself back. "What's going on?"

"We can't stay like this forever. I think not making love harmed our relationship in the first place."

"Whose advice are you following this time, Mahir? May I remind you that you are the one who decided to stop making love back in Scottsdale? So until I know why I was denied your love in the first place, I'm not going to accept it."

Mahir sat on the side of the bed looking up at Yasmin. "Why can't we just forget the past and start over?"

"Forget? That's easy for you to say. If you changed your mind and would like to explain to me why we ended up here, I'm ready to listen."

Mahir sighed and traced a circular pattern on the bedcover with his finger. He was completely lost in his thoughts when Yasmin left the room and returned to her bed.

CHAPTER FORTY

Though Mahir never mentioned his plans, the divorce papers, and the prenuptial agreement after that night, Yasmin did not stop thinking about it for a second. Was Mahir going to consider her ultimatum or just simply ignore her? His divorce papers and the prenuptial agreement were nothing but a cheap attempt on his behalf to gain more control. Such tactics could only come from a sick and devious individual that harbored enormous amounts of contempt and was thirsty for revenge. Did he think for a second how demeaning and offensive his plans were? Never mind his utter disrespect for Yasmin—was he really at peace with the idea of leaving the children behind? Or was he just using them to further twist her arm and force her to submit without any explanations of his past actions and real motives? Either way, it took a very heartless person to proceed with such cruel plans. Maybe Mahir was never the man she thought she married years ago, or maybe he always was but hid it so well. Some people can do that, and at the slight evidence of conflict they snap and return to their true nature, and Mahir proved it day in and day out during the last months. The more Yasmin thought about everything, the more stupid and deceived she felt. It was too late to regret many things she did wrong in her life, especially since they started having problems, but at least she learned one of the toughest lessons life had to teach her. She would not only fight hard but make sure she gained enough power to be the only one deciding her fate.

On March 20, the news anchor announced the invasion of Iraq by the Americans with a sad voice and a grief-stricken face. Desperate as Yasmin was, she had naively hoped that in some miraculous way the war would play a part in her fate and tip the scales in her favor. Maybe the country would be dragged into the war somehow, and then Mahir would get scared, and when the American embassy started evacuating its citizens, the four of them would leave.

During the war Mahir spent longer hours at his parents' house, watching CNN and other foreign news channels. He made sure Sami and Mira had their pajamas on before they left with him every evening. On some nights, instead of going straight to the family room to work on his laptop, he stood by the bedroom door and related to Yasmin the progress of the American troops and pointed out some important facts that the Arabic news stations chose to ignore or even deny.

By the end of the month, Mahir began to speak with frustration about the military news briefings of each side.

"The Iraqis and the Americans are starting to contradict one another. That's ridiculous," he said one night. "I hope it doesn't take too long before we know the truth," he snapped, as if the contradictions were meant to ridicule him personally and as if that were not exactly what he had been doing to her.

Yasmin did not reply. To someone who did not know him, he might have sounded like an honest and decent man who had done nothing wrong in his whole life. As far as she was concerned, he was the last one on the planet that should dare use the word *truth* or demand it.

Tahani told Yasmin that, according to the rumors discussed at the Paradise Mini Market, very few people in town looked forward to the fall of Baghdad. The majority actually believed that the Iraqi Army was going to defeat the evil forces of the Western world. Reason being that the Americans lacked principles and conspired to steal the Iraqi fortunes. Every now and then, she updated Yasmin on similar speculations that she heard at the Paradise Mini Market, at the hair salon, at an engagement party, and at a funeral of a distant relative.

One morning after Tahani and Yasmin put their children on their school buses and were on their way to Yasmin's kitchen, Faridah strolled in their direction. She stopped for a second and sipped from a cup she held with both hands.

Yasmin nudged Tahani and whispered, "I'm freezing. If she starts talking to us, tell her that we're in a hurry. That we're going to a doctor's appointment or something."

Faridah extended her cup. "Cinnamon?"

Yasmin blew a cloud of white breath into her palms and rubbed them. "No, thanks."

Faridah turned to Tahani. "You know our neighbor Um Mustafa?"

"Yeah." Tahani squinted. "Isn't she the one who swore during Desert Storm that she had seen Saddam's face on the moon?"

Faridah opened her eyes wide. "Yes, yes, yes."

"So what's with her? Did she see his face on the sun this time?"

Tahani and Yasmin looked at each other and then burst out laughing.

"No. I saw her yesterday, and she told me that she had a dream about the war."

"Is that right?" Yasmin took out a cigarette from her coat pocket and lit it. "And what did she say?"

Faridah's face brightened when Yasmin gave her attention. She ignored Tahani. "She saw the Iraqi desert and in the middle of it a big sign that read The American Graveyard."

Yasmin and Tahani laughed again.

Faridah stammered, "You'll see. Saddam will not only liberate Palestine but also crush the infidels and make all the Arabic countries prosper—"

"Excuse us, but I really have to go use the bathroom," Yasmin said.

She and Tahani laughed so hard that their eyes filled with tears.

Faridah shrugged and walked away.

A few days later, Tahani told Yasmin that she heard of many other women having similar dreams to that of Um Mustafa. Some claimed that they saw Saddam wearing a turban like Harun al-Rashid, the Abbasid caliph, sitting on a throne, reigning over the entire Middle East. Some went as far as alleging that Saddam was a reincarnation of Hammurabi, the Babylonian king.

On the breezy spring afternoon of April 9, while Yasmin sat on the couch between Sami and Mira watching television, Tahani called and asked Yasmin if she was watching the news and knew that the war had ended. Yasmin immediately changed channels and listened to the aggravated news anchor say that an act of treason caused the Iraqi soldiers to lose their final battle. He assured the viewers that the defeat was by no means a result of the bravery of the American and allied troops. The anchor's face was then replaced by Iraqi civilians celebrating, shouting, singing, and clapping around a few men who were bringing down a statue of Saddam. Once the statue hit the pavement facedown, one of the bystanders took off his slipper and beat their bronze president with it, an act of the greatest disrespect. The rest of the crowd cheered and danced.

At that very moment, Mahir entered the apartment, smiling. He stood close to the couch with his eyes fixed on the screen. "It happened, huh? It finally happened."

Yasmin kept staring at the television too. "Yeah."

"It feels like an evil force has been lifted off this earth, doesn't it?" He set aside his briefcase and then sat beside her on the couch and opened his laptop.

Yasmin agreed and wondered when his own demons were going to be evicted from his head. She got up, walked into the living room, and sat behind her easel. She heard Mira ask him if they were going to see her grandmother, and Mahir said that they were in just a few minutes after he checked his e-mail. Then a few minutes later she heard Sami ask if Mahir could put some Cheerios in a Ziploc bag for him before they left. Moments after, she heard all of them get up and walk to the kitchen. Yasmin was still staring at her painting when Mahir said from the kitchen, "OK, we're leaving. I have to go watch the news. Come on, let's go." He clapped his hands.

Sami and Mira ran back to the living room and gave Yasmin a kiss before running back to the kitchen.

When Yasmin heard the kitchen door close, she lit a cigarette and came back to the family room. Seeing the laptop open on the coffee table sent her heart racing. She looked in the direction of the kitchen expecting Mahir to come barging in, but he did not. She turned the television off, walked to the peacock's room, and looked out the window. Mahir's car was nowhere in sight. She waited a few minutes and then called him.

"Hi, we're flipping between news channels. As usual, it's a totally different story on CNN," Mahir said.

"I'm sure it is. I just called to tell you I was going with Tahani to Share'-el-jama' because I ran out of blue paint. I didn't want you guys to wonder what happened to me if I wasn't here when you came back."

"The sea took all the blue paint," he said.

"What?"

"The sea you painted."

"Oh, yeah, yeah."

"OK, that's fine. I don't think we're coming back anytime soon."

Yasmin had dreamed of this moment for months. She knew from the way Mahir was overprotective about his laptop and closed the screen whenever she suddenly entered the family room that he was hiding something. Without hesitation she sat behind it, and with a trembling hand she wiggled the mouse. The screen opened to his Yahoo inbox. Forty e-mails! It was hard to focus and decide what to read first. She started at the top and opened the first one: a reply from an old coworker discussing the war. The next few were from coworkers and students in Jordan. This was taking time, and she still wanted to go over the suitcase. She scanned the list of e-mail addresses and clicked on one with an Arabic name dated a year back, when their problems began and Mahir started acting weird. The e-mail was a couple of lines in Arabic with no greeting: "I know we agreed on $8,000.00 for your part in the mosque renovation, but we were hoping you would consider your efforts as a donation. Furthermore, the woman in the photos attached is no catch. She has a history of dating Arabic men, and once she claimed she was pregnant and went after the man!"

Yasmin felt her stomach turn. She opened the attachment and saw Mahir in the pictures with a bleached-blond woman in her thirties. Not pretty or prettier than her. It still made her furious to see their intimate poses with glasses of champagne in their hands. What a low-life, cheating, conniving, lying monster Mahir was. Wrecking their lives and putting her though hell all the time—he knew what he had done, and worse, he had tried to blame it all on her. Yasmin forwarded the e-mail to herself before she moved to the briefcase.

She put it on the couch next to her and opened it. It was full of papers, envelopes, and dossiers. She carefully pulled out the whole stack, set it on the coffee table, and examined the first paper: Mahir's contract with the university. When she finished reading it, she placed it facedown before grabbing a large manila envelope.

Going through the documents, she found out that Mahir had transferred $35,000 to his mother's account right before he had traveled to Jordan. She also found two currency-exchange receipts for a total of seven thousand euros, dated around the time of Mahir's trip to Germany with his mother and the children.

Yasmin then opened a dossier that was full of bank statements from America and some from Jordanian banks. She carefully studied a few statements that belonged to Mahir's mother, and from the debit-card transactions and ATM withdrawals, she knew the account actually belonged to Mahir. Next, she opened a small envelope that had a bunch of ATM receipts and checked the time and date on each, and that confirmed her assumption.

When Yasmin came across the agreement of the referee, she put it aside and preceded to the next document, which turned out to be a copy of the divorce papers Mahir's American lawyer had prepared. The papers stated a shared custody and specified the amount of $800 a month as child support. When she read, "The spouse agrees on not receiving any spousal maintenance," she shook her head and continued to the end. There was no mention of the house or of the company shares Mahir owned when he still worked at the firm. The prenuptial agreement stated that, in the case of a divorce, Yasmin would only get $7,000, the equivalent of the five thousand dinars that was specified in her Muslim marriage certificate as her postponed dowry.

She put that aside and picked up a printed e-mail from Mahir's old partner. She could tell from the contents that there were other correspondences prior to this one, but she still concluded that Mahir was going to assume his old position with the firm sometime during the first week of May.

Yasmin's phone rang and startled her. Lina's name appeared on the screen, but Yasmin did not answer. She held up a small envelope, covered with a few stamps and many seals, addressed to Mahir. It looked like it had toured the world before it finally reached Jordan. The phone rang again when she was taking the letter out. She glanced at the screen. It was Lina again.

This time she pressed the green key. "Hi, Lina."

"Where are you? I just called you, but you didn't answer."

"I was in the bathroom. What's going on?"

"I have to tell you something. It's very important. Is Mahir home?"

"No, no. What is it?" Yasmin moved her eyes between her watch and the rest of the stack.

"I overheard Baba and Fadi discussing a reconciliation plan for Mahir and his father."

"What? Why? What's going on between them?"

"I thought you knew that they didn't speak to each other since you guys made up."

"No, I didn't. Well, I knew his father was angry, but I didn't hear any further details. So how come Mahir is at their house every evening?"

"His father is never there. Fadi told my father that, at the beginning, Abu Mahir used to walk out when Mahir and the children walked in. After a while he started leaving before they arrived and only returned after they left."

Yasmin could feel each of her brain cells circling in its own orbit. Millions of thoughts pushed around trying to become of major importance. If Mahir had not spoken to his father since they reconciled, then who made him rent their dilapidated apartment from his father's driver? Who instructed Basim to follow her around and break into their place when she was visiting with her parents? Why had Basim complained to Mahir when his wife, Faridah, failed to befriend Yasmin no matter how hard she tried? Whose orders was Mahir following when he took Sami and Mira every single evening and every weekend to his parents' house? She could not imagine that Mahir's mother, who was silent from day one, was behind it all.

"Lina, can I call you later? Someone is at the door," she lied.

"Sure."

Yasmin threw the phone on the couch and opened the letter, written in English and signed by a "Vicki." The woman wrote to Mahir that she had tried to reach him for a long time but could never get ahold of him. She had e-mailed him numerous times and also called him. Her calls were forwarded to his voice mail, but she never left a message, fearing someone other than Mahir would listen to it. She just needed to talk since he gave no explanation for his sudden break up. They could at least remain friends.

It all started making sense now. Finally Yasmin had found the missing links that completed the horrible story she had to live. But the ending was in her hands now. The mere thought made her light-headed. When she tried to put the letter back in the envelope, her hands shook so badly that she dropped it a few times and almost tore the side of it. After setting the letter next to her on the couch, she opened the last dossier. It contained the refinance papers that Lindsey had mentioned back in Arizona along with two quitclaim deeds. Yasmin recognized her signature on one of them and, to her shock, Mahir's signature on the other. He had quitclaimed the house to his mother back in May. Now it became clear why Mahir had tricked her into signing the deed. He had feared that Vicki would come after him for who knows what reason. Yasmin could think of a million things but did not want to go there. He probably also wanted to be prepared in case Yasmin found out he was cheating, and wanted to make sure she did not get the house in the settlement. Mahir had obviously decided back then that his mother was the only one who could protect his interests from both women, even if she had to ruin her grandchildren's world while doing so.

Yasmin held the stack, carefully placed it in the briefcase, and put it back on the floor. The only thing that came to her mind at that moment was to copy the letter before Mahir and the children returned. She called Tahani. The phone rang for a while, but

Tahani did not answer. Yasmin went to the peacock's room, looked out, and saw Tahani in the front yard with her children.

She opened the window. "Tahani," she shouted.

Tahani turned around, smiling.

"Can you go to the bookstore with me?"

Tahani bit the index finger of her right hand. Yasmin knew she had messed up. She forgot that Tahani did not want anyone in the family, or the neighborhood, to know that she went anywhere near books.

"Sorry, sorry."

Tahani put her finger to her lips, telling Yasmin to lower her voice.

"I mean to the produce market," she said.

Tahani laughed and nodded.

Yasmin slipped on her shoes and her coat, put the letter in her purse, and stormed out the door.

Tahani was waiting by the gate. "What's wrong? You look pale. Are you OK?"

"I'm OK. I have to copy a letter before Mahir returns."

The air was chilly, and the late afternoon had a drab color to it, like the blocks of the buildings they were passing. Yasmin lifted her eyes to the sky and saw slithers of bright blue between the cracks of gray clouds. She took that as a good omen. They paced toward the main road, breaking off a soccer match as they crossed to the other side. One of the boys made it very clear that he did not appreciate the interruption, so he kicked the ball in Tahani's direction, missing her shoulder by inches.

Tahani ignored it and turned to Yasmin. "What kind of a letter?"

"It's from a woman. It's my ticket out of here and back to my house, Tahani," Yasmin said while waving down a cab.

Tahani widened her eyes. Once in the backseat, she told the driver where to take them.

"Inshallah," he said and drove out of the neighborhood.

"I'll tell you everything when we get there," Yasmin said.

Tahani agreed with a smile and a slow blink.

Yasmin took the letter out in the backseat and read it again, as if making sure its contents were still there. The times she had spent running from one dead end to the next, leaving her feeling like she was sifting through mounds of hay in search of a needle, were over. She was right all along, but finally, she had the proof that would help her gain back her life. Now she knew what having power felt like; Mahir would die before he would let her crush his ego and expose the ridiculous manly-man act he had put on from the beginning. He would not tolerate people finding out that he leid about his infidelity. Or invented lies about Yasmin and their marriage to gain support and sympathy.

Mahir had gone out of his way to come across as a wholesome family man, a loving husband that was victimized by an unfair and crazy wife. But this letter and the photos would reveal the truth, would shame Mahir in front of their families and friends.

When they arrived at Share'-el-jama', Yasmin paid the driver, and then both stepped out of the cab. Frying oil, car fumes, and a hint of sewage contaminated the air. Yasmin felt her stomach turn. She and Tahani pushed their way through honking cars, other jaywalkers, and the many street vendors. A young boy followed them, holding up boxes of Lebanese Gandour gum and swearing to them it was real Chiclets.

From their previous trips, Yasmin still remembered that one of the bookstores, the Book Store of Success, had a sign taped to the entrance about having a Xerox copier. She kept her eyes on store signs until she spotted it. Once they entered, Yasmin took out the letter from the envelope, approached a man standing behind the counter, and handed him both.

"Ten copies each, please."

The man turned them over in his hand and then copied them one at a time.

"Long story," Yasmin whispered to Tahani. "When we're done here, I need to go to the Internet café."

"OK," Tahani said, her eyes overflowing with anticipation.

Yasmin paid twenty piasters for the copies, and then as they walked toward the Internet café down the street, she told Tahani about Vicki.

Tahani listened with full attention, sometimes frowning, gasping and lifting her palm to her mouth, and finally slapping her own cheek.

"How are you going to use the letter to your advantage?"

"I don't know yet, Tahani, but I have to be careful. As hard as it is, I'm going to sit on it until I feel it's the right moment."

"Your secret is in a well," Tahani said and then lifted her palms to the sky and prayed, asking God to grant Yasmin the wish of returning to her home.

The happiness Yasmin saw in her eyes revealed a true friend.

When they arrived at the Internet café, the young man sitting behind the reception desk greeted them with a nod and a smile. Yasmin took out a copy of the letter and scribbled her e-mail address on the back of it. She then handed it to him and asked him to scan it and e-mail it to her.

"Sure," he said.

"Is there a vacant computer we can use?"

"Yes. Please go ahead. A waiter will be with you shortly."

"There's no need. We're not staying for long. I need to print out some picture in color, though. Is that possible?"

"Sure. But it's one dinar per page."

"That's fine."

He then motioned with his hand for them to proceed to the big room.

Yasmin and Tahani walked toward a computer in the back, passing many heads that turned in their direction. Yasmin could tell from the murmurs and the puzzled looks on some faces that many were discussing the war.

"Impossible," a guy told another sitting behind a computer next to him. "It doesn't add up."

After Yasmin and Tahani sat down, they each lit a cigarette, and then Yasmin opened her e-mail and checked her inbox. She opened the e-mail she had forwarded from Mahir's e-mail, opened the attachment, and clicked print. She showed Tahani the pictures before she moved to the next e-mail. Tahani made a disgusted face and pretended she was spitting at the photos. They both laughed. Then Yasmin opened an e-mail from Lindsey, their realtor. Lindsey wrote that Mahir had called her, inquired the status of the mortgage, and asked her to help him hire a real-estate lawyer. Lindsey promised Yasmin to write soon if she heard again from Mahir.

Then Yasmin read an e-mail from Ellen dated at least two weeks back. Ellen was concerned since she had not received any mail from Yasmin in a long time and said she was getting ready to leave on a trip to New Mexico. Yasmin wrote back to Ellen, apologizing for not writing sooner and assuring her that she, Sami, and Mira were safe and sound. She also explained why Mahir contacted Lindsey and briefed her on Vicki's letter and the photos.

After Yasmin received the scanned copy, she e-mailed it to Carole and Hala with a brief explanation. Before leaving the café, she and Tahani stopped at the front desk. Yasmin paid for the services and retrieved the copy of the letter she had handed the man earlier to scan.

On the way back, Yasmin thanked Tahani. "I'll never forget this favor. I was too nervous to go out alone. I felt like my heart was going to stop." She opened her purse and handed Tahani the original letter and three copies. "Keep these with you for now."

Tahani put the papers in her purse.

When the cab approached the neighborhood, Yasmin looked ahead and saw Mahir's car parked in front of the building and felt that her heart actually stopped beating.

CHAPTER FORTY-ONE

I t took Yasmin a few minutes to steady her breath before entering the apartment. Thoughts raced around in her head, and she hoped her snooping around went unnoticed, at least for the night. She needed more time to think and plan. This was her first and only chance in a year to get back her life.

Mahir was staring at the television screen when she entered. He looked at her and smiled. "*Ahlan* (welcome)."

Yasmin faked a smile and tried to steady her voice. "Where are Sami and Mira?" She looked around.

"In the living room, drawing." Mahir squinted at the television screen.

Yasmin could hear the shock in the news anchor's voice, reciting the news of the past hours, as if it were just happening that moment.

"Sit down," Mahir said. "I need you to read some papers." He held them out. "They're just copies. Fadi is going to stop by sometime next week with a lawyer so you can sign the originals, and then I will also sign them and have them notarized at the American embassy."

"What papers?"

"The divorce papers I told you about and a prenuptial agreement my attorney in Arizona prepared for us."

"Can we do this tomorrow after you and the kids return from spending the day with your parents?"

Mahir hesitated for a moment but then agreed.

The night took its usual course but not for Yasmin. After putting Sami and Mira in bed, she went to the living room and put the final touches on her painting while going over her findings and how she was going to use them. She was not going to distract herself with predicting Mahir's reaction at this point, although him losing his mind and doing something crazy should be taken seriously. Hours after she heard Mahir go to bed, Yasmin had it all planned. She took her painting outside and packed her easel, paint, and brushes. She then went around making small piles and stacks of things she would pack later. She took her other paintings off the frames and rolled them up. She would do the same with the last painting when it dried.

Yasmin was not sure how long she slept. When she woke up the next day, she could not tell what was dream and what were just the endless scenarios she had thought of.

Right after Mahir and the kids left, Yasmin called Tahani and asked her to come over and have coffee. Tahani brought back the original letter and the copies. They had their coffee in the kitchen for the last time, and it saddened both of them.

"Do you have a plan?" Tahani asked.

"I think so. Mahir wants me to read some divorce papers his lawyer in America wrote for him." Before Tahani finished her gasp, Yasmin continued, "He said he thought we were divorcing back in America and his parents read the papers and now they are insisting on us going ahead with it. Some type of guarantee I guess to protect his assets!"

Tahani shook her head. "When he gets back today, I'll wait a few minutes, and then I'll come stand by the door. If I hear you scream, I'll walk right in."

Yasmin laughed. "Good plan. I hope I don't scream. I'm planning on calling Majid sometime today to come and get me and the kids. So I should be fine."

Tahani seemed satisfied.

"I want to give you something," Yasmin said.

"Give me what?"

"All the new kitchen stuff I bought and something else."

Tahani did not hide her joy. "Thank you so much."

"That's not all. Come with me."

Yasmin walked with Tahani to the living room. She pointed at her paint, her brushes, the new canvases, and her easel. "I want you to have all this. Would you like that?"

Tahani's eyes shone with tears. "I would love to, but I've never tried to paint."

"Try, Tahani, and see what happens. I know you like the verses and anything with calligraphy. I want you to promise me that you will use them and not set them aside. Take classes if you think you need some or find art books in Arabic. Don't miss out on this opportunity of learning how to express yourself without being judged. Do it with a passion regardless of what anyone might think."

"I promise." She gave Yasmin a hug.

Tahani helped Yasmin finish packing clothes, some books, CDs, and toys, and together they dragged the luggage to the living room. Then they carried all the things Yasmin had gifted Tahani downstairs.

"Just in case I don't see you before I leave, I want to say goodbye now and thank you for being a true friend. I don't know how I would've survived this year without having you in my life."

Tahani did not bother hiding her tears. "I'm going to miss you so much. I wish your circumstances were different and you would stay." She wiped her tears. "But at the same time, I am very happy for you and want you to leave."

As soon as Yasmin went back to her place, she called Majid and briefed him on the letter and her plan. She asked him to keep this between them and not tell their parents and wondered if he could come and pick them up. Majid said he was going to leave immediately and hang out nearby until he heard from her again. Yasmin promised to text him when Mahir got home.

It was a little after five when Mahir and the children came home. Yasmin gave them baths and put their pajamas on like she would normally do. She asked them to go sit in the living room and draw until she finished talking to Mahir. Before she went to see Mahir, she sent a text to Majid asking him to come close to the front door and added that he might find Tahani there too.

Mahir was already in his usual spot on the couch in the family room when Yasmin entered the room, a copy of the letter and the pictures tucked in the back pocket of her jeans.

Muir immediately took a stack of papers and handed it to Yasmin.

Yasmin collected her courage and looked Mahir in the eyes. "I've already read them, and I'm not signing them." She threw a copy of the letter on his laptop.

It took Mahir a few seconds to snap out of his shock. The fear Yasmin saw on his face made her think a heart attack was in the making. He suddenly held his head in his palms and shouted, "It was all a stupid mistake."

Yasmin could see and feel his horror. "A mistake? I would have been long dead if I had even come close to making such a mistake."

Mahir grabbed the letter and shredded it to tiny pieces, while his face turned from yellow to pink to maroon.

"Look, I won't show the letter or the pictures to anyone if you fix your mistake now and make everything right again."

Mahir looked up. "You made copies? Damn!" He stood up.

Yasmin jumped back. "Majid is outside. He will be coming in any minute," she said. "So you'd better sit and lower your voice if you don't want the whole world to know about this. Plus there is no need to scare the kids."

Mahir collapsed on the couch out of breath, sweat pouring from his forehead, looking down.

Yasmin could tell that he was seriously shocked and frightened, but she did not feel sorry for him. Let him pay a small price for what he had done to her over the past year. Even though revenge was not what she had on her mind right now or had sought all along, watching Mahir suffer felt good. Now she had to take advantage of the moment she had anticipated for months. She had to make sure that she, Sami, and Mira were going to return to their home and resume their lives.

"So here's the deal," she finally said. "I'm taking Sami and Mira with me to Amman tonight. They already missed a school year, so I don't see the point of making them attend anymore. You will buy our tickets tomorrow and transfer enough money to my account for a few nights at a hotel and to buy furniture and whatever we need to start over."

Mahir banged his head with his palm three times. Still looking down, he said, "What is going to happen then? Are you going to go back, tell everybody about it, and divorce me?"

"You never cease to amaze me. I mean…after everything you've done, you still have the nerve to worry about your image and act like a victim?" Yasmin shook her head. "You need to tame your ego, Mahir. You have to admit your wrongdoing and take responsibility for your actions."

Mahir stayed put.

"I'm sure you still have some common sense to understand that after what you did, and after reading the letter, our relationship and marriage are going to take a backseat for a while. When and if

I decide to forgive, maybe I will consider counseling. The kids and their education are my priority right now."

Mahir nodded. He shut down his laptop and closed his briefcase.

Yasmin walked to the living room and texted Majid that she was OK. Sami and Mira were still in there. Yasmin leaned over Sami to look at his drawing. It was of a house with a pitched roof, a half-circle driveway with a saguaro cactus by the sidewalk and a bean-shaped pool in the back.

Sami looked up. "This is our house."

Yasmin smiled. "Yes, it is. Good job."

"When are we going back?" he asked with the tone of a child who was bored from a long wait at the doctor's office.

"Very soon."

"Really?"

"I promise to do whatever it takes, Sami. We're going to Amman tonight." Yasmin heard the kitchen door slam. She knew Mahir had left, so she texted Majid again to come in from the front door. She let him and Tahani in and told them how the confrontation went.

Tahani sighed with relief. "Thank God he left. Let me and Majid take your luggage to the car. I'm afraid he will return and take out his wrath on you."

"That's a good idea," Majid said. "This is not going to sit well with him."

Tahani cried as if a precious part of her life had ended when she said her last good-byes to Yasmin. "I will never forget you and the days we spent together."

"Me neither, Tahani. I will keep calling you from Amman to let you know what is happening with me. I have a feeling everything will work out just fine. I'm finally able to use a language Mahir understands."

On the way to Amman, Yasmin retold Majid in detail about all the stuff she found in Muir's briefcase and laptop and how she kept the originals. And she told him word for word what she and Mahir said when she confronted him. She made Majid vow again not to mention a word of it to their parents. She did not want anything to influence Mahir's decision and risk her chances of returning to her home in Scottsdale. Majid agreed on the story Yasmin fabricated for her parents.

Once they arrived in Amman, and as Yasmin expected, they were received with endless questions about her sudden arrival with Sami and Mira and all their belongings. Yasmin assured them with a steady voice and convincing calmness that Mahir had decided to send them back first to Arizona and he would catch up when his contract with the university ended. Majid backed her up.

Her parents smiled and sighed with relief when she finished lying to them. Her father went about his usual routine of the evening and watched the news in the family room. Her mother asked the maid, Suka, to make tea and set her hookah in the veranda.

Before she walked away, her mother said, "When I return from the hair salon tomorrow, we'll call Hala with the news."

Yasmin agreed. After she settled in the guest bedroom and put Sami and Mira in bed, she called Carole. Carole had not opened her e-mail and did not know what was going on, so Yasmin briefed her on the letter and her confrontation with Mahir. While Yasmin explained the contents of the letter to Carole, she occasionally gasped and followed with a "What?" or "No way."

Carole laughed at the end. "This is like a movie, I swear to God. I mean…if I didn't know you, I would think you were making this up. I hope everything works out as you plan."

Later that night, Yasmin's mother told her that both Nihad and Samira were extremely pleased with the new developments and promised to visit soon.

The next day, Yasmin awoke to the sound of her cell phone ringing. She rubbed her eyes and looked down at the screen before she answered. Lina apologized for disturbing her at such an early hour but said it was urgent.

Yasmin sat up. "What's going on?"

"Are you going to be home today? Fadi was wondering what time he could come over with the lawyer. He said that you know all about it and that Mahir spoke to him two days ago and asked him to call on you anytime to sign the papers."

The news delighted Yasmin. Mahir had not mentioned the previous night to anyone. Finally, her long-awaited chance to teach Fadi a lesson had arrived.

"Listen, Lina, I'm in Amman visiting with my parents. Tell Fadi he can come over today at eleven."

At around ten, Yasmin's mother went to her appointment at the hair salon and repeated that when she returned in a couple of hours or so, they would call Hala. Yasmin nodded and closed the door behind her, hoping she would not be back when Fadi arrived.

Fifteen minutes before eleven, Yasmin checked on her father and found him still reading on the veranda. She took Sami and Mira down to Majid's house and turned on the PlayStation for them. Then she went back upstairs and waited by the living-room window for Fadi and the lawyer until they arrived. When she opened the door for them, Fadi cleared his throat and introduced Yasmin to Mazen Fahmi. The lawyer looked young, in his late twenties or early thirties. His gel-drenched hair glistened in the sun. He was dressed like Fadi in a three-piece suit and carried a briefcase.

Yasmin shook his hand and invited both of them into the study. She closed the study door, asked them to have a seat, and then sat behind her father's desk. Fadi set his briefcase on his lap, opened it, and took out two small stacks of paper.

"The one on top is the original," he said while handing both to Yasmin. "The other one is just a copy for you. Take your time reading before you sign."

Yasmin nodded and then took her time pretending to read the divorce and the prenuptial agreements. Fadi meanwhile lit a cigar and conversed with the lawyer.

When Yasmin was supposedly done reading, she looked up at Fadi. "So these are the originals, you said?"

Fadi nodded, closed his briefcase, and set it on the floor next to his seat.

Yasmin tore the stack first in half and then in quarters, and then she took each section and reduced it to inch-size pieces while Fadi and Mazen stared at her with their mouths open. When Fadi snapped out of his shock, he scooted himself to the edge of his seat and then stood up. Yasmin gathered the shreds and threw them at his face.

"Now get out of here," she said.

"How dare—"

"Not a word. Take your friend and leave now. If you have anything to say, you can call Mahir and his father."

Yasmin worked her way through the other stack, but this time she dumped it in the trash bin.

Fadi trembled. "I—"

"Out."

Fadi snatched his briefcase off the floor and walked ahead of his friend to the front door. When they stepped out, Yasmin banged the door behind them.

Spring continued to fight away the few days of winter weather that had unrightfully trespassed on the season. A cool wind came a few times and dropped some blooms off the trees. On other days, thin clouds gathered at midday but could not squeeze out more than a soft spatter that scented the air with the smell of first rain. Though Mahir did not contact Yasmin within the next few days, she did not panic or consider a new plan. She knew Mahir well enough and knew he would do as she asked for fear of being exposed.

Lina called Yasmin one afternoon and asked her to go to a room where no one could hear her.

"I hesitated before calling you. I'm sure you don't want anyone to know this. Not even me," she said.

As Lina began to tell Yasmin about a meeting between her father, Fadi, and Mahir that took place a few days earlier, Yasmin listened without interrupting.

It turned out that after Yasmin tore up the divorce papers and kicked Fadi and his friend out of the house, Fadi had immediately tried to call Mahir. When Mahir had not answered, Fadi called Mahir's father and told him what had happened. Mahir eventually had to confess to his parents all about Yasmin finding Vicki's letter and the pictures and her threatening to expose him. Lina said that Mahir's father was enraged. He not only screamed at Mahir and told him he was not worthy of being an Ahmad but also called him stupid for not knowing how to cover his tracks. What if Yasmin decided to expose him? How would Mahir and his parents look in front of Yasmin's parents after the way they had treated them? This would shame not only Mahir but any hot-blooded Ahmad and cause them to bury their faces in the sand. Lina's words turned into pictures in Yasmin's mind. She could see Mahir standing in his parents' family room with a shameful expression on his face, sweat oozing from his temples, his breath becoming faster and faster. Mahir's father ended his screaming session by spitting in Mahir's face and asking him to get the hell out of the house while throwing his shoes at him. Yasmin was shocked yet pleased at the use of one of the most humiliating expressions to demonstrate to someone how insignificant he was. How worthless.

"When Mahir met with my father and Fadi and told them the truth, he actually cried."

Yasmin did not comment but smiled and sighed in content.

Lina continued. Fadi of course did not waste the opportunity to take his anger toward Yasmin out on Mahir. He called him a liar, an idiot, and a loser. Lina's father was not sympathetic to Mahir either. He admonished him relentlessly for the way he had treated Yasmin, the lies he told, the friction he caused between the two families. Mahir was desperate for their support but got none. He needed some kind of assurance that Yasmin would keep quiet about the letter, that she would not divorce him once they returned to Arizona. Lina's father had told him that he was asking for too much and that after all he had done, no one would blame Yasmin if she said or did anything now.

Yasmin's thoughts crashed like waves in her head. She did not know what to say.

"God, Lina. I'm speechless." She ended her call with Lina by thanking her for letting her know what was going on. After she hung up, she smiled again to herself. Though Mahir had gotten some punishment for the pain and losses he had caused, it was not enough. At least she knew now that her chances of getting her way and returning to her home in Scottsdale were greater than ever. For now, she decided not to share the letter with anyone. Maybe one day in the future when the need arose, she would.

The days went by at their usual pace for Yasmin at her parents' house. Not much was discussed regarding the past year, but every now and then her father would drop a comment like, "Be patient with Mahir and the children. Don't overreact. Talk about things before situations get out of hand." Or he would say, "Make sure you stay with a friend until Mahir catches up with you."

Yasmin's aunts Nihad and Samira came to visit and smoke hookah almost every day. No matter what they started talking about, they always switched the conversation to the chaotic situation in

Iraq. They talked about how the mother of all battles had turned out to be the mother of all disasters with casualties on both sides. About the big Iraqi figures seeking political asylum all over the world and about the exiled opposition now returning to claim their share in the long-awaited victory. And of course, about people speculating on the whereabouts of Saddam's wife and daughters. News channels continued to provide the country with a daily barrage of shocking information, like the millions in cash that was found in cottages near Saddam's palaces and the looting of the Iraqi National Museum. Television cameras followed people as they entered palaces and came out carrying whatever they could get their hands on. Some left with big pieces of furniture, while some settled for an expensive painting or vase and some for as little as a toilet seat.

An intriguing topic for Nihad were the playing cards created by the American military to help the troops identify Saddam's government, the high-ranking Ba th Party members, and members of the Revolutionary Command Council. Every time she brought up the subject, she pointed out who was caught, found dead, or still at large. Whenever she mentioned the cards, she added a new possibility to her long list of assumptions on Saddam's whereabouts. Once she said he had fled to Russia or to some country in South America.

One night Nihad said, "They say Saddam left Iraq long before the invasion." She adjusted the coals on her hookah and added, "The person appearing on TV is nothing more than a look-alike." Another evening during a related discussion, she insisted that he was dead, most probably killed by his own bloody hands.

Many Iraqi refugees continued to cross the Jordanian borders, while thousands were denied entry and ended up in camps. Television channels constantly showed families talking about their losses and showing pictures of loved ones misplaced in the chaos. One day around noon, Yasmin went with Fatin to pick up a

FedEx package for Majid. On one of the traffic lights, they were approached by a man in his thirties, holding a small box of SB gum in his hand. He spoke with an Iraqi accent as he swore that he had a degree in engineering from the Iraqi University. Yasmin and Fatin felt very bad for him. There were probably thousands like him in Jordan or even in other countries, struggling to make a living. A few lights down, Yasmin and Fatin passed an Iraqi woman sitting on the sidewalk with an infant in her lap. She held out a sign made of cardboard that read Will Work for Food. It broke Yasmin's heart and reminded her of that woman she once saw in Irbid when she and Tahani were on their way to the Internet café. Yasmin remembered Tahani mentioning that she came across many Iraqis trying to make a living on the streets. Women and children were not only unfairly victimized by the war but were totally neglected, as if they did not count, and that was a big shame.

As usual, every time Nihad and Samira came over, Nihad had some stories to share about her new Iraqi neighbors or their relatives and friends. They told horror stories about kidnappings for huge ransoms, cars stolen and resold to their owners, and people becoming filthy rich overnight and then suddenly disappearing. Nihad mentioned meeting a family of four at one of her neighbors' apartments. The woman cried endlessly over the misfortune that had befallen them. She swore they had left all their belongings back in Baghdad and fled to Jordan with one suitcase. A week later Nihad heard that the family had bought a house in one of the most prestigious neighborhoods in Amman and paid cash for it.

"Now we know what they had in that suitcase, I guess," she said in a sarcastic tone.

It bothered Nihad that shortages were not only at grocery stores now, but she still confessed that the economy was getting a tremendous boost. Some Iraqis lived for weeks, even months, at five-star hotels and made finding reservations at the Dead Sea or Aqaba resorts virtually impossible. Others caused shortages in housing, public transportation, clothing, appliances, and electronics. Rumors about Iraqis paying cash when buying anything, even buildings as tall as ten stories, never ceased. They bought restaurants, big and small businesses, the latest models of expensive and fancy cars, and gold by the kilo.

Though Yasmin participated in most of the conversations with her parents and her aunts, and sometimes with her friend Carole, her life and her return to America remained her most important headline of all. The night Mahir called and said that he had bought the tickets, Yasmin felt a serenity she had never imagined possible. When she told Sami and Mira and saw the joy of looking forward in their eyes, her body started releasing the pain, the sorrow, the horror, and all the cruelty of the past year. Mahir continued to call and speak to Sami and Mira and told them he would drive them to the airport when it was time to leave. On Yasmin's last day in Amman, her mother gave her a lunch farewell party and invited Nihad and Samira, Carole, and Lina. Nihad and Samira arrived around two o'clock with cheerful demeanors, dressed in their athletic uniforms, and with their hair coiffed. Once Carole and Lina arrived shortly after, Yasmin excused herself and went to help her mother and Suka set the table. Her mother carried a large plate of the traditional Jordanian lamb dish and carefully put it in the center of the dining table. *Mansaf* was a mountain of long-grain rice, completely covered with big chunks of lamb and sprinkled with fried almonds and pine nuts. Yasmin spread around it a few small plates of green onions and cold and crunchy cucumber pickles that usually tasted good with all the other ingredients. Suka brought out two bowls of sauce made from dried yogurt. It all smelled so good that Yasmin could not wait to get a taste.

While they were eating, Samira mentioned a rumor she had heard about the prices of fuel going up now that the country would no longer get free fuel from Iraq. After everyone briefly commented on that, Nihad suddenly switched the conversation to Yasmin and said that Yasmin's problems had come to a happy conclusion because she finally wised up and treated Mahir the way every smart woman does her husband.

They all laughed.

"What can I say? You know how it works," Yasmin said.

After they finished eating, Suka cleared the table and then came back with turkish coffee and dessert. *Knafeh* was usually the traditional dessert for the meal they had and was preferred by almost everybody. The thick layer of melted goat cheese topped with a layer of thin red noodles tasted great with or without syrup.

While they had their coffee and sweets, Carole whispered to Yasmin, "I've never seen you happier, but I still could see traces of worry in your eyes."

"I guess I'm afraid of being too happy. I'll be fine once I board the plane."

Yasmin was sure that by the time she landed in Arizona and took one look at the blue sky, not a trace of worry would remain in her eyes.

Before Lina left, Yasmin gave her a long embrace. "Thank you for being so nice to me, Lina. I'll never forget your favors. If there's anything I can ever do for you, you just have to snap your fingers."

"Mahir's parents are devastated, by the way," Lina said. "I heard they feel really bad about the way they treated you."

"Lina, I have one thing to say about this, but I won't. I still have manners."

Lina tilted her head back, laughing. "Take care, and keep in touch."

Mahir arrived from Irbid in his red car a little after four. Yasmin, Sami, Mira, and the whole family were waiting for him out on the balcony. Mahir stepped out of the car and shook hands with Yasmin's parents, Majid and Fatin. Then he placed the suitcases in the trunk while Yasmin and the children said their good-byes.

Yasmin's mother cried when she hugged Yasmin. She held her tight and whispered, "Next time, make sure you let it go. You saw what happened this time."

"You don't have to worry, Mama. I've learned my lesson."

As Mahir eased his way down the hill, Yasmin turned around in her seat and waved to her family. Her father was grasping at the third volume of his book with one hand and moving the other hand as if gently wiping the air. Her mother continued to pat her eyes with a tissue between waves. Majid, Fatin, and their children, Omar and Zaid, kept their palms fanning in the car's direction until they disappeared from Yasmin's view.

Once out of the neighborhood, Mahir took the main road, and they were on their way to the seventh roundabout area. Traffic was mild at that time of the day, save for a few yellow cabs racing one another. Yasmin had mixed feelings about parting with the neighborhood, with the familiar buildings, banks, and shops they were passing for the last time, or at least for a long time to come. It would take her a long time before she would stop associating that road with the many trips she had taken over the past year, only to reach one dead end after the other.

Yasmin felt awkward sitting next to Mahir after all they had been through. Neither one of them uttered a word. She remembered the day Mahir drove them to Sky Harbor and that smile he gave her at the gate. She opened the manila envelope Mahir had set between their seats and leafed through the tickets and the passports.

"Happy you're going home?" Mahir looked at Sami and Mira in the rearview mirror.

"Yeah," they both screamed and clapped their hands.

Their innocent faces radiated happiness, and Yasmin imagined tiny stars flickering in their eyes.

At the end of the road, Mahir turned right, and the seventh roundabout became visible. After a couple of miles, they drove around it and took the highway to the airport.

Spring had claimed every inch of landscape on the way. The vacant lots that usually exposed dirt, rocks, and thorns now yielded an orgy of grass, plants, and wildflowers. Yasmin watched flocks of sheep in the distance grazing in disbelief, running from one plant to the other and from one flower to the next. Not every winter was generous enough to provide them with such an abundance of treats.

Still looking out, Yasmin remembered how the whole ordeal had started in the spring and how it was ending in the same season of new beginnings. She turned her eyes to heaven and whispered a prayer of gratitude. She was finally going home.

Mahir looked in the rearview mirror and sighed. "Are you going to miss this country?"

Yasmin did not answer or look back, as if afraid of turning into a pillar of salt if she did.

Mahir reached out and tried to hold her hand. "I'm glad it's all over and behind us now. We will fix it when I get there."

Yasmin looked down at his hand and then slowly reached in her purse and took out a cigarette. She rolled the windows down and lit it. That was exactly what Mahir had done and said right after their reconciliation meeting, but nothing had changed afterward. Did he really think that holding her hand and saying a few words would make her forget and forgive? Denial was a safe place for men like Mahir. It soothed their swollen egos.

Mahir obviously did not bother to think twice before he cheated on her. He must have been certain she would never find out, but even when she did, he assumed Yasmin would let it slide. He thought of her as nothing but a vulnerable Arabic woman who accepted her fate with gratitude for the privilege of living in the shadow of his greatness. He was not just an attractive man with a good degree: he was an Ahmad! A family name that kept a green light blinking in his head throughout their ordeal. Mahir betrayed Yasmin. Tricked her, took away her children, and made every cell in her body weep and bleed. He made it financially impossible for her to survive without his money, yet on many occasions he had the audacity to claim that he did all of it out of love to keep her and keep the family intact.

Yasmin remembered once reading that the true meaning of forgiveness was about removing the self from that place of sadness so one could move forward. Was that how she had survived her ordeal? It must have been, because otherwise she could never forgive Mahir or forget the hurt he had caused. She turned and looked at her children and sighed. Lesson learned. She would do whatever it took to ensure this would never happen to her or her children again. The first thing she would do once they were back in Scottsdale would be to look for a job, and then she would deal with Mahir one issue at a time.

"What's that?" Mahir interrupted her thoughts, pointing to a tube that lay on the car floor next to her purse.

"One of my paintings. It's the one that has a woman's face underwater and a ship over her head."

"That was a nice one, you know? I think it would make a great book cover. You should try to sell it."

Still looking out the window, she said, "I can do anything if I put my mind to it."

The End

AUTHOR BIOGRAPHY

Reem hopes to inspire change by writing about various life experiences. With a BA in archaeology and a minor in history, Reem has always been interested in exploring various cultures and types of art and traveling to unique places off the beaten path. Reem lives in Scottsdale, Arizona.

www.ingramcontent.com/pod-product-compliance
Lightning Source LLC
Chambersburg PA
CBHW020223180626
46810CB00006B/2029